TRINE FALLACY

THE KINDERRA SAGA:
BOOK 2

By C.K. Donnelly

This is a work of fiction. Names, characters, places, and incidents either are the product of the author's imagination or are used fictitiously. Any resemblance to actual persons, living or dead, events, or locales is entirely coincidental.

First hardcover edition 2021

PHOTO CREDIT: *Mike Harvey/Peak Image Photo*
MAP CREDIT: *Emily Rakić /Emily's World of Design*
COVER CREDIT: *Kim Dingwall*

ISBN 978-1-7350518-4-0 (Hardcover)
ISBN 978-1-7350518-5-7 (Softcover)
ISBN 978-1-7350518-6-4 (Ebook)

Published in the United States by Kibbe Creative Media, LLC

www.ckdonnelly.com

ACKNOWLEDGMENTS

To all my wonderful readers — *The Kinderra Saga* wouldn't exist if it wasn't for you!

Gratas Oë!

2 Maccabees 2:26–27

"For us who have undertaken the labor of making this digest, the task, far from being easy, is one of sweat and of sleepless nights. Just so, the preparation of a festive banquet is no light matter for one who seeks to give enjoyment to others. Similarly, to win the gratitude of many we will gladly endure this labor."

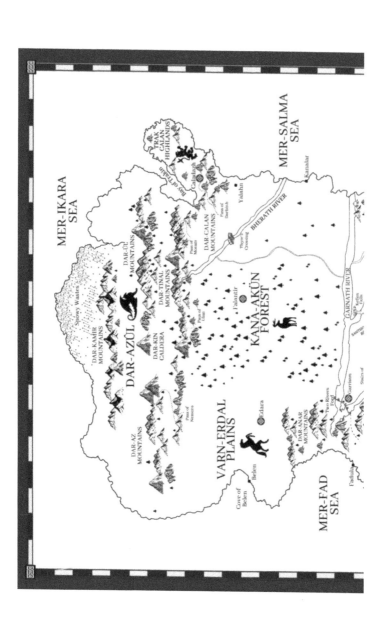

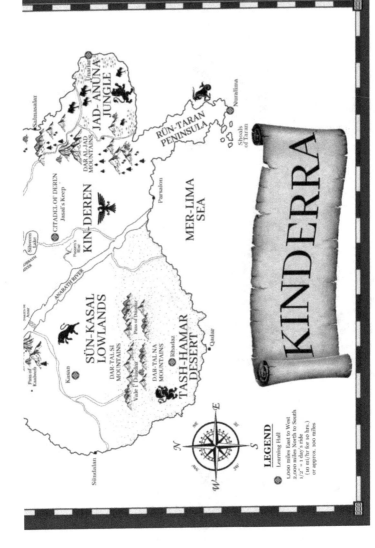

KINDERRA

Salmassáar

Immáat
JAD-ANÚNA JUNGLE

DAR-ALJAD MOUNTAINS

Núralima

RÚN-TARAN PENINSULA

Shoals of Taran

CITADEL OF DEREN
Jassal's Keep

KIN-DEREN

Silvereen Lake

ABBATH RIVER

Paran's Rise

Parsalon

MER-LIMA SEA

ANURATH RIVER

Innecvin Mist

SÚN-KASAL LOWLANDS

Kesan

DAR-TALSI MOUNTAINS
Vale f'Dua_lina
Pass of Duaghor

DAR-TALNA MOUNTAINS

Rhadaz

TASH-HAMAR DESERT

Qádar

Pass of Kaábeeth

Súndalan

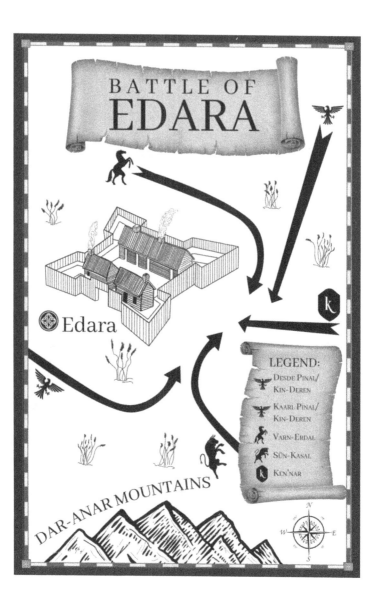

The Trine Prophecy

—The Book of Kinderra

"And it shall come to pass that Kinderra will cry out in such agony as to deafen even her birth. The chosen shall be like a ship without a keel. Aspect will appear where there was none. Light will be dark; dark will be light. One will come forth, thrice-cursed, to destroy. One will come forth, thrice-blessed, to rebuild. End and beginning in one, in both. Only hope shall remain."

CHAPTER 1

"My visions have disheartened me once again."
—The Codex of Jasal the Great

Mirana Pinal curled her fingers around the hilt of a long knife, the blade an extension of her hand, the gnawing ache of hunger chewing her stomach. She had let one of the animals go and stayed on the trail of the other. He was dark, smaller but still of good size. She had missed him twice. She didn't know why she felt it was a "he". It could be a female. It didn't matter. Her prey would not escape her again.

His mind held fear. She advanced, making less sound than the evening breeze through the tall grass of Sün-Kasal province.

She slipped through the dense growth closer to her quarry and licked dry lips as she moved. The Healing Aspect gave her impressions of hunger and exhaustion. She pulled her lips tightly against her teeth in a sneer. That made two of them.

She was close now, almost upon him. In a single, fluid movement, she rose to her feet, parted the grass, cocked her arm to thrust the long knife—and froze.

The newborn roebuck fawn shivered in the grass as its mother stood still in much the same stance as Mirana herself. The doe had tried to lead her away from the fawn. Believing she and her offspring were safe, the doe had circled back.

Trine Tetric Garis came up behind her in silence. … *Go on … Take it down* … he called to her mind.

If she killed the mother, the fawn would die for certain. If she killed the fawn, well, that wasn't about to happen. He was just hours old, still wet in places, his umbilical cord still drying.

She let her hand fall and sheathed the blade in a scabbard strapped to her waist. She couldn't take a life that had scarcely begun.

"Hah!" Mirana clapped her hands. The roe deer and the fawn darted away through the parched sward.

The Trine's long shadow stretched to an even more imposing length by the setting sun. "Why didn't you kill it?"

He didn't need to reveal the displeasure held in his mind; his voice told her all she needed to know.

"I just couldn't."

He balled his large hands into large fists and set them on his hips. "We haven't had a decent meal in sevendays, and you couldn't take down a simple deer?"

Her stomach chose that moment to growl. Loudly. She winced in embarrassment. "I, well, that is, maybe there are some roots we could eat instead." She pretended to search the ground around them for dinner, as that was far easier than meeting her mentor's midnight-black eyes.

"Mirana."

She peered up at him. "He was just a baby."

His mouth flattened into a frown, dark eyes growing darker with exasperation and maybe genuine anger. Remarkably like her father's expression when she would snipe at his corrections, actually. Oh, Aspects Above. She was in for it now. "You cannot hunt an Aspect-forsaken deer to keep from starving?"

She opened her mouth to say something in her defense, but any excuses would be just that. She hung her head. She had never killed anything before. Not before Two Rivers Ford. His rebuke stung more than he probably meant it to.

A hot wind drove the Sixthmonth summer heat in her face. Weather this warm was not unusual in the lowlands, but she had never experienced it before. She had never been this far south, this far anywhere.

She had never done any of the things she had in the past sevendays.

She had chosen an amulet when she swore she never would. She had killed Ken'nar, the ancient enemy of her Fal'kin people, through powers she had spent sixteen summers trying to contain. She had shattered Teague Beltran's heart.

"I will try harder tomorrow. I promise." She more than promised. She would never stop trying to be the Fal'kin she wanted to be, one who bonded with a crystal amulet and used the innate Aspect gifts of the Light from Within. Not the enraged monster she feared destiny might have her become.

A corner of the Trine's mouth twitched, pulling at his dark beard. "How do you propose we bring peace to Kinderra on empty stomachs?"

Had Lord Garis just laughed? Or at least shown a hint of something more light-hearted than his usual morose expression?

Mirana eased some of the tension from her shoulders. "Let me try again. Maybe I can find a prairie grouse or ladahen? Or at least dinner that doesn't have such big, adorable, brown eyes?" She pointed to her face.

"You most definitely will try again, and you will keep hunting until you succeed without help." He lifted his head toward the horizon. "But tomorrow. The sun has nearly set. Come."

They tramped back through the grass to where they had left their horses and meager supplies.

Mirana's warhorse nickered at her approach. "Ashtar," she said, patting his coppery neck, "you have a feast surrounding you for hundreds of miles. It might even be enough for you, too." To say the chestnut destrier was large was a laughable understatement. Standing seventeen hands, he was as fierce a fighter as any Fal'kin defender and a friend as close as family.

Ashtar snorted again and butted her with a velvet nose. She chuckled and kissed his white face.

She hefted the saddle off the horse's back. "We can probably squeeze one more meal out of our waybread. If we get an early start, we should be in Kasan before nightfall tomorrow, won't we?"

"We are not going to Kasan," Lord Garis replied as he unpacked his horse.

She whirled around to stare at the Trine. "But we are almost out of food."

"Are we?" He spread his arms wide. "Did you not say we have a feast surrounding us for miles?"

"I meant *grass*. For *him*." She jabbed a thumb behind her at Ashtar.

"And yet we could be roasting not one but two deer at this moment."

Her shoulders fell with her frustrated sigh. "*Ëo comprende, tuda ben?* I messed up. *My lord.*" She sketched a curt bow.

He did not reply. His glare was a weapon all its own. ... *The humor of your insolence lasts only so long ...*

She rubbed her forehead at the strength of his call. "I am sorry. Truly."

He now exhaled himself and stepped closer, his expression softening. Thankfully. "Think. Why am I pushing you to hunt?"

"So I can survive on my own."

"*Ai.*" He smiled down at her. "And maybe get us a meal or two."

"I wanted to get some apples. They'll last us a long time on the road. That's why I wanted to go to Kasan." She set down her saddlebags. "But I suppose even if we did travel there, it wouldn't do us any good. I don't have any coins for apples or anything else."

"You do not need coins. Any farmer is obligated to tithe to us Aspected whatever we need."

She scowled. "I'm from Kin-Deren province, so I guess I would expect a small tithe there, but Sün-Kasal needn't favor us."

"You now claim Dar-Azûl as your province. But that matters little. You are a Trine. All of Kinderra should tithe to you, as you were born to serve all of Kinderra."

She shrugged. "Tithing. I've never liked that custom. It seems wrong somehow. *Brepaithe* Toban was fair with his tithe requests from Kin-Deren's Unaspected, but I've heard other primes have not run their halls quite so frugally." Or honestly.

"What is wrong is the slaughter that happened at the ford, something the Unaspected will never have to face. I think our sacrifice is worth a few apples," the Trine snarled. She blinked in surprise at his sudden emotion. He sighed and shook his head, dismissing his aggravation. At least his anger had not been directed toward her this time. "I want to stay away from cities and towns as much as possible. There would be too many questions to answer by our presence."

She bit her bottom lip. "About the ford?"

"*Ai*," he replied, "but also about you."

She sat heavily on the ground and stroked Ashtar's fetlock. "My horse was so brave during the battle at the ford. He loves apples. As much as I do." She peered up at the Trine with a hopeful smile.

His mouth sank into the familiar flat line at her attempt to persuade him once more. He wore the expression when he was displeased. Which seemed to be all the time.

He leaned his head to one side, stretching his neck muscles. "Mirana, think about this. We would be seen together in the markets. That information would be passed immediately to Sahm Klai, Sün-Kasal's prime. We would have to meet with him. He would ask why you are with me instead of your mother, the prime of Kin-Deren province. To avoid explaining the true purpose behind our journey, I would have to tell them you are now attached to my province as my *scholaira* to avoid your mother's pronouncement elevating *scholaire'e* far too young to be Fal'kin. Need I continue?"

Prime Klai would no doubt then question why she, and her mother, frankly, would shirk her duty as an Aspected. Then her crime of publicly refusing to choose an amulet, as was required by Aspected, would be known across this land—if it wasn't already. A crime carrying the capital sentence of provincial expulsion.

She shook her head. "No, sir."

Lord Garis gave her a brusque nod and returned to unpacking his mount.

Technically, his stallion was a "he" as well, but the animal seemed to have little in the way of personality as Ashtar did.

Except, of course, when she drew too close. Then he had all the gracious demeanor of a mountain leopard whose fur had caught on fire.

"I'll bet your horse acted bravely during the battle, too. Why have you never given him a name?"

The Trine paused in his tasks and looked at his steed with something like pride. "He needs no name. But, *ai*, he is brave."

The pure black stallion stood placidly as he removed the last of its gear. The steed all but growled at her if she came anywhere near him. Aspects Above help any Ken'nar.

She knelt on the bedding and rummaged through a saddlebag to find something—anything—to eat. "It's all so senseless."

"What is?" He, too, searched his bags.

"This war." She scraped together a few crumbs and some lint from the bottom of the satchel. She frowned and tossed them on the ground. "How can the Ken'nar possibly think their Power from Without is right? Stealing life forces…" She shuddered.

He handed her an entire piece of waybread. "And yet, the Light from Within kills as surely as the Power from Without."

She took the wafer but avoided his gaze. It was a fact she knew only too well.

All the bloodshed. Thousands of summers of it. A choice to give of oneself. Or to take from others. It had been that way for three thousand summers, giving rise to an endless conflict with untold numbers of dead. All over a choice.

If Lord Garis hadn't found a way to stop the Ken'nar after decades of fighting them, it was ridiculous to think that she—all of five feet tall and sixteen summers of dubious wisdom—would ever have a chance.

By all the Light Above, she would try, though. Had she not stopped the Ken'nar at Two Rivers Ford, most of Kin-Deren province's Fal'kin would have perished. It had been a desperate, even foolhardy, act that had nearly killed her, but she had to do something. They were her people, her friends. Her father and mother.

She gritted her teeth so tightly it made her jaw ache.

Unlike her father, Tetric Garis had not betrayed her.

Her father, and her mother, too, had said they did not tell her she possessed the Trine Aspects because they meant to save her life.

The mother deer. She had left her fawn and stood immobile, believing she protected it with her silence. *Ai*, Mirana was still alive, but her mother and her father stood immobile in their silence and had consigned her to summers of self-inflicted torture as she tried to come to terms with possessing three accursed Aspected blessings.

Unlike her parents, Tetric Garis had stayed the knife at her throat and had given her hope that a different future, a different destiny might be possible.

"We must be careful with the fire tonight." Lord Garis reached over and plucked a few grass blades. He toyed with them a moment before letting them fall. They didn't break apart, but they remained bent.

Mirana lifted her gaze skyward. Gabrial, the first of the evening's stars, winked above in the clear heavens. "We had all our rain in the spring. We could use some now."

"*Ai*." He nodded. "It will be a long summer." He sat back against his saddle. "I will keep watch tonight."

"You've led us all day and probably will for the rest of our journey. Let me at least take watch for a few hours. Until midnight. Please, Lord Garis." She smiled at him. "It might make up for my utter lack of hunting skills."

He shrugged his broad shoulders. "I believe your hunting issue is more a bleeding heart than lack of skill, but truth be told, I am tired."

"And hungry. I have the Healing Aspect, too, you know." She continued to smile as she broke the waybread he had given her in half and handed him one piece. "Here. You haven't eaten all day. Even a Trine can sacrifice only so much."

He took a bite and rested his hand on a bent knee. "This journey we are on," he gestured to the grasslands around them with the wafer, "I think it should afford us some informality."

"My lord?"

"Don't call me by a title. We are trying to save the world we know from ripping herself apart. I think that means we can be a bit more familiar."

She was surprised, even uncomfortable with the idea. The great Trine Tetric Garis was a living legend, enigmatic, larger than life, quite literally in many respects.

"All right. If you insist. Tetric."

His given name, speaking it, sounded strange yet somehow empowering. How many others had he invited to use it? Everyone knew Trine Tetric Garis, but how many did he count as friends?

He ate the last of his waybread and gathered some tinder. Cupping his hands over his amulet, he released a thin beam of light at the kindling. He had just thrown more grass on the fire when he tensed. His sudden movement made Mirana jump.

Her hand flew to the hilt of a long knife. "What is it?"

… *Silence!* … He looked down over his shoulder. She didn't move a muscle, not even to breathe. A thin stiletto appeared in his hand. She hadn't seen him draw it. She hadn't even seen the knife on him.

With a blindingly fast move, he struck something beside him. A three-foot-long snake on the end of the stiletto made one last attempt to coil then hung limply from the tip.

She gave an explosive sigh of relief. "*Gratas Aspecta'e Alta*! I don't know what I would have done if it had bitten and poisoned you. I don't know how to heal someone of snake venom."

"Behold. The feast around us." He tossed the dead snake into the fire.

She eyed the roasting snake, her stomach curdling now with revulsion. "I am not eating that."

"*Ai.* You will." He drew his long sword and gently repositioned the blackening serpent in the flames.

She tried to swallow, but her throat wouldn't move. "Can I at least wait until it's cooked?"

He kept the snake in the fire until it blackened and the skin split. He cut off a piece and handed it to her. "Now, eat."

She eyed the reptile morsel as if it were still alive. Closing her eyes, she shoved it in her mouth and chewed. After a moment, she opened her eyes again and smiled. "It tastes like chicken." She wolfed down half of the snake in less time than it took to cook it. "Strange chicken, but chicken."

They finished their meal under a blanket of stars.

Mirana picked at an errant scale stuck in her teeth. "Who would have thought the skin and scales would have prevented the meat inside from burning to ash?" She flicked the reptile flake into the brush.

"All of Kinderra was given to us for our benefit," Tetric said as he rubbed some soil between his palms. "Even snakes have their place."

She glanced at the stains on her saddle blanket from where she had wiped her hands. The dusty soil would have absorbed some of the grease. Why hadn't she thought about that first?

"Would that the Aspects Above had given us a spring lamb to roast instead, but your point is well taken, my lor—Tetric."

As she rearranged the saddle blanket on her bedroll, she scratched herself on the brittle grass. She hissed and sucked at the cut. As tired as she was from the day's long, hot ride, she was not ready to sleep. The days of endless riding had strengthened her muscles. Her limbs, however, felt sapped without the amulet she had briefly held, her chest hollow, less a physical ache than a vacancy in her being. Losing Teague had felt the same way. She touched the mica pendant under her shirt.

She wished Teague were here with some of his mother's numbweed to put on her scratch. Sometimes she deliberately didn't take away her discomfort but let him rub salve on her cuts or bruises anyway. His touch alone would take away the pain, only to ignite a burning elsewhere in her body.

Her throat tightened. Again, she touched the pendant, lying warm against her skin.

Tetric frowned and paused in his own bed-making. His eyes drifting to her hand. "I told you to let him go."

"I have."

"No. You have not. Far from it." He shook his head sadly and sighed. "He will never, ever understand you or your power. Who and what you have been called to be. A union with you will only cause him pain. Is that what you want?"

She sat up, her eyes going wide in horror. "No. Never." She shook her head violently. "Why do you think I let him go?"

"Then you did him a kindness."

Teague's pendant remained in her hand. It had been warped and scorched from the amulet fire she'd leveraged at the ford. The promise of the love he held for her and only her had fallen into the twin river chasms along with the ford bridges, too. Destruction she had created.

Her hand fell away from the pendant. "Then why does it still hurt so much?"

"It shouldn't."

She scowled at the Trine's answer.

"Did he know about your vision of Jasal's Keep?"

She nodded.

"I thought as much." He frowned again. "Did he believe it?"

She looked back down at the pendant. "No. He never believed a word of it."

"I am afraid it is a solitary road we must travel."

"But I thought you meant—" She sighed and rubbed her eyes. She didn't want to think about this anymore. She didn't want to think about anything anymore.

Mirana caught the flash of a memory from her mentor. A young woman with flaming-red hair and arresting green eyes. She didn't have time to sense any emotions behind it. The image was gone as quickly as it came as he closed his mind.

"Who was that?"

"No one." He unfurled his bedroll with a snap, his back to her.

"Did you love her? Did you have to let her go, too?"

He whirled around. ... *I said it was no one!* ...

She winced at the force of his call. "I-I'm sorry. I didn't mean to pry."

He took a breath and shook his head to dismiss her apology. "It was a long time ago. Let us leave it at that."

She pulled Teague's pendant over her head and tucked it in her belt pouch. The whole reason why she had left Teague behind was for his safety. Where would the quest for the missing pieces to the keep lead her? Into danger, probably. But what if it led nowhere? That terrified her as much as her vision of white light.

"What if it's not there?" she whispered. She wasn't certain if she was merely thinking aloud or if she genuinely wanted an answer.

He roused. "What if what's not there?"

"The portion of the keep treatise in Tash-Hamar province. In Rhadaz. That's where we're going, after all. What if, well, there's nothing to find?"

"Are you saying this out of concern that the verses no longer exist? Or your ability to find it?"

She offered him a faint smile. "Both."

He studied her from across the fire. "Jasal meant for us to discover the secrets of his keep. Have faith. We will see this through." He made a curt nod and lifted his cowl over his head. She caught a tendril of emotion from him, not necessarily encouragement, but more like determination. Had he said that for her benefit or his own? Either way, it helped.

Another question sprang up in her mind as she looked up at the stars, one far less fraught with self-doubt.

… *The Archer will be overhead at midnight* … he called and chuckled, sending a picture of stars arrayed in a bow-like curve.

She smiled. … *Gratas Oë, Tetric* …

The simple expression failed utterly to convey her gratitude for his knowledge of southern constellations, hunting skills, and so very much more.

CHAPTER 2

"Mine hands are but ordinary. Yet I am called to use
them for the extraordinary. Why hast Thou not made
my grip stronger?"

                              —The Codex of Jasal the Great

Morning dawned clear and balmy when Teague Beltran collapsed at last on the bank beside a small stream. Dozens of unnamed rivulets and creeks ran down from the mountains through the foothills to the sea. He was grateful for each one. Farther north, water would be hard to come by as the coastal grasslands opened to a broad, arid prairie. He splashed water on his face before taking a drink himself while his horse nibbled on rush grass at the stream's edge.

The banks had been a treasure trove of edible and medicinal plants. In the rush—and frankly, the terror—of the

Ken'nar attack on Two Rivers Ford, he hadn't had a chance to pack any provisions or gear. It had taken him the entire previous afternoon and through the night to collect as much as he could carry.

He rolled up the horse's blanket behind him and leaned against the saddle. It would keep him warm when night came again, even if it did reek of horse and lingering smoke from the garrison fires at the ford. He stored water in a saddlebag. It seeped a bit, but it was better than nothing. He'd figure something else out later.

He took a bite of a raw tuber. "I may end up turning into a rabbit by the time this is all over, Bankin, but at least we have food for our journey."

He had no flint to start a fire to cook his meal, but it was just as well. He didn't want to be seen by the Ken'nar. He frowned at the stalk in his hand. If they were close, the Ken'nar would no doubt have sensed his living presence and would fatally relieve him of any worry about the ill effects from eating a raw water potato.

Teague watched the brook's lazy current. In the sandy mud by the stream were hoofprints. He scowled. Dozens of them, a hundred or more. They sank deep into the mud, which meant the horses were heavy. "Well, that's not good." He swallowed, the tuber scraping the back of his throat.

Warhorses.

The tracks all pointed in the same direction, north. If these tracks were left by the Ken'nar when they came down to ambush the Fal'kin at Two Rivers Ford, they would have been oriented the other way. Furthermore, they would have been washed away by the recent storms.

Teague started to rise, but quickly changed his stance to a crouch. These were made by the Ken'nar as they fled the ford in the aftermath of that terrible battle. Now that the ford bridges were destroyed, the Ken'nar had no choice but to skirt the windward side of the Dar-Anars if they wanted to ride north. As he was doing.

He peered through the grass. Only an ocean of green lay to the north. Unless a hundred Ken'nar lay in the tall grass around him, ready to cut him down where he stood. He forced himself to take slow breaths. He strained with his ears but heard nothing except his too-rapid heartbeat.

"Idiot," he hissed to himself. The Ken'nar would no longer be in the immediate vicinity. They had cut down the Fal'kin who had come to stop them at Two Rivers Ford. They'd slaughtered the herbsfolk who had come to care for the wounded and the dying.

They'd murdered his parents.

His mother and father had held the rare and blessed Healing Aspect. They weren't combatants. They had come to save lives, not take them. Except, in the end, they had. Because of him.

His mother and father had sacrificed their Aspect and their lives by killing Ken'nar to save his life. His unsighted, unhealing, undefending, Unaspected life.

He crawled back to the saddle and took another bite of the water potato. He had a long journey ahead of him, and he'd need to eat.

He frowned again. To where exactly was he journeying? *Ai*, to his death, but even so. He moved toward not so much a destination as a purpose. He looked at the tuber. He didn't care if he had to starve, he would see the Dark Trine dead. For his parents.

For Mirana Pinal.

Maybe he didn't have enough food, after all. He cut off his thoughts of Mirana the way an herbsman would cut off a ruined limb, quick and brutal.

"We need a plan, Bankin."

He nestled deeper into the grass. He would prefer to have camped higher up in the foothills to scout for any evidence of the dark-armored warriors, but they had arrows and amulets and he did not.

That would pose a problem. Attacking the Ken'nar head-on was pointless. He'd be killed before he'd make it two steps into their camp. If he wanted to confront the Dark Trine in person, he'd have to gain access to the Ken'nar army.

Teague reached over and dragged closer the Ken'nar sword he had claimed from the battlefield. The damn thing seemed like it weighed a hundred stone. No, he couldn't bluff his way in as an Aspected defender. He had no Aspects. They would sense that immediately. He'd have to be more creative if he was to infiltrate the Ken'nar camp. Somehow.

He finished the tuber with a smug bite. He had the "what" of his plan. Now, all he had to do was come up with the "how." Simple. He frowned. Well, it was a start, anyway.

Low on the western horizon, the bright star of Gabrial shimmered silver just like Mirana's eyes. So indescribably beautiful, and just as out of reach. The star faded from sight with the brightening of dawn.

He leaned back into the soft grass. A familiar scent wafted on the warm morning breeze. Next to his face grew a small patch of peda blossoms. He picked a flower.

His chest tightened, pulling at the deep contusion from the kick his horse Bankin had given him for spooking her on their ride to Two Rivers Ford. He loved Mirana. He'd told her that more times than he could count. In the end, it didn't matter.

Held by visions he would never be able to see, she chose a potential reality in which he had no place rather than face an actual reality with him.

Teague pounded his fist on the ground, once more, then over and over again, until it hurt too much to keep doing.

He was three months older than her, and those three months were the only ones he had ever lived without her. Throughout their entire sixteen summers, he had been her friend, her confidant, and, he thought, her love. Then a tower of impenetrable stone wrapped in an enigma took her from him. She said the vision that had plagued her for summers showed death and ruin at her hands culminating in an apocalyptic battle at Jasal's Keep. Maybe she did see something horrific with her Aspects, but he knew she could not be the one to deliver the destruction she believed. He, however, had no Aspects of his own to show her anything different. All he had was his conviction and his love.

He blew out another sob. He had been such a fool. He had believed they would join in union. He had thought he could make her his *wife*, forsaking all others for the remainder of his days. He would have done anything for her. He would have followed her through the very gates of the Underworld. He would have remained in the Underworld for her love.

He was the one who had believed in an impossible illusion, not her. Oh, what a hilarious, horrible joke.

He sobbed again, or maybe it was a laugh. Either one would be appropriate.

Hot tears left burning trails down his temples. He gripped the hilt of the Ken'nar sword, longing to plunge its blade into the heart of the Dark Trine. He would not live through the encounter, and in a way, he hoped he would not. Death would end the ache in his heart time would never erase.

Bankin snorted and pawed gently on the ground.

"Rot in the Underworld, you nag."

She whuffled again. He heard voices.

Teague quickly wiped his eyes with the heel of his hand and stuffed the peda blossom into his belt pouch. He grabbed the sword and rolled over, lying perfectly still on his stomach, hidden in the tall grass.

"Could we take a ship? It would be much faster." It was a man's voice.

It sounded like Morgan Jord, Defender Commander of the elite Fal'kin strike force, the il'Kin. Surely, he would have perished at the ford. Teague scowled. What was in the tuber he just ate?

"Faster, *ai*," said another voice, a woman's, in the gently lilting accent of Kinderra's far southern regions, "but we cannot risk discovery."

Binthe Lima, the il'Kin's battle seer? Most of the Fal'kin had been killed at the ford, hadn't they? He was hallucinating.

"Here, we will be caught between the mountains and the sea cliffs. There will be nowhere to run," the man said.

"Varn-Erdal does not run." It was another woman, her voice deeper, richer, harsher.

"Liaonne, Morgan, please. If we are trying to keep the transfer of Fal'kin defenders from Kin-Deren province a secret and avoid letting the Ken'nar know how desperate Varn-Erdal is for fighters—and frankly, Kin-Deren's own lack of protection—we need to stay away from the cities."

Teague stood up. "Binthe?"

Instantly, the grass around him sizzled into blackened ash as the amulet fire from a dozen Fal'kin defenders blazed around him. Several more drew their swords.

"Whoa! Stop! It's me. Teague. Teague Beltran." He held up his hands. With the sword still clutched in his right fist. He dropped it and resumed holding up his hands.

"Teague? Teague! Thank the Light! You're alive!" Binthe Lima cried as she and Morgan Jord ran over to him. The seer woman embraced him warmly.

"We've been looking everywhere for you, son," Morgan said.

He straightened out of Binthe's hug. "You just said you've been marching to Varn-Erdal province."

Binthe's relieved smile faded into one of confusion. "*Ai*, we are going to its capital, Edara, but we've been searching for any trace of you since we left the ford. You weren't among those returning to Deren. This is the only way you could have gone."

He grabbed the sword and climbed back up the hill to get his horse and gear. "How did you know I didn't go south to Sün-Kasal or even Tash-Hamar?"

"It would have been better if you had," Liaonne Edaran said. "It is not safe for you here. You may take some food and water, but then you will head back the way you came and home to Deren."

"No. I'm not going back to Deren." He gathered his things and tossed the blanket and saddle over his horse, tightening the cinch.

"Excuse me?" Liaonne's blonde hair, bleached nearly white by the sun from summers on horseback, made her dark brown eyes all the more penetrating.

"My apologies. I'm not going back to Deren, *Defender Second*," he said, stressing her title.

Morgan Jord glanced with a scowl at Binthe and Liaonne. He probably called something to them, which, of course, Teague couldn't hear. "Vallia Edaran has died. Liaonne is now Prime of Varn-Erdal province."

He'd rather face ten angry Ken'nar than one annoyed Liaonne Edaran. And now he'd just insulted her. Teague bowed. "My apologies, my prime."

Binthe stepped closer, her brows knitted in concern. "Are you all right?"

"It depends." He cinched his sword to the saddle within the folds of the blanket. "What do I have to be all right for?"

"Let me get you some food," Morgan said. "You must be starving."

"I already ate."

"We do not have time for this," Liaonne growled under her breath. "Give him some provisions and send him on his way." She stomped back to her troops.

"Liaonne," Binthe sighed. She returned her gaze to Teague. "I'll be right back." The seer smiled and ran farther into the camp.

Teague was both elated and frustrated at the unexpected appearance of the Fal'kin. He would have been hard-pressed to escape if he had been attacked, but now the Fal'kin would complicate his plans of infiltrating the Ken'nar.

Morgan put a hand on his shoulder, examining him for wounds. "You aren't injured, are you? We saw—"

"Ken'nar. Riding north. About a hundred. *Ai*, I know."

"They didn't attack you, did they?"

Teague gave a humorless laugh. "I don't think they would even waste the time."

"Then what the bloody hell is this?" The defender flipped back the saddle blanket to reveal the broadsword.

"I can't fight them with my belt knife, now can I?"

"Fight them?" The man threw the edge of the blanket back down. "You think you are going to ride into the midst of the Ken'nar army and fight them?"

"No, of course not. That would be stupid. I have a much better plan than that." His voice turned brittle with sarcasm as he lifted his leg to the saddle's stirrup. Morgan grabbed the collar of his shirt and dragged him back down.

"There is no plan you could possibly make that would not be stupid."

He pulled himself from the defender's grip. "I'm not going to fight the entire Ken'nar army. Just one in particular." He turned to his horse again.

"You think you can kill the Dark Trine? Walk right up to him and cut him down with that hatchet of yours?"

"Isn't that what you want to do? Why can't I feel the same way?"

"Teague, you can't possibly do this."

Anger boiled up within him. "You don't think I could." He pressed the side of Morgan's neck with his index and middle fingers. "If I press here for a few moments, you'll pass out." He touched the other side of the man's neck with his thumb. "If I hold you like this long enough, you'll die."

The defender batted his hand away. "Stop this foolishness. Now. Your parents died so that you could live, and this is how you honor their sacrifice? By committing suicide through revenge?"

He clenched his jaw. "Isn't that what you've always longed for?"

Morgan lanced him with a murderous gaze. "You have no idea what I long for, boy."

"I am not a boy." Teague's fury exploded. He swung at the Fal'kin. The defender sidestepped out of the way of his blow, but Binthe could not. His fist struck her jaw as she had come up behind Morgan, carrying food. She spun to the ground, waybread and dried beef spilling around their feet.

"Binthe!" Teague struggled to free himself as Morgan restrained his arms behind him. "Oh, Lights, Binthe, I'm so sorry. I didn't see you. I didn't mean to hurt you. I'm so sorry."

"We do not have any food to spare, so I would caution you against wasting it, Herbsman Beltran," she said, her sea-green eyes colder than he had ever seen them before.

He had always wondered how Binthe, who seemed so mild and kind, could fight as an il'Kin battle seer. He swallowed. He'd never wonder again. Morgan finally released him, and he rushed over to help her up.

"I'm sorry. I'm so, so sorry." He ran his fingers through his hair, thinking. "I need something cold to take down the swelling. No. Wait. I have some numbweed left. I think. Maybe I can—"

"I am all right." Her expression softened. "But you must rid yourself of this anger."

Morgan held his arms out at his sides. "If you will not listen to me, at least listen to her."

Teague folded his own arms and lifted his chin. "You have your calling and I have mine."

"*Ai*, you do," Binthe replied. "You are an herbsman. You care for the wounded and the sick. Soon, we will need those skills more than any Seeing or Defending Aspects."

He scowled. "What do you mean?"

"The Dark Trine may not have gained Two Rivers Ford, but his plans most certainly extend far beyond that. We believe his next target will be Edara."

Morgan nodded slowly. "If he conquers Varn-Erdal, half of Kinderra will be under his control. We are all but certain Kana-Akün fell to the Ken'nar during the winter."

The Fal'kin's words sank into his mind, the enormity of their meaning making his thoughts lurch to a stop.

"Teague, the men and women you see here are all that stands in the way of the Ken'nar overrunning Edara," the seer said.

"So few?" Then he remembered the butchery in the Kabaarh Pass leading into the valley near Two Rivers Ford.

Morgan gave a curt nod. "Prime Kellis Pinal and Prime Edaran resorted to a cleaving."

"A cleaving? But a cleaving takes away half a hall's Fal'kin. There can't be more than twenty-five people here." He gestured to the men and women resuming their trek to the north. His arm fell. "Then Deren's all but unprotected, too."

Binthe nodded slowly. "That is why Edara must not fall. I know you want to avenge your parents' deaths. But you must set that aside. Liaonne will need you to help keep these people alive."

He stepped back and snorted a laugh. "Me? She doesn't need me. Prime Edaran has her own herbsfolk."

"*Ai*, but none trained by your parents. Please help us."

Liaonne trotted her snow-white mare over to them. "We have to move now."

"I have good news, my prime," Binthe said, smiling as she pulled Teague forward. "Teague Beltran wants to put his herbsman's skills in your service."

The young defender woman sat back in her saddle. "Is that right?"

His mouth hung open. He looked from Binthe to Morgan, and finally up at the prime. His gape fell into a frown. "*Ai*, my lady. If you'll have me." It was a bald-faced lie, but if the Fal'kin could sense it, they made no point of saying so. He could at least help lay in supplies before an attack.

And if the Ken'nar planned to march on Edara, then that was exactly where he wanted to be.

Liaonne grunted an acknowledgment. "Very well. I will need herbsfolk. It's too bad, though. It is not often an Unaspected lands his mark on an experienced battle seer. You would make a good Varn-Erdalan."

Teague made a half-smile. "*Gratas*. I think."

CHAPTER 3

"The traitor does not come as an enemy but as a friend."
—The Book of Kinderra

Kaarl Pinal raced his horse over the grasslands of Sün-Kasal. His mount, a spirited little brown and white three-summer-old, had the heart of his big chestnut warhorse, Ashtar, but not his stamina. Stopping to rest the beast had slowed his journey to Kasan, time he could ill afford to waste.

The freshness the rain had brought to Two Rivers Ford had long since disappeared in the southlands. The oppressive heat of the early summer season had made the ride sweltering. He was a defender, not a seer, but if the temperature was already this warm, the season would be a long, hot one.

The pungent, almost musty smell of soil filled Kaarl's nostrils as he neared the main thoroughfare. Kasan, the province's largest city in Sün-Kasal province and home to its learning hall, had no outer defenses to prevent an attack. Only the hall itself had protective ramparts. He grimaced. Such a lack of protection only invited disaster, but other than occasional raids on traders and farmers, the Ken'nar seldom made any concerted efforts to attack this far south. At least until now. If he could not convince Sün-Kasal's prime to aid him in preventing Varn-Erdal from being sacked and its fabled warhorses stolen, the Dark Trine's Ken'nar would sweep over the southern provinces like a wildfire. He tapped the sides of his mount, picking up its pace.

The streets inside the city were crowded. It was just past midday, and the markets and businesses bustled at their peak. Kaarl resisted the urge to scream at people to get out of the way, wanting to keep up the horse's charge. He settled into a swift canter as he approached the Fal'kin learning hall.

Tall timbers filed to a point ringed the learning hall complex. Wood from deep in Kinderra's forests must have been dragged for hundreds of leagues centuries ago to the province. Other than the cultivated orchards, there was not a proper tree for hundreds of miles. While nowhere near as sturdy as Deren's legendary iron gates and stone walls, the timbers used for Kasan's gates and walls were some of the largest he had ever seen. Perhaps that was due to more than just the pitch. He smiled. It was, after all, a Fal'kin learning hall. It would take a battering ram with Aspects of its own to bring them down.

As Kaarl approached the stockade battlements, he called a greeting to the sentry Fal'kin. Sün-Kasal's learning hall always underwhelmed him with its appearance. The hall in Deren was a grand if rambling fortress, built to be as beautiful as it was secure. This hall looked more like an ugly stepsister than a true sibling. Cobbled together with daub, thatch, and mud mortar, its lumpy appearance reminded him of some enormous toad rising from the grassland.

Incongruously, the hall had many windows. Fantastic shapes and designs, in hues of green and gold flecked with red and blue, the glass panes glinted in the afternoon light. He wondered if the artisans who crafted stained-glass windows in the library at Deren had made these.

Inside the hall's tamped-earth courtyard, Kaarl dismounted and handed the reins of his horse to a young girl. He reached into his saddlebag to give the girl the last of his dried apple to feed to the horse when his shoulder hitched painfully from the arrow wound he sustained at the Battle of Two Rivers Ford. The girl caught the dried fruit before it reached the ground.

He smiled down at her. "No seeing the weather for you. You are a defender."

"*Ai*, sir," she answered brightly.

"How many summers have you seen?"

"It will be eleven next month," she replied. "*Paithe*, *Maithe*, and my *siba'e* are with the Aspects Above now, but I am hoping Prime Klai will allow me to choose early. I want to show my family how brave I am. I know they are looking down on me."

Kaarl forced his smile to remain. "I am certain they already know how brave you are."

The girl—all wheaten hair, meadow-flower-blue eyes, and freckle-dusted cheeks—was as much a casualty of the Ken'nar as any Unaspected orphan. At least she would be taken care of by the rest of the Fal'kin in the hall. How many more children, Unaspected *and* Aspected, would become orphans if Sahm Klai wouldn't listen to him?

He nodded his thanks to the girl and strode to the hall's entrance. The grand doors to the hall itself were made of the same wood that comprised the stockade and gates. The impressive beams were bound together with bands and pegs of iron and stood taller than twice the height of a tall man. Carved into both doors were the bulls of the province's heraldic.

As massive as the doors before which he now stood was the defender prime of the province himself. Sahm Klai was not so much obese as he was giant in all dimensions. White streaked through his brown hair and beard, but both were as thick as the grass of the province. His broad face and brow sank into a scowl as if a potter had tried to sculpt it from the Sün-Kasalan clay but added too much water in the mixture.

Kaarl fought a frown of his own. The man's expression, to say nothing of what little he perceived of his mind, told him he was ready for a confrontation. By the Aspects, Sahm Klai didn't even know yet why he was here. The prime's second was an extremely adept seer, however, so maybe he did.

"Pinal," the big man said.

Kaarl kept his forced smile and gave a slight bow. "Defender Prime, *ben dië*. I trust you are well." He reached out to grip the man's brawny forearm in greeting. They had fought together but not often. Sahm Klai had a reputation as a staunch pacificist. It took nothing short of a direct assault on his province for the man to engage his Fal'kin. He hoped the Aspects Above would give him the words to convince the man to act this time.

Sahm Klai kept his fingers wrapped around Kaarl's forearm. The prime's mind pushed against his own. "I was. Then I heard of your arrival."

No sooner had the defender prime finished his words when a tall, thin man with reddish hair emerged from the hall. His skin was tanned from long days in the sun. The pale scars on his chin, chest, and hands, however, did not come from working in the fields.

This time, Kaarl's smile came from genuine admiration. "It is very good to see you, Rabb."

"My Sight has not deceived me. Defender Commander Pinal," Rabb Plout said. "To what do we owe the pleasure of your visit?"

"There is nothing pleasant about his visit," the prime said, glowering.

He would explain his new station and title later. "Sahm is right. I need to speak with you both. Now."

Rabb Plout's eyes went unfocused for a moment, the russet-colored topaz amulet around his neck glowing. He nodded, his face grim. "So it's true?" Kaarl nodded. "Come."

When they entered Sahm Klai's chamber, Kaarl did not waste time on a guest's good manners. He nodded his thanks to Rabb for the offered chair but remained standing.

"Sahm, our situation has grown perilous."

"What happened at the ford?" Sahm Klai asked.

"Probably everything Rabb saw," he answered. "Two Rivers Ford has fallen."

The prime looked from his seer second to Kaarl. "How is that possible? That is the very reason why we leave a garrison there. Furthermore, it was Varn-Erdal's tour. They'd never let anything get through."

"The Varn-Erdalans were overwhelmed. We all were. Thousands of Fal'kin were killed by the Ken'nar."

Rabb Plout's eyes widened in shock. "Thousands were killed? But the attacking force I saw was not that large."

"A second force of nearly five thousand hid in the Kabaarh Pass. After they cut down the Varn-Erdalans en route, they attacked us while we were engaged with the five hundred black-armored bastards you saw. We were caught between the two phalanxes." Kaarl's hand went to his amulet, the red crystal glowing softly at the memory he did not want but which would never leave his mind. He walled his thoughts away from the other men. Kinderra would find out how Mirana stopped the thousands of marauding Ken'nar soon enough.

The seer shook his head in disgust. "The vision was all but impossible to understand. It was unclear, it took place at night, and yet there was an unmistakable sense of peril. It didn't make sense that the Ken'nar would have made a play for something as strategically important as the ford with such a small number of troops. Even if they didn't know Varn-Erdal was expected, they would have needed at least two thousand to remain to hold it once it fell into their hands. Sahm, I told you we should have sent—"

The prime raised a broad hand, silencing his second. "You told me you saw five hundred Ken'nar. Between Kin-Deren's forces already stationed at the garrison and the relief troops from Varn-Erdal, that should have been plenty to deal with the Ken'nar menace. I may have been wrong, but I was still right holding our troops back. They would have been slaughtered at the ford like the others. What if those bastards kept coming south? Who would have protected Sün-Kasal then?"

Kaarl was not surprised that Rabb Plout had counseled action despite seeing a seemingly small number of Ken'nar at the ford. He knew the man was an intelligent seer, and Sahm Klai was either too much of a fool or too weary to care. Kaarl suspected he was both.

"We should have gone," the seer said, his voice soft. "We could have made a difference."

It was all he could do to not cheer at the seer's words. "You still can."

"How?" Sahm Klai said, scowling.

"Desde and Binthe both believe Varn-Erdal will be the Dark Trine's next target," Kaarl replied. "After the ford, neither Edara nor Deren have the numbers to repel him. Your defenders are at full strength. You need to move north. Together with what resistance Varn-Erdal still possesses and the handfuls we have left, we may be able to keep him from advancing on Edara."

The big defender's scowl deepened further. "Do you not lead the il'Kin? Interprovincial conflicts are your affair. Not mine. And Edara is Vallia's concern. Not mine, either. Talk to Tetric Garis. Is he not still Trine of all Kinderra?"

Kaarl gritted his teeth. He had hoped corroborating Rabb Plout's vision would have shocked the man into action.

"Tetric's scant hundreds of Dar-Azûlans will be no match for the thousands Desde sees advancing on Edara. And the il'Kin—" The words were harder to speak than he thought, too. "Morgan Jord and Binthe Lima are all that are left of the il'Kin. The rest perished at the ford."

Rabb Plout shook his head and bit back a curse. "*Ëo ten Oëa pián.*"

"*Gratas Oë, Ëi cara.*" He was grateful for the man's condolences, but he doubted anyone could hold that particular pain.

The seer poured a cup of water. "Here. You had a long ride." He brushed Kaarl's hand as he offered him the drink. ... *What have you not said?* ...

... *Later* ... he returned privately. He nodded his thanks and gulped down the water. "I am here not as defender commander of the il'Kin. Toban Kellis elevated me to Steward of the Quorum of Light upon his death. So, *ai*, you are correct. Interprovincial conflicts are indeed my affair. I am here because I need you. I need your troops to help us safeguard Edara."

The big prime sank deeper into his chair and regarded him for a moment. "Your private army is gone so you are trying to lay claim to the rest of ours as steward?"

Kaarl opened his mouth in shock. "What? No, Sahm, of course not!"

"And yet you have the audacity to come here and order me where to send my troops?"

He raised his hands, palms up, gesturing helplessly. "I am not ordering you at all. I am trying to impress upon you our situation."

"Or your ambition? Trying to make up for twelve hundred summers of cowardice, eh, Pinal?"

His eyes widened. "How can you—?"

"Sahm," Rabb Plout said, holding up his hand. "Did you not hear what happened at the ford? We have a chance to prevent that from happening in another province, one that borders our own, I may add."

Kaarl wanted to cheer a second time. The seer was pragmatic, the complete opposite of Sahm Klai. He wondered how the prime ever chose the man to be his second. Maybe he should give the defender a bit more credit. Perhaps he knew his weaknesses.

"My duty is to this province and this province alone. That is the responsibility of a prime." Sahm pointed firmly to the floor with a finger.

Kaarl shook his head. "You can't mean that. How many times has Edara ridden to the call of Kinderra? Varn-Erdalans have been a part of every major campaign since its hall's founding."

"If Vallia Edaran cannot safeguard her province, that is her own affair."

He could not look at the prime for the moment and fixed his eyes on his cup instead. He swallowed the rest of the water along with his anger. "Vallia is dead. Her daughter Liaonne now leads Varn-Erdal."

"If anyone could be more vicious than Vallia, it would be Liaonne," Rabb Plout replied.

"Maybe Bystra?" he offered gently. He meant it as a compliment. Sahm Klai's wife, now long dead, had been a formidable defender.

The prime glared at him a moment, then exhaled explosively. He rubbed his face with his hands. "Think about what you are asking, Kaarl. I am not an imbecile. I know the Ken'nar are almost within sight on my lands if they march on Varn-Erdal. But I guard the breadbasket of Kinderra. If I send my forces out to meet the Ken'nar at Varn-Erdal, who guards our food? If I fall, the rest of Kinderra will starve, not just Varn-Erdal. I cannot afford to throw my troops at a conflict that does not directly affect me. Not just for the sake of Sün-Kasal, but for the sake of Kinderra."

Kaarl took the chair at last. The big man was right, to a point. He rested his forearms on his thighs and hung his head. "You cannot afford not to, Sahm," he said at last. "If I still had a full complement of il'Kin, I would order them in straight away, but I no longer have that option. You must act now. Not even a sevenday hence. Now."

"I would have expected a move like this from Tetric Garis, but not from you."

He no longer felt the need to be polite. He pinned the defender prime with his silver gaze. "You may have to do more than just expect it. Garis will ask the Quorum to declare him Primus Magne."

Sahm sat up, nearly falling out of his chair. "What?"

"He asked me to support him in his bid. He would have me serve as defender commander under him."

"You can't be serious?" Rabb Plout said. "The last thing Kinderra needs now is another Aspected trying to become her overlord. What did you tell him?"

"I flatly refused."

The seer chuckled under his breath. "Oh, I bet our Lord Trine liked that."

Sahm Klai, however, did not laugh, nor even smile. "So, this is what it has come to? You or him?"

"What do you mean?" Kaarl demanded.

"How many times have you and Tetric clashed over the il'Kin? He either wanted the unit dissolved or absorbed into his forces. Only because your wife's father held the reins of the il'Kin did they survive," the defender prime growled. "You would do anything now to keep the unit going. What easier way than to use mine and Varn-Erdal's and block Tetric once and for all. I will have no choice but to vote for a Primus Magne to stop you or vote for you and prevent losing our right to self-governance."

Kaarl's blood chilled in his veins. He had never been on close terms with Sahm Klai, but he respected the man's abilities as a fighter and his honesty. He had thought Sahm respected him as well. Did he really believe that he was the kind of man to make a power play like this?

"Listen to yourself, Sahm," Rabb Plout said. "I've been at Quorum with you for more than a few summers. Garis is as ambitious as he is brilliant. But more than that, Toban Kellis was steadfast in saying Kinderra needed more defensive forces, not less. And I agreed with him. I thought you did, too."

"I did. When old Toban was the steward."

Kaarl tore his gaze away from the large man to stare at the seer in hopelessness. The other man returned his expression. He turned back to the prime. "I do not want your Fal'kin any more than I want Varn-Erdal's. I only want to stop the Ken'nar from killing innocent men, women, and children. Is that not what you want, too?"

"That is the conviction that enables me to draw breath each day," Sahm Klai snarled. A quicksilver thought of four graves sparked from the defender's mind to Kaarl's. "And I will protect them. My people. My way."

Kaarl slumped his shoulders in defeat. "After the massacre at the ford, Liaonne asked for a cleaving of Kin-Deren's Fal'kin. Deren does not even have one hundred fifty left to guard its borders. If you do not help us, Desde will muster Unaspected volunteers."

Once again Sahm Klai lurched forward in his chair, stunned. "Un-Unaspected?" He turned to his second. The seer looked ill.

"*Ai*," Kaarl replied. "Desde may save Varn-Erdal, but she could lose Kinderra in the process."

"I cannot believe Desde would commit such sacrilege."

"Is there no time to pull from Tash-Hamar or Jad-Anüna?" Rabb Plout asked. "Nambre Dinir has an even larger complement of Fal'kin than we do."

He shook his head wearily. "Desde feels it is only a matter of sevendays before the Ken'nar will advance. They will most certainly attack while Liaonne is weakened."

"Then what choice does Desde—and Liaonne, for that matter—have but to ask the Unaspected to fight?" the seer second asked.

He did not answer right away. "Without you? None."

"I refuse to collude with such heresy," Sahm Klai said. "If Liaonne cannot keep the Ken'nar at bay, the Dark Trine will sweep south. With what you're telling me, I have no choice but to remain here to guard my province."

"If the Dark Trine does come southward, then you will not need to guard your fields. There will be no one left to feed." Kaarl rose silently and left the defender prime's chamber.

*   *   *

Kaarl stroked his horse's neck as the animal drank. The stable was all but empty. Sahm Klai conditioned his warhorses by having them work the farm fields when they were not on the battlefield. It was unorthodox, perhaps the only unorthodox thing the big prime ever did, but he couldn't argue with the results. Unlike his little mount, Sün-Kasalan steeds never seemed to tire.

"Aspects Above know you deserve at least one night's rest, Patan. Unfortunately, we don't have the time for that." He gave him another pat then hefted the saddlebags across his mount's brown-dappled back.

"Good. You're still here." Rabb Plout hurried over. "Give Sahm some time. I'll try and talk some sense into him."

"I very much appreciate the effort, though I don't think it will matter."

The seer made a gentle, low noise and patted the horse's flank. "Ashtar shrank?"

Kaarl laughed lightly at the man's comment, then grew serious. "Ashtar is with my daughter."

"Thank the Aspects she is safe in Deren."

"She's gone, Rabb." Grief welled up and threatened to smother him. He gripped the side of the saddle and shoved the emotion aside as he had so many other thoughts of late. Sinking into despair would solve nothing and only steal what strength he had.

"She was at the ford? She wasn't—?"

"No." He placed the saddle on Patan's back and kept his hands on the seat. "No, she is alive. She is the reason you are not fighting the Ken'nar right now."

"What do you mean?"

He hesitated. To keep Mirana safe from the Dark Trine now would require a miracle. All the summers of his lies, his silence about her Trine Aspects could do nothing to protect her any longer. Maybe it never really had.

"When I said Two Rivers Ford fell, I wasn't just speaking in terms of the battle. She destroyed it. The ford itself, the bridges. With the Aspects. Mirana is a Trine."

The seer leaned back against the paddock, awestruck. "By the Light. The Prophecy." His hand flew to the ruddy topaz in his amulet. "We have Tetric Garis. And-and the Dark Trine. Three Trines? What does this mean?"

"It means one of them will die. If Tetric perishes, then Mirana will have to face the Dark Trine herself. Or the Dark Trine could strike her down before Tetric—" Kaarl's heart constricted so tightly in his chest it hurt. He turned his gaze from Rabb to stare at nothing. "Her whole life, I hid the truth. We did it to save Mirana's life. We expected her to come to us first when she figured it out for herself. She never said a word. After destroying the ford, every soul in Kinderra will learn who and what she is. The Dark Trine will stop at nothing to kill her now."

The seer fidgeted with the chain of his amulet. "Do you think this means he will succeed at eliminating Tetric?"

Kaarl gave a harsh exhale and shrugged. "I don't know, *Ëi cara*. Maybe. And if Mirana is Tetric's, well, *heir*—" He shook his head. "For sixteen summers, I did everything I could to keep her safe from the Ken'nar bastard. In the end, I drove her straight into his sword. I may never see her again."

He shut his eyes against the pain of the memory of her bitter leave-taking and gripped the saddle so tightly the leather creaked.

"If I had a child, I would have done the same thing," Rabb said softly.

They were quiet for a moment, watching Patan eat fresh hay. "Where is she now?" the seer asked.

Kaarl shrugged, his shoulders feeling as though millstones lay on them. "I don't know. I begged Garis to take her from the ford garrison before the fighting broke out. I can only hope he did, and they are someplace far away. The eyes of the Dark Trine are upon him, too, however. Her life is still in danger."

His amulet warmed the skin beneath his shirt, stoked by his frustration. He slammed a fist down on the stall, causing his horse to start.

Rabb placed a gentle hand on Kaarl's arm. "We have always been in complete agreement about Garis's naked ambition, but he is immensely powerful. She could be in no safer hands, whatever the threat."

"I wish I could believe you."

"That does beg a question or two, though." The other man held his amulet, tracing the setting's edges. "If Garis is points unknown with your daughter, where are his Dar-Azûlans?" He let the amulet fall to his chest and looked up at Kaarl. "Who is leading them now? Not Sido Rendel, his weasely seer second?" The seer grimaced. "No Fal'kin, especially one who's not even a defender, should fight with that much, well, *enjoyment*."

"That does say something coming from a battle seer like you." Kaarl laughed ruefully. He then considered the seer's questions, valid both. "Fifty of Garis's troops came down with us from Falantir and were with us at the ford. When we regrouped afterward, I saw none of his men. He could have ordered them to follow the Ken'nar fleeing north when the ford fell. Sido Rendel and the remainder of his five hundred, I thought, were still in Kana-Akün trying to ferret out information on the Dark Trine's forces there. That's the other arrow in my side. Falantir fell to the Ken'nar during the winter."

"What?" Rabb stared at him in wide-eyed shock. "What in the nine levels of the Underworld is going on in this land?"

Kaarl rubbed at his shoulder. It ached. "We think the Dark Trine is encamped at Falantir. We haven't even begun to put a strategy together to liberate the Kana-Akün province. I don't know what direction Garis took after the ford. I lost contact with him during the fight." His hand slipped from his healing shoulder to his amulet. "I never saw him again after the fighting started. Nor Miri."

The seer smiled sadly. "That took courage. To give your child to the man you hate."

"I don't hate him. To be honest, I don't know how I feel about him."

"You're not seriously considering supporting him as Primus Magne?"

Kaarl leaned heavily on the stall gate and hung his head. Light Above, he was tired. "If he can keep my daughter safe, maybe it is time to re-examine some things."

The small cut in the hollow of Mirana's throat. From the knife she had placed there. The knife Garis had stopped. He squeezed his eyes shut once more and, once again, blocked the memory with the shield of his will. He had spared his wife this truth. He wished he could have remained ignorant himself.

"After the ford, maybe uniting Kinderra under one leader isn't so anathema after all," he said. "The Ken'nar seem to grow despite our best efforts. Something has changed over the summers, Rabb. I no longer even feel fury from most of them. Just an insatiable will to kill. They hack away at us. Then we are forced to hack away at them. This is not war. It's butchery."

"All the while, Sahm has us sitting here harvesting wheat when we should be fighting. And he has the gall to call me perverse." Rabb added a curse under his breath.

"Sahm knew of your choice of companions long before he elevated you to be his second," he replied. "That was as much a sign of respect as it was one of trust. He knows you are a good second and an even better man."

The seer smiled. "Can you help me find another?"

He returned his grin. "If I do, yours will be the first name I recommend."

Rabb Plout leaned his forearms on the railing of the paddock and hung his head. "What is happening to our world, Kaarl? Can we Fal'kin no longer carry out our sacred duty? Has it truly come to choosing between uniting under a man we detest or asking our Unaspected to save us?"

"'Hope shall remain,'" Kaarl said, quoting the Book of Kinderra's Trine Prophecy. Hope was all he had left.

CHAPTER 4

"The Aspects Above hath called me, but am I enough?"
—The Codex of Jasal the Great

Teague wished fervently they had taken the ship Morgan had suggested. Liaonne Edaran had set a pace even a grynwen couldn't match. The good thing was, if any of those four-hundred-pound carnivores, as much fangs as flesh, decided to hunt them, the beasts might not be able to catch them.

When they finally stopped for the night, he all but fell off his horse as he dismounted.

"We'll make camp here," Liaonne said as she surveyed the plateau. "The hills will provide us some protection if the Ken'nar make the mistake of returning south for us."

They were somewhere beyond the northern edge of the Dar-Anars, Teague figured. They had made good progress toward Edara, but he didn't much care. He wanted to sleep even more than revenge at the moment.

He and the others had seen no further signs of the Ken'nar. Binthe, however, had been strangely quiet for days. That had made him more than a little nervous, and that made him angry. If he was ever going to kill the Dark Trine, he had better start growing a spine and stop jumping at the mere mention of the dark-armored warriors.

A young moon grinned overhead at the sprinkling of stars. He collapsed on a grassy knoll, shut his eyes, and tried to will away his exhaustion. Apparently, unrelenting grief and vengeance really did take a toll on one's body.

The toe of a boot tapped his leg. "Attend to your horse first, Herbsman Beltran. Then you can sleep."

Teague frowned and peered up at Morgan in the faint moonlight. "I was just taking a moment."

The young il'Kin commander started to say something, then shook his head. "Do you need some help?" He reached down.

He swiped away the man's hand and hauled himself back up to his feet. Morgan sighed and turned, leaving him to uncinch Bankin's saddle. He tossed it heavily on the ground.

"Damn you, boy," a defender snarled as he rose from a tall stand of grass, kicking away the saddle. His pale-yellow amulet faded out.

Teague jumped back in surprise. "Sorry. I didn't see you."

"The prime has set a watch."

"Right on top of me?"

"Just be more careful."

He couldn't see the Fal'kin's expression in the darkness. He didn't need to. He could hear it in the man's voice. So, Liaonne thought he was incapable of taking care of himself? He had his Ken'nar broadsword. It was all the bodyguard he needed.

He set down the saddlebag with the water in front of Bankin and took a long draught from a waterskin Liaonne had given him.

The night was warm and humid, and the breeze felt soothing on his face. He stretched out again on his saddle blanket, laying a hand on his blade next to him. He fingered the blade's grip. The thing looked like it could fell a tree. He had never used a sword before, but what was there to know? He just had to hack at anything that wasn't himself or one of the Fal'kin.

No, he wasn't a swordsman, but he was, however, something else: completely forgettable. He huffed a laugh under his breath. He never in his life thought his invisibility could be an advantage. He was at least as tall as most men, though perhaps thinner. Last summer, he shot up a hand, but the rest of him had yet to catch up, it seemed. His hair was neither dark enough to be brown nor light enough to be blond, instead, it was the brownish coloring of hundreds of thousands of men in Kinderra. His eyes were not green nor brown but a sort of mixture of both. He had no scars or tattoos to add character. His voice was mild, and he'd never picked up his mother's Tash-Hamari accent.

He was thoroughly unremarkable in every way. He looked like no one because he looked like everyone. He smiled. No one would make a better spy—or a better assassin.

He sat up and hefted the sword. No, he didn't have to be a swordsman. He just needed enough skill for one perfect strike.

Dark excitement chased away most of his exhaustion and all of his sleep. Snatches of soft conversation drifted over the knoll and lulled him into semi-consciousness.

"How is your wound?" It was Binthe. "The arrow could have gone through your back."

"No. My kidney, most likely," Morgan's voice answered.

"That is in no way humorous." There was a pause. She must have called something to the defender. "You still haven't answered my question," she said in her lilting Rün-Tarani accent.

"I can still fight if we are attacked."

Had Binthe seen something? Teague rolled over onto his belly and crawled down the hill a bit closer to the couple, Ken'nar blade in hand. If the Ken'nar were coming, he wanted to be ready. Or at least not run screaming in fear like a little girl.

He had learned to be extraordinarily observant of nonverbal communication. A gesture or a glance was often all the warning he had to fend off a sucker punch from those Aspected children at the hall who knew he was not. In the darkness, though, he couldn't see the Fal'kin's faces.

He strained his ears to listen to what else Binthe and Morgan were saying, but their conversation became disjointed as they alternated between calling and spoken words. Mirana seldom called in front of him. He frowned. Morgan and Binthe were not calling in front of him; he was the one eavesdropping on them.

The two il'Kin sat close to each other farther down the hill's slope, a dozen paces away from him, their legs touching. Teague raised an eyebrow. He didn't know them as well as Mirana did. Were they coupled? Morgan Jord was the sort of Fal'kin men wanted to be and women wanted to, well, be *with*. His brown hair was dusted with lighter streaks from long days of riding in the elements, which sometimes gave him the appearance of being much older than his thirty summers. His blue eyes were a shade that reminded him of the summer sky. They peered above a chiseled nose and beard-traced jaw. He stood a good head taller than Teague, but he wasn't overly muscled like some defenders. That gave the defender a sort of predatory litheness, like a mountain tiger waiting to pounce. The man held a somberness, though. During Quorumtides, plenty of women—Aspected and Unaspected alike—appeared to want nothing more than to make Morgan Jord happy. Now that Teague thought about it, the only time the defender did smile was in Binthe's presence. Lucky bastard. He had it all—looks, brains, talent.

"You should have gone back home. Rün-Taran needs you," Morgan said to the seer woman as they sat on the knoll. "Your grandmother is ill. She will need you to take over the province."

"Syne Develan is *Bremaithe*'s prime's second as well as the defender commander of her provincial forces. He will take the primeship when she passes, not I. I am a seer of the il'Kin."

"There are no more il'Kin, Binthe."

Oh. Right. The man also had grief. So many of his friends had died at the ford, men and women under his command. Teague gritted his teeth. No, he wasn't jealous of Morgan Jord. Well, not completely anyway.

"All the more reason why you need a seer. You do not know what dangers may lie ahead. For Edara. Or for you."

"What dangers could there be that I have not already faced?"

Grass rustled. Teague propped himself up a little higher to look down the hill at the Fal'kin. The defender commander had risen and walked off into the camp, leaving Binthe to sit alone. She bowed her head, long hair covering her face, as her shoulders shook. Was she crying?

He got up and started down the hill to comfort her, then he thought better of it. What could he say? He wasn't supposed to have heard their conversation.

What in the name of the Aspects was he doing with these people? He could do nothing for them. Liaonne did not need him. She had herbsfolk of her own, ones that knew something. He should leave tonight, now.

"You rode hard today. You should get some rest," the seer said over her shoulder.

He plopped down beside her. "I wanted to check on Bankin."

"I thought you hated horses."

"I do, but I figured I better be nice to her. The way Prime Edaran is running us, I need her in good shape. An ocean voyage might have been better after all." Moisture shone on Binthe's cheek in the pale moonlight. The bruise on her jaw where he had accidentally slugged her was visible, too. He frowned. Should he say something anyway?

She turned to look out at the western horizon where the Mer-Fad Sea shimmered under the stars. The breeze caught a tendril of hair, and she tucked it behind one ear. "It would have been nice to be back on the water again."

"You sailed?" That was a stupid question. She was from Rün-Taran province, a peninsula surrounded by ocean. Of course, she had sailed. Was she related to whomever the sea was named after?

She laughed lightly. "*Ai* and *ai*. The Limas were maritime seers." She plucked a few blades of grass and began to braid them into a seaman's knot. "Maritime seers were quite common in Rün-Taran, helping to guide ships through the treacherous shoals, to forecast the weather, even to protect trade ships from Ken'nar raids. Now there are none to spare from the battlefields."

Unlike Morgan, Binthe smiled often—and when she did so during the Quorumtide festivals, she had her share of would-be suitors, too. However, she seemed to reserve her most arresting smiles for Morgan Jord.

Teague certainly thought she was beautiful. Any man would—tall and willowy, with rich auburn waves of hair that caressed her fair face and made her sea-green eyes even more alluring, soft lips that all but kissed words as she enunciated them. Her warm personality, though, made her different from so many of the other Fal'kin he knew. She possessed a compassion, an honest kindness that reminded him of his mother. He simply felt more comfortable around her.

He often wondered why his parents never had any more children—well, they probably felt one Unaspected mistake was enough—but if he were to have a sibling, he would have liked a sister. And he would have liked that sister to be just like Binthe Lima.

"You were a maritime seer?"

"No, not really, but my father was for a time. My mother was a defender and frequently gone, so I spent much of my childhood with my father at sea. He taught me everything I know about my Aspect."

The light breeze made the silver-gilded grassland ripple almost as if it were water. Teague had sailed a few times with his parents when they spent their healing sabbaticals in Rhadaz with his mother's people.

Mirana had begged him to take her away from Deren and her visions. He should have. They could have sailed to Rhadaz or Unadar or anywhere. It wouldn't have mattered, as long as they were together. That seemed so long ago now, it could have been a request made by another girl. Maybe it was.

"Why did you become a battle seer? You don't seem like you enjoy it." He grimaced. "What I mean is, you're not like the others. Well, you are, of course. I mean, you're one of the best il'Kin."

Binthe laughed again and patted his hand. "I know what you are trying to say. And you are right. I did not seek to become an il'Kin." She then took a slow breath. "The il'Kin did not have a battle seer for a long time. After my parents died, my grandmother thought it best I leave Rün-Taran for a while."

"Oh." The thought had never occurred to him that a Fal'kin might not like where or how she served. "Do you regret joining the il'Kin?"

"*Ai,*" she paused, looking off into the camp, "and no."

Some comfort he was. He wracked his brain for something, anything, to say. "How is your jaw? Binthe, I'm so sorry."

"Teague, you've apologized every morning and every night. I know it was a mistake. A stupid mistake but a mistake nonetheless." She squeezed his hand. "The bruising is almost gone. Your numbweed is unlike anything we have back in Nuralima."

"Numbweed is made from peda blossoms. They don't grow well in Rün-Taran's humidity. The essential oils need drier air to concentrate. At least that's what my mother said."

"Speaking of skills that don't come naturally, where did you learn to throw a punch like that?" She put her fingertips to her jaw.

He winced again. "My father showed me a few things." He fiddled with a long blade of grass between the fingers of his left hand, tying it into a surgeon's knot. "You know. Courtyard bullies." He tossed the knot in front of him.

Binthe picked up the knot. "One hand? Your left hand?" She pointed to her jaw. "But you're right-handed." He shrugged and said nothing. "Where did your father learn to fight? He is— was a healer."

"Everyone on my father's side was a defender. He was sort of an anomaly." His father, however, was the most gifted mistake the Aspects Above ever made. "I guess growing up he had a few courtyard bullies, too." He rose and bade her good night.

"Please stay."

"I'm just going back to my blanket."

"I know what it is you wish to do. If Morgan is ever wounded again, I want nothing more than you to care for him."

"He has his Aspect. He sure as hell doesn't need me." Teague stalked back over to his blanket and wrapped it around himself to shut out the night.

m

CHAPTER 5

"Defendeä ísi mor tha Iës amula o Iës clae. Ië ísi mor tha Iës Aspecta. Defendeä ísi virtú crearé aspecente."
("A Defender is more than his amulet or his sword. He is more than his Aspect. A Defender is courage made manifest.")

—Ora Fal'kinnen 48:1–3

Someone kicked Teague's thigh, hard. "Cut it out, Morgan. Can't you just wake me like a normal person?" He opened his eyes. It was not Morgan Jord.

A tall warrior encased in black armor stood over him. "Scream, boy. It will be the last sound you will ever make."

He did scream. He also grabbed his sword. The Ken'nar, however, stomped on it with a heavy boot before Teague could begin to put up a defense.

The black warrior laughed and swung his own sword. Teague spun away, narrowly missing the blade as it came down where his head was a moment ago. He kicked out at his attacker's knee. The Ken'nar stumbled back, howling in pain. Teague snatched up his sword and scrambled to his feet.

Shouts rose throughout the camp. The Ken'nar patrol. Liaonne and Binthe were right. They had doubled back and attacked them. He hadn't expected it would be so soon.

He dashed for Bankin and tripped over something in the grass. The defender Liaonne had assigned to him lay dead in the grass.

The moon had set, taking with it whatever bit of light it had offered. Silhouettes struggled against each other in the darkness. He could not tell friend from foe. Amulets flared around him then went dark. When he reached his horse, a black shape appeared next to him.

He swung his Ken'nar blade. "Take one more step, and I'll run you through."

"Easy. It's me," Morgan said. "Ride north. Do not stop until you reach Edara. Go, now!"

He was about to protest when another form rose out of the gloom. "Morgan! Behind you! Look out!"

The defender whirled around and cut down a Ken'nar before he could cleave him in two. "Hurry! Go!"

"I'm not leaving." He heard an eerie whistle.

"Get down." The il'Kin barreled into him, knocking him to the ground. Three arrows quivered in the sod where he had been standing.

"Get off me." He pushed Morgan from him and started to dash off into the fray.

"Ride!" The il'Kin defender grabbed his collar and shoved him toward Bankin. "This is not your fight."

Teague wrenched himself from the man's grip. "*Ai*, it is. As much mine as yours."

A woman screamed.

"Binthe." Morgan turned to Teague. "Go!" He ran to the seer.

Teague was not about to be mollified nor run like a coward. Not when the bastards were within arms' reach. He grabbed his sword and took off running after the il'Kin defender.

Another dark shape loomed near him. He flailed his blade. "You'll pay for what you've done."

"Put that thing down before you hurt yourself." A yellow amulet glowed, revealing Prime Edaran's face. "Get out of the camp. Go to Edara." Her amulet went dark again.

A shape moved next to her, closing in. A raised blade glinted in the moonlight.

"Look out!" Teague shouted.

She hissed in pain and whirled around, blocking the blow meant to sever her arm. She loosed brilliant yellow amulet fire at the Ken'nar. The warrior collapsed to the ground in a heap of ash and smoking armor. Morgan's face glowed in the violet light of his amulet. Binthe held a long knife at the ready.

He swallowed, his heart racing. "Prime Edaran, I—"

"You have attached yourself to Varn-Erdal," she said. "That makes me your prime. The next time I give you an order, you will follow it immediately, without question, or you will leave my province just as quickly. *Oë comprende?*"

He nodded, not daring to look the young prime in the eye. "*Ai, Ëi primus. Ëo comprende.*"

The fight was over as quickly as it started. Several defenders sustained injuries. Two were dead.

Teague finished tying a bandage around the defender prime's arm. "You should be fine."

He didn't know if her wound would heal properly—he had very few supplies with him and no needles or sinew—but felt the need to say something. Thank the Aspects, the wound wasn't life-threatening. Any apology he could think up now after his blunder during the skirmish sounded ridiculously inadequate.

He frowned and shook his head in disgust at himself. The young defender prime had sustained the cut on her shoulder because of him. Even the defender ordered to guard him was dead. He was more than a distraction; he was a downright liability.

The Varn-Erdalan woman nodded her thanks and beckoned to the two il'Kin. "We had better leave this place. They may have called for reinforcements."

As Teague packed away the medical supplies, he hefted his Ken'nar blade. Flailing the sword around was utterly useless. He needed to learn how to use it. Finding a teacher would be easy.

The hard part would be convincing Morgan Jord.

CHAPTER 6

"The life of a Fal'kin is not his own. It is of Kinderra.
It is of the Aspects Above. So, we were called to be."
—The Book of Kinderra

"Succulent rabbit is on the menu tonight." Mirana held up her trophies. "Or at least scrawny, stringy desert hare we can pretend is succulent rabbit."

Tetric did not look up from piling kindling for a fire. "It took you long enough. I was growing worried."

Drawing her mouth into a flat line, she tossed the hares down and drew her belt knife. "They were very clever." She had to eat to live, but she didn't have to like how it came to her plate. "I also searched for some more of those chokecherries you showed me the other day." She emptied on the ground a saddlebag containing a dozen walnut-sized cherries. "They're not apples, but if we're not going to stop in Kasan or anywhere else for a while, I figured we needed every edible thing we could find."

"Good thinking. Especially since the weather in the Dúadar is unpredictable and we might be held up for a day or two."

"Wait. What?" She dropped a chokecherry. "We're going to take the Dúadar Pass?" The Dúadar Pass was treacherous, even deadly, but its destination was far more fearsome. The pass would take them straight into the heart of the foreboding Vale i'Dúadar. "Wouldn't it be easier to go around the Dar-Tal Si Mountains?"

"*Ai*, it would be easier but not quicker. We would face a long trek through the open desert. We could never carry enough water for both us and the horses. If there was another route, I would have us take it."

"And that's supposed to reassure me?" She turned her head toward the pass. "They say it's haunted. So much death. After the battle."

"It's not haunted. There's no such thing as ghosts." He, too, now faced the pass. "But it is a hostile place. We will need to be cautious and travel fast."

The Dúadar Pass. They'd probably find nothing to eat for dinner there but Aspect-forsaken insects just for good measure.

Kneeling beside the rabbits, she bowed her head and sent a prayer of thanksgiving to the Aspects Above.

"You used your belt knife?"

She sat back on her heels at his interruption. "How did you know?" Was there no end to the Trine's skill with his Aspects? Or had he been spying on her with his Seeing Aspect, making sure she followed through with the hunt?

He pointed. "You didn't clean it."

She glared at him. "Why bother? It would become bloodied again a moment later." She plunged the belt knife into a hare and began to gut it. "Throwing one of my long knives with any force would have cut the thing in half."

"Good thinking."

Oh, she so hoped he read her mind right now.

Tetric walked over and knelt. "Why are you so filled with anger?"

She studied the knife in her hand. "It's just, well, I hate death." She gestured to the hare. "This kind of death. The sudden silence. The abrupt emptiness." The emptiness at Two Rivers Ford. She swallowed and turned away from the hares and her mentor.

"*Ai.* So do I. More than you can know. But it is a necessary part of the circle of life."

"Death is, *ai.* But not this. Not killing. A day does not pass without me missing my *Brepaithe* Toban. But his death was natural. Sort of an echo that softened beyond my hearing. Not like—" Not like the ford.

As he regarded the dead animals, he nodded, a sparse gesture, barely moving his head. "*Ëo comprende com Öe dici. Verda.*" His thin lips lifted in an equally spare smile. "This kind of killing, however, allows us to survive. It is not so different than the use of the Light from Within and the Power from Without."

She fell back on her backside, dropping the small blade. "What?"

"We Aspected give of our innate gifts. The world around us," he gestured wide, "also gives back to us if we decide to choose it."

Mirana's eyes widened. "Hunting and the Power from Without are not even remotely the same thing."

"No?" He pointed to a hare. "These died, gave their life force if you will, so we may live. Life around us sustains us. Think, Mirana. Is it any different from the way we must use the Aspects?"

She worked a jaw a few times before the words came. "*Ai! Ai*, it is!" She wanted a much more emphatic response and certainly one more eloquent.

"No, it is not," he replied. "It is war, the endless cycle of hate we have endured, that is reprehensible. We, too, have a role to play in the cycle. We, as Trines, must also be willing to die so others may live as well." His voice had grown distant with his last words.

She searched his dark eyes, rolling back the walls protecting her mind. "I am. I swear to you."

He rested his large hand on her shoulder "*Ëo comprende Oë isi.*" He smiled, a genuine one.

She favored him with a smile of her own. Her stomach growled, breaking the poignant moment. "Sorry." They both laughed.

"Hurry up before the fire dies down. We need a good dinner. Tomorrow will be a long day."

The temperature fell rapidly with the setting sun as they finished their meal and with it their conversation. As she watched the fire, Tetric's words about dying for Kinderra came back to her. She had indeed been willing to sacrifice herself at Two Rivers Ford to save the Fal'kin—she nearly had, too. But what about so many others?

"Tetric?"

He took out a whetstone and began to sharpen his long sword. "*Ai?*"

"Did any—" She swallowed as some of her dinner tried to hop up from her stomach. ... *Did any Fal'kin die at the ford when I—because of what I did?* ...

He looked intently at her. ... *Fourteen* ... He returned to his sword, drawing the whetstone along the length of the blade with swift, violent strokes.

His answer crushed her. She felt faint. The fire ate away at the kindling, appearing all too similar to the amulet fire she wielded at the ford. "I was trying to save them."

"*Ai.* I know you were. Such losses, such *travesties* as that, are why we must end this war. Even when we control Jasal's Keep, it will not be easy," the Trine said. "The only way we can even begin to do that is by uniting. All the provinces must come together as one, under one leader." His voice had dropped low. A tendril of emotion escaped from his mind to hers. He had not whispered to keep a secret, but in humility, even a bit overwhelmed by the thought. He should be. It was insanity.

Mirana's jaw dropped. "You can't be serious?"

"Do you think I chose to be responsible for so many lives? I don't want to be Primus Magne; I *have* to be." He thrust his long sword into the ground. She started at the action.

What could he possibly be thinking? As Primus Magne, every prime would have to show fealty to him alone. Self-rule was the reason why there were nine provinces in Kinderra in the first place. It was the threat of the Ken'nar that held together the loose confederation of mutual aid. Only in times of extreme crisis was a Primus Magne elevated from among the primes.

She looked at the Trine, searching his mind. It wasn't the determination she found there that surprised her, she had expected that. But as much as that emotion pervaded his thoughts, it was the apprehension tinged with weariness residing there as well that shocked her. Could even the great Trine Tetric

Garis be uncertain, even uncomfortable with his own destiny? "Even as desperate as Kinderra is now, we don't need a dictator."

He laughed, a sort of exhaled bark that sounded anything but humorous. "Were you not at the ford? That is just a taste of the coming conflict."

In that, he was correct. A siege would surround Jasal's Keep someday. A siege she might bring herself. In her keep vision, Tetric Garis was not there. Would she fail him? Would he die because of her?

Her chest clenched in dread. The Trine Prophecy, written so long ago the name of the prophet was no longer known, spoke of only two Trines: the thrice-cursed, come to destroy, and the thrice-blessed, come to rebuild. Tetric Garis was the thrice-blessed, and the Dark Trine who led the Ken'nar was the thrice-cursed. No writing, no scripture anywhere spoke of three Trines. What, then, was she? Would Tetric die at the hands of the Ken'nar Trine, leaving her to fulfill his role? Or would he defeat the warlord but not be able to turn her from her destiny of destruction at Jasal's Keep, leaving them enemies—Oh, Aspects Above, no! She killed the thought like a ravenous grynwen breaking the neck of a deer.

"I know you want to end the war, but please do not do this," she said. "You could die."

Tetric smiled down at her. "I am not so easily vanquished."

"Maybe not, but are you so certain I can aid you?"

"More than aid me. You are the most important thing in Kinderra."

"Because of this." She pulled the Codex of Jasal Pinal from one of her saddlebags on the ground.

"Your ability to detect Jasal in his writings is exceedingly important, *ai*, but," he spoke slowly as if he were unused to revealing such thoughts they were so foreign to him, "you, yourself are important. To me."

Her jaw worked on several sentences before one came out. "I-I don't understand."

He took the ancient journal from her and set it aside, then held one of her hands in his. "You are the only person who has ever truly understood the blessing and the burden of being a Trine. In you, I see hope. For Kinderra. For me. You are a gift to me from the Aspects Above I never hoped to receive."

"I won't fail you."

He nodded minutely. "No, Mirana. It is I who must not fail you. For the good of Kinderra."

CHAPTER 7

"Brother fought brother, the vale between the hills turned red by the work of swords and amulets."
—The Book of Kinderra

She backs away as the tall swordsman levels a blade at her chest. Teague shouts a warning behind her. She calls again and again for Tetric Garis. The swordsman speaks to her. She cannot hear. The raging storm, the siege far below, her grief, blots out his words. His sword comes at her with blinding speed. She blocks it, blow for blow, each impact reverberating through her entire body. He strikes again. Her desolation makes her response slow. He rakes the tip of his blade across her stomach. She sinks to her knees, groaning in agony. Her blood flows hot over her hand.

The truth overwhelms her more than any physical blow. She failed. Failed Tetric Garis. Failed Kinderra. Failed herself.

The Ken'nar stalks over to her. With a mockery of gentleness, he brushes the hair back from her neck with fingers like ice. He lifts an object from her.

"Don't give it to him!" *Teague collapses then lays still.*

Pain. An ocean of it. A nothingness follows it, seeping in. A loss so profound it silences her heart. A brilliant light flares and consumes everything.

"Mirana, wake up."

Mirana bolted upright and swung her fists.

Tetric grabbed her wrists, steadying her. "Mirana? Wake up. It's all right."

"Oh, thank the Aspects Above! It hasn't happened yet."

He scowled. "What hasn't?"

"Nothing!" she answered far more emphatically than she meant to. "Nothing." She shook her head to dismiss, well, everything. "It was just a nightmare."

The crushing sense of guilt permeated through the vision of Jasal's Keep. It had grown, if that was possible.

He frowned. "You are lying to me. Why?"

"It was no lie." She rose to her feet and stretched. It was still dark with just a faint brightening on the eastern horizon. "It was the worst nightmare I've ever had."

"What was it?"

She turned her back to him, as much to pack for the day's journey as to avoid his gaze. "I don't remember now. It was just frightening. That's all."

He was not happy with her response—was he ever happy?—but he did not press her.

Mirana rode for several hours with Tetric guiding his black stallion carefully ahead of her up the rocky path of the Dúadar Pass. Steep shale walls towered on either side of her and blotted out what little light made its way into the narrow canyon. Soon, they were forced to dismount as the pass constricted. Storm clouds thickened, deepening the shadows. The wind began to whisper through the crevices. She did not like this place. Even a long, hot, thirsty trek through the open desert would be better.

She picked her way through the high ledges. Her feet threatened to slide out from under her on the loose rock. Her hands and knees became cut and bloodied from slipping on the gravel.

The Trine led her to an exceptionally narrow stricture in the rock walls, forcing her to turn sideways to pass through. The horses whinnied as rock scraped at their sides in the tight opening.

She hesitated a moment. This would either be a horrible or an excellent place for an ambush, depending on which side of the amulet one was on. No warning came. She strained her ears but heard nothing save her heart rattling like a baby's toy. The flatness in the Aspects around her made the pass feel more like a tomb. Tetric's anxiety grew the farther along the pass they traveled. That didn't exactly calm her fears either.

Once through the stricture, she hissed against a stinging sensation across her chest. She looked down, expecting a scrape. There was nothing wrong with her. She looked at the Trine. He had several cuts across the skin of his chest. "You're hurt."

"These do not worry me." He pointed ahead. "That does."

Her jaw dropped. The pass dead-ended into a rough-hewn wall of stairs. They climbed nearly straight up high into the mountains and disappeared from view as they crested a peak.

"Oh. Tetric. How are we ever going to get over that?"

"Slowly and carefully."

"How are the horses going to make it?"

"*Ai*, they're sure-footed. It is us that might find the way more difficult. This part of the pass is called Deven's Stair, after an ancient seer. I think the illusion is less the handiwork of some creative seer and more that of miners searching for amulet gems. These mountains used to be filled with them." He looked up at the sky. "The steps are broken in places and will become treacherous with the rain, though. Be careful. Come."

She sucked in her breath and grabbed his sleeve, remembering a history lesson from her mother. "Deven was a seer known for meddling with the minds of Aspected and Unaspected alike. Are you sure it's safe?"

He nodded. "I have been through here before. Once. A very long time ago."

She hoped he had a good memory. "What if the path has changed since then?"

He curled up one side of his mouth. "You think I'm not up to the task?"

"Not at all," she said. "I'm not sure I am."

"There is only one way to find out."

"*Ai.*" She tried to sound confident. She knew she did not.

The Trine bade her follow. "Step where I walk."

The sky grew darker overhead as the wind moaned louder and tugged at Mirana's cloak. She inched up Deven's Stair through the mountains, clinging to Tetric like a shadow, leading her nervous mount.

The clouds continued to thicken and lower as the wind grew to a keening wail. Thunder echoed through the pass. She smelled wet stone. Rain was coming.

Tetric was correct, the stairs lay uneven and missing in many places, making them as dangerous as if they were vertical.

After hours of climbing, her legs burned and wobbled. The wind whipped pebbles and sharp gravel into her face. The air grew colder, and rain fell in uneven taps. Frigid drops hit her skin so hard they stung.

When they reached the summit, she released her breath in an exhausted exhale. "Thank the Aspects."

"Do not thank them yet," the Trine replied.

She scowled. "What do you—?" She groaned. The stairs now led straight down. They were already slippery, and the cliffs held no sheltering outcroppings where they could wait out the storm. "These stairs will become impossible to descend if it rains much harder."

As if to give evidence to her words, her foot slipped on a moss-covered step. Tetric whirled around and caught her wrist.

He pushed her against the rock wall. "What did I say?"

A hand's breadth away, the rough stairs dropped to nothingness. "You said to be careful."

"No, I said to step where I walk." He let go of her wrist. "Now, do you understand what I mean?"

She nodded vigorously and said nothing.

Deven's Stair jagged in curves through the Dar-Tal Si Mountains to end, at last, on a small flat of shale. From her vantage point, the Vale i'Dúadar below stretched from horizon to horizon. Lightning revealed a broad expanse of cracked earth devoid of any living thing. The land appeared to be scoured clean by the Aspects Above themselves. The tailings of war lay strewn over the split and pitted ground. Broken armor, lances, shields, and swords of every description were embedded in the cracked earth. Here and there, boulders sat like huge, hunched timber bears, just waiting to pounce on unsuspecting travelers and rip them apart limb from limb.

Ahead of her, Tetric stood unmoving, his shoulders tensed. "What is it?"

He didn't answer but raised his hand to silence her. His mind remained open to her, and this time, she wished it was not.

He was wary, even nervous. More so than he had been before the start of the Battle of Two Rivers Ford.

She waited long moments, but the Trine said nothing as he continued to search the valley below. "Tetric?" she whispered finally. She wasn't sure why she felt the need to be quiet. Little from the vale reflected in her Aspects. Dead. No, not dead. More like life, suspended. Either way, the sensation made her skin crawl. "Traders say the Vale has monsters. But that's just a silly rumor." She bit her lip. "Right?" Maybe the few merchants who did brave the Vale i'Dúadar mistook the boulders for creatures.

Tetric glowered at the valley. "I think it would be best if we put on our armor."

So much for the boulder theory.

She waited for him to give a further explanation, but he did not. Did he always have to be so cryptic? "Why? What's down there?" She searched one of Ashtar's saddlebags, then pulled out her pectoral guard and wriggled into it.

"Monsters." The Trine adjusted his sword belt and swung a long leg over his mount's back.

"You choose *that* to tell me plainly, *Ëi patrua*?"

"Hush. Ride." He kicked the sides of his stallion to pick up its pace.

Mirana shook her head and climbed onto Ashtar's saddle, grateful to have all seventeen hands of his height between her and the accursed valley floor.

She rode down the remainder of the pass to the valley. The rain struck the dry earth, stirring up little puffs of dust on impact. The only sounds in the valley were the rain and the soft thud of the horses' hooves on the hardpan. Even the wind had quieted. The silence was deafening.

"Tell me something," Mirana said, as much to hear her voice as to seek information from her mentor. "How did these boulders get here? I could see if they fell from the mountainside and rolled down some, but the slopes are miles away."

Tetric hesitated before he answered. "They were thrown. By defenders. During the battle."

She glanced down. To give credence to his explanation, some armor lay squashed flat under a large stone. She quickly turned away, not wanting to see if what was left of its wearer remained. Squeezing her knees against her horse's side, she cantered to ride next to the Trine. "How do you know they were thrown? My parents said you didn't fight in the Battle of the Vale. That it took that very massacre to bring you back to us from your hermitage."

"I know exactly what happened in the vale." His jaw tightened. "The memories still haunt me."

She blinked. "So, you did fight in the—"

He reined in suddenly. "Wait. Do you sense that?"

She reached out with her senses, physical and Aspected alike, and gave a small gasp. "*Ai.* Everything feels sort of—" She took another breath. "Overwhelming. Almost like there's too much of the Aspects."

Tetric stiffened. "*U'Nehíl.* Ride!" She jabbed her heels into Ashtar and galloped across the barren plain, a breath behind the Trine.

Mirana held Ashtar's reins tighter in one hand and gripped the hilt of one of her long knives with the other. A deep, visceral tug pulled within her as something glinted in the dirt below her stirrup as she raced by. She glanced at it but saw only a shield half-submerged in the ground. She held Ashtar's reins tighter. The glinting flashed again. Lightning reflecting off the metal? It was green.

"Tetric?" she shouted above the drumming of the horses' hooves. He said nothing and continued to ride. Below her right boot, she saw another spark of light, yellow. Then red. Blue. Then dozens more surrounding her.

The amulets. Any amulet could be theirs, not just one like most Aspected. She swallowed. They were the amulets of those Fal'kin and Ken'nar who perished during the Battle of the Vale i'Dúadar, thirty long summers ago. Their need wrenched the breath from her lungs. They were calling her. By the thousands. She clutched at her pectoral armor and groaned. The whole valley floor erupted in an explosion of rainbow colors.

"Run!" he shouted.

Her Defending Aspect rose sharply.

A monster blocked her path.

She screamed.

It was a man but unlike any man she had ever seen. He was brawny and leather-skinned. Tatters of a Sün-Kasalan uniform hung from massive shoulders, and his eyes held a ferocious gleam that matched the maniacal grin twisting his maw. His body appeared corrupted into a brutish monster by the endless summers in the unforgiving valley. His appearance was fearsome enough, but it was his mind's sense that was truly terrifying. Demented bloodlust had supplanted any reason. No, this was no longer a man; it was a monster.

From behind boulders crept other corrupted men and women, other twisted monsters, swords held in gnarled hands, amulets hanging from scarred necks. They advanced on her.

"Tetric!"

Ashtar reared, pawing at the air in terror, and threw her to the ground. The feral men and women surrounded her. The horse kicked out with his hind legs, sending two of the ghastly warriors flying.

Mirana slashed at one of the feral men with her long knife, but it spun away before her blade did any damage. Long knives were not nearly long enough. She spied a sword sticking out partway from the ground and called it to her with an urgent intent in the Aspects. As it sailed toward her, a feral woman caught the hilt. The creature gripped her amulet and struck out, blade and deadly light, lightning-fast. Mirana yelled and ducked the twin blows. She wrested another sword from the hardpan. Two more feral warriors closed in. She swung at her attackers, slashing them before they could focus their amulets on her.

The rain now came down in torrents, turning the valley into a river of mud. She brandished the sword and the knife, trying to move closer to the Trine, but the mud sucked at her feet and greedy hands grabbed for her. Claw-like fingers clutched at her cloak, gagging her. She staggered backward and dropped her sword. With her knife, she cut off the feral man's hand holding her cloak.

Another feral woman brought the hilt of her blade on Mirana's wrist, forcing her to drop her long knife. Three more untamed warriors advanced, amulets aglow. She wrapped her Aspects around them and flung out her free hand. The three gruesome fighters flew away, smashing into boulders to collapse unmoving in the mud. She called to her fallen long knife and drew her second blade as another ghoulish warrior rushed her. She sliced each knife in opposite directions, decapitating her attacker.

One after another, the crazed warriors surged toward her. "Tetric! I can't hold them off!"

As she fought, she touched amulets, brushing the toe or heel of a boot against one as she wove her body away from her attackers. The crystals begged for her, pulling, grasping, clawing at her Aspects to join with them whenever she made contact.

She couldn't breathe. She couldn't fight off the feral folk and fend off the amulets that implored her to bond with them. She swung hard at a tall man wearing the shreds of a Tash-Hamari uniform. The force of her blow caused her to slip in the mud, and she fell to one knee.

"Mirana!" Tetric whirled his stallion around, attempting to ride back. Blood-crazed warriors pressed in and swarmed over him, throwing him to the ground.

She cried out as the Trine went down under an onslaught of demon fighters. An instant later, an intense draining sensation ripped the air from her lungs and the Aspects from her body. She pressed her hand against her chest and sank to all fours. A dark-tinged silver fireball exploded, destroying the fighters surrounding her mentor, sending mangled bodies flying. She staggered to her feet and ran toward him, his hematite amulet still clutched in his hand.

"Go. Make for the pass straight ahead," he gasped.

"But—"

"Go!"

She vaulted onto her horse and took off at a dead run. Ashtar dodged amulet fire and demon fighters, slipping in the slick mud. She clung to his neck as he righted himself and regained his gait.

The remainder of the pass lay just ahead. She steered her mount through knots of feral folk. Her armor saved her from a glancing strike from a lance. Both she and her steed received cuts and scrapes and burns from swords and amulets wielded by murderous hands. Washes of color scintillated across the valley in her wake, a river of iridescence created by amulets.

At last, she reached the southern portion of the pass. She reined Ashtar around to search for Tetric. A last line of feral warriors rose, blocking the Trine's way forward. Others came at him from the rear, preventing escape.

"Tetric!"

She had to save him, but how? She would never be able to beat back that many wildfolk with just her long knives.

An amulet.

In her keep vision, death and destruction lay all around her, annihilation that could only be wrought through an amulet. But had she not chosen an amulet at Two Rivers Ford, most of the Fal'kin from her home would be dead.

Her keep vision. Tetric Garis was gone.

She would not let him die.

An amulet lay ahead of her, sparkling a deep blue, its beauty utterly incongruous to the horror swirling farther within the vale. Mirana screamed and dug her heels into Ashtar's sides and charged back across muddy flats. She leaned low from her saddle and snared the amulet. The sapphire flared instantly.

The world slowed as she slipped its chain over her head. The blue gem burned against her chest. It pulled at her Aspects, demanding them, coalescing, focusing, merging with them. Her breath rasped in her ears as all other sounds faded away. The amulet willed her to release her power, the three-part harmony of her Aspects building into a deafening swell of life music.

She raced toward the hideous warriors and opened herself to the irresistible pull of the crystal. With a cry of victorious release, a jet of deadly blue light erupted from the amulet and struck at the monstrous horde attacking Tetric. Oily ash melted in the rain as bodies disappeared in a pyre. His stallion shot out of the fray, neighing in terror as it ran for the pass. More ghastly warriors continued to advance. Tetric's pain seeped from his mind to hers, beckoning to her Healing Aspect.

Mirana called another amulet to her free hand. Her Aspects surged through a deep golden topaz, modulating her life's harmonics with its own. The sapphire and the topaz battled for supremacy over her power. At last, she let them take from her. Azure and golden flame exploded from the amulets. The twin jets of deadly light blended, green fire now washing over the skeletons, consuming them, turning them into muddy gray ash.

The remaining feral folk howled and gibbered to each other and shrank back from Mirana's brilliant amulets. They retreated across the mire to disappear into the crags and crevices in the mountain slopes in the distance, moving far too quickly, far too agilely for creatures who were once human.

The tall Trine lay on the ground, bleeding from a dozen wounds. She tossed the amulets aside and leaped down from Ashtar's saddle.

"I'm here." She dragged him over to Ashtar and hauled him to his feet. He fell over the horse's back.

They charged out of the valley, Tetric's black stallion ahead of them, running for its life. The violent colors of the amulets of the dead flared in their wake then went dark once they reached the safety of the southern portion of the pass.

She slowed Ashtar to reach for the reins of the Trine's stallion, preventing it from racing away. Tetric fell to the ground as he tried to dismount from Ashtar.

She jumped down, cradling him. "You're injured." She looked out over the vale. The closest amulet lay half-buried more than a hundred yards away. Could she make it before another phantom phalanx rose against her? She bit her lip. She would *not* fail him. "I'll be right back."

"No, Mirana. It's too dangerous."

Under her palm, his wounds cried louder to her Healing Aspect. A laceration across his chest was deeper than she had first thought. "You're cut nearly to the bone. I need an amulet to heal you." She tried to stand, but he held her wrist.

"They'll attack you if you go back there." He released her hand, tightening it against a wave of pain that sang through his body to Mirana's sense. "Use mine."

She wanted to debate the offer, but every moment she wasted was one more moment Tetric bled.

Cautiously, she lay one hand over the hematite amulet and the other over the deepest of the wounds. Like walking from a dark room into the noonday sun, the need from her *patrua's* injuries slammed into her Aspects. Her head swam and she steadied herself against a rock.

"I-It's so deep," she said, breathless. "I've never healed anything this serious before." Tears began to scald her eyes. "I-I need you to show me."

He nodded, his breaths coming from between pain-clenched teeth. Again, he stifled a groan. "It may feel very strange at first, but I need you to trust me."

"I do trust you." She scowled. She trusted him with her life. *… Don't you know that by now? … What are you going to do? …*

He placed both their hands over the hematite amulet. *… We shall use it together …*

Vitality left her as a deep draw pulled from within. She had used the Healing Aspect before, albeit just to block pain, but it had never felt this way. It wasn't as brutal a sensation as she had felt when they tried to save Vallia Edaran's life, but it was still as disconcerting. It seemed like she were the one bleeding, more and more being taken from her, leaving her *less* somehow.

Slowly at first, then faster and faster, blood vessels reattached their severed ends. Muscles knitted their fibers back together. And Mirana felt herself disappear, bit by bit.

… Tetric … I think … I think I understand … I can— …

... I need you for one more moment ...

Torn flesh continued to mesh back to wholeness, while she became more empty. One by one, the Trine's bleeding wounds sealed themselves to thin red lines, some disappearing altogether.

This couldn't be what it was like to heal? It felt, well, all *wrong*. She certainly had been ill, and even sprained her wrist once, and when Teague's parents healed her, she felt as if she were floating in a pool of sunlight and warm honey. Not like *this*.

She began to take her hand from his amulet to find a new purchase of strength within herself from which to continue the healing on her own when he drew his hand from hers. He lay back against the rocks, recovering his breath.

"Tetric, *Ëi patrua*, are you all right?"

He nodded. *"Ai. Gratas a Oë."*

Had he taken her life force to heal himself? Now she gasped. He *had* taken her life's essence. Just like—O Aspects Above!—just like the Ken'nar! Why would he do such a thing? Or was it something else? Had he been too injured to call to the Healing Aspect on his own?

For once, *he* needed *her*.

Tetric smiled at her. "You chose an amulet, two amulets. You used mine. To save me. You have been terrified of nothing else. All my life, men and women have sought my power for their own ends. But you did this for me. Just. Me. *Gratas. Gratas Oë."*

"I can't bear the thought of losing you."

He embraced her, his mind full of pride and gratitude. Of love. ... *You won't ...*

CHAPTER 8

"To see may be a blessing, but to gift the skill of Defense in continuity with the touch of Healing? Therein lies a dilemma with no solution. Therein lies damnation."

—The Codex of Jasal the Great

A multitude of stars winked overhead in the dark firmament by the time Mirana and Tetric reached the end of the Dúadar Pass. The rain had stopped, and they made their camp in a niche of rocks above the high desert of northern Tash-Hamar.

The Trine had not spoken since their harrowing ordeal in the Vale i'Dúadar, and her mind burned with questions.

She rummaged through her saddlebag and retrieved some scrub berries and seeds they had foraged. She held out a few of the all-but-inedible tart fruit to Ashtar.

"Here, boy." The chestnut warhorse ate greedily from her hand. "Aspects Above know you deserve something far better than just some berries for fighting so bravely."

She kept several back from Ashtar. The horse tossed his head. "You must learn to share, you big brute."

She approached Tetric's black stallion. The imposing animal just glared down at her. Cautiously, she held out the berries to the horse. She received the eerie impression that it was contemptuous of her and would as soon bite off her hand as take the fruit. She backed away and stole a glance at her mentor. Thankfully, he faced the pass behind them and did not see her. She popped them in her mouth.

"You should eat something," she said to him. She handed him some of the seeds and scrub berries. He took them but did not eat. She found his actions to be remarkably similar to his horse at the moment.

Mirana suppressed a shiver in the chill air and scrounged the rocky ground for something with which to build a fire. Frowning at the sodden lichens in her hand, she said, "I think we're in for a cold night."

He nodded minutely. She sighed. She would just have to speak up and ask him her questions. "Will they follow us?"

He shook his head. "No, I don't think so. I think they've been mollified enough for the moment."

He *thought* so? Would it kill him to honey-coat the truth once in a while?

"Tetric, what happened in the vale? Those-those men and women? If you can still call them that."

He pointed to the lichens in her hand and called to her to get busy. After she had scraped together a small pile of kindling, he cradled his amulet and closed his eyes. A thin finger of silvery light reached out and licked at the brush. A flame erupted. He reached into a nook between the rocks and found some dry leaves and twigs, and added them to the blaze. He still hadn't answered her.

"Tetric?" she asked again.

"The Soul Harvest," he said at last. He handed her a waterskin and kept his gaze on the vale a moment longer before sitting beside her.

She took the skin but was too stunned to drink. "The Soul Harvest?" She laughed. "That's a myth. Something *Brepaithe* Toban threatened me with when I was misbehaving. A rather horrible thing to say to a child, if I might say so."

"It's not a myth," Tetric said, his voice subdued. "'Soul' might be the wrong word. It is not life's essence that is destroyed but will, self-determination. Conscience. It renders living victims without the will or thought of self-preservation." He turned away from her to gaze out into the night. "It destroys part of one's mind. But it can destroy much more." He cracked open some of the seeds and chewed them before eating the berries. "Eat."

Those that had been harvested would be mindless slaves, fully alive as any man or woman but acting without regard for themselves or anyone around them. Fighting without conscience, ignoring pain. Relentless. She no longer had an appetite.

Flame bit into an air pocket in the wood and flared brightly. Mirana squeezed her eyes shut and wrapped her arms around herself.

"Who could be so evil, so desperate, as to steal the mind of another? And why, for Aspects' sake? Even a Ken'nar cannot be that evil." On second thought, maybe she didn't want that question answered.

He propped his bedroll against a rock and regarded her before answering. "The Soul Harvest is not a skill exclusive to the Ken'nar. Only someone with the Healing Aspect."

She shook her head, incredulous. "The Soul Harvest is about as far from what the Healing Aspect is supposed to be as one can get. It destroys everything that makes a person, well, *a person*."

He nodded his head. "*Ai*, but do not think that the Ken'nar are the only Aspected who bear responsibility for all the evil in this land. The Fal'kin are as much to blame for this war as the Ken'nar."

She opened her mouth to argue the point but shock stole her words. Two Rivers Ford. No Ken'nar destroyed those bridges. Not even their Dark Trine.

"Mirana, there are many things we wish were not true, but to ignore them is a fallacy leading to self-destruction." His voice had dropped to a whisper. "Accounts of such a skill exist in ancient, long-forbidden texts."

She raised an eyebrow. "If they are forbidden, how do you know about it?"

He threw another twig into the fire. "No knowledge is truly forbidden. It is only how one uses such knowledge that makes it damning."

"I cannot even imagine anything more damning than the Soul Harvest."

"*Ai*, perhaps. But does it not mean an Aspected can continue to be in service to Kinderra? If he or she is truly dead, what use is that? From one perspective, the Soul Harvest is a waking death. From another, it turns one's enemies into allies. Of a sort."

She sat back. "You don't believe that, do you?"

"I am trying to get you to think beyond the obvious, beyond black and white, beyond the narrow views of your heart." He poked the fire. "And, *ai*, Mirana, you are right. It is an act of desperation. Terrible and wonderous. But desperate." He reached over to his stallion with a handful of berries. The animal gently lipped the fruit from his palm. "Go to sleep. We should be in Rhadaz within two nights if we get an early start and keep up our pace."

Sleep? She would never sleep again after this conversation. She unfurled her bedroll with a snap. "Your bedtime stories are abysmal, *Ëi patrua*."

He chuckled. The sound comforted her. Unfortunately, not enough, not after his explanation of the Soul Harvest.

She burrowed into her bedroll, covering herself with the saddle blanket and watching her mentor stoke the fire with his stiletto. "That's a beautiful knife." Even concentrating on a weapon was less unnerving than some horrible corruption of the Healing Aspect.

The thin blade, as long as his hand, held a hilt of exotic ebony wood from Jad-Anüna inlaid with pearl from far-off Rün-Taran.

He nodded. "It's forged from Tash-Hamari steel. They are the most skilled swordsmiths in all of Kinderra."

"Where did you get it?"

He shifted and moved his gaze away from her to the fire. She caught fleeting images of an old man with the soulful, canted eyes of a Trak-Calander.

"My father."

"Your father?" she replied with more surprise in her voice than she meant to include.

"Why is that so strange? Did you think I was hatched?"

Mirana laughed. "No, of course not. *Ëo culpa*. I just meant—well, that is, I guess I have a hard time picturing you as a child."

"Well, that was a very, very long time ago." She caught his gentle sarcastic reference to her earlier jibe about his age and ability to trek through the Dúadar Pass. "This was presented to me by my foster father when I was eight summers old. It was the first Quorumtide I had ever celebrated in Deren." He peered into the fire again. "I never knew the man, nor the woman, who gave me life."

She watched the fire for a moment. "Sometimes, our families are those we choose, not those to whom we're born."

"Well said." He smiled at her, a warm, genuine smile. "Now, get some sleep."

She curled into a ball and shut her eyes. Her own smile faded, however, as thoughts of the Soul Harvest rose like feral folk on the attack. If the Ken'nar Dark Trine used the Soul Harvest to destroy his enemies, would he try to harvest Tetric?

Or would she be harvested?

No longer caring for what she once loved. Tetric. Teague. Her parents. Kinderra. All gone in an all-consuming white light. Terrible and wondrous. Like she might become.

Mirana's hand slipped into her belt pouch to touch the mica pendant held within.

No. She would not let that happen. To those she loved. Or to herself.

CHAPTER 9

*"She mounts to the stars on hoofs of Light, the Sixth
Sister. Varn-Erdal, the celestial mare of the Aspects
Above."*

—The Book of Kinderra

A chill roused the Ain Magne from his meditation. The
campfire had all but died. He poked at the embers with a stick,
adding it to the glowing coals, whereupon they extinguished
themselves with an anemic wisp of smoke. He sighed.

He rose to his feet and stretched. He had journeyed far
from his Ken'nar troops in Kana-Akün, bent on securing the
more delicate parts of his plan of conquest. His healing
meditation had done wonders to beat back the weariness from
long days of traveling, but it could do nothing to slow time, nor,
frankly, to start a fire without kindling.

He searched the area around his camp for something with which to build the fire anew, his familiar nemesis, frustration, visiting him once more. Two Rivers Ford had been destroyed, leaving him no other viable option than to make a more direct albeit slower march from Falantir across the Garnath River toward the citadel-capital in Kin-Deren province. He had had to channel his fury over the loss of the ford to other, more constructive uses.

Deren and the enigmatic Jasal's Keep it held were at the heart of his plans. With Deren and whatever power that dwelled within the watchtower firmly in his grasp, Kinderra would finally be at peace. Oh, certainly, some prime would attempt to unseat him even as he controlled the citadel, but he or she would fail. No other Fal'kin would dare rise against him again.

He piled some brush on the ashes of the fire and cupped his amulet in his hands. Calling to the Defending Aspect, he let it swell within him a moment. A thin beam of light shot forth from the crystal to ignite the kindling. The dried bits of lichen curled into a bright orange flame. Tiny tongues of fire licked at the rest of the fuel to create a small but comfortable blaze.

Starting a fire was such a simple use of his Aspect, certainly not something that required drawing in life forces with the Power from Without. The Light from Within. The Power from Without. Two very different paths both leading to the same destination—manifesting the gifts of the Aspects. Neither was better or worse, good or evil. Just different. Why could the Fal'kin not see that? Why did they force his hand to fight them, harvest them, *ai*, even kill them? Did not many roads lead to Deren? None of those were considered nobler over another. They were simply other ways home.

Whether it was the Power from Without or the Light from Within that would ultimately control Jasal's Keep, he would use either to ignite its light and flame to end the long millennia of conflict.

Mirana Pinal, however—ah, she would ignite the light, the flame within the heart of Kinderra itself. When Deren was his, when the tower and its power were his, she would deliver the continent into his hands for the rest of the age. When she knew him at last, he would mold and shape her as his heir, ensuring his ideals would live on long after he was gone.

Someday, he would ride through the streets of Deren, no longer veiled in anonymity, but with his head held high, his visage for all to look upon.

He did not want the laud of the people, and certainly not their worship. He was a man, not a deity. He was, however, a Trine. *The* Trine. Most believed the Trine Prophecy spoke of two Trines. They were wrong. Only one true Trine would fulfill the prophecy in its entirety. End and beginning in one. Power from Within and Without. Him.

The Fal'kin and the Ken'nar would be united once more under him, their philosophical differences erased, and the Unaspected would no longer be harmed by their conflict. He would become the ultimate protector of all the peoples the Aspects Above had created. The *Primus Magne Ultimus*. Fear and hatred would ebb away, and all Kinderra would come to understand what he had done for the land. When Deren was his. When Mirana Pinal knew him.

Time continued to march on like an army, relentless and unforgiving, while his designs to conquer Deren remained in a precarious balance that could not be rushed. They would only unfold when they were ready. When *she* was ready. And so he would bide his time. But he didn't have to like it.

The Ain Magne stirred the growing flames with a stick, coaxing the fire to build but willing his impatience to die back.

To make siege on Deren, he needed to get his army there. For that, he needed horses.

Edara. He could see it in his mind's eye as his mortal eyes watched the flames lick at the kindling. Edara, the capital of Varn-Erdal province, was little more than a collection of crude habitations ringed by a moat and stockade fence. The learning hall there did not protect much more than shepherds' huts and hunters' lodges scattered over the high plains. The hall and the habitations were worthless to him, but the province did have one treasure: horses.

Raised in the cold highlands, the horses of Varn-Erdal were as sturdy as the draft horses of Sün-Kasal, as smart as the warhorses of Kin-Deren, and could run at full stretch for twice as long as the lithe, elegant mounts from Tash-Hamar.

Constant skirmishes with his troops and now the massacre at the ford left Liaonne Edaran, the province's new defender prime, with few Fal'kin to command.

Still, she was a charismatic figure to her people, the strength of her presence almost as powerful as her amulet. Far too independent of mind and steadfast in belief, she would never accept his plans for Kinderra willingly. Nor could he risk her rising against him, regardless of the paucity of Fal'kin she commanded. Harvesting her would also destroy her most valuable asset, her leadership qualities. Therefore, he made the only decision he could make, but it was not without regret.

He slipped into communion with the Seeing Aspect as his fingertips traced the jagged edges of his amulet's setting. A nebulous sense of light and heat surrounded Edara, vague with the fluidity of a time to come. He smiled. Maybe light and flame would deliver Varn-Erdal to him, just as they would Deren someday.

He let his bond to the Seeing Aspect slip away and drew his sword, making no sound as he pulled it from its scabbard, preparing to sharpen it. He paused, hefting the blade in his hand. Perhaps metal was not needed to conquer Kinderra but only light. He wanted to believe that was true. So very much.

A presence brushed his mind, faint but needful. The Ain Magne set down his sword and raised a hand to his amulet again to open his mind to the Aspects and allow the connection.

… *Lord Trine, your contact is long overdue* … his seer second called. The distance swallowed the strength of his mind's words but not their urgency.

He sensed the enormous effort his servant put forth to contact him. He did not know whether to be flattered or irritated by this. Since he disregarded flattery, he chose the latter. … *I will call you at a time of my choosing* …

… *Ai, of course, Ain Magne* … *I was concerned for your welfare* … *I sensed danger* …

… *My welfare is none of your concern* … *Growing my army is* … *What has been your progress?*…

… *The Soul Harvesting of the Kana-Akün Fal'kin is nearly complete* … *Those that we captured from the ford have been most resistant, however* … *Until they are within our fold, I am not sure how long we can keep harvesting at this rate* … *The old one grows weaker, my lord* … *She will not last* …

He considered his second's words. The healer that had been Prime Belessa Tir of Kana-Akün was integral to his designs. If she did not survive to take his other assets, he would have to resume harvesting the Fal'kin himself, something he could no longer afford to do.

… *Give the healer rest* … *Then make sure she harvests the others at all costs* …

He needed her to make as many fighters as possible. Or perhaps not.

He sent an image to his second's mind. ... *We may yet have assistance* ...

... *She will never accept the Ken'nar way* ... the seer second returned.

... *Even you did not understand the Power from Without once ... Now you stand at the head of all my armies* ...

... *You showed me power beyond all imagining ... I shall always be indebted to you* ... The sense from the young seer's mind was muted, the words struggling to free themselves from the emotion that engulfed them.

The Ain Magne knew his warriors' innermost thoughts, deepest desires, darkest deceits. He could find any mind that belonged to him and encourage it—or destroy it. The Ken'nar now knew he rewarded them for the absolute fealty he demanded. The only other alternative was death. They had long since stopped testing him on this simple edict. Killing traitors and those who wished to expose him to Kinderra, making an example of their infidelity gave him no pleasure, but it was necessary to keep the loyalty of his troops. Respect, however, elevated loyalty to apostolic devotion. Like that of his seer second.

The boy had learned well from him, and so he had placed the young seer above all the others. When others tested his second's youth, they quickly learned not to do so again. There was never a third time.

Once the Ain Magne sat at the apex of Kinderra's Aspected, his lieutenant would also be praised. This, the boy knew as well. *Ai*, the seer idolized him, but at the core of that adoration was ambition, and he was never so much a fool as to forget how easily one could eclipse the other.

... We must rely on the healer while we can ... the Ain Magne returned. *... Time will work for us and against Edara and Deren ...*

... We must take Edara and Deren now while they lie weakened, Lord Trine ... his seer second called, the connection straining. *... Come back to us ... We suffered grave losses at the ford ... The old one cannot harvest and heal us both ... Come back and build your armies as you were meant to ... I shall drive Edara to its knees and then Deren ... We must move our plans ahead much sooner without the ford ...*

... We have time enough for this ...

... Forgive me, Lord Trine, but if we wait until autumn, the river will become impassable with the rains ...

He sighed. How could his seer be so adept at his Aspect and still not see? *... What are siege towers constructed of, my second?...*

Confusion and wariness slipped from his servant's mind to his own. *... They are ... Made of wood, my lord ...*

... Wood floats, does it not?... He continued, his mind's voice deceptively paternal.

... Ai, Ëi Trinus ...

... We have time, Ëi Seconde ...

The Ain Magne sensed the seer's lingering apprehension. *... You thought I died ...*

It was a long time before the youth answered. *... I sensed your distress ... I was too far to have helped ... I grew concerned ...*

... Obviously, I am well ... Your unnecessary apprehension led you to make the wrong conclusion ... Am I to no longer rely on your Aspect? ...

... No, lord ... You need me now more than ever ... The vision of Jasal's Keep does not leave my sight, my Trine ... Have you seen past the explosion of light? ...

He pursed his lips. Past the explosion? Why should he have searched beyond this? Once he harnessed the power in the keep, the war would end. *... What have you seen? ...*

… A future skein … It is no more substantial than the wind, but it exists nonetheless … Deren lies in ruins … Mirana Pinal stands victorious … I stand with her … I was wrong to suggest killing her … I will always grant you victories, but only Mirana and I together can give you Deren …

The Ain Magne wanted to laugh at such a blatant power play. *… Have I not told you … Several times, in fact … that Mirana Pinal is not your concern? …*

… Ai, lord … But I felt this prescience was important— …

… What would you do with the girl if you had her? …

… What? … My lord, I did not mean to suggest— …

… I know what you do with women … I tolerate it because most of the time, they are willing … The Ain Magne fought the temptation to lash out at the young man for the mere suggestion of coveting the girl, but too many reprimands might destroy his second's loyalty. Still, a verbal rebuke was more than appropriate. *… Mirana Pinal is not some harlot to be used for your pleasure … You have no concept of what she means to Kinderra …*

… My lord, please! … I do not look upon Mirana Pinal that way … From my vision, I saw that only together will she and I give you Kinderra … All I want is that you bring me into closer confidence with her so together we can give you your victory at Deren … I bring you this news for the sake of your ultimate conquest of the continent … Please, Lord! …

The Ain Magne eased his grip on the young man's mind but did not vacate it. The boy did believe he saw something of importance to their plans, but it was the sensations of longing interwoven through the seer's testimony that could not be denied. On some level, his servant now wanted Mirana Pinal for himself.

… I have taught you the difference between dreams of desire and visions of truth from the Seeing Aspect since you were younger than the girl …

… Ëi Trinus, what did you ask of me when I first came to you as a broken, starving lad from Kana-Akün? …

It was the Ain Magne's turn to be taken aback. What was the seer getting at? To understand a game, one must play it. *... I had you kill your parents as a show of fealty ...*

... Ai ... And I did ... If I committed such an act without question when I was little more than a boy, when I hardly knew you, how much more do you think I am willing to do now that I am your second? ... You do not need to question my loyalty ... If I were going to usurp Deren from you with Mirana, why would I have told what I saw? ...

The Ain Magne froze at the observation. The young seer was correct. It was not often such simple logic eluded him. He was growing careless, distracted. He would not let it happen again. Furthermore, his plans for bringing peace to Kinderra still had many skeins of time yet to be woven. He needed his second now more than ever.

... Ëi Seconde ... Our efforts to end this war weigh on me ... At times, it is difficult to see friend from foe ...

... I owe you everything, Ëi patrua ... I ask nothing more from you than to trust the insight I have with my visions ... Insight you helped to instill in me ... I know what I saw ... Mirana and I are in Deren ... After the siege ... If I am standing with her, we must have won ...

His second's reasoning was sound but not ironclad. Other conclusions could be made—several flitted before the mind's eye of the Ain Magne—but they were so extreme as to be almost preposterous. Almost.

... Before we can begin our assault on Deren, I need you to bring Varn-Erdal into the fold ... I have one last command for you, Ëi Seconde ...

... Ask anything of me ...

... Kill Liaonne Edaran ...

CHAPTER 10

"The Unaspected know not how blessed they are!"
—The Codex of Jasal the Great

A scattering of sod farmhouses peeked out from small clearings cut in the tall prairie grass as Teague and the Fal'kin neared Edara and the learning hall of Varn-Erdal. Bulwarks soon rose on either side of him, sharp poles bristling like an angry porcupine's quills.

Ahead of him, the Fal'kin formed up into a single line to cross a narrow drawbridge set within the stockade fence. He looked down. Big mistake. The wooden planks spanned no mere ditch or culvert. A moat, as deep as three men stood tall, held no water but was filled instead with jagged rocks and sharpened poles. He grimaced. He'd rather drown than be skewered to death.

Ahead of him, Morgan Jord chuckled under his breath. "I agree."

Dammit. If there was one thing he wished he could do, it was close his mind to others.

He reached down to his belt pouch, then paused, leaving the peda blossom inside. After destroying the ford, the Dark Trine had to be searching for Mirana. Was she safe?

What a ridiculous notion. She was a Trine, with three Aspects to protect her. She was with Tetric Garis, the greatest Fal'kin in Kinderra. And she wanted nothing more to do with him. Aspects Above knew he certainly couldn't defend her or anyone else. He barely knew which end of a sword was which. That, however, was about to change.

He followed the others up to a second tall stone and timber stockade fence, homes and buildings nestling against it. Wide, iron-strapped doors slowly opened to receive them. Someone must have called to the sentries.

As he rode through the gate, Teague frowned at his first underwhelming glimpse of the learning hall of Edara. Its walls stood massive, like all of Kinderra's halls—long, multi-storied sides arranged in a square surrounding a central courtyard—but the wooden edifice, with its dormers rising at regular intervals, appeared more like an overgrown hunting lodge than a proper Fal'kin learning hall. He had visited the hall in Kana-Akün once as a small boy with his parents. It bore a vague resemblance to Falantir's compound, as builders had constructed both from enormous timbers, but that's where the comparison ended. It had none of the woodland province's intricately carved logs nor proud rampant-stag gates. Deren and Rhadaz were the only other halls with which he was familiar. Edara was no fortress like Deren, and certainly no palace like Rhadaz.

If the Ken'nar planned an all-out assault on Edara, Liaonne wouldn't stand a chance. The moat might be effective, but everything else was made of wood. A battering ram could splinter the inner and outer fences like twigs. He wouldn't even give them a day against an army like the one that massacred the Fal'kin at Two Rivers Ford.

Morgan looked up at the tall fences as he rode beside him. He didn't look any happier about the Varn-Erdalans' prospects.

"This isn't going to go well, is it?" Teague asked.

The il'Kin defender commander inhaled and paused a moment before replying, still looking up at the palisades. "The Varn-Erdalans have elevated war to an art form."

From what he had heard, that was no exaggeration. "*Ai*, but the Ken'nar don't strike me as the kind of people who enjoy art."

Morgan eyed him but said nothing. He tapped his horse's sides and jogged up ahead to where Liaonne and Binthe rode at the head of the group entering the courtyard, leaving Teague to ride alone in the rear. He reached down to touch the Ken'nar broadsword he had under his saddle blanket. He hoped the defender was a connoisseur.

An hour later, Teague had washed most of the journey off him. He had been given a plain but comfortable room in the hall. He couldn't remember the last time he had a proper bath. Bankin probably smelled better than he did.

He rested the sword against the wall in the corner. After he changed into a fresh pair of leather breeches and a second shirt, he tossed his dirty clothes on the floor next to the blade. He sipped some water, cool from an earthenware jug, and eyed the bed. It was a simple, linen-covered white rectangle stuffed with straw and wool, but it looked achingly inviting after sevendays of sleeping on the ground. He walked over and fell spread-eagle on the mattress. A knock came at the door. He cursed under his breath.

"Teague?" It was Binthe. "You are to come with us to the council room."

"Why?" He put the pillow over his head, not caring to hear the answer.

"May I come in?"

He didn't answer her. He hadn't locked the door, and it wouldn't have mattered if he had.

The seer entered. "Prime Edaran is gathering her senior staff to plan a defense strategy."

"And that concerns me how?"

"Teague, take the pillow from your head."

He sighed in frustration and complied. He could never be truly mad at Binthe. She was one of the gentlest souls he ever met. When she wasn't on the battlefield.

He sat up on the edge of the mattress. "What?"

"You came to give aid to the herbsfolk. I should think you'd want to hear the state of her affairs. You might be able to offer some suggestions."

"Me?" He laughed, genuinely tickled by her comment. "I've been in exactly one battle and did nothing but run for my life. I don't know anything about this kind of preparation."

"I think you do. More than you realize."

"I'm tired, Binthe."

"And just how tired do you think Prime Edaran is? She has reminded you once about following orders."

He looked down at his boots. "I have nothing to say to these people."

"You don't have to say anything. Just having a Beltran in their presence will give them comfort."

"I'm not the Beltran they want." He curled his hands into white-knuckled fists. "I-I couldn't save the Beltrans they want."

"I'm sure you did everything you could to find help." She sat down on the bed next to him. "I should have said something the other night. I am heartily saddened by the deaths of your parents. I was older than you when my parents died, and it still shattered me. I didn't want to go on without them."

"I'm sorry, Binthe." His gaze remained on his boots. He didn't want to see his own heart-numbing grief reflected in those kind, sea-green eyes. "I know I've been an ass."

She put a hand on this shoulder. "*Ai*, but it's understandable." He raised his head to her warm smile. "Come."

Teague followed Binthe down a long hallway, then she gestured down a side corridor. It ended at a pair of doors that opened to an expansive great hall. The council room was filled with dozens of men and women. A long wooden table stood in the center, flanked by twenty chairs. More seats lined the walls.

Prime Edaran and Morgan were already there, as were the cleaved Fal'kin and a dozen other people he assumed were ranking Fal'kin of Varn-Erdal. His brows rose in confusion. Some weren't wearing amulets. She let Unaspected into her councils? Such a thing never happened in Deren. An all-but-impenetrable wall of culture stood between the two peoples.

"Ah, Binthe, Teague, good. We can begin," the young prime said.

She had changed out of her armor and into a simple white linen shirt and dark brown leather leggings. Her white-blonde hair was pulled back into a complicated series of braids. Without her armor and the fierce scowl that usually lidded her brown eyes, she looked far younger than he had initially thought. Summers of fighting the Ken'nar and the harsh weather of

Varn-Erdal's high plains had sculpted her body into a savage sort of elegance.

Liaonne must have called something because the men and women immediately stopped their conversations and took their seats.

"You know by now Prime Vallia Edaran was killed by Ken'nar in the massacre at Two Rivers Ford," she said, her voice faltering for a moment. "I want you all to know I never sought nor wanted my mother's primeship. I was content to serve Kinderra in our provincial forces as is my duty as a Fal'kin."

Teague played with a loose thread on his shirt. A sobering thought struck him. She, too, had been orphaned in that horrible battle.

"We are in a precarious situation," she continued. "After the massacre at Two Rivers Ford, we have few defenders other than our youngest *scholaire'e* and the three *brepaithe'e* the Aspects Above have left with us. To bolster our defenses against the Ken'nar attack, I have cleaved twenty-five defenders from Kin-Deren province. At great cost did Derén honor us this way. They, too, suffered many losses."

He shifted nervously in his chair. He was not alone. Several Fal'kin turned to each other, concern written on their faces. Quick words and phrases were met with intense expressions. He wished he could hear what they were calling. Then again, he had a pretty good idea anyway.

"*Ai.* It is when, not if," Liaonne said, confirming his notions. "There is no time to ask for additional cleaved forces from the other provinces. There is little we can do to defend Edara against even a moderate attack force. Our only hope is to give up nothing. The Ken'nar may storm our bulwarks, but when they enter our gates, they will find little to conquer."

The room fell dead silent. Moments later, a man began to laugh.

"So, our fox has already outwitted the hounds?" the man said. "You truly belong as our prime, Liaonne il'Edaran."

A Fal'kin woman stood up, the deep pink of her tourmaline amulet winking in the light of the oil lamps. "I see nothing to laugh at, Horsemaster."

The man was dressed in buckskin breeches and a sleeveless leather tunic. Grizzled hair, bleached blond from the sun, stuck out in all directions. His bronzed, sinewy arms reminded Teague of burnished tree limbs more than flesh. From the lines on his face, he must have seen the passing of sixty summers if he'd seen a day. Other lines in the form of scars etched his arms. Another scar on his cheek was lost inside the tangle of his beard. A particularly vicious one ran across the bridge of his nose, from left eyebrow to right cheekbone. Teague was certain no horse's hoof had created it.

"Grenne, sit down. I disrespect no one," the man said. "Will our Fal'kin be evacuating with us?"

Teague sucked in a breath. Was Prime Edaran thinking of surrendering before the Ken'nar had even marched into the province? He didn't think such a thing would even be possible for her.

"No, Eran," she replied, "the blackhearts will be expecting some resistance."

Another man, one of the Fal'kin from Kin-Deren whose name Teague did not know, rose to his feet. "My lady, I came to Edara to defend it, not to commit suicide."

"I have no intention of having anyone sacrificing his or her life needlessly."

An ancient man with an amber-colored amulet stood slowly. He had scars just as vicious as the horsemaster's. "Then what is your plan? To sacrifice Edara instead?"

"Don't be so thick, Nathen," the wild-haired horsemaster Eran said. "She means to empty Edara and the countryside of Unaspected and probably your sorry arse as well after that comment."

Teague shook his head, sighing in disgust. "They could not care less about your overgrown cabin, imbeciles. With the ford gone, they'll have to cross the river, then ride to make up for lost time," he muttered under his breath. He pulled at the loose thread. It unraveled a bit of his shirt's weaving.

"What was that, Herbsman Beltran?" Liaonne asked.

Startled, he looked up from the thread. "I, uh, what I said was, without the ford, the Ken'nar will have to cross the Garnath River to march on Deren. They'll need horses to pull barges and supplies across the river. And probably mount as many of their defenders as they can. I think. My prime."

"Eran, Teague, you are both correct." She looked down at her hands for a moment and back to the council members. "We will evacuate the Unaspected from Edara and the surrounding region. We will also gather the horse herds and move them northeast, as far from Edara as possible. The Ken'nar have no use for the Unaspected. It is our horses they are after. They need them to conquer Deren."

Horsemaster Eran Talz unfolded his tree-limb arms to grab the side of the table. "Deren? You said they're going to strike Edara. They wouldn't dare attack Deren."

Binthe rose. "Edara is just a step on the Dark Trine's march across Kinderra. His ultimate prize is Deren." Again, shocked voices ricocheted around the room and were met by intense stares. "All of this—Two Rivers Ford, Edara, even Kana-Akün—is merely a prelude to a siege upon Deren."

"Kana-Akün?" An old woman bearing a deep magenta amulet struggled to her feet. "What are you saying, girl?"

Seer Grenne stood again. "Then we seers were correct. Falantir fell into Ken'nar hands."

Binthe nodded. "*Ai.*"

The Varn-Erdalan seer splayed her hands flat on the table, leaning forward toward the prime. "I warned Vallia. We had sevendays. Perhaps if you had supported my information, Liaonne, we could have done something to save Falantir. Then we could have had Kana-Aküni archers with us at the ford. And your mother would still be sitting in that chair."

Teague pulled hard at the thread in his shirt, creating a small tear. So, they could see Falantir collapse under the weight of the Ken'nar, but they could not see what happened to his parents, the healers of Kinderra? "Blind fools."

"An impressive tongue for one so scrawny. Who is this boy?" Eran hitched a thick thumb in his direction.

"Teague Beltran," the defender prime growled. "The son of Tennen and Niah Beltran. He has agreed to lend his herbsman's skills to our hall. I am rethinking my acceptance of his offer."

All right, maybe he had overstepped his bounds with that snipe.

"The healers?" Eran snorted. "The least Kin-Deren province could have done was send the healers along with their defenders."

Teague clenched his fists and shot to his feet. "My parents are dead, so that makes it a little difficult for them to do their job, now, doesn't it?"

"We had not heard," the horsemaster replied, looking from Teague to Liaonne and back. "All of Kinderra will mourn this loss."

"You mean your seers didn't see what happened to them at the ford?" He swept a hand out, indicating the destroyed bridge complex far to the south. "They couldn't even see the healers of Kinderra slaughtered?"

"Teague," Morgan cautioned. "Horsemaster Talz may not have had a chance to speak with the seers."

"Of course not. He's not a Fal'kin, so he would never have gotten the call. We never know what the hell is going on."

"Please sit down, Teague," Binthe said gently.

"I will not sit down. I'm sorry if you all are in too much denial to want to hear it, but Edara is nothing more than a minor nuisance on the way to Deren. Isn't that bloody obvious? The Ken'nar merely want to plunder your horses. It's the only thing in this Aspect-forsaken province anybody would want. What good are you Fal'kin? You can't even protect yourselves, let alone a bunch of nags. The healers are dead. Don't you understand? They're dead. You couldn't even protect my—"

"Teague. Sit. Down," Morgan ordered, clipping each word.

Prime Edaran remained sitting, but the way she tensed her shoulders, it must have taken all her effort to keep in her chair. "Herbsman Beltran, you are here at my pleasure. At the moment, I am displeased. Very."

He stared at the stone floor in front of him, trying to avoid the looks of shock, anger, and downright fury. He let out an explosive sigh. "I am sorry, my prime." He sank onto his chair.

"No, you are not sorry. Not one bit," she replied. "*Ai*, we saw an attack on the ford. We sent all we could. I had no more Fal'kin to send."

He kept his eyes on the floor. "*Ëo ad culpa, Ëi Primus. Ëo comprende.*"

"We would have had even fewer if we had gone to Falantir," she continued. "Was that not also a possibility you saw, Grenne? As did the other seers?"

He peered up at the seer woman, who nodded at Liaonne's words and retook her seat.

"I am well aware Varn-Erdal has little in the way of riches to offer the rest of Kinderra." The new prime appeared to deflate in her chair.

He frowned. This was probably the first time she had addressed the council as Varn-Erdal's leader. Aspects Above knew he felt awkward. Was she nervous, too? She took a breath and squared her shoulders. He doubted the defender woman had ever been nervous a day in her life.

"Our horses, however, are priceless. They mean as much to us as the Aspects. Maybe even more so." She turned her hard sienna eyes to him once more. "This land that sustains them, sustains us. We live and die for our horses and our land. So when you dare insult my province, you insult us."

Oh, Lights. "My prime, I—"

She held up a hand, silencing him. "You are not a child, Teague Beltran, so I will not treat you like one. I will not tolerate such an outburst again. If you do, I will have you expelled from the province with the full weight of that sentence on your shoulders. Either you stay and help us through the coming conflict or leave now. *Oë comprende?*"

He did want to leave. He wanted to run straight from the room and hide in a broom closet somewhere. He couldn't make a bigger fool of himself than he already had. He clenched his jaw as he nodded.

"I did not hear your reply."

He nodded again. "*Ai*, Prime Edaran. *Ëo comprende*."

He understood plenty. If he was expelled, he would be banished from the province, to be killed on sight if he even stepped foot inside its borders again. Banished. From the province. If he were, he could resume his plan to infiltrate the Ken'nar forces and assassinate the Dark Trine. But if he had to travel through the province on some phony Ken'nar mission and was caught by the Varn-Erdalans, his head would fly from his shoulders like a melon tossed from a farmer's cart. He frowned. No, better to stay in Edara. Besides, the Dark Trine just might come to him. Maybe in a matter of sevendays. He rubbed a palm against his breeches. Both plans would probably leave him dead. He barely knew which end of a sword was which.

Eran Talz snorted a laugh. Teague didn't think any of this was funny. "I met his *paithe* and his fair *maithe* summers ago. That tongue of his is wholly his own. Still, the lad is correct, if a little blunt." Teague looked up in shock. The horsemaster winked at him. "A river crossing will take time, mounted or not. They will have to move up their timetable to attack us if they want to grab our horses and make a play for Deren before the winter. The Ken'nar bastards will be here sooner than we think."

Prime Edaran rubbed her chin and tugged at her lower lip. She nodded. "I agree. Seer Lima, do you have any sense of when they might come?"

The Fal'kin in the room, many several decades older than Binthe, eyed the young woman with curiosity and, in a few cases, expressions less charitable. It was largely on the il'Kin seer's word that Liaonne believed Edara would be attacked.

She shook her head. "Not yet, my prime, but I search for nothing else."

Grenne the seer woman sat back in her chair as her lips curled into a humorless smile. "Perhaps the summers spent in short-sightedness in battle as an il'Kin has left you wanting in proper seer's skills."

Binthe did not change one nuance of her expression or her posture. "Perhaps. In that case, I will defer to your gift. Please. Tell your prime when you expect these events to unfold."

"The granddaughter of Eshe Pashcot knows her Aspect," the prime said. Her raised voice—and probably something more—rattled Teague's molars. The room immediately stilled. "Because she is a battle seer is precisely why I intend to rely on her. We will be attacked, but I do not intend to give up Edara without a fight. And, Aspects willing, we will not be alone. Seer Prime Desde Kellis Pinal might have only given us twenty-five Fal'kin now, but she has also given me her word she will come to our aid with a much larger force."

Another old man stood. "So, she gave you a handful of fighters and some pretty words." He shook his head. "Liaonne, *biraena*, no one has ever come to our aid. It has always been Varn-Erdal that rides for Kinderra, but Kinderra has never ridden for her."

The old man wore no amulet. What role did he hold at the hall that allowed him to speak so frankly?

"I shouldn't have to remind you that Kin-Deren province has borne the brunt of almost every battle on this continent as well. You've treated their wounds as much as ours, Palen," she replied. "Edara's safety means Deren's as well. She will come. I trust her word with my life. But I am not a fool. Every Fal'kin apprentice who has seen at least thirteen summers and every amuleted Fal'kin who has seen fewer than sixty will stay and defend the hall." She gestured to the ancient Fal'kin with the amber amulet. "Nathen, I would ask you, Wesal, and Piol to remain as well. I wish I could make it otherwise. I so wanted you three to enjoy the rest you earned from your long summers of fighting."

"*Ëo defende*," the ancient man said. Two other old men nodded.

Her gaze shifted to him. "Master Beltran, you'll remain as well and work with my herbsfolk."

Teague stared at Liaonne. Some too-often-unused corner of his brain registered the fact that he had been given a great honor, but another thought rose and quickly snuffed it out before he had a chance to feel something like pride. He was to stay. During the conflict. He had gotten his wish. He would confront the Ken'nar. For real.

Was it too warm to break out into a cold sweat?

A gray-haired woman rose, although it was hard for Teague to tell. Her dowager's hump gave her the appearance of bending over. "And what of us?" she said, her voice grating like a door badly in need of oil. She gestured to several older women and men.

"You will go with Horsemaster Talz and the Unaspected."

"What?" the old woman cried. "You cannot send us from our hall."

Again, the young prime tightened her shoulders. This time, the sinews in her neck tightened as she clenched her jaw. She wouldn't use her amulet, would she? "Nomenne, you are too old to fight the Ken'nar hoard that will surely come. And I will need seers after the conflict."

By the tone of her voice, Teague wondered if she wanted to add "if the hall remains standing."

"But more to the point," the prime continued, "the horsemaster will need help with the horse herds. And so will the Unaspected. If you feel your duty as a seer is being cheapened by offering what protection you can to the people of this province, then you need not return. I realize my leadership in this role is new, but these are my orders. You can abide by them or leave the province, but either way, you will leave this hall. *Ëomus fin.*"

The old woman nodded her head. Whether it was in acceptance of Liaonne's order, as an acknowledgment of understanding, or simply a bow of leave-taking, Teague wasn't sure.

At the defender prime's words, the Varn-Erdalans filed sullenly from the gathering room. They weren't happy, but how much more could they object?

How could he possibly render any meaningful help to these people? And during a raging battle, no less. He had taught Mirana some healing techniques for the last few summers now, but no one had been shooting amulet fire at him or trying to lop off his head at the time. At Two Rivers Ford, it was all he could do to keep himself and Bankin alive and not soil himself. Now, he'd be expected to do something.

What if one of the wounded died in his arms because he suddenly forgot everything? Or because he did something wrong? Or did the right thing but too late? Or a Ken'nar tried to kill his patient as he tended to him? Or tried to kill him?

Teague ground his teeth. He didn't know how to save a life any more than he knew how to wield a sword. And if Morgan stuck to his decision and refused to teach him?

He should have left when he had the chance. He shoved the chair from him and stomped out of the council room.

Teague returned to his room and slammed the door shut. He threw himself on the bed and pounded a fist on the mattress. He had called the Varn-Erdalans imbeciles and fools, but he was the real imbecile, insulting them to their faces. By the Light, he was a rackin' idiot!

He growled in fury and punched the plaster wall. "Son of a bitch!" He grabbed his fist and squeezed his eyes against the pain. All four knuckles on his right hand were bruised and cut. He sucked at a bloody knuckle. At least it wasn't a total loss. He'd left a dent in the wall.

Liaonne deserved an apology from him. No, everyone deserved an apology from him, but he'd start with the defender prime.

He searched for his sword belt. Maybe it'd make him look a little more respectable and a little less of a cow's hind end. It would certainly help hold up his breeches; he'd lost some weight during sevendays of hard travel. "Where is—?" The clothes he left in the room's corner. They were gone—and so was his Ken'nar broadsword. He needed it to kill the Dark Trine, or at least try. Or at least prove to everyone he could. Or maybe prove to himself that he was willing. "Damn you, Morgan."

He flew to the door and nearly ran over a young woman standing there.

She steadied him. "I need your help."

"I'm the wrong person to ask," he replied. "If you'll excuse me." He pushed past her and continued down the hallway.

She ran to catch up to him. "Please, Herbsman Beltran. My horse. She's dying."

"A horse? I don't know anything about horses. Besides, they hate me."

"Herbsman Beltran, please. If you'll just look at her."

He stopped abruptly and the girl ran into his back. He held her back from him. "Why don't you ask your herbsfolk?"

Her dark brown eyes held desperation. "I have. They say there's nothing they can do for her."

"Then I doubt there's anything else I could do." He resumed hurrying down the corridor.

She ran ahead of him, blocking his way. "But you're the healers' son, aren't you?"

He sighed in frustration. "*Ai*, but I'm not a Fal'kin."

She shook her head. "I don't see what that has to do with anything."

"I don't know anything about horses." He stepped around her and rushed out into the hall's courtyard.

She ran after him again. "You took care of Prime Edaran's wounds. She probably won't even get a scar."

He searched the courtyard, trying to find Morgan or the armory. "Her wound was superficial."

"Herbsman Beltran, please. I have nowhere else to turn."

The hot breath of the summer wind blew a lock of honey-colored hair across her face. She tucked the loose strand behind one ear. "Your parents were known for miracles as much from their knowledge as from their amulets. Surely, you must know something of their skills?"

Emotion flushed her cheeks. Her fine nose, sculpted cheekbones, and chin were tanned golden from the sun. She took a step to stand closer to him. She was nearly as tall as he was. He could look directly into her eyes. If he wanted to. Which he did. They were a deep brown, warm and inviting, like a soothing tea on a cold day. No! He was angry. And grieving. And embarrassed because he was angry and grieving and couldn't resolve either one.

"We must evacuate the hall soon on Prime Edaran's orders," she continued. "If Hamriah cannot walk, I will have to put her down. They said you are a good man. Please help me."

She asked for his help. No, she asked the son of healers for help. He had none to give.

"I'm sorry, I really am, but I don't think there's anything I can do. Where is the armory?"

Her bottom lip trembled as she scowled in confusion. "Wh-What?"

"Never mind. I'll find it myself."

She straightened her shoulders, composing herself. "It's over there." She waved in a direction over his shoulder. "Third door. Next to the washhouse."

That was quite clever. Excess heat from the crucible bellows could be piped in somehow to boil the water for laundry. He shook his head, dispelling the notion. He wanted his damn sword back, not to help a pretty girl, and certainly not to learn more about plumbing.

Across the courtyard, he saw a woman carrying a bundle of clothes and a dark scabbard.

"Hey!" Catching up to the woman, he held her arm, stopping her from entering the armory. "What are you doing? That is mine."

"I did not mean to intrude on your privacy, Master Beltran. I knocked and no one was in your room. It was open, so I thought it would be all right to do your laundry. It looks like you brought half of Varn-Erdal back with you." The woman gestured with a filthy sleeve. "You have come with the others to save us. The least we can do is give you a nice clean shirt. But this thing?" She nudged the broadsword held in the crook of her arm. "This should be destroyed." She proceeded to enter the armory.

He followed her. "Y-You can't just take that. It's mine." Heat from the fires and his anger made the room sweltering. He tried to grab the sword from her.

"Herbsman Beltran!" The woman pulled out of his grip.

"Don't call me that. I'm just an apprentice." He didn't know what he was anymore.

One of the old defenders, Nathen, stepped back from an anvil, his amber amulet glowing. "That's a Ken'nar blade, boy. The same kind that murdered so many of our Fal'kin." He took it from the washerwoman. "The same kind that murdered our defender prime, noble Vallia Edaran. I don't even want its slag to be reused."

Teague grit his teeth in rage, glaring from the washerwoman to Nathen. "It is mine. Not yours. Mine. I'm taking it back." He gripped the hilt.

Instead of backing away, Nathen stepped closer. "You are Unaspected, boy. You have no business touching a blade, least of all an accursed one like this."

"Herbsman Beltran, please understand, war trophies such as this are not allowed in Varn-Erdal. I'm sure Defender Keldir here will find you something—" the washerwoman started.

"This is *not* a trophy. It is a weapon. And it's mine."

He heard footsteps behind him.

"What seems to be the trouble?" Morgan entered the armory, frayed leather dangling from his scabbard.

He pointed at the washerwoman. "She stole my sword."

"Defender Commander, Ken'nar war trophies are against the law in Varn-Erdal. So many of our people have perished from Ken'nar weapons." She held the bundle of Teague's dirty clothes close to her chest. "I took it to Defender Keldir," she gestured to old Nathen with a tilt of her head, "to see what should be done with it. I didn't mean to steal anything."

Morgan gave his broken scabbard to the old defender. "And you have not, *siba*."

"Morgan—"

The il'Kin commander's blue eyes turned hard. "That is enough, Teague."

"Take it," Nathen said, his amber amulet brightening. He threw the Ken'nar broadsword down hard. The blade sang when its tip pierced the earthen floor of the armory a finger's width from Teague's foot. "Get him out of my sight."

"Come." Morgan yanked the blade free. He grabbed Teague by the back of his neck and dragged him outside. He pushed him down to sit on a low wooden bench. "You've insulted the prime and her hall, now left the washerwoman and another girl in tears, and nearly had an amulet flashed in your face by a man who is sworn to protect you. Tell me what is troubling you. Now."

Teague peered around the Fal'kin to the armory. The old defender watched them a moment with angry, narrowed eyes, and slammed the armory door without lifting a hand. Teague sat back, fuming, and said nothing.

The il'Kin commander crossed his arms. "I am waiting for your answer."

He shrugged and shook his head.

The other man sighed and sat down beside him.

"Son, you've been through more in the last few sevendays than many people twice your age. Because of that, I was willing to excuse these outbursts. But no longer. If you won't tell me what is troubling you, I'll respect your privacy, but you've got to move past this anger. Liaonne is well within her right to send you packing for Deren. In a way, I wish she would. You remain here under her request, however, not mine."

"Even primes can make mistakes." Teague refused to meet Morgan's gaze, staring instead across the courtyard at two young boys practicing with wooden swords. He rubbed at his face. "I don't know if I can help these people."

Morgan tossed the Ken'nar blade on the ground in front of Teague's feet. "A good friend once told me the tighter you hold on to anger and grief, the tighter it holds you until you cannot grasp anything else."

Teague pointed at his chest. "My anger and grief are all I have left."

The il'Kin commander stood. "All you have left? Your father said those words to me and saved my life with them. You have your life. One they gave you. Twice."

"To do what?" He shot up from the bench and threw his arms out wide. "I couldn't even save my parents."

Morgan clamped a hand on his shoulder and forced Teague to face him. "You cannot kill. You have been consecrated to save lives. Your parents taught you everything they knew so you could help these people and others. They gave their lives so that you could continue their calling. How dare you squander their sacrifice with this death wish of yours!"

Teague pulled himself away from the man's grip and snatched up his sword. "And I will die unless you show me how to use this thing properly."

"Absolutely not! You are Unaspected and an herbsman. That's why there *are* Fal'kin. I will make certain myself if I must that you will not be killed. You. Cannot. Fight."

"No. I am nothing. I have always been nothing. I will always be nothing." He spun away from the defender.

The il'Kin defender grabbed him once more and slammed him against the wall of the hall so hard, he dropped the blade. "You listen to me, Teague Beltran. Most of the people on this continent are Unaspected. Kinderra thrives as well as it does because of them. When you speak in shame of what you feel you are lacking, you insult most of the people who live and toil and love and die in this land. I reminded you of your father's words for a reason. You can be every bit as good a man as he was if you choose to be. But first, you must get past this self-loathing of something that is neither your fault nor something to be ashamed of." He gave him a last shove, then turned on his heel and stormed away.

"That's easy for you to say. You're a Fal'kin."

Morgan stopped and turned around, venom in his eyes. "My wife was Unaspected. As was my son. And a Ken'nar blade killed them both."

Teague's mouth fell open. He blinked. Once. Twice. It took several heartbeats before words found their way to his tongue again.

"Morgan, wait!"

The defender paused, his back to Teague.

"I…I'm sorry."

The other man turned his head slightly to look over his shoulder and gave a curt nod. He then left the courtyard.

Teague looked down at his broadsword. It was a long time before he picked it up.

CHAPTER 11

"U'deán rosa crese te derra sterílis?"
("Does not the rose bloom from barren soil?")
—Ora Fal'kinnen 52:38

Teague wandered the learning hall of Varn-Erdal until long after the sun had set. After his mortifying show at Liaonne's council meeting that afternoon and the fiasco at the armory, sleep wouldn't stand a chance against all his offenses repeating themselves in his head. He found himself outside of the hall's stables. Unlike Deren, Edara's stables didn't make up the ground floor of one of the learning hall's sides. The separate wooden edifice sprawled farther than the learning hall itself, stretching into the night far beyond what he could see.

He entered, intending to see to Bankin, when he heard a noise definitely not made by a horse. It sounded like crying.

"*Ben kin*? Is someone there?" He heard a small gasp. He walked in the direction of the sound. In a paddock in the middle of the long row of stalls, he found the brown-eyed girl sitting in the hay next to a mare. The horse lay on her side in the straw.

The girl angrily wiped at her eyes. "Please go."

"I didn't mean to disturb you. I was just going to pack my horse."

She stroked the mare's neck. "Which one is yours?"

"Bankin. The nasty little gray one."

"She is not nasty. She is intelligent and spirited. If you continue to treat her like a beast, that's how she will treat you."

The girl continued to run her hand down the horse's neck. The mare's deep chestnut coat and black mane were still glossy despite the labored breathing. He knew horses about as much as he knew girls, but the mare was a beautiful animal.

"What was her name again?" he asked quietly.

"Hamriah."

He smiled faintly. "That sounds like a Tash-Hamari name."

The girl nodded. "It is. Her dam was full-blooded Hamari. Every few generations, we like to introduce some fresh blood. It keeps our herds strong."

"I'm part Tash-Hamari, too."

"You don't look it."

"My mother was born in Rhadaz, but my father was from Kin-Deren. I guess I look more like—" He didn't want to think about his father —or mother—right now. Instead, he picked at the wood of the paddock for a moment. "I, uh, never did learn your name."

"You never asked."

He screwed his mouth into an embarrassed smile and scratched the back of his head. "*Ai.* You're right." He opened the corral and knelt next to the girl. The horse nickered and tossed her head. The girl cooed to the mare to settle her.

"I am Illenne il'Talz."

He sat back on his heels. "Talz? As in—?" He pointed over his shoulder in the general direction of the council room.

"*Ai*. Eran Talz is my father. There is no one on the face of Kinderra who knows more about horses, more about their breeding and their training than he."

He closed his eyes and made a soft groan. "Illenne, I am sorry."

At last, she looked up from the horse. "You are only sorry because you disrespected the daughter of one of the most prominent men in Varn-Erdal."

He gave another lopsided smile. "You're right again, but I do want to apologize anyway." He reached over to rub the mare's nose. She jerked away from his hand. He pulled it back and hissed, the sudden movement sending an aching throb across the bruises on his knuckles.

Illenne scowled. "What happened to your hand?"

"Fell into the wall. How did she get lacerated?" he hurried along before the girl could ask for more details. The horse's movements reminded him of a patient in pain.

"Why do you care? You already said you wished to do nothing."

"No. I said I didn't think I *could* do anything." He smiled again. "I very, very much *want* to do something."

She did not answer him right away. "She caught the edge of a scythe on her left hind fetlock."

He crawled down to the mare's hind legs. "How did that happen?"

She tried to stifle a sob but failed. "We were riding. I was lost in thought. I didn't see it."

"Never mind. It doesn't matter," he said quietly. "Hold her head." He gently lifted the crude poultice on the horse's left fetlock, grimacing as it stuck to the wound. The horse kicked out at him, and he ducked just in time.

Illenne gave an appraising nod. "You move fast."

"I've had a lot of practice." He frowned again, this time at the wound itself. It was raw and red, its edges black, and it oozed pus and serous fluid. The summer, though dry, was a hot one. It had already begun to fester. "When did this happen?"

"Two sevendays ago."

He sat back again. "What have they done so far?"

The girl stroked the horse's head. "Numbweed for pain. A mud poultice to draw out the infection."

Teague shook his head. "That doesn't work nearly as well as one would think. We clean wounds from the battlefield. Why? To get rid of the dirt. It doesn't make sense to introduce it back in."

She ran her fingers through Hamriah's mane. "We don't have many herbsfolk left in our province. Many have been captured or killed on the battlefield in recent summers. The Ken'nar keep coming and keep coming." She took a breath. "The rest of us do what we can."

He bit the inside of his cheek. Illenne was the one who made the poultice.

The laceration reminded him of the injuries his parents had once treated on the brewmaster of Deren and his apprentice. The still had exploded, throwing the master into a trough of fermenting sugarcane. The apprentice was blown clear. Both were cut from the metal fragments. Oddly, the brewmaster's wound did not become infected. The apprentice's wound did, however. His parents tried making a paste of the fermenting sugarcane and applied it to the apprentice's wound. It healed.

Where would he get fermenting sugarcane in Varn-Erdal? Most of it grew in Jad-Anüna, thousands of leagues away.

"I won't lie to you. This doesn't look good, though maybe there's something we can try."

"Really?" A smile lit up her face.

Heat rushed to his cheeks. "Uh, maybe. *Ai*. What have we got to lose? I need, um, what?" He ran his fingers through his hair. "Is there a brewery near the hall?"

She sat back, aghast. "Are you trying to get drunk or make my horse drunk?"

"No, no. I need fermenting sugarcane."

"We are a rural province. We don't have the grand market squares and taverns of the southern provinces."

"Well, doesn't anyone make beer or liquor in their home?"

Illenne shook her head. "Bringing cane all the way from Jad-Anüna is difficult and expensive. We sometimes get molasses though."

"That might work. Where can we get some?"

She shifted uncomfortably at his question.

"I know it seems odd. There's something in the fermenting cane that might stop the infection. I'm hoping it's in the molasses, too."

She frowned. "My father might have some, but I don't know if he will give us any."

He scowled. "Why? I thought you said he loved horses?"

"He does. He also makes the best ale north of the Garnath." She held up her chin. "Molasses is his secret ingredient."

"I'll bet he'll give you some if you ask."

Illenne caressed her horse once more. "He won't even let me use some to make bread."

"I'm sure your father wants very much to see you smile again."

She nodded and smiled. "*Ai*. You're right."

Once, he could make Mirana smile. But she was a Trine, and at the ford, she had finally embraced that fact. The one fact he had begged her to accept since they were twelve summers. She hadn't left him; he had unwittingly helped her to realize the truth about their lives. She had all three Aspects and he had none. He could have no place in her life because of that. And so, Mirana had made the choice he had forced upon her.

Illenne, however, was just as blind to the Aspects as he was.

She squeezed his hand. "*Gratas Oë.*"

"For what?"

"For thinking of something clever. For attempting a cure. For even just wanting to. When my—" She lowered her gaze to her boots. "When people I cared about were killed, it was all I could do to remember to breathe. For a long time. I was useless." She lifted her eyes to his and smiled. "You are not."

Maybe it was time he made some choices of his own.

CHAPTER 12

*"The Light from Within. The Power from Without.
One giving, one receiving. Are they both paths to the
same calling from the Aspects Above? Or does one
lead the way to sin? Which path? Which sin? So very
much the same, so very much different."*

—The Book of Kinderra

Mirana awoke with a start, shouting and striking out with
her fists.

… Wake up … You are safe … Tetric Garis's call came into
her mind, soothing away the nightmare.

She sat up, panting, and wiped the sleep—or lack thereof—
from her eyes. Stars faded as the sky to the east glowed with
approaching dawn.

He had already packed half the camp. Who knew what other dead armies they would encounter on the road ahead, and it would be her luck he would be too tired to fight them. "Why didn't you wake me?" She could make a flat-lipped frown in irritation, too.

"I wanted to let you sleep, but from the sound of it, it didn't matter."

She rubbed her face. "I guess I was dreaming." She gathered her bedroll and cinched it to the saddlebags.

"It was the same nightmare, wasn't it?"

"I don't remember."

He swung up onto his saddle. … *I will allow you your silence for now … But soon you will tell me what it is that you have been seeing …*

"It's just a nightmare," she replied. She would not let the vision become anything more than that.

She climbed onto Ashtar's back and followed the Trine into the desert.

As the sun rose higher in the sky, the temperature rose steadily along with it. Mirana had covered her head from the sun with her spare shirt like Tetric taught her to do. Her cheeks, forearms, and the bridge of her nose, however, had turned bright pink.

Small shrubs gave way to scrubby plants as they rode on, then no plants at all, just shifting sand. Far off to the south, the regular shapes of buildings appeared. They seemed insubstantial, blurred by heat shimmers dancing on the horizon.

She and Ashtar paused on a high dune, the sand painted bronze by the setting sun. "Are you sure Rhadaz is really there? It never seems to get any closer."

The Trine chuckled. "That is what the Tash-Hamari hope you think. There is no easy way to get to Rhadaz. An invading army coming through the Dúadar Pass must trek a day through this desert, as we are, before reaching the city, and then fight hot, tired, and thirsty. If they try and circumvent the Dar-Tals, it is days longer. You can see why Rhadaz has been sacked just once in recorded history." He clicked his tongue and guided his horse down the dune.

What if that invading army was one of Soul-Harvested fighters? The heat would mean nothing to them.

"There's not a living thing in this desert for Ken'nar to use against the Fal'kin. That's why Tash-Hamar hasn't been sacked," she said perversely. "The Ken'nar deserve to perish out here if they are going to use the Power from Without."

The Trine reined his horse to stop and looked over his shoulder at her. "Are those the words of a Trine of Kinderra? Or a haughty child trying to justify away her culpability?"

She blinked, startled by his question and its vehemence. "What?"

He now drilled her with a dark-eyed gaze. "You killed one thousand forty-seven Ken'nar when you destroyed the ford using the Light from Within you champion so strongly."

Her mouth went dry. "I-I *what?*"

"You asked me how many Fal'kin died at the ford by your actions. You never even gave a thought to the Ken'nar lives you took." His ire pulsed against the walls of her mind like a wild amulet.

"I-I had to save the Fal'kin. They were trapped on the bridge. The Ken'nar were slaughtering us. I had no choice." Righteous anger tried to vindicate her against the guilt growing in her conscience.

"No choice other than genocide?"

"No, of course not. I don't want to kill every last Ken'nar."

"Oh, don't you?" She tried to come up with a protest, but he beat her to it. "Both the Fal'kin and the Ken'nar have tried to destroy each other for three thousand summers. Tell me how that has solved anything?"

She rode downhill to him. "Why are you defending them? The Ken'nar are the ones who want to wipe us off the face of Kinderra. *They* kill *us*."

He leaned in the saddle toward her. "Your father can slit the throats of nine men in a line and the tenth will have never heard a sound until he attempts to scream himself. I know. I've seen it."

She sat back, her face twisting in revulsion. Surely, the Fal'kin did not use such barbaric tactics? Not her father? Was that just another of the many secrets he had kept from her? She didn't want to think about him now. She didn't want to think about any of this.

"We are Fal'kin. We use the Light from Within. We defend, we protect, we steward," she said instead. "Using the Power from Without isn't a selfless giving of one's life force from within the Aspects, it is a taking." She defined herself by this belief.

"So, using the Light from Within makes killing at Fal'kin hands less heinous?" he challenged. "The Fal'kin kill just as the Ken'nar do. And so the cycle goes on and on and on."

"Why do you think we're fighting? We're trying to break that cycle."

"Are you? Think, Mirana. You were at Two Rivers Ford. Was that peace to you?"

She shook her head, avoiding his gaze. "No."

"It takes two sides to make war or to make peace. Aspects Above know unleashing amulets at each other is not the answer. You are a Trine. Kinderra will be yours to protect someday. How will you bring peace?"

She said nothing, cutting little half-circles in the saddle's leather with her thumbnail instead.

"I want your answer."

She didn't have one to give. She'd killed one thousand forty-seven people. One thousand forty-seven lives. The fact that she used the Light from Within to kill them made no difference.

Could she ever find a way to bring peace? Should she even try?

He grabbed her arm. She jumped. "Answer me."

"We would," she swallowed, "we would all have to lay down swords and quiet our amulets together."

The Trine released her. "*Ai*. All of us. Together."

"But a truce like that is all but impossible."

"Is it?" He shook his head, his irritation intensifying to downright anger. "If that's what you believe, why are you by my side? Why are you even bothering to find out what the keep holds in store for us?"

She hung her head. "Because it's the only hope we have." The only one she had.

"*Oë verda*." He resumed riding down the dune.

It didn't matter that he said she was correct. Guilt swallowed her whole. With one action, she had taken one thousand and forty-seven living, breathing people. People who may have had loved ones, children, hopes, even their own dreams for some kind of peace. Did it even matter where the power came from to do what she had done? They were all dead now. Killed. By her.

… *Why did you bother saving my life?* …

He reined in his stallion, but his back remained to her. … *Because I believe in you … I believe in what you can become if you choose to* … "You are a Trine, no different than I. You must decide if you will accept the fullness of the burden the Aspects Above have given you or not." He lifted his head toward the deepening sky. … *If you do not, I will fail as well* … He tapped the stallion's sides with his heels and continued across the sand.

Mirana sat motionless in the saddle. Was accepting the Ken'nar's philosophy as righteous and equal to the Fal'kin's beliefs the only way to save Tetric's life? Would peace only come to Kinderra if every Fal'kin, if *she*, consented to the Power from Without's use? It didn't change the fact that the Ken'nar took life from around themselves to lend power to their Aspects. There had to be another way than to let the Power from Without continue to decimate Kinderra. There just had to be.

Accepting the Power from Without was a path she didn't think she could follow.

CHAPTER 13

"Tash-Hamar rises like a white dove from the desert,
fourth among her sisters, but none fairer."
—The Book of Kinderra

Mirana and Tetric walked the last mile to Rhadaz as the sun embraced the western horizon, each step feeling like a mile to her saddle-weary muscles and her burdened thoughts.

The setting sun painted the whitewashed buildings of Rhadaz scarlet. Diluted blood. Like in the rain puddles at Two Rivers Ford. In the keep vision. She shook her head to clear it.

Tiles rendered in a riot of colors and tangled patterns covered the steps and stoops of homes and shops. Their intense colors and violent designs swirled in her mind like so many amulets at her ill-fated Choosing Ceremony. Or those of the overwhelmed Fal'kin at the ford. The dead in the Vale i'Dúadar.

The scents of exotic spices from cooking fires hung cloying in the air, heavy and pungent as burial incense.

She trailed behind the Trine, thoughts running in relentless circles, searching for a noble answer to the abomination that was the Power from Without.

Around her, the short, squat homes, tall rectangular shops and inns, arabesque arches, and lofty domed towers created a curvilinear patchwork quilt of habitations. Their designs were as disorganized as her emotions. Teague had been to Rhadaz several times with his parents. His mother was born and raised here. He never spoke of the city's exotic, overwhelming, almost oppressive character. All he said when he returned to Deren was that it was hot and how glad he was to be back home. And how much he had missed her.

Would Teague find something righteous in the Power from Without? She shook her head slowly. Tetric was right. If Teague didn't understand her, he would never understand something like the Power from Without. His love for her was now gone, she'd seen to that. He would despise her after he learned she killed a thousand men and women through the sacred connection of Aspects and amulet to the Light from Within.

"Mirana, this way."

She turned her head. The Trine's voice had come behind her. He had taken a turn down a side street as they wound their way to the learning hall in the city's heart.

"You've been quiet," he said when she rejoined him. The streets slowly emptied as market vendors closed their carts and shops for the evening.

"I've been thinking about what you've said. About the Ken'nar. The war. Everything."

"And?"

"You were right. I never gave a thought to the Ken'nar lives I took. I am trying to understand the Ken'nar and the Fal'kin as you do. I just don't. Yet."

He smiled down at her, pride and sympathy brushing her mind. "It has taken me many painful summers to have come to the conclusion I have. I don't expect you to arrive at one overnight. To change one's beliefs on something held so dear for so long is never easy, but at least you're willing to try. For that, I am grateful. Kinderra will be as well."

She looked up at him with quiet desperation. "I'm grateful to you, too. I just don't know if I understand you." Aspects Above knew she wanted to.

"You will." Tetric might have told her things she didn't want to hear, things to challenge every one of her beliefs, but he had never lied to her. Unlike her father. "Come. Tash-Hamar's learning hall is the most beautiful in all of Kinderra."

She followed him around another corner, walking between rows of buildings, then down a side street. After a few paces, he reined in the horses.

Mirana stopped and gasped. The learning hall of Tash-Hamar appeared like something from a minstrel's tale, too beautiful to be real. The enormous domed structure was made of pure white stone and glowed in the soft light of the rising moon. The courtyard's watering trough was designed as a reflecting pool, its sides, even its interior covered in intricately patterned tiles. Not that Ashtar cared. He tugged at the reins, and Tetric let him loose to trot over to the trough to drink, while the Trine's horse waited for a command. Once given, it followed Ashtar and drank. Lush trees lined the courtyard, their branches sagging low with pendulous oranges and pomegranates. Flowered vines spiraled around portico columns, clinging to them as a child clings to his mother leaving for battle. *Maithe.*

She shook her head and walked a few steps closer to the tiled trough. Tetric's description of the hall as "beautiful" was ridiculously inadequate; it was breathtaking.

"So. The calls from the streets were not wrong," said a voice off to one side.

A man sat on a stone bench under a portico. He peeled an orange with a blade much too large for the job.

"Defender Second Sadhi." Tetric inclined his head in greeting. "*Kin ísi Öea.*"

The defender placed a wedge of the fruit in his mouth then tossed the peel aside as he walked across the moonlit courtyard.

He gripped Tetric's forearm in greeting. "*Ëi Trinus.*"

Mirana smiled. "Defender Sadhi, how good to see you again."

She remembered Timir Sadhi from Quorumtides. He had seen only a few summers past thirty, but her father once said the defender wielded a blade and an amulet with as much skill as those half again his age. He was of good stature but not of Tetric's height. No one was that tall. Compared to her, though, everyone seemed tall. A balmy breeze ruffled his dark, wavy hair. His handsome face held a chiseled chin and strong mouth, which were further defined by a close-cropped beard and mustache. Both of which were tugged down in annoyance. She bet his dark brown eyes missed little. Like now. He watched them as if they were thieves in the night. She scowled. Why? They hadn't done anything. At least, not yet.

"We've missed you at Quorumtide in Deren for a few summers." She reached out to take his arm, but he made no move to return the gesture.

"Ask your father about that." He turned to Tetric. "Why have you brought her here? Pinals are not welcome."

What was going on? She was unaware of such open animosity between Defender Second Sadhi and her father.

"I have a very good reason," her mentor replied.

She lifted her chin. "I am Lord Garis's *scholaira* now."

Timir looked from Mirana to the Trine. "Is Kaarl Pinal dead?"

Again, she inhaled to speak and again her *patrua* mentor stopped her, sending an intense command to be silent.

... Do not give him a reason to ask uncomfortable questions where you'll have to give uncomfortable answers ... Tetric shook his head. "No. But the il'Kin have been all but destroyed."

"Yet he still lives." Timir released Tetric's arm and curled his thumbs in his sword belt. Near his sword. Really? *Really*? "Tell me, were there any amulet burns on his chest? Or on his back?"

Mirana shrugged out of the Trine's hold and stepped forward, standing toe-to-toe with the defender. "My father may be many hateful things, but he is no coward."

The Trine pulled her back by the shoulder. *... Silence ...*

Timir laughed. "At least one Pinal has some courage. Too bad it has been wasted on this slip of a seer."

She advanced again, and once more, Tetric dragged her back, more forcefully this time. She winced at the warning he pounded into her brain.

Timir chuckled again. He called two boys, who came for the horses. "The prime is waiting for you."

She glared at the tall Trine for not letting her speak but held her tongue. The defender second ushered them through the learning hall and into the prime's chamber. As they entered, a beautiful young woman gave Timir a brief smile and left. The prime himself fussed with a kettle on the fireplace hearth. When he turned, though, his expression was more bemused than annoyed.

"My prime, your visitors," Timir said. He bowed and left.

She watched Timir leave. Jasal Pinal had been accused of treason, abandoning his people to build the keep then disappearing during the siege. Her father betrayed her, too. However, that didn't make him any less brave. If anyone else in the Pinal line was capable of foul actions, it was her.

Tetric's elbow nudged her arm. "Do not be rude. The prime just welcomed you."

"What? Pardon me," she said and quickly bowed. "*Kin ísi Öea*, Prime Aldi." The man might be nearing seventy summers, but he was just as handsome as his nephew—and probably still just as adept with his sword and amulet.

"Mirana Pinal is your *scholaira* now?" Fasen Aldi asked, cocking up an eyebrow. He then glanced over his shoulder to the bed chamber a moment and pulled the carved separation screen closed.

"*Ai*, although I am beginning to regret that decision," the Trine replied. "I apologize for her behavior with your nephew."

"I am sure his own behavior was less than hospitable. That skirmish two summers ago is seldom far from his mind. Nor mine. I, however, understand that even great swords can be defeated now and then. It is time he understands that as well."

The prime indicated two chairs. When she and Tetric settled in them, the elder defender poured fragrant tea from a kettle into three cups. He placed the kettle back on the hearth of the small, round-bellied fireplace that squatted in one corner of the chamber. Above it, a beautiful mosaic of a woman lay embedded in the plaster. The tilework was so fine it looked like a painting. It seemed to stare back at her.

Fasen Aldi handed a cup to Tetric. "I suppose there's no one better for her learn her Seeing Aspect from than a Trine. I must say, though, I thought I would see the Ken'nar lay down their amulets before I'd see Pinal handing over his only child to you to be trained."

The tall man accepted the tea from the prime and nodded his thanks. "It is true we seldom see eye to eye, but respect can overcome much."

She took the cup the prime offered her, nodded, and took a quick sip. It was sweet with honey and fresh with mint, and it almost made up for the irritation of being discussed as if she were not in the room. She should be searching for the keep clue and finding a way to protect Kinderra, not sipping tea and staring at pretty tile pictures.

In her earliest geography lessons as a child, she had learned the Tash-Hamari brought as much back to their province in trade as they did in bringing Tash-Hamar to other provinces. Defender Prime Aldi's chamber was a geography lesson in and of itself. Earthenware dressed in subdued glazes from Sün-Kasal and wooden figurines from Kana-Akün sat displayed on shelves molded right into the plastered walls. The prime's chairs, table, and other furniture were made of black ebony from the jungles of Jad-Anüna. A carved wooden panel depicting a mountain scene from far-off Trak-Calan screened the sitting area from the sleeping chamber. She caught a glimpse of a large bed, veiled by gossamer curtains, filled with silk pillows, and overlaid with a damask coverlet. The chamber seemed so feminine for the suave, bachelor prime. Not to mention a bit messy. She recalled the young woman who left when they had arrived.

Oh.

Embarrassed shock heated her cheeks. Apparently, his undiminished prowess extended beyond the battlefield.

"What brings you to Tash-Hamar?" the defender prime asked.

When Tetric's mind nudged hers, she panicked. She'd assumed he addressed the Trine. She didn't have a cover story.

"Well, um, sir, I am afraid we bring sad news. My grandfather returned to the Aspects Above last Twelfthmonth. My mother is now prime, and he also named my father as steward in his stead until the Quorum of Light convenes in the autumn. I am, er, I am here as the prime's emissary to give formal greeting and announcement as to the status of Kin-Deren province. My mother felt it was important, in light of such a sweeping change in governance, we should also hearken back to traditional custom."

Prime Aldi smiled and inclined his silvered head. "A beautiful gesture and a worthy one. I would have expected no less from your mother. We in Tash-Hamar will mourn your loss with you so you will not grieve alone."

"*Gratas Oë.*" Although her words had been a simple ruse, the prime's were heartfelt, and she was truly grateful.

"I also know your mother to be as skilled in politics as she was with long knives."

Her mother was also skilled in lying. Maybe that's why she was so adept at statecraft. She clenched her jaw and kept her comments to herself.

Again, the mosaic of the dark-haired woman seemed to reach out to her. If she studied the mosaic, she wouldn't have to think about home. Or her parents. She took another sip of her tea.

"I highly doubt you came all this way with Lord Garis in tow to inform us of something we'd heard from traders months ago," the prime continued. "What happened at Two Rivers Ford?"

Before she could reply, Tetric said, "The Ken'nar massacred the garrison at the ford and the installation fell. Varn-Erdal and Kin-Deren lost most of their Fal'kin in the conflict. Both provinces are vulnerable."

Silence in the room fell like a hammer. She tensed. She had not expected her *patrua* mentor to be so frank. Thankfully, he did not give the prime further details on exactly *how* the ford was lost.

Prime Aldi held his cup but did not drink. "My seers saw a battle to the north. We were still analyzing the vision, trying to get a timeframe."

She had been confused at first, too. Until she stopped denying what all three of her Aspects had shown her. She studied the exquisite tile picture of the beautiful woman and slipped further behind U'Nehíl, hoping neither man would notice.

The prime sat back in his chair. His polite smile vanished. "Vallia Edaran is no more?"

"*Ai.*" Tetric nodded. "They were ambushed in the Kabaarh Pass. Only Liaonne survived."

The silver-haired man stroked his beard, frowning. "That is a great loss, not only to Varn-Erdal but to Kinderra. Thank the Aspects Above Liaonne was spared. Timir will be grateful for the news."

Mirana scowled, confused. Other than meeting at Quorumtide, how did Timir Sadhi and Liaonne Edaran even know each other? She hardly saw them much at all during the celebrations. The Varn-Erdalan was often in the company of a middle-aged seer woman from her own province. Come to think of it, though, Liaonne and Timir always seemed to disappear together as soon as the festivities began, not to be seen again until the concluding ceremonies, both looking strangely happy. Oh. *Oh.* So, it was roosters *and* hens for Liaonne.

"The il'Kin are gone, too. Perhaps Timir will be even more grateful for that news," the Trine added.

Prime Aldi sat back in the chair. "They all perished as well?"

"Nearly. Seer Lima and Defender Commander Jord survived."

"Defender Commander, eh?" The older defender gestured with his cup to Mirana. "Your father made a wise choice. Jord is a good man and an even better defender."

Tetric's mouth thinned to a line. "Perhaps. Perhaps not." When the prime lifted an eyebrow in question, he answered, "He lost his entire command in one battle."

Whose side was he on? "My lord knows well that was a battle unlike any other," Mirana said. "We were outnumbered."

She adored Morgan Jord. He was as much a reason her father still breathed as her father's own Aspect. She clenched her hands tighter, her fingernails digging into her palms. The new il'Kin commander was her father's closest friend and even he had never been told about her. Was there anyone her father hadn't lied to?

The tall Trine stared down at her, his Aspect-weighted glare a physical sensation. "Quite. Right." She averted her eyes and squirmed in the chair.

"So, there's no chance of retaking Two Rivers Ford, then?" the prime asked.

Tetric shook his head. "It was destroyed."

She whipped her head around to stare, wide-eyed, at him. What in the name of the Aspects was he doing? She gave a wan smile to the prime, but it was pointless to cover her reaction. It was pointless to hide the ford's destruction anymore, either.

Sooner or later, trade caravans would light up the continent with the news quicker than a defender's amulet. She turned her gaze once again to the mosaic.

Prime Aldi did not move as the blue sapphire of his amulet began to glow. "Destroyed? You mean the actual bridges are gone?"

Her mentor nodded. "The earth itself fell away, carrying the bridges with it."

She wished fervently Trines had the power to disappear because if there were ever a time she wanted to be invisible, it was now.

The prime's shoulders now fell in shock. "Did you—?"

"Days of rain made the ground unstable," she interjected before Tetric could respond. "It could not support so many fighters." It was the truth. Partly, anyway. "Without the ford, however, the southlands will have a measure of safety for a while."

"So, what do Desde and Liaonne intend to do now?" Prime Aldi asked, looking from her to the Trine.

He shrugged. "I suspect they are thinking about that right now. Their provinces lay virtually emptied of Fal'kin."

Mirana had not thought about Kin-Deren's predicament until this moment. All eligible Fal'kin *scholaire'e* had already gone to fight at the ford. Many had died.

The mosaic truly was exquisite. The woman in the tilework had jet-black hair and penetrating, soulful amber eyes, and resembled how she imagined Antiri Amil Pinal, Jasal's wife, would appear. Antiri was from Tash-Hamar. She gasped, then covered with a cough.

Jasal Pinal. His presence. It was in the mosaic.

"Pardon me, Prime Aldi. The air is much drier here than I am used to." She laid a hand on the Trine's elbow and feigned clearing her throat. … *Jasal is here … Behind the mosaic …* She took another sip of tea. … *I need to check the tilework … The keep paragraph … I'm sure it's there …*

He moved his long leg, lightly touching hers. … *I will search for any openings …*

… *I really think I should be the one—* … He rose and walked over to the fireplace. She bit her lip.

"How long has Falannah been gone?" He touched the side of the mosaic. "Twenty, twenty-five summers now?"

"Twenty-three summers, six months, two sevendays, and three days, but what does my sister have to do with Varn-Erdal and Kin-Deren?"

He turned back to face the prime, but instead of giving Mirana some inkling as to whether the mosaic had an opening or slot of something, his eyes rested on a collection of exquisite swords from Kin-Deren's smithies hanging from the opposite wall.

"Falannah was a battle seer, was she not?"

"You know she was. You were there when she lost her life. We never recovered her body or her amulet, so thorough were those Ken'nar *vermihn*."

Tetric turned around to face them. She opened her mind, waiting for instructions, but he called nothing. "Your sister was a brilliant tactician. She would have understood. Two provinces are desperate for fighters. Three, really, with Kana-Akün under Ken'nar control. The il'Kin have been decimated. I cannot guarantee our safety alone. Kinderra is in jeopardy, *Ëi cara*."

Fasen Aldi looked up sharply. "Falantir fell, too?"

He nodded.

The prime wiped his face with a hand and was silent for a moment. "It will only be a matter of time before the ills of the north spread southward."

"War will indeed come south. I have another concern," Tetric replied. "The only real power the steward ever had was the command of the il'Kin. With Desde and Liaonne in such dire straits, and Kana-Akün, too, for that matter, Kaarl will be in a difficult position trying to rebuild the unit."

Prime Aldi toyed with the chain of his amulet. "The il'Kin have come from all over Kinderra, not just Varn-Erdal and Kin-Deren."

"*Ai.* Are you willing to sacrifice the best and the brightest from your provincial troops? Will you offer up Timir to rebuild the personal guard of the Steward of the Quorum of Light?"

She tore her gaze from the tile picture. Personal guard? What was he getting at? She might despise her father for the lifetime of lies he had told her, but he would never even consider, much less use, the il'Kin to further his own agenda. He didn't even have an agenda. Did he?

The description of her father silently slitting men's throats slashed through her mind. He was indeed capable of things she had never imagined. Did he hold something of Jasal Pinal's sins, too? He'd once told her good men turned evil when they sought power above all else. Was that kind of all-consuming ambition within her father? Was it great power tethered to great ambition that killed her ancestor?

Tetric was not at the keep in her terrifying vision of white light. Had she sought power and found she could not control it? Was that why she sensed so many desperate emotions from that future self?

And what of her mentor's desire to become Primus Magne? Did he seek such power, believing he could master it? What if he couldn't?

She shook her head and coughed lightly to cover for her sudden movement.

This was all becoming too much. Maybe they should just ask the prime if she could chisel away at the mosaic in his chamber and be done with it.

Prime Aldi chewed his lip and regarded the Trine with hooded eyes. "It is no secret, *Ëi Trinus*, that you do not believe Kinderra needs the il'Kin while we have your troops. It is equally obvious you do not want the unit to be reformed. What is it that you do want?"

"I want to create a single, unified army." His conviction gave all the weight his quiet words needed.

"Under your sole command," the defender prime continued, not skipping a beat. His sapphire amulet glowed brighter.

… Tetric, be careful… His amulet … she warned.

He shook his head and sat back down. "It is not like that."

"Then what precisely is it like?"

"If we combine our strength under me, I can guarantee this war will end."

"How?"

"I know things the Ken'nar themselves do not know. Truly, it is about strength in numbers. It's as simple as that. United under me, no enemy shall dare oppose us."

Mirana could no longer keep silent. That role was too much power for any one person to wield. It was suicide, moral suicide if nothing else. "No war is simply about numbers. Even I know that."

Prime Aldi nodded. "The girl speaks the truth. I have been the underdog in many a fight. I used my smallness to my advantage. I was also the victor. So was Kaarl. So were you." He shook his bearded head. "No, my friend, I cannot support you in this endeavor. *Ai*, I agree with you that Kinderra is in great peril, but the last thing we need now is a Primus Magne taking away our ability to govern ourselves." He raised his teacup to emphasize the point then took a sip.

"You were the victor, you say?" Tetric's voice dropped to a lower register, sending shivers up her spine. "The force that attacked the ford was more than twice what you have sleeping in your hall tonight. If you could not protect your sister, how will you protect her son? He barely walked away with his life two summers ago, no thanks to Kaarl. Are you still so willing to rely on your smallness?"

The older man jumped to his feet. … *How dare you?* … His call reached her mind as well.

She didn't think Defender Prime Fasen Aldi was the type of person to make idle threats. "My lord." She plucked at Tetric's shirtsleeve, sending along an intent of caution. "It's been a long day. Perhaps some rest for all of us will give us time to consider this news."

The Trine ignored her. "I dare because I am trying to make you see reason. Whom will you rely on? Varn-Erdal? Kin-Deren? That thick-skulled pacifist Sahm Klai? Kaarl and his failed il'Kin? This war will only end if we unite. There is no other way, Fasen."

The prime tightened his hand. The delicate teacup gave a sharp snap then shattered, falling to the floor in pieces. "So," he bit off the word, "we would no longer be our own men under this unified force? All our orders would come from you?"

Tetric held up his palms. Those large hands that could turn into large fists in the blink of an eye. "You are being unreasonable."

"No, I am not. You are talking about Primus Magne, for Aspects' sakes. You want to create a dictatorship. I fail to see what advantage we have owing supreme allegiance to you." He took a step closer to the Trine, the shards of the teacup crunching under his boot.

Mirana moved to Tetric's side. "It is late, my Trine. Let us leave." She held his elbow in an attempt to guide him from the room.

He gripped her shoulder, his fingers digging painfully into her collarbone. "You have the advantage of surviving the coming conflict. Or not."

... *Let's go* ... *Please!* ... she called.

He let out an explosive exhale and loosened his grip on her. He stepped back from the prime at last. "I do not want to run your province. I do not care how many bushels of wine grapes you harvest or whether the terms of your trade contracts are acceptable. I only want to keep you and your people safe. Kinderra needs your support, Fasen. I need it to stop this war."

The prime held his gaze a moment longer, then took a cleansing breath of his own. "And you would fight for us?"

"Haven't I already?"

She didn't know whether to be relieved or alarmed. The prime had backed down, but he was on the brink of accepting Tetric's bid to become Primus Magne. Fasen Aldi was a powerful man and his words carried weight in the Quorum. He could very well convince the council to elevate Tetric to the role.

Tetric wasn't in her keep vision. Maybe Primus Magne wasn't the mantle he was supposed to wear. Maybe it was meant for her. The thought left her cold. Could taking such an awful burden from him save his life? Was that why she faced the swordsman alone in her keep vision? Was he safe, somewhere else away from the conflict? But to become Primus Magne. Aspects Above, she did not want that kind of power.

"Oh!"

The men looked at her. Mirana waved a hand at her mouth and gestured with the teacup. "Hot."

She did *not* want that power. Maybe that was the way around her destiny. Seeking the very thing she wanted least. What a cruel irony. But with all the rage, agony, desolation in her keep vision? Maybe it was too soon to feel elated.

"You fought with me last summer in southern Jad-Anüna," Tetric continued. "The Ken'nar had never advanced so far south in such numbers. Was my calling of the battle so onerous?"

"No. If you hadn't arrived when you did, I would have been killed. Timir, too," Prime Aldi replied. He then pointed an accusing finger at him. "But you came late."

Tetric smiled faintly, then his expression grew serious. "I am sworn to protect Kinderra. It is why the Aspects Above made me who I am. Fasen, I am out of options. This is all I have left."

The silver-haired defender nodded slowly. Was it in acceptance or defeat? Maybe it was both. "I cannot give you my word now. This decision is far too important to be made so quickly. I will speak to Timir as well, as he is my second. I promise you, though. I have taken your words to heart."

Tetric nodded. "Even as a Trine, I cannot be everywhere at once. With all of us working together, I can be."

The men rose from their chairs. Prime Aldi gripped her mentor's forearm. "I will not vote in favor at Quorum unless Timir agrees as well. I daresay you had an easier time convincing me."

Mirana gazed once more on the tile portrait as they left the prime's chambers. Once she found the secrets to the keep, Tetric might not have to convince anyone to become Primus Magne. That job of convincing people might fall to her.

CHAPTER 14

"They asked me to take the mantle as the sole defender
of the Sisters, and I accepted its unspeakable burden,
its terrible sacrifice. Now will they do the same for me?"
—The Codex of Jasal the Great

Mirana and Tetric were escorted to their rooms by a
scholaire. She waited a few moments until the boy had left before
she slipped back out into the hallway. She crossed the empty
corridor to Tetric's room. She paused before knocking. A
fragment of Jasal's keep writings was in Prime Aldi's chamber.
She knew it; she could feel an echo of her ancestor there. And
she and her mentor were going to do what? Break in and steal
it? She frowned. Maybe they could say she lost something in the
room and needed to retrieve it. Oh, like a lie was so much better.
Why couldn't they just ask the prime if they could search his

chambers? Tetric, however, had said the keep's power and the intentional separation of the instructions on its use were information people would kill for. She bit her lip. Why was everything always so bloody complicated?

Mirana knocked on the Trine's door and waited, but there was no answer. He laid her palms on the door and reach out with her mind. The room was empty. Where could he have gone so quickly? Did the man become part of the night? He must have already headed to Prime Aldi's chamber on his own. She had hoped he would have waited for her.

She crept down several thankfully empty hallways then turned the corner near Fasen Aldi's room.

Before she could enter, she heard footsteps and voices. She ducked into a door alcove and peered down the hallway. The defender prime and Timir Sadhi spoke in low tones. The older man gripped his nephew's shoulder and squeezed it. If Tetric was in the prime's chamber, he would be found out. She sought his mind. He was close, but his damnable hold on U'Nehíl didn't reveal where.

... *Tet—* ...

... *Be still* ...

She jumped. The Trine stood behind her.

The prime and his second continued down the corridor out of sight. Once they were gone, she breathed a sigh of relief. Tetric crossed the hall quickly and placed his palms on the chamber door. A soft click broke the stillness of the hallway. He opened the door and went inside, motioning her to follow.

"So, the mosaic?" He stood in front of the tile picture.

She ignored his question and stepped next to him. "Are you trying to get yourself killed?"

He glared at her and pointed to the open door. She grimaced and closed it gently with the Aspects.

"You are putting your life in danger with each person you reveal your plans to," she whispered harshly. "Wait until we've collected all the stanzas. Maybe once we figure out what the keep is, or what it can do, no one will have to be Primus Magne. Furthermore, that might not be the role—"

… We do not have time for this … Fasen will not be gone long … he called. *… Find the verse…*

… This discussion is not over … "It's somewhere behind the mosaic. But wait. Aren't we violating Prime Aldi's privacy by doing this? Not to mention that of a province?"

"If you're right and there is a keep verse behind that mosaic, we will be one step closer to peace. Any wrongdoing we perpetrate pales by comparison."

"I suppose you're right." She shrugged. "Still, maybe we should just ask?"

"This secret is so long forgotten, I doubt he knows it's here."

"This seems wrong somehow. Sooner or later, everyone in Kinderra will know about Jasal's Keep."

"*Ai*, but we need to know before our enemies do."

The Trine's words came back to her. "If you say the Ken'nar want peace just as badly as we Fal'kin do, who then is our enemy?"

His dark eyes burned with smoldering fury. "Anyone who would prefer war."

His words struck her. War had been Kinderra's way of life for three millennia. Were there those who preferred it to peace? Aspects Above knew she didn't. If Tetric became Primus Magne, there would undoubtedly be Fal'kin who would object, to say nothing of the Ken'nar. Would he end up continuing the war in that role instead of stopping it? If she became Primus Magne to spare him, would she? All the more reason to find the keep writings as quickly as possible. Maybe no one would have to become Primus Magne and carry that kind of power.

He walked over to the tile chip rendering. "Falannah was a beautiful woman."

"I don't think that's Falannah. Unless Jasal's writings were kept elsewhere until twenty-three summers ago when Falannah died and they made the likeness of her, I believe that is Antiri Pinal. Her father was prime in his day." She gestured around the chamber. "This might have been his room at one time."

Tetric traced around the edges of the tile with his fingers again. "I would think Fasen would know if he had a likeness of his sister in his chamber or not." He turned and scowled at the opposite wall.

"He never said that was his sister."

He smiled. Mirana smiled wider.

"Let's get this over with." She climbed onto the hearth and stood on tiptoes and ran a hand over the smooth, tiny squares, searching for a way behind it. There were no breaks in the grout lines or any other way of getting underneath the bits of stone. For all she knew, the treatise could be embedded in the plaster, not simply lying underneath. She took out her belt knife.

"Wait." The Trine grabbed her wrist. "Are you so sure you want to just dive in and pry the thing off? Search further."

She eyed his amulet, hesitating. "All right. Give me your amulet for a moment."

She laid her palm flat against the mosaic and called to the Trine's amulet. She sucked in a breath as its harmonics vibrated roughly against hers then quieted as her mentor decreased his control. The sensation. It felt just plain wrong. Two people should not hold one amulet, but seeing there was no other way to get to the passage, she endured the discomfort. She reached out with her Seeing Aspect. The hematite crystal began to glow a dusky silver. Instead of a vision, however, her Healing Aspect conveyed the sense of stabbing pain in the small of her back. She gasped and turned to face the opposite wall, a hand still on the tilework. "The swords! I think they are a trap—"

A shearing agony flares in her back. Pain, a universe of it, envelopes her from the waist up. She can no longer sense her legs. Half of her body is still; no life music comes to her. Half of her body shrieks in the dischord of mortal injury. The world disappears in a brilliant white light.

Mirana gave a small cry and stumbled off the hearth. As she fell, she reached for her Defending Aspect to steady her, her flailing hand hitting the tile portrait. Tetric's amulet brightened.

"Mirana! Down!" the Trine shouted, pulling her to the floor.

A grinding noise, like stone on stone, came from behind the mosaic. A small section of the tilework swung open on a hidden hinge—and a sword flew across the room to embed itself in the hearth plaster, just where her back had been.

Mirana peered from Tetric's arms at a metal coil vibrating from the sword's bracket. "*Excra hale!*"

She forced her breathing to slow as she climbed to her feet.

"Spring-loaded." He nodded. "Clever."

"Or cleaver. As in the back." She handed him back his amulet and shook herself as much to dispel the experience as to calm herself over the suddenly broken connection from his amulet. Her mentor hadn't seen the fragment of her keep vision. Or maybe he wasn't revealing that he had. Mirana took a long knife and carefully pried open the little tile door farther, her gaze shifting from the mosaic to the opposite wall. When no other weapons attempted to bury themselves in her body, she sighed in relief. A piece of parchment lay in a small depression in the wall. Tetric reached for it and unfolded it.

"What does it say?" She read the parchment around his arm as he held it:

With a great price do we labor on the Tower, for while we toil, our enemy gnashes at our heels like mongrel dogs. While we build, the Ken'nar tear down. Our numbers dwindle as we lay mortar, stone, and aught else we have to give. I knowest that which makes my heart tremble. I have seen Their divine plan. Woe to the enemies of the Light! They will be their own undoing!'

She sighed, frustrated, and took the parchment from Tetric. "Well, this is no help. The 'divine plan' is probably the tower itself, but we already knew that. 'Aught else'? What do you think that means?"

He shrugged. "Their lives, perhaps."

"*Ai*, but no." She bit her lip, thinking. "No doubt some died during the keep's construction. 'Our numbers dwindle.' There's something else to it, though. One thing's for sure, he's frightened. To his core." She studied the writing again. "'Aught else.' I sense some sort of overwhelming sacrifice but not necessarily death."

"We have two more provinces to visit. We may need a few more stanzas," Tetric said. He abruptly looked at the door.

She sensed a presence approaching. She refolded the parchment and slipped it under her shirt, then closed the little tile door. "They're coming. Give me the sword. I need to reset the protection."

He worked it out of the fireplace. "Here. And take my amulet, too." He began to remove it.

"Not everything needs the Aspects to be fixed. I think if I just—" She placed the sword back on its bracket, but the spring mechanism refused to stay coiled, forcing the blade to hang in the wrong position. "Uh oh."

Now, she heard voices.

The Trine made a growling noise in the back of his throat that didn't sound remotely human. "Come." He grabbed her by the wrist and dragged her out of the chamber.

When she started to run down the corridor, he grabbed her shirt collar, yanking her back. "If you act like a thief, you will be treated as one." They walked back to their rooms.

"I'm sorry," she said before the Trine entered his room. "I really thought I could do it without your amulet."

"The next time I give you an order, you will follow it immediately, without question. *Oë comprende?*"

She had become used to his intense gaze when he was displeased with her. Which was as often as not. His black eyes now held a cold, merciless expression she had never seen before. It frightened her. She nodded quickly. "*Ëo comprende, Ëi Trinus.*"

He sighed and stretched his neck. "You need to follow my orders because I may perceive a danger ahead of you and save your life."

Like the sword booby trap.

She nodded and slipped into her room. Closing the door behind her, she headed toward the bed and paused. What if she sensed a threat ahead of him? Would he listen to her? Like becoming Primus Magne. Whenever she thought of him assuming that role, a shiver went down her spine. It almost felt like—no, it *did* feel like the whisper of a distant premonition in the Seeing Aspects. It was wrong, but how?

She walked back across the hallway. The door opened on its own and revealed him standing in the middle of his room, long arms folded across his chest, a bemused smile tracing his lips.

"I'm not so sure Primus Magne is the answer."

"Why?" His arms remained folded.

She stepped farther into the room. "I don't know. You could be killed."

"That is no different than any other day."

"All right, maybe you won't be killed. Maybe something else."

"I have faced every evil mortal life has." He straightened his broad shoulders and brought himself to his full height. His very tall full height. The man changed moods like a Tash-Hamari trader changed terms. "And I do not fear for my life."

"I do." She sought his mind. ... *Please do not do this* ...

"Creating peace is only the first step. Keeping it, making it last, that is our true struggle."

"What do you mean? Once we have peace, why in the name of the Aspects Above would we want to return to war?"

He shut the door behind them. "Mirana. Think. What would the Aspected do when they no longer had to fight each other? What would the *Unaspected* do when there was no reason to support the Fal'kin any longer?"

Her jaw dropped. "You mean to rebuild our very society."

"I would have to." His voice became soft, humbled by his own words. "If I do not, it would be war again."

Her mind returned to that very possibility she had thought of earlier. "Doesn't that prove to you that becoming Primus Magne could do more harm than good? It's too much responsibility for any one man or woman to shoulder."

"We Aspected know no other trades. We can't suddenly become farmers and weavers and bakers. When the war ends, we need time to adjust. How much more time do you think the Unaspected will give us? We've had three thousand summers. The Unaspected would rise against us, striking back at us for all our failures, real and imagined. This time, it would not be the Aspected who would perish."

Teague.

"No."

His face became hard. "You are still in love with him. I told you before, such things cannot be."

She turned away from him. "I'm trying to put him behind me. I need to." She laughed painfully and stared up at the ceiling rafters. "Aspects know he couldn't possibly love me again for the things I've done." She pulled out her peda blossom pendant. "But I still don't want him to die."

"Listen to me. You must forget him." The Trine placed a hand on her shoulder and turned her to face him. "Your role in Kinderra will demand all of you. I know this."

"So, you've never had anyone in your life?" She turned back to face him and folded her arms. "I think you did. And you lost her. And it hurts you. Even to this day."

He shut his mind so quickly, it made her wince. "Think of who you are. You will be guiding a continent someday. And Teague Beltran? He is an Unaspected herbsboy."

She had held onto some shred of hope that maybe if she managed to save and not condemn Kinderra, Teague would understand her and her power. They could be together, at last, joined in union as husband and wife.

"If he even outlives the coming conflict," he continued, "you and he will be on different paths, an ocean apart."

She backed away from him. "If we finish what we are attempting to do, Kinderra will be at peace, and it won't need to be guided by any Trine, certainly not a Primus Magne."

"You can't be that naïve." He stepped closer to her. "He will never understand. If you persist in keeping him in your life, he will grow to resent you and your powers." His voice was as soft as his mind was not. It pressed down on her, a smothering blanket of crushing sadness and profound regret. "Every day with you will be a reminder of what he should have been and is not. And you will live the rest of your days knowing you could have released him to a better life, but your selfishness chained him to your side."

Hadn't Teague's father said the same thing? If anyone knew Teague's inner heart, it would be his father. Tetric was right. And she wanted to beat the "rightness" out of the man with her fists. "I will hear no more of this." She thrust out her hand and the door flew open, banging back against its hinges. She stomped from the room.

... Someday he will no longer be able to bear it any longer ... the Trine continued. *... Then he will leave you alone, in the cold, with a babe in your arms that he will not acknowledge ... What will you tell your child when she asks the question of why her father left her? ...*

"Stop it. Leave me alone." She ran across the hall to her quarters.

... Will you tell your child that her father hated you both and the power you both possess? ... Because you constantly had to choose Kinderra over him? ...

She whirled around and attempted to slam her chamber door closed with the Aspects. He stood inside the threshold and repulsed her actions with his powers.

... Would you tell her lies? ... What then when the child seeks the truth for herself? ...

"Get out."

... You think you feel hatred for your parents for lying to you ... They thought they were protecting your life ... The anger you bear against them is nothing compared to the hatred your child will hold for you for your own lies ... It is better she is never born ... Mirana, if you love the boy, let him go ... Truly ...

Anger rose within her, igniting her Defending Aspect. She shoved Tetric away from her with her arms and her

Aspect. … *I said get out!* … He flew across the hallway and slammed into the doorjamb of his room. As he recovered his balance, his midnight-black eyes drilled into her with that cold fury she saw earlier. Light glowed and ebbed within his amulet.

Mirana swallowed with a mixture of fear and loathing, expecting a rebuke, even a physical one. None came. Instead, his expression softened into one of pain and sadness. He stepped into his room and quietly closed the door.

She walked into her room and held the door, uncertain if she wanted to rip it from the wall, slam it, or shut it like a mature person. She tried to push away from her imagination the scenes he had painted but they remained. They lingered not because they were lies but because they were possible.

CHAPTER 15

"U'tuda fin'e iré a Mortea."
("Not all ends lead to Death.")
—Ora Fal'kinnen 133:3

Mirana awoke the next morning to shouts outside her room. It was just as well. She had slept fitfully, her dreams filled with desperation, pain, and garish light. She sensed confusion and anger and fear. She rubbed her eyes, unable to discern for a moment if the raised voices came from her nightmare or the hallway.

Someone banged on her door.

"Mirana?" Timir Sadhi's voice came through the door, taut with urgency.

"*Ëo hac.* Just a moment." She rushed out of bed and threw on a tunic and stomped into her boots. She hurried over to the door and opened it. "What's the matter? What's happened?"

He held his sword as he shouted over his shoulder to another Fal'kin, "She's safe. Inform Lord Garis." He turned to her.

"A trap set for marauders was tripped."

She swallowed nervously. "Did you—did you catch them?" She closed her mind against intrusion, hoping the defender second would not notice.

He did. He smirked. She frowned. "Not yet." His smug humor now disappeared. "Why would you have gone back into my uncle's chamber and ransacked it?"

Mirana thrust out her chin in an attempt at righteous indignation. "Why would you assume it was me?"

"If you were innocent, why would you have covered your mind?"

"Well, I—" She tried for the door. "Where is Tetric? Is he all right?"

The defender stepped in front of her and prevented a convenient escape. "Why were you in my uncle's chamber?"

"I left something there that belonged to me."

"To you? What?"

"You see—" She held up her palms as she formed and discarded several answers. The truth could be far more damaging right now but lying seemed just as wrong.

She exhaled and slapped her palms against her thighs in defeat. "The Pinals are so identified with Kin-Deren province, the two are almost synonymous with each other. There's this whole other side to us, though. The Tash-Hamari side. The mosaic in your uncle's chamber."

Timir scowled. "My mother?"

Mirana shrugged. "Maybe. Do you know when it was made?"

"No."

"It could be your mother. It could also be Antiri Amil Pinal. I wanted a closer look. How could she have so dearly loved a man that had fallen so far from grace? Then I noticed your uncle's swords. The one from Kin-Deren is crossed over the one from Tash-Hamar. They were so beautiful, I touched them. Then, um, a tile fell away." There was enough truth in her words that Timir would not sense a fabrication. She hoped. "I am sorry. I should have just asked."

"You could have been killed."

Mirana huffed a laugh. "No kidding."

He sheathed his sword at last. Was everyone's sword as long as she was tall? "Why are you really here? Especially with him? I don't think it's to look at my uncle's artwork."

What could she say that was not a lie but still kept their real purpose unknown? "What do you mean?"

He crossed his arms. "I have a very hard time believing Kaarl Pinal would willingly let his daughter roam the countryside with a man he dislikes only slightly less than the Ken'nar."

She set her mouth in a thin line. "I no longer care what my father likes or dislikes. I am no longer beholden to him. Or my mother. I am Trine Garis's *scholaira*. I am now bound to Dar-Azûl province."

The defender second did not change his expression one bit. "Dar-Azûl. Really."

"My reasons are my own." She clamped down on her mind like a vice. "Apparently, the Lord Trine is not the only one who disagrees with my father. Why do you?"

"I, too, have my reasons. Sixty-three of them," he hissed through clenched teeth.

She meant to deflect his questions, not antagonize him. She took another step back. "That skirmish in the Trak-Calan highlands was savagery, I know that. Many were killed."

Timir took a step closer. "That 'skirmish,' as you call it, was not some accidental meeting of a Ken'nar raiding party. We knew their location. Because of information from your father's il'Kin."

"And the il'Kin got that information from Tetric Garis," Mirana challenged.

"When we arrived, there were no il'Kin to be seen. But there were Ken'nar. We ended up fighting for our lives." The deep orange citrine gem in his amulet flared with his anger like fire.

She blinked. "What?" She had never heard this. "Are you saying my father never came?"

Again, a corner of Timir's mouth jerked up, only this time into a most unhandsome smile. "Oh, he came. Too late to do any good. He said he was dogged by a group of Ken'nar from the same unit that attacked us. He didn't want to lead them to us and make a bad thing even worse. Your master, our blessed Trine, came even later. He, too, had seen the attack but was too far from us to have arrived any sooner. At least he called a warning to us. The il'Kin didn't even do that. We were slaughtered, defending a province that wasn't even our own."

She looked down at her boots. Good men could and did become evil. Tetric said ending the war was just the beginning. The real work would be to undo wrongs and create lasting peace. "I am sorry."

"Sorry?" He stabbed a finger at her. "Your father could have called us. Warned us. We would have had time to pull back. Instead, he did nothing." He exhaled in disgust. "Why am I wasting my time with you? You are nothing but a child. What would you know of war? I will tell my uncle you tripped the protection by accident." He turned to leave.

If he only knew the things she had seen, the things she had already done. The things she might still do. "If what you say is true, the Ken'nar attacked the il'Kin miles from where they expected to meet the main host. They were fighting for their lives, too. What would you have had them do?"

He whirled on her. He stood close enough that his amulet touched her chest as he breathed down at her. A soft tug pulled at her. A forlorn invitation. A need. From his amulet.

"How dare you presume—" He gasped and backed away.

No. Not now. Dear Aspects Above, not now. Her Trine powers forced a connection to the man's amulet straight from his chest.

She stared back at him, terror in her own eyes. "I-I can't help it."

He clutched his amulet, sunset-colored light leaking between his fingers, his dark eyes wide in horror. "What in the Nine Levels of the Underworld are you?"

There was no longer any reason for secrets. After the ford, the whole of Kinderra would know about her soon enough, including the Dark Trine. Answers to her destiny certainly had never come from secrets. Maybe it was time to speak the truth.

She shook her head sadly and averted her eyes. "Why do you think I'd be apprenticed to Lord Garis?"

"You-You're a Trine?" he whispered. She nodded. "We have Lord Garis. And the Dark Trine. What are you?"

That was indeed the question. "I just want to do what I can to help Tetric stop this war and save Kinderra. To save your people. To save all of us."

His hand remained on his amulet. "We've seen what happens with a Pinal Trine."

His insults cut deeper than even he probably meant them to. Maybe her ancestor had died in shame, with hundreds of Fal'kin falling before the Ken'nar, but his keep did ultimately save the land. People always seemed to forget that part. Even so, if her keep vision became reality, Jasal Pinal's failures would seem like a child's mishap.

Mirana turned and walked from him, as much to separate herself from his amulet as his emotions. A carved panel of fragrant dark wood made up an entire wall in her quarters, screening a balcony overlooking Rhadaz. She stepped outside.

"Did you know what it was meant to protect?" Timir and his uncle had to have noticed the little safe was now empty.

Timir moved to stand next to her. "My uncle used to keep valuables in there, things he wanted to give to a, um, special friend during Quorumtide." He shrugged. "There used to be a bit of poetry in there, but it never made any sense." He raised his gaze to the cloudless blue sky. "I don't think he's used the safe since my mother died." He sighed. "There's nothing in there now. I suspect it's been empty for summers."

The sunlight on the city made it shimmer like something out of a dream. To see Rhadaz, the crown jewel of Kinderra's fairest sister, overrun like the ford was unthinkable. "Your seers must have told you what happened at Two Rivers Ford."

"The ford was annihilated."

"I want nothing more than to prevent another Two Rivers Ford. War is coming, Defender Second. It will make all battles before look like a game unless Tetric and I can do something to stop it."

"What would you do?"

She hesitated. Her *patrua* had said knowledge of the keep was information people would kill for. Would Timir Sadhi? If he knew, would his own life be in danger? She didn't want to know the answer to either question. He did, however, deserve something of the truth. She had indeed ransacked his uncle's private residence.

"Tetric has his own plans. I, however, hoped to find a bit of my legacy here. Jasal Pinal may have damned my family for fifty generations, but he did save Kinderra from the Dark Triumvirate. His keep somehow saved Deren when Ilrik the Black returned to destroy the city. I hoped I could find here something of the good man that Jasal had been in the home of his beloved wife Antiri. Something I could use to save Kinderra yet again."

He looked out over his city, his home. "Did you find what you were looking for in my uncle's chamber?"

"I don't know." That was the honest truth.

She traced the stone railing of the balcony with a fingertip. The air was already warm despite the early hour, but the limestone was still cool from the night. Far to the south was the shimmering silver line of the Mer-Lima Sea. The ocean. Vast. Indifferent. It had no responsibility to be anything other than what it was, free from having to make choices. She could leave now. Just slip out of Rhadaz's learning hall, away from Timir's prying questions, away from Tetric's abominable truths, and never turn back. She should jump on Ashtar's back and ride away, now, before she could take another thousand lives.

But how would escaping to the ocean solve anything? How would running away keep Tetric alive? How would disappearing save Kinderra?

Timir shifted beside her, maybe imagining the same horror she had of his beloved city being sacked by Ken'nar. "What could Trine Garis do to stop the war that he has not already done?"

His question was probably rhetorical, but she answered him anyway. Or almost. "As I said, he has his own plans. If the Dark Trine isn't already trying to kill him because he is the Light Trine, any larger action Tetric takes will certainly make his life forfeit. I will do whatever I must to keep that from happening."

Timir leaned on the railing. "The Aspects Above gave Lord Garis to us to save Kinderra. Even so, your father was not the only one who arrived late to that damnable highland massacre. When Lord Garis finally came, the Ken'nar ran in retreat, putting an end to that fight. He saved what few of us managed to survive. I would stand with him against the Dark Trine if he would have me."

So would she. Oh, Light Above, so would she. "I can't imagine what it must be like to go from person to person and decide who can be saved and who cannot."

He nodded. "I went back the next day. I couldn't help myself. Fewer of my—" His jaw worked for words that would not come easily. "Fewer bodies remained on the battlefield than the previous day. Far fewer. I have never known carrion feeders to act so quickly. Or thoroughly."

A chill rippled through Mirana's body despite the heat of the day. "You think the Ken'nar took the bodies? Whatever for?"

He curled his amulet hand into a fist. "Target practice."

She sought his mind, both to comfort him and to find out if he was being facetious. He remained closed to her.

"I cannot pretend to understand the decisions my father and Tetric made that day that left so many of your defenders dead. I am only beginning to know our Trine. But my father? I'm no longer certain I ever knew him." Her father had always been her hero. When he would ride up the long road to Deren, his chain mail rent, blood staining the purity of his white uniform, she would send endless prayers of thanks to the Aspects Above that he was still alive despite what he had faced. Had the long summers of war killed the parent she loved? What had it left in his place? "There is nothing I can do to change the Pinal blood in my veins. All I can do is try to accomplish something good with the Aspects I have."

He patted her hand. "I will tell my uncle no harm was done. It was just a mistake made by a curious girl whose heart was in the right place." He turned and headed for the door.

"Defender Second Sadhi, I am sorry. Truly."

He paused by the door. "For what?"

"For the deaths of those close to you."

"Why are you sorry? You didn't take their lives."

No. Not theirs. Not yet. "If I could bring their heartbeats back, I would." The heartbeats of Timir's friends, Tetric's flame-haired girl, her dead Kin-Deren compatriot whose amulet Mirana had used to destroy Two Rivers Ford, and so many others. "All of us have lost men and women—friends—in this horrible war."

He regarded her for a moment. "Sometimes, in the heat of battle, it's all one can do to survive. Other actions, even warnings, come second." He nodded and left.

Tetric's mind nudged hers, bidding her to hurry. He wanted to leave as soon as possible.

She took one last look out the balcony at Rhadaz. Timir had held onto his anger towards her father for two summers, blaming him, in part, for the deaths of his comrades. When she helped him look at the brutal skirmish from a different point of view, much of that anger disappeared. Although Tetric's words during their argument the previous night had been harsh, even he had said her father—both her parents—thought they'd save her life by lying to her.

Maybe she didn't know her father. Maybe he was not a hero, above reproach. Nor was he an accursed betrayer. Maybe he was just a man trying to do what he thought best for others.

Wasn't that what she was doing, trying to do her best for others? Pushing Teague from her life by breaking his heart to save him? Trying to convince Tetric that pursuing a magnistate was dangerous? Disagreeing with her mentor that any noble use of the Soul Harvest existed so he could see just how wrong it was? Stealing a precious bit of parchment that might be the key to unlocking peace in Kinderra? In her own heart?

Maybe it was time for her to change her point of view on so many things, too.

CHAPTER 16

"The Ken'nar marched ever closer, like Doom itself.
We hardened our lines, but it would not be enough to
defeat our foe."

—The Book of Kinderra

Kaarl Pinal galloped his dappled horse over the grasslands of Kin-Deren province. For the first time in his life, he dreaded coming home. Each hoofbeat pounded dully like a death knell.

When he reached the learning hall in Deren, he handed the reins to a young boy.

"Taddeus, isn't it? A seer?"

"*Ai*, sir," piped the boy, "but everyone calls me 'Taddie.'"

After the ford, Deren had become home to a handful of old seers and little children. Kaarl had been just a few summers older than the boy when he became a scout and saw for the first time what happened in war. The memory of bloated corpses rotting in the sun remained etched in his memory.

"Is there some other service I can do for you, sir?"

"No, Taddie. You take care of Patan well, all right?"

"*Ai*, sir." The little boy started to walk toward the stables when he paused and turned around. "Sir, where is your other horse? The one as big as a house?"

Kaarl smiled. "My daughter rides Ashtar now."

"When is Mirana coming home? She helps me with my lessons. I miss her."

"I do, too." He turned away so the child could not see the pain written on his face.

He climbed the stairs that led to the hall's residential corridors. He used to run them two or three at a time when he was the seer boy's age, sometimes more when he was older and Desde awaited him. Today, his feet felt like lead.

When he reached his and Desde's chamber, he found the door already ajar. He pushed it aside. His wife held her amulet with both hands and touched his mind with hers. He said nothing. He had no words to speak.

She turned from him and cried silently into her hands.

He wrapped his arms around her. ... *Hope shall remain* ... The mind-words sounded comforting, but he no longer believed them.

Kaarl held Desde close and wept with her.

CHAPTER 17

"When I fought the Dark Defender, I emptied my
amulet upon him. And still he came anon. Either I
was weak, or he was strong. And yet the Aspects we
touched were the same."

—The Codex of Jasal the Great

The ocean.

Mirana smelled its salty tang in the air. It was not an entirely pleasant scent but distinctive, brackish yet invigorating.

As she rode behind Tetric through the streets of the port city of Qadar in far southern Tash-Hamar province, she glimpsed the water between buildings, the moonlight fractured to ribbons on its swells.

The ocean was both a lie and a reality.

She'd once begged Teague to take her away from Deren, to ride to the ocean to start a new life together, away from Jasal's Keep, her parents' lies, away from her own lies. She once thought to walk into the ocean's embrace and find a different kind of freedom from her destiny. The ocean couldn't give her a home with Teague, it couldn't give freedom from responsibility, not really. The ocean of her dreams was an illusion. The ocean of her reality held no answers nor absolution. It was nothing more than water.

Tetric had been correct about her relationship with Teague. The whole reason why she had pushed him from her life was to save his own. She had done the right thing, the good thing. She was out of his life; now, he would be safe. It was time he was out of hers. The Trine needed her help to save Kinderra. That was the only reality that mattered now.

She tapped her heels against Ashtar's sides to urge him next to the Trine's stallion.

"My lord? About the other night. My behavior. It was inexcusable. I want to apologize."

He shook his head and brushed off her comment. "It is not often I find myself in a physical altercation I did not choose."

"I'm so sorry—"

"But rarely is one so brave as to stand up for what she believes in against me."

Her mouth hung open. Her *patrua* mentor had the perplexing ability to crush her and build her up at the same time. She would leave well enough alone. She gave him a vague nod and concentrated on guiding Ashtar through the crowded thoroughfare.

Where Rhadaz was a sculpture, Qadar was a tool. The port city's seedy streets had none of the splendor of its fairer sister to the north. Most of Qadar's inhabitants worked hard to ply a trade on the Mer-Lima Sea, buying and selling its bounty. She wrinkled her nose. That bounty was fish.

As they rode past a boisterous tavern, a scantily clad woman cooed a proposition to Tetric. Mirana watched for his reaction out of the corner of her eye and found him as stony-faced as usual.

"I think she liked you." She wanted to hear him laugh again after the fiasco in Rhadaz.

He kept his gaze straight ahead. "She is unworthy of our notice."

"Would that be because she was a pleasure woman or because you did not find her attractive?" She grinned as she needled him.

He still did not turn to face her. "What would you know of pleasure women when you've scarcely been outside the walls of Deren's learning hall?"

Ai, the people of Qadar worked. Any way they could. "She said she wanted a little companionship."

The Trine straightened in his saddle. "I do not need her companionship."

The image of a young woman with copper hair and emerald eyes again filled her mind. As it had before, it left as quickly as it came. He then shrouded his presence deeper behind U'Nehíl.

She blinked at the intense but fleeting image. "Who was she?"

"Leave it be."

She had meant to tease him, not upset him, and certainly not call up a painful memory. Had he once lost his heart to the copper-haired girl? "I just wanted to—"

He whirled his horse around so quickly she nearly rode into him. ... *I said leave it be* ... She started to call an apology when he shook his head. He reined his horse to a halt. ... *She was ... important to me ... I have never been able to erase her memory ... And so*

I have a wound that still bleeds … I don't want you to bear this kind of pain …

Mirana reached across to place a hand on his arm. … *I'm so sorry, Ëi patrua ama … Gratas … For telling me this …*

He straightened his shoulders as if he had just donned armor. Maybe he had. "Come. There is an inn down the road where we shall stay the night."

Soon, she and Tetric arrived at a nondescript building and handed their horses' leads to stable attendants. Voices tumbled out of the open double doors. A few sailors just off their boats lingered by the doorway, fish stains still on their clothes. They were Unaspected, but even if they were not, they did not seem like the type of men who cared to censor their thoughts. Which they did not. Regarding her. She clung to the Trine like armor as they entered the inn. Armor. Why hadn't she thought to put hers on?

He led her inside to a table in a dark corner. "Wait here and do not speak to anyone." He disappeared into the crowded tavern room.

The pressing bodies made the room sweltering. A whisper from her Defending Aspect set the hairs on the back of her neck on end. A sailor watched her from the middle of the tavern. His mates bickered with each other over a card hand. The sailor ignored them as he packed a long-stemmed pipe with tobacco. His amber-eyed gaze took all of her in as if she were a prize catch trapped in his net. His mind decided on a closer investigation. Oh, no.

She searched frantically for the Trine. The sailor picked up his mug of ale and wound his way through the crowd toward her. … *Tetric?…* Her mentor was nearly seven feet tall. How could he be lost from view?

She wrapped her mind within itself and focused on the table. Nice table. Wood. Worn. It had nicks on it. Hopefully from ale steins and not knives. A presence drew close, nearer than the rest of the tavern patrons. She peered up without lifting her head.

The sailor's tawny eyes were framed in his face by a close-cropped dark beard and mustache. A linen shirt wrapped arms of corded muscle knotted hard by working boat rigging. That shirt was open to nearly his waist, revealing a muscled chest bronzed by the southern sun. Tucked in the belt around that waist was a dagger, long, handsomely crafted, and definitely dangerous-looking. Just like its owner, come to think of it.

Mirana swallowed. She was used to curious glances because of her exotic silver eyes, but stares based on physical attraction were new. Why was he even eyeing her in the first place? The Aspects Above gave her far more powers than curves.

Her heart pounded in her chest. She searched the room again for Tetric as her hand slowly drifted under the table to one of her long knives.

When the sailor reached her table, he took the pipe from his mouth and regarded it for a moment. He then slipped the pipe into his belt next to the handsome, dangerous dagger. "You are looking for a boat or looking for work." His voice was surprisingly pleasant, an easy baritone accented with the sultry cadence of the province. But his words were not a question. She tensed.

"Well, sir, that is—"

"People in Qadar ply only two trades." He put his leg up on the chair next to her and leaned on it, cutting off her only escape route. Under the table, she gripped the knife's hilt. He raised two fingers. "Sailing a ship," he dropped one finger, "and other pursuits equally physical. In which trade are you?" He took a long sip of ale from his mug as his eyes moved from her face to her breasts. Which were thoroughly unremarkable. Her lack of a figure didn't seem to deter his gaze, however.

Her heart thudded against her ribs. She peered around the man, scanning the tavern with eyes and Aspects to find her *patrua*. Well, was she a Trine or was she a Trine? "I am not from Qadar, so I have different choices of occupations. I am Lord Garis's *scholaira*. I am accompanying him on official business." She placed a hand on her thigh, conveniently—and obviously— close to the hilt of a long knife.

"May I help you?" The tall Trine appeared on her left, seemingly out of nowhere, with two mugs in one hand.

The sailor jumped. His mustached smile fell as he made a deep bow. "Lord Trine Garis. I-I am surprised to see such a noble man in such humble surroundings."

Tetric set down the mugs and pushed one toward Mirana. "Bartus?" The man nodded. Her *patrua* smiled and grasped the sailor's forearm in greeting. "Bartus Alhambre. When I last saw you, you were hardly older than Mirana here."

Bartus straightened, and any lascivious thoughts he had promptly disappeared. "Ah. So, the silver-eyed jewel has a name. Mirana. She is with you?"

She grinned and took a sip from her mug. She expected ale but found it was some sort of fruit juice. She frowned. She could have used something a lot stronger.

"Come. Sit." Tetric offered the sailor the remaining empty chair at their table.

"What brings you to Qadar? Not the Ken'nar, I hope."

"We seek passage to Nuralima. Is your father's vessel available?"

Bartus hesitated. She sensed uneasiness from the sailor. "My father sleeps with the Aspects Above. When he lost his eyesight, he could not sail. The Aspects Above calling him home was a blessing."

The Trine nodded. "A pilot without his eyes is not a pilot. I am sorry for your loss."

The handsome sailor hurried on. "Now, this trip to Rün-Taran. Is it just you, or does the jewel go, too?"

Tetric looked down his aquiline nose at her and smiled. Well, not quite a smile, but an expression more encouraging than his usual flat line. "*Ai.* Her, too."

The sailor bowed his head toward her. "I have not carried such fair nor such brave cargo in quite some time. It will be my pleasure, Lady *Scholaira.*"

Apology accepted. "*Gratas*, captain, but we also have horses." She ignored the Trine's questioning expression.

"Horses, eh?" Bartus smoothed his mustache with his fingers. "Well, that does cost a little more, of course. I have to make room in the hold, I have to dump ballast, I have to—"

"I'm sure you will do it *a Gratas* as a gesture of goodwill to the Aspected who serve you." Tetric's amulet winked in the candlelight.

Wait. He wouldn't. Have the man ferry them for free? This was way beyond the bounds of a tithe.

The Tash-Hamari man blinked, his smile now gone. "Surely you don't mean that, *Ëi cara.* I have wages, supplies."

The Trine raised an eyebrow. "Were you or were you not taking a shipment of produce to Nuralima tomorrow?"

"How did you—? Ah, well, *ai.*" Bartus now toyed with his own mug. "Produce? My customer and I hadn't agreed yet on shipping terms. We might not sail for days."

The conversation paused momentarily while a serving girl placed a board of flatbread and cheese on the table. After she left, Tetric rejoined, "Then why did your first mate say you were sailing at dawn to stay ahead of a storm in the south?"

"Tarq. I will gut him like a carp," Bartus growled, then cleared his throat. "You'll have to forgive my first mate. Tarq occasionally forgets to tell me when he closes on a contract. Especially one of my own." He sighed as his shoulders slumped in resignation. "*Ai*, of course, I am pleased to offer you and the jewel the hospitality of my ship in gratitude for all the Fal'kin do for Kinderra."

Mirana took a piece of bread. She had accused her mentor of being a thief, a dictator, and now, an extortionist. If Bartus was already going to their destination, it made perfect sense that they tag along for the ride. Still, they and the horses would eat and drink from their stores during the trip. Shouldn't they pay Bartus at least something? She considered the bread in her hand. Tetric could do as he pleased, but she would do something for the crew, perhaps some service with her Aspects.

A chill slithered down her spine. Her gaze shot around the tavern, but no threat appeared. Tetric seemed unconcerned. She swallowed down bread that didn't want to move. Vague nudges from the Seeing Aspect were always the worst because there was no information, no images attached to them, just a sense of diffuse wariness.

"*Gratas Oë*." Tetric extended his hand again.

The sailor took it and laughed. "Would that the Trine thanked me with coins instead of words, but alas, a Fal'kin's heart is known only to the Aspects Above. We leave at first light, though. I do not intend to donate the tide to charity as well."

The Trine nodded. "We will be there."

*   *   *

Mirana awoke before dawn. Sweat covered her body. Her shoulders and abdomen ached. Ashtar dipped his great head and nuzzled her. She rubbed his velvet nose. They had spent the night in the stables. Many of the ships were in port because of a storm off to the south, so there were no rooms available.

"What have you seen?" Tetric stood over her as she rubbed her eyes. He had kept watch over the horses and their packs while she attempted to sleep.

She climbed to her feet and brushed the straw from her clothes. "It was a dream."

"Enough of this. Tell me what you saw."

"I didn't see anything. It was just a nightmare. I'll saddle the horses." She stretched her neck and worked out the soreness between her shoulder blades.

He caught her arm. "You will tell me. Now."

She sighed. He was only trying to help. And if anyone needed help, it was her. "It's a nightmare. *Ai*, happens every night, but that's what nightmares are, I guess." She gave a weak laugh, one the Trine did not return. "I fight a swordsman. A Ken'nar, I think."

His obsidian eyes widened. "You what?"

"A Ken'nar. He bests me."

He released her with a gentle squeeze, but his face was set like flint. "What did he look like?" He swallowed.

She picked up Ashtar's saddle. "I never see his face."

"Mirana, after all this time, do you still not trust me? You must tell me the rest of this."

"I do trust you." She just didn't trust herself. Or rather she was relearning how to do that. She bent her head away from his gaze, studying the scars on her palm as she rubbed them. "I don't remember the rest. You should have awakened me sooner. We don't want to miss the tide."

… If you are to face a Ken'nar, I need to know about it … All of it … He threw his saddle on his horse. The animal snorted and took a step sideways from the sudden weight. The Trine grabbed the stallion's reins and dragged the animal out.

She had barely opened her eyes and already she had let him down. She frowned. It was going to be a long day. "Come on, Ashtar."

They met Bartus by his vessel. Despite the shabby appearance of the dock, to say nothing of the crew, the ship looked good and sturdy, for which she was ridiculously relieved.

The bow of the longboat curled upward, ending in a leopard's head, the standard of Tash-Hamar. The wooden spans of its hull bore only minor scrapes to mar them. Two large triangular sails, each painted with a sunburst, swelled from their masts, already pregnant with the wind. A third, rolled tightly, hung from near the bow.

"Ah, the jewel," Bartus said effusively and helped her off her horse. Whatever his desire at the tavern regarding her, she now sensed only a desire to be amicable. No doubt her being the Trine's *scholaira* had something to do with that.

The captain greeted her *patrua* and called for two of his crewmen to take the horses below decks. The stallion went willingly but Ashtar balked.

"Ashtar, what's the matter with you?" She ran over to her mount and took back the reins. "You would never believe he's a trained warhorse, would you? Come on now, you big brute." She tried to pull him, but he would not budge.

"Your horse. He's afraid of the water, eh? Maybe he can't swim?" Bartus reached for the reins to help her.

She stroked the big chestnut's neck, trying to soothe him. "I've never seen him like this before." When Ashtar would not move, she covered his head with her travel cloak and led him onboard. Moments later, Bartus shouted orders to his men, and the boat eased away from the harbor.

The rising sun lent its warmth to the sultry air. Small downy puffs of clouds floated in a morning sky washed in pink and gold. The reflection of the pastel hue painted the sea a dusty rose. The vista stretched to the horizons, leaving Qadar behind her to slowly shrink in the distance. Maybe land wasn't the only thing she was leaving behind. Maybe it was time to leave other things as well. Truly.

"You've never seen the blue water, eh, my jewel?" The captain tightened a rigging line near her.

"No." She leaned over the gunwales and watched the ship slice through the waves.

He looked up at the sky. "Blood at dawn, weather's Ken'nar-spawn. The other ships reported angry seas to the south. Summer storms can be treacherous."

"But we're sailing east, aren't we?"

"*Ai*, for now. We'll tack south before the Mother River Anarath empties into the Mer-Lima near Parsalon. We have to stay in deep water because the entire coastline of the Taran peninsula reads like a grynwen's jaws." He turned to yell at his mate. "Tarq, let's use the wind while we can, eh?"

A sword split the air. It landed, ringing, in the gunwale next to her. She whirled in shock.

Tetric stood in front of her, his long sword leveled at her chest. "You said a swordsman bests you in your nightmare. We are going to change that."

She stared at him, wide-eyed. "You-You could have killed me."

"Indeed. Take it." He gestured to the embedded blade with his chin.

Bartus shouted a warning. "Where did you get my sword?" The Trine said nothing. "Just be careful with that. It cost me more than a Fal'kin's amulet."

She worked the blade out of the wood. "Don't worry," she shouted over her shoulder. "I'll be careful."

"If my crew, or worse, my boat gets damaged, we'll see if you swim any better than your horse, eh?"

She laughed and waved. Something sharp poked her chest.

"You are dead." Tetric was not laughing. "When an enemy has a sword leveled at you, never look away. You may watch his eyes, his face, his arm, and not his weapon, but never look away from him. Never. Look. Away."

Mirana frowned. "I wasn't ready yet." She forced the tip of his blade down with hers.

"You must always be ready." He stood back from her and straightened. All near seven feet of him. She swallowed. "Let us begin."

CHAPTER 18

"Great Prime, they named him, Halen the White. To him, they gave their swords, their allegiance, and their lives. And thus, he was able to turn back the onslaught of his brother, the dread Lord Hafen."

—The Book of Kinderra

Tetric slid his long sword into the scabbard at his waist. "Pain is merely a warning. Once felt, it no longer serves a purpose."

Easy for him to say.

Mirana winced as she wiped off the blood leaking from her nose and split lip with the back of a shaking hand. She had no idea taking a sword hilt to the face could hurt so much.

"You did as well as can be expected." Which wasn't "well" at all.

She clenched her teeth, irritated, and winced again. That hurt, too. "I was training as a battle seer."

He folded his long arms, arms that had half again her reach. "For how long?"

"About six months."

"And how long ago was that?"

She frowned. "You've made your point."

"Precisely. Which means you haven't been trained at all." He ladled a mouthful of water from a barrel.

"I was good, though." She sighed. "Back then."

He held the ladle out to her. "You showed some promise today."

She slid her sword into its sheath and took a sip of water, hissing at the sting it made on her split lip. "Sometimes I ended in a draw with Defender Second Corran and Defender Commander Koehl before my parents put a stop to my training."

"I am not Dav Koehl or Niall Corran, and you are not a battle seer. I am training you as a Trine. Rest now. We will begin again tomorrow." He left and went down into the hold.

She shook her head slowly and stumbled over to the ship's gunwales, gripping the rail in exhaustion and pain and shame.

The sun cast the clouds in a deep orange as it dipped below the horizon. Its reflection quaked on the waves, a false impression of itself. She was some false impression of Tetric Garis. How would she ever learn to rise above her failures when she could barely keep her sword upright?

Exhausted, she sank in a heap onto a coil of thick rope. It was cozy, like a nest. After sparring with the Trine all day, she could have stretched out on the barnacle-encrusted ship hull and found it comfortable. She sucked at a blade nick on her knuckle.

The pale moon and stars made a brief appearance only to be blotted out, one by one, behind thickening clouds. The blue ocean turned to ink and the sky faded to the color of hearth ash. Far to the south, heat lightning flashed.

Bartus lit a mast lamp near her. "His sword is as long as you are tall, eh?" He stuck the mouthpiece of his pipe in the corner of his mouth.

"I think it's longer." She tried not to sense his emotions. After all, he was an Unaspected and could not block his thoughts, but she couldn't help herself. They were loud and strong. He was concerned, even wary, maybe frightened. Surely not of her? Of Tetric, then?

"Here. Eat." He reached into the pocket of his baggy trousers and tossed her a piece of dried fruit.

She nodded her thanks and bit into it. It was sour but pleasant. She hissed again as the tangy fruit stung her lip.

"You got better by the end of the day. Much better, actually."

"I started to remember a few things." Not that it made much difference.

He clicked his tongue. "The jewel has lost her sparkle, eh?" She did not answer. "Our Lord Trine was not easy on you."

"What do you mean?"

"I would not call what he is doing 'training.' He is beating you."

Mirana tried to laugh but grimaced in pain and grabbed at her ribs. The flat of her mentor's blade hurt as much as the point. "*Ai*, he is beating me. I think that is more than apparent. I didn't win a single round."

"I do not mean in terms of winning or losing." He grew serious as his voice dropped low. "I mean he is beating you like a stray dog in the street."

She looked up at the sailor, taken aback. "Don't be silly. I'll admit, I hadn't expected our Trine's teaching methods to be so, well, physical, either." She looked back out over the water. "I am learning, though."

"Tetric Garis. He can be—" The sailor did not finish. His unease leaked out from his mind once more. He was as worried for her as he was for his crew. He cast a glance toward the hold where the Trine had gone.

"He can be what?" she pressed.

He pointed to her chest with the pipe. "How come you don't wear one of those?"

"I haven't chosen yet. What is it about Tetric?" She asked again, foiling his attempt to change the subject.

Bartus chewed on the end of his pipe for a moment before answering. He looked one more time toward the hold. "He can be a hard man."

"*Ai.* But I've seen another side of him. One he does not often show."

He raised an eyebrow. "He has another side?"

She smiled at his comment. "He saved my life. I owe him so much."

He patted her knee. "You train hard, and you choose yourself a jewel as beautiful as you, eh?" He pointed to her chest where an amulet would lie. When she looked down, he tapped the tip of her nose with his finger. They both laughed now. He walked off to take the ship's wheel from his mate, Tarq.

Mirana curled up in the nest of rope. Far off to the south, heat lightning pulsed in white flashes. She did not care if her vision of the keep would come again tonight. She now held a real sword. She would be ready for the Ken'nar. Someday.

CHAPTER 19

"Genten u'vide vide mor tha genten u'comprende."
("A blind man sees more than an ignorant man.")
—Ora Fal'kinnen 142:12

Heat. Heat. Heat.

The Ain Magne meditated, allowing the Seeing Aspect to fill him, impervious to the heavy night air that surrounded him. The men with whom he traveled kept their distance, giving him the solitude he needed. Spring in Kinderra had taken her own time in coming, and she hadn't stayed long. The summer season now held sway.

His journey had taken him farther south than he had been in a long time. Setting the stage for his final act of bringing the Fal'kin into submission demanded he travel the breadth of Kinderra. The moment for playing the last gambit was still months hence, however, it was coming ever closer nonetheless. He hoped and prayed he would secure an alliance with the Fal'kin at last. He dreaded, however, that it would be a bloody, forced surrender. Either way, Kinderra would finally be at peace under him. Whether the Fal'kin wanted to be a part of that peace or to be wiped off the face of the continent was their choice, not his.

He cupped his amulet in his hands and reached for the Seeing Aspect. It was that gift from the Aspects Above he cherished the most. While the Defending and even the Healing Aspect gave him strength, the Seeing Aspect gave him knowledge. Knowledge was where true power was found.

Edara would be an easy mark after so many of its provincial defenders had been lost at Two Rivers Ford. He now sought a future skein of Deren. Detailed prescience, however, eluded him. Sight merely whispered to him a notion of caution, a warning. Was it for his enemies or him?

The sense that something worked just outside of his reach frustrated him. Exceedingly. Perhaps the skeins of time were so unsettled, no more could be revealed. A threat could exist, both inconsequential and dangerous, until time wove itself more tightly. The Ain Magne stiffened.

The Unaspected. Inconsequential yet dangerous. They were powerless, however, they did have numbers. Millions of them. The Unaspected had always lurked as a danger to his plans. He felt the dark thrill of wariness course through him. Those without the powers of the Aspects outnumbered his armies by a thousand to one. Kin-Deren province's Unaspected alone numbered in the millions.

Certainly, the Unaspected tried to fend off his Ken'nar from their farms and pastures as his warriors took what they needed. Even his army needed to eat, and his warriors did not have the largesse of a tithe to feed themselves like the Fal'kin. Farmers and homesteaders were no match for the might of his Ken'nar. Banding together, however, their numbers would be overwhelming. To fight against him as an army, however—to fight at all—was anathema. If they did, the bedrock of Kinderran society would be fractured.

As he traversed the breadth of Kinderra, cementing the more delicate facets of his plans for the continent, joining up with travel companions was sometimes unavoidable, however unfortunate. The men that surrounded him now were afraid of him, preferring to take their evening's rest elsewhere. They did not know him, though they would, at a time of his choosing. All of Kinderra's people—her Aspected and her Unaspected— must show him fealty if the war were to truly end. Only then could he usher in the lasting age of peace and enlightenment the Aspects Above meant for Kinderra to have.

… *Hearken unto me, my servant* … the Ain Magne called.

… *Ëo hac*… his seer second returned.

… *Beware of the Unaspected, my second* …

… *We are too late* … *The bitch in Deren seeks the Unaspected to fight for her*…

His servant's words left him cold. Dark dread and even darker fury called to his Defending Aspect. The heat from his amulet burned his chest. … *And just when were you going to inform me of this?* …

… *Your mind has been hidden, my lord* … *I have only just seen this myself* … *If she succeeds, we will be hard-pressed to turn them back* …

He grabbed his amulet, allowing its connection to calm him. … *How many have answered her summons?*…

… *Past skeins of time show a few hundred, but my Sight has shown me more will come* … *Much more* …

… *Is Edara following that course of action as well?* …

… No … Activity outside of Edara has been all but nonexistent … Given what is happening in Deren, however, we cannot wait any longer … We must attack Edara now …

The Ain Magne considered his second's sense of urgency. They had lost thousands at Two Rivers Ford. The harvested healer that had once been Prime Belessa Tir needed time to rebuild their numbers in Kana-Akün.

Heat. Heat. Heat.

Heat not from his amulet but of a different kind. A drought had begun to parch northern Kinderra. The waving prairie grasses of Varn-Erdal would be reduced to so much broom straw. His second scoffed at the use of the Aspects for an action so banal as forecasting weather. But seeing the weather was important in planning any attack. Using the weather in an attack was paramount.

Heat. Heat. Heat.

The Ain Magne smiled.

… We cannot yet … We have yet to replenish the numbers we lost at the ford with harvested fighters … I told you, time will work for us … Especially when the rain refuses to come … Our conquest of Edara will be slower but certain … In the meantime, continue to search for the horses …

It was a moment before his second's mind returned to him. *… There is danger in your plan, my lord … It will be successful if that future skein and only that future skein proves to be the actual course of events …*

His second was correct, however, there were always risks in war. *… With my plan, we will gain not only Edara but Deren as well … in one battle …*

… Great One, please consider other time skeins … We must strike before Desde Pinal can give aid … Edara lies weakened now, nearly crippled beyond hope … Ai, we, too, have been weakened, but the horse

whore will not be expecting us to attack so soon … There is nothing Kin-Deren can do to help … Let me strike now …

The Ain Magne sent a searing reprimand into his seer second's mind. … *You will obey my orders or I will find another who will …*

… *Why do you punish me? … Did you not train me to give you counsel? … I am telling you, your plan of attack is wrong … Time will not do the work of our amulets … It will only bring us closer to defeat …*

Rage swelled within the Ain Magne. His second had grown bold in his absence. The young seer tasted too much of his own power, guiding the Ken'nar armies outside of his presence. It was time for a lesson—the more painful, the quicker it was learned.

He seized the Aspects with the Power from Without and struck his second's mind, using his servant's life force to feed his torture. He sensed the young man's agonized scream.

… *Please, Lord, stop … I beg of you … I am only telling you the truth …*

… *There is no truth but my truth!* … The Ain Magne stormed through the young seer's mind and crushed his will. Mute with pain and terror, his servant could only send a feeble notion of comprehending obedience.

He released the seer and allowed the young man's presence to fade into the miasma of minds in Kinderra.

Perhaps Desde Pinal's use of the Unaspected was an unexpected boon. Once these peasants experienced firsthand the destruction at the amulets of his Ken'nar, they would never support the Fal'kin again. The slaughter he envisioned on what troops she did manage to bring would leave even less to defend the citadel later.

He gritted his teeth. Why? Why did everyone test him so? Did they not understand he was trying to *stop* pain and suffering, not inflict it? If anything drove him close to weeping, it was lessons such as these. He could afford to wait before he struck Edara, but first, he must endure the painful lessons the Aspect Above had ordained for him.

"Forgive me, my lord."

He turned his attention from the Aspects to the man, one of his traveling companions. He stood back, perhaps in respect. The Ain Magne sighed. No, the man was frightened.

"I did not wish to disturb you, but we are concerned. About the weather," the man said, his words coming slow. He knew he made an overly simplistic request of a Trine. The Ain Magne hated that people feared him so; he would much prefer respect. What he wanted more than anything was their understanding.

"I am concerned about the weather as well but have no fear. All will be well," he replied.

"*Gratas Oë.* I will tell the men." The man dipped his head in a bow and left, trying but failing to keep his stride measured.

The Ain Magne settled back into a light meditation, letting the Aspects wash through him.

Heat. Heat. Heat.

Ai, he would wait for Edara to fall on its own.

CHAPTER 20

"Kin a Vide, Kin a Defende, Kin a Sanare."
("The Light to See, the Light to Defend, the Light to Heal.")
—*The Exultantae*, Ora Fal'kinnen 12:2

A blistering series of moves put Mirana's sword underneath Tetric's as he forced her blade down with his own. He did not let up and her wrists bent painfully.

"You must reach out with both Sight and Defense," he ordered. "Even without an amulet, you will still have some measure of control."

She grimaced, fighting to keep her sword up. Time for a different tactic. She called to her Healing Aspect.

Tendons pull. Muscles flex. Nerves suddenly quiet.

The Trine hissed and dropped his long sword, shaking tingling, limp fingers.

"Hah!" She held the point of her blade at his chest and smiled victoriously. "You are always telling me to think. I'm thinking I have you."

Any trace of his expression, however, disappeared, as did his presence. "This will end in a draw."

"A draw?" she laughed. "I don't think so. You're already down—"

A sudden pull within made her lose her breath. He loosed a thin tendril of fire from his amulet to lash at her shoulder. She cried out in pain and astonishment. He called the long sword back to his hand and swiped at her, leaving a deep cut on her leg above the knee. She staggered back, never having a chance to block him. With a wide sweep of his hand, he tore the weapon from her and sent it spinning across the deck. His blade was now leveled at her throat.

"That was a clever move, I'll give you that, but just because your opponent does not hold a weapon does not mean he is unarmed. Especially one who is Aspected." He stepped back. "We will try again tomorrow when you can keep your overconfidence in check." His midnight-black gaze bored into her, and he slid the long sword into its scabbard with a decisive snap. He glared at the vessel crew as he went down into the hold.

The sailors had stopped talking. She turned around. They stared at her. "Well, I thought it was a clever move," she muttered.

"Back to work, boys," Bartus said. "Mustaf, you have the wheel." He walked over to a storage locker and rummaged through it.

She held her burned shoulder and limped over to her rope pile. She tried to sit down but her leg gave out and she collapsed.

The Tash-Hamari captain came over with some strips of cloth and a jar of ointment. "Let me see your leg."

"It was a stupid mistake, one I'll never make again. But dammit all, he didn't have to go this far. I'm fine. It's not deep."

He kneeled in front of her. "It is deep, and you made no mistake. You had him, and you made him angry."

She smiled at his efforts to soothe her pride. "I suppose I did cheat by using my Healing Aspect." She gasped and bit her lip.

He scowled. "He is teaching a healer to fight?" He sat back on his heels. "He said to use both Sight and Defense. Together. You are—" He swallowed. "You are like him?"

She rubbed at her blistered shoulder. "Bartus, please, it's not—"

"The Fal'kin speak of a prophecy—"

"Tetric is the Light Trine. The one leading the Ken'nar is the Dark Trine."

"Then what are you?"

A failure? A protector? A curse? A hope? She did not know. Her shoulders sagged. An unanswerable riddle. The time for secrets was long over, that she knew for certain. "Honestly, I don't know. I just want to help Tetric save Kinderra. That's all." That was everything.

A flash of lightning flickered far off on the horizon but brought no thunder. The storm was still a long way off.

The sailor fidgeted with the bandage. "Should I, ah, still tend to your leg?"

She nodded, anything to move past the conversation. The gash reverberated its painful song through the Healing Aspect. She didn't think the mica in her little peda blossom pendant would be strong enough to heal the wound. She'd just have to settle for letting the laceration heal according to nature's way. Along with all the other gashes, scrapes, contusions, and cracked bones.

She took the jar of ointment from him and gagged at the odor. "Are you sure that's still good, whatever it is?"

"Not exactly rose water, eh? It's made from a rare seaweed that grows only in Qadar near the bottom of the ocean."

She raised a doubtful eyebrow.

"Or at least the bottom of the ocean that is reachable by wading offshore a few steps."

She smiled.

"The seaweed will cut the pain and help draw out any infection."

Mirana daubed some on the cut and hissed at the ointment's stinging cold. Immediately, the pain dulled to a manageable throb as the cool sensation surrounded her thigh. "It works better than numbweed."

Bartus tied a strip of cloth around her leg. "There. Good as new."

"It already feels a little better. *Gratas Oë*." Another flash of light illuminated the clouds to the south. A second and a third flash arched across backlit clouds. "The rain will reach us tomorrow."

He studied the sky. "If that is the storm the other ships warned of, it will do more than rain." He drew a pipe from his pocket and packed the bowl with tobacco. He clenched the tip in his teeth, his eyes on the darkening horizon.

She sat back in the rope nest and studied the Tash-Hamari a moment. "You don't really smoke it, do you?"

He shrugged. "Smoking makes me cough. I like the smell of tobacco. It reminds me of my father."

She rubbed absently at a bruise on the meat of her bicep. "Did your father ever lie to you?"

"Of course." He laughed. "What father doesn't lie to his child? Until I was your age, it was the only way he could get me to do any work."

"I supposed it matters more why a parent lies." She clenched her jaw. "Regardless, it still hurts."

The pitching and rolling of the ship comforted her, like being rocked by her mother. She ground her teeth together. Much of her anger focused on her father, but hadn't her father and mother *both* betrayed her? Had her mother known she was a Trine when Mirana was an infant? When she was in her womb? Had her mother known all that time and still never said anything? All the nights spent in terror, held by a vision that refused to release her. Had her mother even known then, hearing that terror as it tore through her mind, and said nothing? *Nothing*?

Bartus was quiet for a long time. "How long have you known the Trine?"

"I have traveled with him for many sevendays. I wasn't born to him, but," she watched the distant lightning, "I love him more than the man to whom I was."

"Maybe I should have asked how well you know him."

It was an interesting question. In truth, she knew very little about the Lord Trine Tetric Garis. She had no idea where he grew up, where and how he had trained, even what his learning hall in Dar-Azûl was like. Her parents had said he had left Fal'kin society for a long time, and it took the horrors of the Battle of the Vale i'Dúadar to bring him back. He alluded to the fact his youth was difficult as there was no one to show him how to understand all three of his Aspects together.

Regardless of the length of time she had been with him, her devotion and gratitude were as deep as if she had known him her entire life. It didn't matter that she had yet to agree with some of his beliefs. He'd saved her life. He believed in her. He gave her hope where she had none to give herself. That made Tetric Garis the most important person in her life.

"I suppose I know him as well as he is willing to let anyone. Why?"

The sailor glanced over his shoulder toward the steps that led down into the hold. "Summers ago, when my father was captain of this boat, Lord Garis and a few of his men sought passage, only north, up into the cold waters of the Mer-Fad. My father refused. We carry cargo, fish, not people—well, maybe the occasional jewel, eh?" They both smiled. "We don't sail those waters. The Trine offered my father some money, but my father still refused. Then, quite suddenly, my father changed his mind. He took Lord Garis, his men, and their horses up the Sün-Kasalan coast past the Dar-Anars. It wasn't long after that my father began to lose his eyesight."

She leaned back from him, shocked and angry by turns. "You're not accusing Tetric of taking your father's eyesight because he refused him passage, are you?"

He chewed on his pipe for a moment. "Mirana, I have sailed to every port from Sündalan to Kanalar. I have come across many dangerous men." His voice was low, barely above a whisper. "That look in the Trine's eyes. When you made him drop his sword. I have seen that look before. In men who kill. You be careful, eh?"

"How dare you?" She struggled to her feet. "Tetric Garis, *Trine* Tetric Garis has laid down his life for everyone in Kinderra. Including Unaspected like you. Of course, he is a dangerous man. Dangerous to those who would prefer the war last another three thousand summers. He is the only one capable of bringing peace to our land. We all owe him a debt."

"*Ai*, of course, of course. I meant no disrespect, Lady Trine." He made a curt bow and left her for the ship's wheel.

She sank back down into the pile of rope. How could anyone blessed with the Healing Aspect use it to take away a man's eyesight? But had she not caused Tetric's hand to go numb? That was no lifesaving act.

The Soul Harvest. That erasure of self-preservation and free will could only be done by one with the Healing Aspect. How in the name of all Creation could the Ken'nar Trine perpetrate such evil? How could Tetric even agree with a shred of logic in it?

Would the beautiful and deadly white light of Jasal's Keep also require the Healing Aspect? Hers?

Mirana gave a soft cry and hid her face in her hands.

CHAPTER 21

"Through the healer, the cure of Kinderra was wrought."
—The Book of Kinderra

"The interesting thing about maggots is they only eat dead flesh." Teague Beltran picked out a wriggling worm from Hamriah's wound with a set of tiny forceps. "This looks much better compared to a sevenday ago."

"I thought this is what you wanted my molasses for?" The horsemaster, Eran Talz, leaned against the paddock wall and stood with his arms folded while his daughter Illenne knelt next to Teague. She held a cup into which he put the maggots.

He nodded. "I did. The maggots eat the dead tissue. The molasses treats the infection."

"It didn't matter that my molasses went bad?" Eran frowned. "I haven't had much time for brewing. Damned Ken'nar."

He sat back for a moment. "No. That's why I wanted it. It was a theory my parents were working on. When certain foods go bad—oranges, cheese, sugarcane, even bread—they noticed the rot staves off some illnesses. People who ate a bit of blight sometimes didn't catch fevers."

The horsemaster ran thick fingers through his beard. "How the hell did they figure that out?"

Teague didn't answer right away. He spread some of the fermented molasses on a fresh poultice. "They were Fal'kin, sir."

"And I breed horses. That doesn't mean I know everything about the oats they eat."

He concentrated on picking out the last of the maggots. "With their Healer's Sight, they saw or sensed tiny creatures, for lack of a better word. Tinier than anything that could ever be seen with mortal eyes. When these creatures mixed with the mold extracts, they died, and the infection stopped spreading. My parents are—" He took a breath. "My father and mother were still trying to understand all of that before they died. I'm hoping they were right."

The horsemaster grunted an acknowledgment.

Illenne, however, beamed a smile. "I don't care if you said grynwen spit would work, as long as it does."

Her hair was lighter than he remembered from his first impression, streaked with gold from the sun. Her smile was warmer than the sun.

"There's some truth to that, too. Did you ever wonder why a dog licks its wounds?" He gently laid a fresh poultice on the horse's wound and secured it with a bandage. "Do you want to try getting her up?"

She jumped to her feet and clicked her tongue. Hamriah struggled for a moment to get her legs under her, then she pushed her way to a stand.

Illenne cried out and threw her arms around the mare's neck. Teague smiled at the girl's joy, his heart turning somersaults in his chest.

Eran opened the paddock door and walked down the row several feet. "Let's see how well she walks." He whistled. The horse perked up her ears and walked over to the horsemaster. She favored her left hind foot a bit, but her steps were true. He made a low, soothing vocalization and stroked the mare's nose.

"Ille, why don't you get up on her?" Eran waved his daughter over. "See how she does with some weight."

She nodded and swung effortlessly onto the mare's bare back.

Teague laughed. "No stirrups, no bridle. What, were you born on a horse?"

She returned his laughter with her own. "*Ai.* Nearly." She gently tapped Hamriah's sides with her heels and walked the horse down the row of paddocks.

Eran stood close to him. "You did a good thing, lad."

He shrugged. "I think we had luck on our side."

"That's not what I mean. I haven't seen Ille smile in more than a summer. Not since Drei died."

He scowled. "Drei?"

"Drei Carada. He was one of our youngest and most promising defenders. They were young, too young. But even an old mule like me knows love when he sees it. Drei's group rode out on patrol spring before last and never came back. We found his sword, signs of a fight, ash. The Ken'nar bastards didn't even leave us their amulets. When Ille packed up the things from his room, she found the gold union bracelet he was going to give her. She buried it. Along with her heart."

Teague sought furiously for some poignant or at least comforting words to say but none came. "I'm sorry," he mumbled.

Eran turned to watch Illenne ride slowly through the stable. "Her mother died bringing her to me eighteen summers ago. I love that girl more than all the horses in Kinderra. I will not have her heart broken again. *Oë comprende?*"

His mouth fell open in shock. He wasn't sure what he felt for Illenne—there was little left of his own heart to feel anything—however, he was certain he would never willingly inflict that kind of pain on anyone. "*Ëo comprende.*"

Illenne brought the mare to an easy trot then pulled her to a stop with a gentle tug on her mane. "Well, *Paithe?*"

The horsemaster nodded and clapped Teague on the back with roughly the same amount of force as a battering ram, either a companionable gesture or a show of the considerable strength he would face if he stepped out of line with the man's daughter. Probably both. "If you don't run her like the wind, *ai*, she'll make the ride."

Again, the girl shouted in triumph. She leaped off her horse and embraced Teague, kissing him on the cheek. "You said you couldn't work miracles. This is a miracle. To me."

He was too stunned to refute her compliment.

"I'm going to take her to the near pastures for some fresh grass. Would you like to come with me?" She smiled.

He looked from Illenne to her father and back to the girl. "I, um, I suppose I need to watch her for any signs of a secondary infection. *Ai*, I will come."

Her smile grew. And so did his.

CHAPTER 22

"Love made us brothers. The Aspects will make us enemies."
—The Codex of Jasal the Great

Mirana's eyes burned from lack of sleep as she stumbled up out of the hold. She rubbed her face. Her head ached as the afterimage of the keep's white light lingered behind her eyelids.

Bartus Alhambre tightened rigging lines with quick, sharp tugs, and did not speak with his men. Some of the crew cast furtive glances at the sky, their movements likewise hurried. Why were they nervous? She swallowed against the anxiety wriggling through her belly.

The captain had changed the ship's heading to a more southerly direction. Thick clouds blanketed the sky, and a hot, humid wind sighed against the sails. The very air seemed too heavy to allow the sea to rise beyond the barest of swells.

She glanced again at the Tash-Hamari pilot. The coming storm had replaced his casual confidence with concentration.

Before she finished swallowing a quick breakfast, Tetric emerged from the hold, sword in hand. "Come."

Knowing him, he'd be aware of the exact moment the squall would hit them and would render her suggestion pointless. The last bite of food only riled the nerve serpents in her stomach.

She did not move from her rope nest. "I thought we could take the day off. That storm's going to move in. We should probably help them. It's the least we can do since we're not paying them."

His mouth flattened. "Are you tired?"

Oh, he had no idea! Then again, he had the Healing Aspect. He just might have an idea. "That's not the point."

"*Ai*, it is. You didn't sleep again. I've watched over you all these months. Your vision. It's growing stronger. Why don't you want to tell me what it is that you've been seeing?"

Mirana clawed some of the straw from the hold from her hair. "You...you're not in it." She bit her lip and winced as she reopened a cut. "And I don't know why."

He crouched in front of her. "You think I'm dead?"

She turned away, fighting back tears, and didn't answer.

He gently guided her chin to face him. "Maybe I'm fighting elsewhere. Did you think of that? Or maybe I decided to help that poor pleasure woman in Qadar find something better to do with her life?"

She laughed, swallowing back the tears. "I understand the Seeing Aspect well enough to know the simplest explanation is often the correct one."

"*Ai.*" He smiled and stood. "Now, come." He helped her up. "Do not think, however, I'll be easy on you because you didn't sleep well."

*   *   *

He wasn't kidding.

The Trine's sword came at her much faster now. He turned his blade in a complicated series of maneuvers pushing her to make increasingly defensive moves. Twice during their practice, his sword cut her, once on the forearm and again on her side.

He stepped back and pointed at her hand pressed against the cut on her ribs. "Pain is merely a warning. Once felt, it no longer serves a purpose. Ignore it."

"So you keep telling me."

"Then learn it."

Tetric wove his sword in a blistering series of moves. Mirana blocked them, blow for blow, but he pressed her back. She tripped over some rope, falling as she beat back his lunge. Her mentor drew back his arm, ready to strike. She kicked, catching him in the knee, and sprang to her feet. He collapsed, his sword tumbling from his hand. She gripped her blade with both hands for a final blow. Tetric made a noise deep in his throat, more a snarl than a cry of pain. Mirana hesitated.

He was unarmed. Should she strike an unarmed man?

He flung out his hand as his amulet flashed and shot to his feet. She flew back into the mainmast and cracked her head on the spar. Mirana fell sprawling to the deck.

Tetric stood over her. "Get up."

Her eyes would not focus. She tried to push herself up, but her arms and legs refused to coordinate themselves because her head was about to explode. She groaned in pain and collapsed back to the deck.

The Trine sheathed his sword with a snap and hauled her up under an arm. He shoved her down on her pile of rope. "Why didn't you strike at me?"

The pounding concussion made her see two Tetrics. She wasn't sure which one to answer. The boat spun, and her stomach clenched. So much for breakfast.

Both Tetrics frowned. "Hold still."

He covered her forehead with his large hand and gripped her temples. Blinding pain flared in her head. She cried out and grabbed his wrist, only to have the pain dissipate a moment later. She blinked and took a cleansing breath.

"Why didn't you strike? You had the perfect opening when I was down." He pointed to the deck.

"I was going to, but you were unarmed." She shrugged. "It didn't seem fair."

"Not fair? No Aspected is ever unarmed." He gave an explosive sigh and wiped at his face. "Fighting is always a last resort. Make damn certain you win. At all costs. There are no second chances with death."

Why fight at all? All right, maybe using the Healing Aspect to tweak an opponent's hand wasn't exactly what the Fal'kin sages intended for the gift, but it was better than injuring someone. Far better than the Soul Harvest. And far, far better than killing. "Why can't I just render my opponent unconscious, never having to draw a sword or fire an amulet at all? He won't be able to attack me then."

"Why not just stop his heart? Then he will never be able to attack you."

She blanched. To use the Healing Aspect to kill? Even to inflict pain? That seemed as far from healing as one could get.

"Tetric, that's wrong. The Healing Aspect must only be used for healing. Or at least not to do harm."

"Yet you compressed the nerves in my wrist to make me drop my sword with your Healing Aspect."

She frowned. "I made your hand go numb. I think that's a wee bit different than stopping someone's heart."

"Is it?" He folded his arms as he stood over her. "You've already chosen to use the Healing Aspect for something other than healing. There's no going back from that now."

He was right. But still. "Using the Healing Aspect to kill? That cannot be right. The name alone sets its purpose."

He laughed ruefully. "The name of the power means nothing. Consider the Defending Aspect. There is no 'defending' whatsoever. It is the Attacking Aspect, the Fighting Aspect. The Killing Aspect. Is using the Healing Aspect to do what we must any more wrong than this? Killing is killing. It does not matter how the act is done."

Her shoulders fell in defeat. "I have already made that choice. One thousand and sixty-one times. Including fourteen of my people I meant to save."

"I have crossed that line more times than I can count. Each one left its mark." He knelt in front of her again. "Mirana, we are the Trines of this age. We are not masters of the Aspects. We are slaves to them. To the Aspects Above. We are their tools. Our lives are not our own. We have been created for one purpose and one purpose only. The Aspects Above have demanded you and I free Kinderra. We have no choice but to free Kinderra by force. Regardless of the abominations required to do it."

She shook her head. "I disagree. There's always another choice."

He squared his shoulders. "All right. How would you *choose* to end the war?"

Mirana sank deeper in her rope nest. "I don't know." She then thrust her chin out. "But I will find a way. Someday."

"Someday." He tilted his head to one side, stretching neck muscles. She didn't even need to read his mind to know she was beginning to annoy him. "Now. Why didn't you strike when you had the chance? The truth this time."

Bartus watched them. He held the hook he used to repair a torn net with white knuckles, no longer tying knots. Concern and anger were etched upon his face and within his emotions. She shook her head, warding off his chivalry and dismissing Tetric's question.

Mirana exhaled and rubbed her eyes. "I can't strike you." Her hand dropped to her arm and held the wound there. His brows furrowed in a question. "I can't because you're, well, *you*."

"What does that have to do with anything?"

"You believe in me. My—" Dare she use the word? "My lightness. You saved my life."

He knelt in front of her and wiped the blood from her cut with the sleeve of his shirt. "And you saved my life. At the vale." His amulet brightened and a soothing warmth like liquid sunshine enveloped her arm.

"I only distracted those feral folk. You saved yourself."

He ran a thumb across her split knuckles. "You chose not one, but two amulets. And destroyed my attackers." Her hand tingled, and the wounds faded. "I told you before, finding the keep extracts is your only concern, not my wellbeing."

"It is." She nodded. "But I can't do that without you."

He shook his head slowly. "Only you can sense Jasal."

"That's not what I mean." Mirana held his forearm. "The only way I can finish this journey, to *do* something with the

writings we find, is if I learn how to be a Light Trine. From you."
She lowered her head. ... *Without you, I am lost* ...

He gently lifted her chin. "You will not fail me nor
Kinderra."

"How do you know?"

A slow, sad smile crept across his mouth. "Because you
know you must succeed." He brushed the hair from her face.
His amulet glowed as he drew his thumb across a cut on her
chin, releasing a sense of warmth.

She took his hand in hers. "I know I must. I don't know if
I can."

He sighed and shook his head. "I cannot teach someone
unwilling to learn. Even a Trine. What do you want?"

She wanted to bring peace to Kinderra. For everyone. She
wanted to stop the endless summers of bloodshed. She wanted
to learn if Jasal Pinal's weaknesses ran in her veins. She wanted
to prevent the horror she saw at the keep wrought at her own
hands. She certainly did not want to kill more people. Tetric was
wrong about his powerlessness against destiny. He had to be. If
she remained a slave to the Aspects, her vision of Jasal's Keep
would become reality.

She rose painfully. "I want to practice some more."

"No, Mirana. What is it that you truly want?"

She glanced over her shoulder at the sailors. "I want a
successful conclusion to our journey."

"That's not good enough."

Lightning flared in the distance, followed by a low rumble
of thunder. A successful conclusion *would* be good enough. To
find all the pieces that spoke of the keep's construction, find out
what it truly was, how it saved Deren. To save Deren—all of
Kinderra—again. That would answer so very much.

She leaned on the gunwale of the ship. A flash of lightning duplicated itself in a reflection on the ocean's surface.

He followed her. "What has you so frightened that you continue to hide it from me? Something has plagued you since we reviewed the vision of Two Rivers Ford together. I have respected your silence. I had hoped you would have come to me by now."

He had been honest with her since they began their journey, sharing his plans to save Kinderra by becoming Primus Magne, his deepest beliefs, putting his trust in her. She had lied to him from the start. She could not hide the fears of her destiny from him any longer. Maybe Tetric Garis was where the Hope remained. It was time for the truth.

Lightning flickered. She squeezed her eyes shut.

"If I answer the call of my destiny, if I become what I see, all that I love will be destroyed," she whispered.

"I told you before, you are not the Dark Trine."

"I killed a thousand men and women at the ford. I meant to do good, but I caused so much death. That cannot be a sign of blessing. Maybe I'm even something worse than the Ken'nar's Dark Trine. Maybe whoever wrote that damn prophecy got it all wrong. Or-or somebody should have written about two Dark Trines instead. I don't know." She buried her face in her hands.

He sighed and lowered one of her hands. "Mirana."

"Do not dismiss what I'm telling you as childish foolishness. Too much is at stake. You said you saw the vision of Jasal's Keep exploding in white light, but you haven't really. Not all of it."

His expression changed from one of curiosity to one of guarded concern. "Tell me what it is that you've seen. Please."

To speak the words, to give voice to them, would make the vision real, no longer just images. The vision was a disease, a cancer growing inside her, becoming more malignant with each passing day. There was no cure for cancer but to cut it out. Or die.

"I am on the pinnacle of Jasal's Keep. Deren lies under siege. I sense I knew that I could have stopped the attack. I could have stopped everything, but I failed. I fight a Ken'nar swordsman. He is not just any swordsman. I know that now. The crushing, unrelenting will. It is the Ken'nar Dark Trine. It must be. I am consumed with rage, guilt. Desperation. Just as Jasal is in his final writings. I need to stop the swordsman, stop the siege, but I cannot. I feel a weight around my neck, at my chest. An amulet, maybe? I keep calling for you, but you are not there. Teague. The Dark Trine strikes him. He falls and does not move. He is bleeding, dying. The Dark Trine cuts me down. He wants something from me. I don't know what. I don't want to give it to him, but I can't stop him. The siege continues down below. Death surrounds me. I can't stop it. I am dying. I'm in pain such as I have never felt. Then everything disappears as I am consumed by a white light. Teague, you, all the Fal'kin and the Unaspected fending off the siege. They die because of me. I could have stopped it all, but I didn't. How can I possibly be a Light Trine of the Prophecy when this is what I see?"

All the terror and desperation she had locked in her heart for so long erupted into a cry. She hid her face behind her hands again as if they could somehow forestall the onslaught of her destiny.

Tetric enfolded her in the safety of his arms and stroked her hair.

"I am afraid I will fail you. I will fail Kinderra. I'd rather die than let that happen. My parents—" Her broken sobs stole her words. "My parents orphaned me with their silence, with their lies. You have filled my heart as much as they ever did. If you die, I will—I cannot survive that kind of loss a second time."

He laid his cheek on the top of her head as his mind reached for hers. ... *This vision shall not come to pass ... I will not let it ... Remember, I promised you, we will go forward together ...*

She held onto him. He was the anchor in the tempest of her life. ... *It is not a future you control, Tetric ... I'm not sure if I do ... I've done everything I can to stop this fate from becoming true ... But it remains ... This is my destiny ...*

"No. It is not." He stood back and held her face. ... *I was created to save Kinderra ... You are Kinderra to me ... Mirana ... Ëi Trinus ... Oë ísi Ëi biraena ... You are my child ...*

CHAPTER 23

"Acceptente te ain a dam a anelies ëllenas u'ai voide."
("Taking from one to give to another fills no void.")
—Ora Fal'kinnen 216:13

Mirana's hand hit something hard. The sudden pain and a flash of light jolted her awake. A storm and not a vision raged outside.

The ship pitched violently, forcing her to steady herself against the vessel's hull as she searched for Tetric. He was nowhere to be seen. Ashtar pawed at the deck and whinnied in fear. She patted him then ran up the stairs out of the hold.

Sheets of rain and windswept sea spray drenched her as she stepped onto the deck. As the ship flailed on the waves, lightning and thunder crashed around it, threatening to strike the vessel. Towering swells slammed into the hull and threw Mirana to the deck. She screamed and slipped as the vessel rolled at an oblique angle. Her fingers searched for a handhold to prevent herself from washing overboard. She stuck her feet out and slid into the gunwale of the ship, its port side turned to the water.

Bartus and his first mate Tarq grappled with the ship's wheel and fought to keep it steady. "Get back down below."

The ship righted itself, then faster and faster, it came down and slapped its bow back onto the water. Terrified, she scrambled on her hands and knees and clung to the wheel pedestal.

"Where is Tetric?" She braced herself for the deluge of another wave.

"At the bow."

She choked, spitting out seawater, and squinted through the storm to make out a black figure standing with his arms outstretched. Tetric had lashed himself to the forward mast. The hematite amulet at his chest set the rain aglow in its pewter light.

She held onto Bartus's waist. "What is he doing?"

"He's attempting to keep the ship on course," he shouted above the storm. "We've already reefed the mainsail and furled the jib. But the storm, she refuses to play fair."

She had no idea what he meant, but it didn't matter as long as he did. Another wave pounded over the gunwales swamping the pitching boat and her crew. Mirana coughed and gagged with the seawater and shook the hair from her eyes.

"Dammit! Mustaf, the trysails! Tarq, go forward! Help him!"

The other sailor crawled to his mate, a rope tied around both men's waists.

Through the garish lightning, jagged, dark columns appeared like black fangs.

Mirana gasped. "Where are we?"

"Just where we don't want to be." Bartus shook off another wave of seawater.

The Taran Shoals. "Oh, Lights. We're going to crash."

The captain shook his head, defiant. "Not if I can help it."

"What are we going to do?"

"*We* are going to do nothing. *You* get below decks, jewel. I'll get us out of this. I've had lovers more fickle than Lady Weather."

As if to argue the point, an enormous gust of wind threw the ship headlong toward a mountainous wave. Bartus hugged the pilot wheel, fighting both the wind and the waves, as Tarq and Mustaf grabbed their safety lines for dear life. The hurricane-force winds pushed the vessel straight into the deadly rocks.

Mirana bit her lip and squinted through the spray at the Trine. Whatever he was doing, it wasn't enough. Keep vision be damned! Their quest was too important, Kinderra was too important for her to hide like a coward below decks when she could do something to help Tetric.

She struggled across the wildly pitching deck toward the Trine.

"Mirana! Where are you going?" Bartus yelled.

"This storm is too much for Tetric to handle alone! I need to help him!"

When she reached Tetric, she grabbed his legs to keep from sliding overboard. "Tetric! Give me your amulet! We're headed right for the shoals!"

… *Tie yourself to me!* … he called to her mind and dragged her up. She fastened the remaining length of rope around them both. … *Work with me … We need to move the ship away from the rocks …*

If she could destroy a stone bridge, she could destroy rock shoals. ... *The wind's too strong for that ... Give me your amulet ... I need to clear us a path through the shoals ...*

A gust of wind blew the ship towards another lethal outcropping.

... *I can't have you risk yourself like that ...* His amulet shone painfully bright.

... *Tetric, please ... I can do this ...*

A flurry of strong emotions shot from his mind to hers as he nodded. She tore Tetric's amulet over his neck and threw it around her own as he held her with iron arms. She opened herself to the Aspects. Her powers labored to shift the harmonics in the hematite crystal. She willed her Aspects through the amulet and destroyed the crags that stood in their path. The amulet scintillated wildly in her palm. An ethereal beam of black-edged silver fire shot from the crystal and knifed through the razor-sharp rocks. Moments later, the ship wallowed through the tight passage she created.

Another enormous wave crashed into the ship. Again, she lashed out with amulet fire, striking basalt and sending a myriad of sparks in the air. Stone shards blew into her face, cutting her cheeks and chin. A large basalt column loomed directly in front of the ship's helm.

Mirana screamed as she released an enormous jet of flame mediated by her Aspect. She gasped for breath and her knees buckled, the ropes preventing her from sinking to the deck.

He held her close to him. ... *You cannot save us that way ... You nearly killed yourself at the ford ... I will not let you come that close to dying again ... Your Light from Within is not strong enough alone ... You must use the Power from Without ... It is the only thing that can save us now ...*

"I can't! I mustn't! The Power from Without is an abomination!"

… How can something be evil if it can save lives? …

Could the Power from Without be used for a noble purpose?

… Use the life around you as if it was your own … he intoned in her mind. *… Life itself is your amulet … Use me … As a father gives life to his child …*

Was it a sin if he willingly gave of himself? Whether she poured out her Aspects on her own or used what was freely given, what truly was the difference if lives were spared?

… Do you still not trust me? …

The ship slewed away from the remnant of the basalt column. The bones of other vessels that had not been as agile stood like skeletons in the lightning.

… I am afraid …

… Mirana, you must! … You have no choice … The power you hold from Within is not enough … It is never enough … You must use the Power from Without … He took her hand now and placed it over his heart. *… Trust me … Please …*

She did trust him. With her very life. Just as he entrusted his to her. "I will not fail."

Mirana grasped the Trine's power, wrenching it from him, blending with it, merging it with her own Aspects. The screaming gale faded from her hearing. The cold drops of the rain ceased stinging her skin. Her breath quickened as her heartbeat thudded dully in her ears as his presence surrounded her, blended with her. His Aspects merged with her, growing, building, igniting her soul. She could no longer contain the power.

With a cry, she released the Power from Without through the dark silver crystal. Their combined Aspects transformed power into a fist of fire that smashed whole blocks of stone larger than the ship. Boulders crashed into the water, their waves swallowed up in the swollen sea.

Under Bartus's skilled hands, the ship passed through a small strait. Another powerful storm surge smashed into the ship and buffeted it against the jagged shoals. The scraping and straining of the ship's hull rose above the howling wind.

She pulled more power from her *patrua* mentor, allowing it to fill her until the ephemeral energy burned within her. When she could no longer bear the pain, she poured out their combined power through the crystal, destroying the rocks that threatened to rip the ship apart. It was not enough. The rocks were too many. She could never destroy them all. She must move the ship itself. Tetric could not do it on his own. But together, with the Power from Without, they could. They must—or they would all die.

Mirana wrapped the Aspects around the vessel, pulling at Tetric's essence now, at his life's music, grasping it, clutching at it, tearing it from him, gathering more and more into her, and drove the ship between the shoals. The tempest-tossed ocean fought against her, the fury of natural life wresting control back from her.

Glorious pain and grievous power filled her, terrified her, enraptured her.

She would not fail Tetric. She would not fail Kinderra. She would not fail herself!

She drew in life from around her, forcing the ship through the waves, dragging it away from the rocks that would destroy it.

She was a living amulet!

Tetric fell slack against the ropes. A theme sounded in her mind, a dark counterpoint to the guidance of the ship. The notes of his life turned to dissonance. He could not breathe; his lungs burned for air, their need wailing to her Healing Aspect. His heart worked faster but could not keep up with the demands she put on his body. His pain resounded through her.

She needed more power than he could give her if she were to move the ship clear of the shoals. She needed more life to save lives.

She demanded it!

Bartus. The sailors. If she were to succeed, she needed their life's essence to fuel her.

The power she forced through the crystal of the Trine's amulet seared her palm. A sailor's fear sang out to her. She latched onto his life's music and pulled it into her. His essence coalesced with her own. She held it, the power swelling within her, and thrust it out through the hematite crystal.

The more she poured herself out through the amulet, the emptier she became, and the more she craved life to fill that emptiness. Crags exploded on either side of the ship, shards of rock falling on the deck like flaming hail.

A cry lifted above her voracious, frantic need for power, one that only she could hear from within the Aspects. A shriek in the music of life, like that of a child in torment. The echoing dissonance ripped through her, overwhelming her ability to perceive anything else. The Aspects rent themselves apart within her, a shattering of life and light. One heartbeat later, all was silent.

The ship heaved over another wave, reaching the safety of open water, at last.

The rope binding her to the Trine had burned free. She fell to her hands and knees, and Tetric collapsed to the deck with her. Where the agony of sound had enveloped her, now its deafening antithesis of silence surrounded her. The dark amulet hung heavy from her neck. The hematite crystal's dusky table facet had ruptured, a crack bisecting the gem.

"Tetric?" She knew she had spoken, but she could not hear her own voice. He lay still. "Tetric." What had she done? The Power from Without. Aspects Above, what had she done?

She pulled him into her arms. "Wake up. Please." She put a hand over his heart. "Tetric!"

His eyelids fluttered as he slowly opened them. His breath came in labored rasps. ... *You-You have saved us* ...

The retreating lightning reflected in the broken facets of the amulet against her chest. "What have I done?"

"You saved us."

"I nearly killed you. I took your life."

"But you did not. You did not take from me. I willingly gave you my Aspects and my life. They all did. As all life does."

Mirana whirled around. Bartus slumped over the ship's wheel. Abject terror imprinted the faces of the other sailors. Tarq lay unmoving at the Tash-Hamari captain's feet.

Bartus's face pulled taut with shock and pain. His emotions, however, froze her heart. Horrified disbelief. Revulsion. Betrayal. Hatred.

"No." She staggered over to the fallen man. She placed her hands on his chest, ignoring the pain of her burned palms. "No, no, no." She called to her Healing Aspect. And heard nothing.

She turned to the Trine. "Help me!"

He shook his head weakly. "He's gone."

"What have I done?" Her desire for power had consumed her. "Why didn't you stop me?"

She reached again for the Healing Aspect, but no life essence sang in Tarq. His heart remained still, his body quiet.

Tetric crawled over to her, the weakened music of his life whimpered to her Healing Aspect. "If I had stopped you, you would have never believed in yourself. You would have never understood the Power from Without."

What had she done?

"No. He can't be dead. Tarq. Please wake up. I didn't mean to do this. I didn't mean to take it all." Hot tears fell over her cheeks and merged with the cold rain. "Bring him back. You must."

"He made a noble sacrifice, and we are alive because of it." The Trine closed the fallen man's eyes. "Be at peace, *Ëi cara*."

Mirana opened her mouth in another useless protest as the silence of Tarq's death continued to condemn her.

She gripped the dark amulet and flooded the sailor with the Healing Aspect, desperate to bring back the rhapsody of life that had been there. Aspects Above, what had she done?

Tetric wrapped his hands over her shoulders. "You did nothing wrong, Mirana."

Bartus sank to the deck. "Tarq was like a brother to me. Get away from him, you Ken'nar witch." He pulled the body of his mate from her.

"I am sorry. I am so sorry. I didn't mean to kill him. I swear it. I didn't understand. I didn't know until it was too late." She meant to do good, she meant to save lives. Instead, she killed. The sailors stared back at her in silent terror and hatred. "Bartus. All of you. It was an accident. I swear. I was trying to save us."

She clawed at the amulet still hanging about her neck. "Take this from me. I will destroy Kinderra. I told you that. The only way I could is with an amulet. Please. Take it from me."

Tetric held her hand and prevented her from removing it. "Mirana, listen to me. Listen to me. You did nothing wrong. You used the life the Aspects Above gave to you to save lives. That is a worthy act."

She struggled with him, trying to rid herself of the hematite that somehow burned and yet felt cold against her palm. "I killed a man with the Power from Without. That-that power, it is a taking. Not a giving."

He pulled her hands away from the amulet's tarnished chain and held both of them in his. "And had you not, none of us would be alive. None of us. Do you understand? One was sacrificed for the many. *Ai*, it was a painful choice to make, but you made the right one. You saved our lives by using a power stronger than yourself. A power, a life given to you by the Aspects Above for this very purpose. Saving lives. Is that not why they have created us as Trines?"

The emptier she had become, the more life, the more power she hungered for. The more life she emptied from herself, the greater the void in her soul. So she had demanded more and more of the sailor's life essence to fill the expanding chasm within her until he had none left to give.

Yet Bartus and the rest of his men were still alive. Tetric was still alive. How could using the Power from Without be an act of goodness when it caused so much pain? Her mind burned in torment.

Tetric wiped away the saltwater and the tears from her face. "*Biraena*, we're alive because of you. Because you were willing to see past the lies so many others have believed."

"But a man is dead," she wailed in anguish.

… *You fought your fear and naïve convictions to save our lives* … His call was hushed in awe. … *To save my life* … He reached for her, to draw her into the solace of his embrace.

Mirana shied from him. "The Power from Without. Tetric, it is a taking. I cannot, I will not touch it again."

… *You must, Ëi biraena* … *Now you understand what it truly means to be a Trine* … *Just as the Aspects Above are a trinity yet a single whole, so are we … The Light from Within, the Power from Without, separate yet together make a whole … Defending, Seeing, Healing, separate yet whole … Oë Trinus … Thou art Trine …* He smiled down at her, tears brimming in his own eyes. Pride and love emanated from him—a faith and trust in her she rejected yet so desperately needed. … *Oë Ëi Trinus …*

CHAPTER 24

"A sin must save us. My sin."
—The Codex of Jasal the Great

Kaarl rolled in bed once more. Desde rustled beside him but did not wake. Her days were spent with the other seers, attempting to decipher the Dark Trine's plans, while her nights were spent in tortured visions.

The recent months had not been kind to her. Her father's death and the deaths of Niah and Tennen Beltran, the battle at the ford, the agonizing decision to ask for Unaspected volunteers, and Mirana's bitter parting all weighed heavily on her.

He rose and paced in their chamber, uncertain if he wanted to lie down again or go to the prime's study.

With Sahm Klai's refusal to come to Varn-Erdal's aid, they had no choice but to ask the Unaspected to fight.

The muster itself had been fraught with danger. They couldn't stand in the public square and shout for help. The call-to-arms had been given under a certain amount of secrecy. Much of Desde's plan relied on the element of surprise.

They had asked the hall's Unaspected staff to make their intentions known to those they trusted and hoped the word would spread from there. A few volunteers came almost immediately, which had heartened him, but each day after that brought only a handful more. So far, only five hundred had answered their call.

He chided himself for his impatience. It had been little more than a sevenday since word had gone out. More would come, wouldn't they? His stomach knotted.

He rubbed his eyes. Five thousand would only leave them matched with the Ken'nar forces Desde and the seers had perceived. Five hundred, however? He huffed a quiet, vengeful laugh. These were not seasoned defenders. They were farmers and seamstresses. The largest blade any had held served to carve a chicken, not a Ken'nar. If they didn't get significantly more fighters, they might as well let these go back to their homes and farms. He and Desde were desperate, but he would not let innocent men and women throw their lives away on a useless action.

He inhaled, long and slow. The muster's secrecy wouldn't hold out forever, but he intended to use every advantage they had, no matter how slight.

He and the handful of provincial Fal'kin who had survived the battle at Two Rivers Ford had begun to train the volunteers in the courtyard within the learning hall's walls. At some point, however, he would have to increase the target distance, which meant moving the training to the fields outside of the city itself. Travelers and those who didn't know about the muster would see this. Soon, all of Kinderra would suspect something odd was going on. What excuse could he and Desde give? Could they say they were holding some sort of archery contest?

He wiped at his face. "By the Light, that's bloody awful."

If they were blessed to have Unaspected skilled enough to shoot at targets from a distance, their secrecy was over. There was nothing for it. He didn't think his hope could extend that far.

Kaarl sank into one of the chairs near the empty hearth. The firebox was dirty. He hadn't had it cleaned since they had left for Two Rivers Ford months ago.

He finally had to admit to himself the Unaspected muster was not what kept him awake. Of all the matters that should be concerning him, his thoughts dwelled on their daughter. He had not heard anything from Mirana in sevendays. Not one word. Not even a precocious nudge against his mind. He had hoped she would have at least tried to understand that he and Desde had kept her Trine Aspects a secret to save her life. Perhaps it was for the best. Perhaps her silence would keep her safe where their silence could not.

He raised his hands to his face again and kept them there this time. … *Oh, biraena … I was just trying to protect you … My tiny child …*

He curled his fingers as he had so many times gripping a sword, digging them into his eye sockets. He was Steward of the Quorum of Light, a role that gave him the power to intercede on behalf of every province on the continent, yet he was powerless to ease his wife's slumber or to save his child from the ravages of war.

Desde woke abruptly.

"Are you all right?" He walked over and sat next to her on the edge of the bed. "Was it a vision?"

She pushed the flaxen hair from her eyes. "Maybe. I thought I heard Mirana cry out. Something powerful held her and refused to release her." She sat up, her topaz amulet piercing the darkness with its golden light. She gripped it with both hands. "Whether it was a nightmare or a vision, I don't care. We've heard nothing from her in months. I must find her, Kaarl. I will leave this madness of preparing for war behind and find her. She is my child. My child! The Dark Trine has never had to fight a mother's wrath! He will not have her!"

He held his wife's shoulders and searched her eyes in the sulfurous glow of her amulet. "Have you seen something? Tell me where she is, and I will leave this instant. What have you seen?"

"I don't know. I didn't *see* anything. I only felt her terror. Then something—" she fought for a word "—something enraptured her only to be lost again in terror. I don't understand it."

He swallowed. "Is she—"

"No!" She shook her head violently. "No. We would know. I would know if my *biraena* were dead." She rubbed her eyes, then crossed her arms to hold herself. "Maybe it was a nightmare. One of my own, for once." She raised her gaze to meet his and sent a compassionate intent to his mind.

His nights hadn't exactly been quiet, either. They never had been, not fighting a war for as long as he had.

Kaarl wrapped his arm around his wife. If there was more she wasn't telling him, he didn't want to know. "As terrifying as it was, if you had a vision of her, then she is safe. If it was just a dream, she is still safe. Our *biraena* is safe."

She nodded slowly and sat up out of his embrace. She squared her shoulders. "It was a dream. *Ai*. Only a dream. Mirana is safe with Tetric. *Ai*. She is safe. *Ai*."

He leaned over and kissed her forehead. "Go back to sleep."

"I can't. Edara plagues me. I see the dark line of black armor, yet all is still. Does the Dark Trine mean to sack Edara or is it just a feint meant to draw me out and make Deren even more vulnerable? As your illustrious ancestor wrote, 'If my eyes are cast to the east, who watches the west?'"

He tightened his jaw. He hadn't considered that possibility.

She threw back the bedcovers and shrugged into a robe. She poured some water into a cup from an earthenware jug on the side table and walked over to the window embrasure. A warm breeze tugged at her hair as she took a sip. Some brilliant prime long ago had a portion of the window casing fashioned in such a way that it opened to let in the fresh air.

She traced the rim of the cup with a finger. "Have we done the right thing?"

He knew his wife very well. She was never one to give in to defeat, ever. Indecision, though? This was new.

He followed her to the window. "No, but we have done the only thing we can."

She sent her cup floating in the air and set it back down on the small side table by the bed. She turned, rested her forehead against his chin, and nodded. "Do you think I've made a bad plan even worse by enlisting Deren's magistrate for help? Taul Brandt governs the province's Unaspected, after all. Legally, he had to be the one to ask for volunteers. I just worry about our secrecy."

He held her tighter. "This amulet strike may come back to burn us, *ai*. The only thing Taul Brandt cares for more than his magistrate's chair is the gold in his pockets. He went rounds with your father for summers on interprovincial relations."

"He cares for his life most of all, *ísi verda*, but he's not stupid. He has no love for the Ken'nar, either."

Kaarl shrugged. "I suppose. But the young man who lost his family and his herds to the Ken'nar is long gone. Besides, the argument is moot. We've brought him into our plans and our confidence, and now it's up to him to bring in volunteers."

When Desde had brought Brandt to the hall and showed him the one hundred and forty-two Fal'kin, all that remained to protect Kin-Deren after Two Rivers Ford, he quickly saw how precarious their situation was and readily agreed to help. The man was a greedy, deceitful manipulator but a smart one. He would do whatever it took to keep the province safe, especially if he could elevate his popularity among the Unaspected should they be victorious against the Ken'nar. It was another matter entirely if the allied army lost, but then there wouldn't be anyone alive to hate or support the politician.

She nodded and turned back to face the moonlit citadel and tent-filled courtyard below. "Do you think there's any way we could reach out to Sido Rendel? Didn't you say Tetric left his seer second and most of his Dar-Azûlans to keep an eye on the Ken'nar garrisoned in Falantir?"

He gritted his teeth. "I'd had to risk a message runner getting captured. And I don't know Rendel's mind well enough to call to him."

"And Mirana is, well—" His wife swallowed audibly and took a breath. "I don't know Rendel well enough either."

"Of that, I am very glad." Kaarl chuckled, hoping to alleviate some of Desde's concern for Mirana. "He's an odd one. The few times I've fought with him, I've never been certain if the young man's passion for fighting is fueled by idealism or sheer bloodlust."

Her mouth turned down in a disapproving frown. "But he is one of the better blades on the continent." She sighed.

"We need thousands, *ama*, not these few hundreds. They have never fought, never held swords. They will be going before lethal warriors.

To Kaarl, the dark piles of straw at one edge of the courtyard looked more like grave mounds in the moonlight than targets for archery training. He agreed with his wife, wholeheartedly, but she did not need his agreement. She needed his optimism. He had none to give her, so he would give her reassuring lies instead. "Our Unaspected *sibe'e* may yet surprise us."

"Perhaps." She smiled. "We do, however, have one thing the Ken'nar do not."

"And that is?"

"We have the greatest defender in all of Kinderra to train our Unaspected."

He embraced her around the waist. … *I am glad you have confidence in me to do what must be done* …

… *You have always accomplished what must be done* …

… *I have tried* … *But our fate is in the hands of the Aspects Above now* …

… *Any fate is better than one ruled by the Dark Trine* … *I would rather set aside my amulet forever and pull a plow like an ox than see the Dark Trine as Kinderra's overlord* …

Kaarl rested his forehead against his wife's. … *If all of this means I can hear Mirana's laugh once more, I will be the ox* …

CHAPTER 25

"Periclaem ísi luveclae il'aspecaem. Quen Id engren, nehíl cinstandan Id. E en len potem, etís comprendea." ("Fear is the tempest of the soul. While it rages, naught else can stand against it. And in the calm afterward, there is understanding.")

—Ora Fal'kinnen 265:63–65

Mirana lay balled up in the straw as Ashtar stood next to her, a sentinel armored in a copper coat. The slats of the ship's hold pressed against her back, her shoulders scraping the rough wood as they shook. The Power from Without had violated her, a violation she had perpetrated on herself.

She had meant to save their lives. She had to. Kinderra depended on it. Did that not justify using the Power from

Without? And yet to save lives with that awful power, she'd taken life, killing an innocent man.

If she had not used the Power from Without to guide both Tetric's Aspects and her own through his amulet, if she had not taken the life force of Tarq to augment that power, the ship would have crashed into the jagged rocks. Her *patrua* mentor would have died. All the sailors would have died, instead of just one. She would have died. No one would be left to find Jasal Pinal's keep treatise. The secret to its power would remain hidden forever. And Kinderra would perish in an abyss of war and death.

But she took a man's life without thought.

She held Tetric's amulet. It was crudely made, almost childlike. The metal was of some silver alloy, tarnished to a deep greenish-black patina. The chain's links were uneven and ragged, and the setting around the crystal wrapped the gem with a jagged border. Glyphs were etched into the metal's edge. She squinted. *Ëomus ísi as Ëomus nome; Ëomus Cëosan.*

Mirana stifled a cry. "'We do as we are called; We are the Chosen.' Oh, Tetric. You forgot the most important part of this Book of Kinderra verse: 'We are Fal'kin.'"

Except he had not forgotten. He left it out on purpose.

In the faint light of the hold, the hematite gem shone a dusky silver, the crystal's disorderly facets reflecting like a piece of the winter midnight sky. A fissure ran down its center, other smaller cracks spiderwebbed from the middle.

She had created that flaw. She'd fractured the crystal with the Power from Without, pouring more of the Aspects through it than it could focus. It was Tetric's, it was a part of him. He had said, although Trines could wield any amulet, not just one, there was an ocean of difference between choosing and using. He had chosen it. She had used it. She took something perfect, a jewel borne from Kinderra's earthen body, and corrupted it. Violated it. As she was flawed and broken from using that power. Ruined. Violated. Corrupted.

She buried her face in her hands. The Power from Without. It was as magnificent as it was monstrous. Using it just that once, she had glimpsed its limitless potential.

"What have I done?" She squeezed her eyes shut. Remorse overwhelmed her, locking the breath within her chest. "Aspects Above, what have I done?"

Had Jasal Pinal been tempted in his desperation to use the Power from Without to save his people, too? Had he been more than tempted?

He'd died in sin, a coward who took his own life, abandoning his people to the swords and amulets of the Ken'nar. His words within the Codex were so imbued with despondency, it could only lead her to that conclusion. And yet his keep saved Deren from destruction at the hands of Ilrik the Black and the Ken'nar. Jasal had been hailed a hero for most of his life, some even whispered him divine. Then his weakness erased all his greatness, his goodness. A single act of supreme cowardice destroyed a lifetime of heroism. He admitted through the words in his journal he was not strong enough to stop the Ken'nar bent on laying waste to Deren, even though he was a Trine. Just as Tetric had said her innate powers were not strong enough to save the ship and its crew.

Maybe Jasal hadn't given in to weakness and cowardice. Maybe he gave in to something else entirely.

Had he tasted the Power from Without, as she had, to make himself stronger? Legend said Jasal's body had never been found. Had he pulled so much power to himself, the energies killed him, turning his own body into ash? That didn't seem to be quite the right answer, and yet, a sense of truth rang through the notion.

She pushed herself up to sit against the hull, her limbs resisting the movement.

"What if Jasal had been strong enough?" Her whisper grated against her ears.

The thought chilled her. What if, in his final moments, Jasal Pinal had not viewed himself as inadequate for the role the Aspects Above had chosen for him? What if he had the power to do what they had called him to do? That felt right in a way her Aspects whispered to her. What if he had enough power? And craved more? As she had.

"What if he did not want to be stopped?" Had she wanted to be stopped? Truly?

No.

Bitter understanding froze her lungs.

To empty herself through an amulet and the Light from Within for the sake of Kinderra, to surrender back to the Aspects Above all she was—that was the absolute and utter union of her own life and her Aspects bequeathed on her as a Fal'kin. That path to her power, that connection was also absolutely and utterly finite. To give completely of herself, to completely empty herself, she would die. She nearly had. At Two Rivers Ford.

The Power from Without, however, was endless. The only limit imposed was the demand she release it as soon as she pulled it within herself. To hold such unceasing power within her too long would kill her as certainly as if she were struck by amulet fire.

The Power from Without wasn't a giving as the Light from Within was but a taking. Instead of using herself as the source for her Aspects' power, she used the life around her. Tarq, the sailor. An innocent man.

The Power from Without wasn't a surrender but a domination. The emptiness created as she bled the life from the sailor only magnified the desire to pull even more life to her to fill it, an unending addiction. Using it made her crave more power. The more power she poured out through the amulet, the more she wanted. The need became an obsession, unstoppable. Had the amulet not fractured or had she not sensed the sudden stillness of Tarq's life music, she would have killed everyone on the ship in an unquenchable thirst for power.

She buried her face in her hands, crying out the shame in a silent scream. This pain could never be vented by mere sound.

Tetric had said her Light from Within was not strong enough to save them. What if he was wrong? She destroyed the bridges at Two Rivers Ford with nothing more and nothing less than the power she alone possessed. Hadn't she, in fact, already destroyed some of the rocks in the Rün-Taran Shoals, allowing the ship to sail through safely? If she chose to push herself to the limits of her Light from Within, she had only herself to pay the price. Could she have saved Tetric, Bartus, Tarq, and every one of the sailors with her Light from Within?

It was Tetric who had begged her to use the Power from Without, not her Light from Within. Tetric hadn't suggested they work together using the Light from Within to destroy the larger rocks or even guide the ship.

He hadn't even tried to stop her from bleeding a man's life force from him.

She sucked in her breath as a thought broke through her like the ringing of a blacksmith's hammer on steel. Her brain demanded she make a connection, an understanding.

Tetric Garis had dedicated his life to saving Kinderra from itself. Yet he saw a noble purpose in the detestable Soul Harvest. He didn't even seem to hold the Ken'nar accountable for their part in the war. He embraced the corrupted, perverted path of connection to Aspects that was the Power from Without, naming it as part of the divine directive of the Aspects Above.

The Power from Without. The Soul Harvest. The Ken'nar. More than accepting all three, Tetric held them as necessary, even bearing a sacredness of their own.

It was wrong. All of it. Wrong. All her questions bled away. Only one truth remained: there had never been three Trines. Only two. Tetric. And her. Her mother and father had been right all along. Even Tetric himself had said it: she couldn't possibly be the Dark Trine.

Because he was.

"I am such a fool," Mirana sobbed. "Such a naïve, trusting fool!" His deception bloomed further in her mind. Since the night they had first viewed the vision of the Battle of Two Rivers Ford, he had used her as some sort of tool for his own ends, an amulet in human form. Instead of the Trine Prophecy ending in some cataclysmic confrontation between a Dark Trine and a Light Trine, Tetric tried to circumvent that battle by defusing it altogether. He had tried to turn a potential enemy into an ally by turning the Light Trine into a *second* Dark Trine.

Her.

She let out an enraged scream and pounded her fist again and again against the ship's hull, beating her knuckles raw.

"Mirana? Are you all right?"

She fought for composure and staggered to her feet, Ashtar's muscular body steady under her trembling hands.

Her mentor descended into the hold and stood next to her. "We have arrived at Nuralima."

"Here." She took off his amulet. "Take it back. It is yours, not mine."

He closed her hand over the crystal. "I do not need to wear it. Its presence is always close to me. As you are, *Ëi biraena*. It is now ours."

"No." She held the amulet out to him. "I do not want it."

"Why do you persist in believing you committed some sacrilege?"

"I said take it back." She took a breath to calm herself. "Please," she added more gently.

"You must wear it. To heal. And to understand." He took the chain from her and began to place it back over her head.

She stepped back. "How can you, of all people, stand to use the Power from Without? You are Trine! You are supposed to save us! Not allow the killing of a man by taking the very forces that make him alive!"

His face drew down in sadness, but something died in his midnight-black eyes. He knew. He knew she understood who and what he really was.

"The Power from Without is the complete connection to the creation of the Aspects Above," he said, his voice soft, as if he no longer had the strength to continue living his lie in front of her. "*Ai*, it is overwhelming, even frightening in its potential. But you must accept it if we are truly to save Kinderra."

No, the Power from Without wasn't part of a duplicitous alter ego. It was a part of him, integral to his true self.

She shook her head. "It is the taking of life, Tetric. Have you become so jaded by all your summers of bloodshed in this Aspect-forsaken war you no longer care?"

His dark eyes bored into her. "Every breath I draw, I do so to see Kinderra free of that bloodshed."

"Yet you commit bloodshed to stop it. To use the Power from Without makes us no better than the Ken'nar."

Emotions leaked from his mind to hers. Confusion. Grave concern. "Mirana, please try to understand—"

"No, Tetric. I will not use the Power from Without ever again." She took Ashtar's reins and ascended the stairs out of the dark hold into the sunlight.

Once on the deck, she blinked against the brightness. The sun sat high in the sky, a flat disk turned milky with thin, high clouds. She caught her reflection in a puddle of water on the deck. Her dark hair had matted in tangles from the saltwater. Dark circles hung under her eyes. Her face was pale, as if the terrible storm in her soul had washed away who she once was.

The sailors stopped their work. When she sought their gaze, they quickly turned away.

"Our food was ruined by the water that leaked into the hold," she said as the Trine came up behind her with his own horse. "Get us some more supplies. I will be along shortly."

It was a ridiculous request, so completely out of context to what she now understood about her mentor, she might as well have asked him to turn her into a fish so she could swim away in the ocean.

Her gaze drifted beyond the vessel. The ocean. Its limitless blue arms beckoned her. Maybe Jasal wasn't a coward for killing himself. Maybe he'd done the right thing. If she were gone, however, who would find the remaining keep stanzas? She was the only one who could prevent further evil. Once she did find the missing writings, what then? Would Tetric use the knowledge, even the keep itself, to control Kinderra with an iron fist, believing his precepts, like the Soul Harvest, were benevolent? Did he even recognize evil anymore?

She pulled out the peda blossom pendant from her belt pouch. Teague. That was the one good thing she had done, removing him from her life.

Tetric placed a gentle hand on her shoulder, but she shrugged it off. "Mirana, *biraena*."

Prevent further evil. If she were gone, who would be left to prevent further evil? She curled her hand around the pendant, its edges biting into her fist.

"Mirana, these men—" He gestured to the crew repairing the storm damage to the ship. "—they live because of you."

"Tarq does not."

He stood too close behind her, his amulet whispering to her with its nearness. The bond she had that only hours ago felt ecstatic now sickened her.

"He gave his life so that others could live."

"He did not *give* anything. I took his life from him."

He remained silent for a moment, then slipped away behind U'Nehíl. He left her and disembarked from the ship.

Bartus knelt, patching a hole in the deck. He now wore a sword strapped to his waist, the same one she had used to practice with the Trine. He jumped to his feet as if pulled. "Get off my boat."

"Bartus, please." He backed away as she approached. She stopped. "I am so sorry. I know my words cannot possibly undo what I have done."

His hands tightened around the hammer. "Did he teach you how to do that?"

"It doesn't matter if he did or not. I swear to you, though, it was an accident. I did not understand until it was too late. I don't expect your forgiveness, so I won't ask for it. I meant to save us, not kill a man. What I did was an abomination."

She was an abomination. As she had always known.

"You are no better than a Ken'nar," the captain spat. "Is that not what he is training you to be?"

"Lord Garis doesn't look at the Power from Without that way. To him, it is part of the cycle of life to ultimately preserve life. But it is not. It is—" No words could describe the horror of what she had done. Of what he had done to her. "It is murder. The most heinous form of killing there could be."

Bartus stepped back farther from her and pointed to the boarding ramp. "Leave. Now." As soon as he spoke, his shoulders stiffened.

His fear and anger leaped to her mind. He expected she would attack him for his remark. She didn't blame him. She had no idea where to go, what to do with her own evil let alone that of her conclusions regarding her mentor. She had no idea how to repair Bartus's view of her. The only thing she had ever held of value was Teague's love. She looked at the pendant in her hand. It no longer held the promise of a beautiful future for her. But maybe it would for someone else.

She held out the pendant. "Here. I want you to have this."

"What makes you think I want that trinket?"

"Because it represents everything I once held dear. I don't have the right to wear it any longer. I don't know if Tarq had any family, but maybe you can sell it and give them the coins. I know it's a laughably useless gesture, but I don't know what else to do."

"No gesture can make up for what you did. That," he jutted his chin at the pendant, "won't even make up for your fare. It's worthless."

"Not to me."

"Did he give this to you? A pretty bauble to keep the pretty jewel by his side?" His mouth twisted into a sinister grin. "Or maybe someplace even closer?"

"What? No! He's my—" Mirana shook her head. What was Tetric to her now? She had no idea. "No. The boy I once loved gave me this." She held it out to him a moment longer. When he made no move to take it, she slipped it back into her belt pouch.

Bartus's angry grimace remained. "What happened to him?"

Her shoulders fell, the sudden lack of tension in them causing her chest to ache in strained weakness. He wondered if she had killed Teague like she had Tarq. The pain wouldn't be much different if she had. "I broke his heart. I meant to save his life from the Ken'nar. Now, I know I had to save his life from me." She wanted to cry, but the depthless shame locked in her heart held such an expression a prisoner. "I don't want to hurt anyone. I know you won't believe me. I want to find a way to stop this endless war. I'd rather die—I am willing to die—than see this violence continue to destroy Kinderra."

At last, Bartus relaxed, setting down the hammer. "What you did. That cannot be the answer for this land."

"It's not. I know that. Now."

"Take this." He unfastened the blade from around his waist.

She held her hands up. "I can't. Not after everything I've done."

"It can't protect me or anyone else from you. You could kill me with a single thought."

She shook her head. "I would never do that."

"You already did. With Tarq. Take it. Use it instead of the accursed crystal that hangs from that man's neck." He glanced out at the docks. "If he even is a man."

She slowly reached for the sword, admiring again the graceful flow of its simple lines. "Where did you get a sword like this? This is a military weapon."

"The Fal'kin are not the only ones who love Kinderra. Many would fight for her." He paused. "Many have had to. Even the Fal'kin cannot be everywhere."

"Bartus, please don't hate other Aspected because of my crime. Please. Hate me if you must, but Kinderra needs good people like you. As do the Fal'kin."

"Mirana, jewel, leave that man," he replied. "If killing good people like a Ken'nar is what he expects from you, then there is no hope for Kinderra."

She reached for his forearm but sensed he did not want the gesture. She bent in a bow to him instead and held his sword close to her heart. "*Ben íre*, Bartus il'Alhambre."

Bartus was right. The Power from Without could not be the answer to bringing peace to Kinderra. There had to be another way. Or not even hope would remain.

CHAPTER 26

*"Does it not go against everything they hold dear,
everything I believe in? And yet, if I do not, if they do
not, there will be no hope."*
                         —The Codex of Jasal the Great

Nuralima. What a forlorn and dreary place. It suited her
perfectly.

Weariness had sunk into Mirana's bones, leaving her too
fatigued to sigh in dismay. The port town was nothing like how
her mother and Binthe Lima had described it. Her mother had
spent a few winters here as a small child. She had told Mirana of
the beautiful sea cliffs. Binthe was born here, grew up here. She
had said she loved to watch the ships in the harbor, admiring the
multitude of colors and designs on their sails.

Mirana, however, only saw a grim seaport and the bleak learning hall high on a bluff in the distance. Constructed from the same black basalt of treacherous shoals, the hall sat apart from the village like a brokenhearted mother observing her remaining children but unable to find joy in them after the loss of a babe.

Her mother never mentioned anything so somber as this place. Her mother hadn't mentioned a lot of things, swearing she kept the truth about Mirana's Trine Aspects from her to protect her. That wasn't the truth from which she needed to be protected. But ignorance, like suicide, never solved anything. It was just another, less final form of continuing lies.

She had begged Tetric Garis in Deren's library to prevent her from becoming a monster as he took the knife from her throat. Begged him! An innocent man lay dead because the Power from Without she wielded had become a power that superseded all else.

Her father's words haunted her. He had said good men and women became evil when they sought power above all else. And she had learned that lesson oh so well from her mentor.

Tetric pulled his black stallion alongside Ashtar, although the Trine's face was obscured by his cowl. "Your mother has some of the sea province in her, doesn't she?"

"What?"

"Your mother has some Rün-Tarani blood?" he asked again.

"She's distantly related to Seer Prime Eshe Pashcot and her granddaughter, Seer Binthe Lima, but it's been many, many generations."

She turned her attention away from her tall *patrua* and back to the road on which they traveled. Nuralima's harbor hugged the rocky coast, but the sea cliffs prevented the city from encroaching farther inland. Even though Qadar was a working port as well, it still held an air of the exotic. Austerity draped Nuralima, drowning out the vestiges of grandeur. Once-vibrant buildings now stood pale and gray, their painted colors scoured away by the elements. Shops, taverns, and what she assumed were homes were made of similar whitewashed shell plaster and earth as in Qadar. The habitations of Nuralima, however, held none of the Tash-Hamari port city's decadent excitement as they tumbled down to the shore from the high cliffs. Here and there, scrubby little weeds tried to bloom and would have been pretty if not for the stony soil into which they had sunk their roots.

The city sat in mourning, unable to rise above its grief. That was the only way she could describe its character, its sense of place. It felt just like she did.

Few people bustled along the streets and alleys despite the sun being past its zenith. A man dressed in a drab brown cloak ducked into an inn. An old woman swathed in a somber gown and shawl paused by a barrel of potatoes outside one of the market stalls then scurried into an adjacent shop. Other than those individuals, Mirana saw no one. Rock and seashell gravel crunched uncomfortably loud under their horses' hooves.

"I'm glad you took the sword. You need a weapon more substantial than a long knife. We may encounter difficulties in the remaining learning halls."

Difficulties? As if fighting an army of feral men and women and suffering in torment within an existential nightmare weren't difficult enough?

"We should have enough supplies to see us through Salmasalar in Jad-Anüna," he continued. "We will most likely have to forage after that as we travel north."

She ignored him, listening instead to the stones grinding under Ashtar's hooves.

They passed no one as they rode. Maybe they had learned what she had done. "The people. They are afraid," she said.

The Trine, closed behind U'Nehíl as always, plodded his horse along, and looked neither right nor left. "They are. Of me."

"Why?" Did they know what she knew?

"The Seer Prime of Rün-Taran and I had a tragic falling out."

She reined Ashtar to a stop. "Is that because you used her people to feed your Power from Without?"

He reined in his horse as well but did not turn. His long back and broad shoulders remained iron-rod straight. "Had I not done what I have in the past, thousands would be dead. Had you not done what you did, we on the ship would be dead. It was a choice of the greater good. You made the right choice. As I have. I did not say it was an easy choice."

She tapped Ashtar's sides and trotted up next to the Trine. "I trusted you. I put my life in your hands. You were supposed to stop me from becoming a murderer. Not turn me into one. Like you."

"Like me?" He now turned in his saddle to face her, his amulet glinting in the diffuse sunlight. "So, you are blaming me for your guilt? I told you to use the Power from Without. I did not tell you to kill that man."

Rage exploded within her, fed by a storm of the Defending Aspect. She struck a scarred hand across Tetric's face with every ounce of strength she could muster. He took the blow full on, the force of it knocking his cowl back and making him grapple for his saddle to keep from being unseated.

Slowly, he turned his face back to hers. In his eyes was that look—flat, black, devoid of mercy. The look he had leveled at her when she made him drop his sword, the one Bartus had warned her of.

Mirana tried to swallow in a tight throat. She had never truly feared Tetric until now. *Ai*, she had held him in awe, he confused her, overwhelmed her, but he had not frightened her. Her anger, now without focus, transformed into tears she did not want to release.

She slipped off her saddle and buried her face against Ashtar's neck.

"You're right. I do want to blame you," she said, her voice broken by emotion. "You told me my prescience about Two River Ford was wrong, even though, deep down, I knew I was right. You told me I wasn't strong enough, my Light from Within wasn't strong enough to save the ship. Only the Power from Without could save us from the storm. In my heart, though, I knew I could save us with my Light from Within alone. You *are* wrong. For leading me to believe I am something weaker than I am. And you are wrong for so very many other things. But I can't blame you for my believing your lies. That's my fault. Tarq's death is no one's fault but mine. My choices are my own. I must live with the consequences."

Once again, she was lost. Only this time, there would be no hero to save her. No, if she wanted to be saved, she would have to do it herself.

He dismounted from his horse and stood close. Too close. His amulet. She needed its embrace as a traumatized child needed the embrace of a loving parent. ... *If I had told you, you would not have done what was necessary* ... he called gently. ... *We would all be dead ... I told you, we are slaves to our Aspects ... The Power from Without is what the Aspects Above require of us to free Kinderra ... And, ai, sometimes, we must pay this terrible, terrible price ... That is what it means to be a Trine, Mirana ...*

She stepped back from him, anything to put some distance between her and his amulet. It repulsed her, yet she wanted it even more because its connection would be the only thing that would quiet the torment and help connect her once more to the life that thrummed around her. "We haven't paid anything. Bartus's friend did."

Answers were supposed to bring knowledge, even hope. Instead, the answer to the enigma of Tetric Garis was far more convoluted than the riddle. The only thing certain was that denial of that answer, with its false comfort, would be what would truly kill her. To believe such as fallacy was a sin as great as killing. It was the suicide of one's conscience.

"*Ëi biraena*, something has broken in you. I can feel it. Tell me how I can fix it?" His sadness pervaded her senses, a soul-weary melancholy and something more, all but elusive. Fear.

Fear? *He* was afraid of *her*? *Ai*, he was afraid of her, but not of her Trine Aspects. He was afraid she would reject him and all he had tried to teach her.

He should be well afraid.

She gazed at his amulet a moment and gasped as a shudder overtook her. "Do not use the Power from Without, Tetric." She took his hand and held it. She wanted him to sense her life's music, as he once had done in Deren's library. He needed to feel life, so he could remember why claiming it for the Power from Without was the gravest sin of all. "It is wrong. So very wrong."

He wrapped her hands with his. "And sacrificing yourself for no reason on those jagged rocks would have been right?"

She stepped back and crossed her arms, holding her shaking body against the need to choose his amulet. "It is my right to choose that sacrifice if I wish. We have no right to take that choice from others. I cannot follow you on this path. I will not."

"You fight it now as your Aspects beg you to open yourself to the life around you." Again, soulless fire glittered in his obsidian eyes. "So, you will let the Ken'nar swordsman from your vision kill you? How will that save Kinderra?"

Her eyes widened in shock. "I—"

He leaned closer. … *You speak of sacrifice? … You do not yet know the meaning of the word! …*

His anger billowed out beyond his efforts to hide it behind the walls of his mind. She backed away. Woven within that fury, however, was a dark harmony, a descant so soft she almost missed it. She caught a wave of moral agony such as she had never felt from anyone. No one except Jasal Pinal.

"Tetric, what happened to you?" she whispered. "What could have possibly happened to you to allow you to justify such an abhorrent use of the Aspects? Do you even recognize your Light from Within anymore?"

The enraged flame behind his eyes was stoked once more. "Perhaps you should remain here. Wait until I have engaged Eshe Pashcot, then find your way into the learning hall and find the keep extract."

She had to ask him. She needed to ask him, however, the words would not come. It had to be wrong. It just had to be.

"I once asked you if you believed in the Trine Prophecy. I realize now you never answered me. You led me to believe you thought it was just nonsense written down by a forgotten seer. The truth is you do believe in it. Wholeheartedly. Don't you?"

"There is no Light or Dark Trine, Mirana," Tetric replied. "It is a fable. There is no good or evil from within the powers of the Aspects. They simply are."

She laughed in disbelief. "No Light or Dark Trine, you say? The Power from Without. The fact that you not only validate it but embrace it without hesitation. Your use of the Power from Without is no myth. Are these things not what the Trine Prophecy foretells about the thrice-cursed?" She leaned closer to rivet him with her gaze. ... *You lied to me! ... You lied to all of Kinderra! ...*

"I have never lied to you, *biraena*," he said. "I have told you things my second does not know. I have saved your life, and you have saved mine. We are bound together by this. By the Aspects Above. By Kinderra. You are far more to me than just my *scholaira*. You are the child, the daughter, I never thought I would have."

She gripped his arms. "If you love me like your child, if you say you've never lied to me, then tell me you are not the Dark Trine. Say it. Say it with your own lips, and I will believe it. Please, Tetric. I am begging you."

He looked down at her, pity in his eyes. "It is only the lies of your beliefs that have created a Dark Trine."

She hung her head. It was unthinkable. Not her beloved *patrua*, a man she once looked to as her moral compass, a man she loved as much as her father.

And yet it was the truth.

Tears burned in her eyes. "What would you do if I left you now?"

"You won't leave." His voice was soft, like a parent correcting a wayward child. But his mind held other, more frantic emotions. Again, he was afraid. Afraid she would leave him behind? Leave his beliefs behind? Afraid she'd tell Kinderra's Fal'kin leadership of his treason? Afraid he'd lost his most cherished disciple? Maybe all of them. "You want to find the next clue to the keep as much as I do. And the only way to find it is at the end of that road." He pointed with a long finger to the learning hall looming in the distance. Tears streamed down her cheeks, their salt biting into the cuts on her face from the rocks she exploded. With the Light from Within. She welcomed the sting. The pain was honest.

"You're right. But you didn't answer my question."

The Trine closed his eyes and swallowed noisily. Tears of his own flowed over dark lashes. When was the last time he'd cried? Did he even know right from wrong anymore? Was this the great sin? That increasingly desperate choices and a desire for power above all else would leave one's soul empty?

"Mirana, I am the same man I was a moment ago, a sevenday ago. I am the same man who stood next to you at the Choosing Ceremony. In the Vale i'Dúadar. In the library."

No, he wasn't. And he never would be again.

He reached to wipe her tears away, but she pulled her face from him. His hand fell limply to his side.

"Mirana, after we find what we can in Nuralima, we still have thousands of miles yet to journey to Trak-Calan. Do you know the way there? Do you know the jungle trails through Jad-Anüna that do not end up in deadly swamps? Do you know how to find food and shelter in the bitter cold of the mountain passes through the Dar-Calan Mountains?"

She lowered her head to stare at her boots and clenched her fists tighter, allowing the stinging pain of her nails biting into her palms to fill her mind.

"Then I suggest you think longer on how much leaving me will cost you. Come." He climbed into his saddle and headed for the learning hall.

She had told him—was it only days ago or a lifetime?—that she needed him to become who she wanted to be so she could use Jasal's writings to understand the keep and use it to stop the war. She had told him she needed him, depended on him to help her find a new destiny. And he had, with his greatest lesson to her. He was a prime example of how *not* to use the Aspects.

Tetric Garis was indeed the same man he had always been. Only now she knew exactly who that was.

Tetric Garis was the Dark Trine.

CHAPTER 27

"Oscuil'e vide e u'vide."
("Eyes can look and still not see.")
—Ora Fal'kinnen 293:45

Mirana rode Ashtar up the path that led to the learning hall of Rün-Taran province, Tetric's black stallion a few paces ahead of them. The hulking edifice loomed above them, standing barren on the high, windy bluff.

"You said you and Seer Prime Paschot had a falling out? What happened?" she asked, hoping to deflect her mind from the impasse growing between them.

"It was a long time ago."

She huffed a laugh. Yet another of her mentor's non-answers. "Did you lie to her, too?"

He pulled back on his reins and pinned her with a black gaze, saying nothing. The strength of his mind pressing against hers was enough of a reprimand. And, *ai*, now was not the time nor the place for a serious confrontation.

Someday. But not now.

Mirana averted her eyes and continued riding. "Do you think Seer Prime Pashcot knows why we are here?"

He cocked his head in acknowledgment. "Perhaps. The prime sees more, knows more than any other Fal'kin in the land. *Ai*, sometimes more than me."

She trotted up to ride alongside the Trine. "I have known Prime Pashcot since I was born. My mother and Binthe idolize her. She has always been kind to me during Quorumtide, even if I didn't always understand her." She concentrated on the rocky road for a moment. "Still, I have often wondered if she is not quite lucid. She is very old."

Tetric made a derisive laugh. "Eshe Pashcot is the most lucid person in Kinderra."

She gripped the horse's reins tighter. "Then she'll know about the keep." Would she know about the sailor as well? Did she know about Tetric? Would she tell the prime what she now knew? Mirana shivered despite the warm, humid air.

"Perhaps." He shrugged, the casual gesture not squaring at all with the wisp of wariness she caught from him. "Perhaps she knew about the keep long before we knew ourselves. She may know our intent but not our full purpose, which will make her even more formidable. Think long and hard before you answer anything she asks you. What she does not know, she will want to find out. And she has ways and ways again of obtaining answers."

Caution lurked behind his words, certainly, but something else as well. Anger. And sadness. Sadness? Why?

"You make it sound as though she were our enemy."

"She may yet be. Never presume that just because someone fights alongside you, he or she will be your ally forever."

Like Tetric.

"What if she does know about the keep and our purpose? Wouldn't she want to help us?"

"Would she?"

She laughed at his question. "Of course, she would. The keep will save Kinderra." Unless he didn't truly want to save Kinderra. She cut her laugh short.

He fixed his eyes now on the learning hall ahead of them. "Only if it stays in the right hands."

Oh, if he only knew how true that was.

She pulled back on Ashtar's reins. "Was Eshe once an ally who stopped supporting you? Is that why she makes you sad?" Like her and him.

The Trine's back stiffened as he continued riding. "Remember what I told you."

Mirana did not follow him. "I have nothing to fear from Prime Eshe. I know she will help me."

He gazed over his shoulder and laughed darkly. "I once thought as you did." He turned. "Come."

When they arrived at the learning hall's entrance gate, Defender Second Syne il'Develan awaited them. His face was battle-scarred and a patch covered one eye. The blue eye with which he regarded them now was hard.

Mirana remembered the old defender from Quorumtide visits. She had never seen the serious man laugh during the season's festivals. Where focus served as the foundation of Tetric's, and even Morgan Jord's, stern demeanors, Syne Develan's was care-worn.

"*Kin ísi Oëa*, Mirana il'Pinal, Trine Garis," he said in a gravelly voice.

"*E Oë*, Defender Second," she replied with a smile. She dismounted Ashtar and gripped the old man's forearm in greeting. Several young Fal'kin *scholaire'e* arrived to take the horses.

Tetric swung off his saddle and reached for the old man's forearm. "*Kin ísi Oëa*, Syne. I trust the prime is well."

Syne Develan made no move to return the greeting. He gave a curt bow instead, his orange citrine amulet winking in the diffuse sunlight. "I am certain the Lord Trine is well aware of the prime's welfare given his communion with the Healing Aspect." His ruined face wore a smile. His voice, however, was devoid of warmth.

Mirana bit her lip to keep from gaping at the man's remark.

"The seer prime has been expecting you. Please follow me."

As she handed the reins to a little boy, she made a sidelong glance at Tetric to see what he made of this news, but his expression was as flat as the hard line of his mouth.

The old defender led them through the hall's courtyard, his progress slowed by a pronounced limp. A battered sword hung from his waist. How many battles had he lived through? Defenders that had seen his number of summers were not many.

As they walked, she noted the province's hallmark, a mythical sea-ram capricorn, chiseled into reliefs around the walls. That was about the only thing magical she could see around the hall.

Tetric laid a hand on her shoulder. ... *Defender Second Develan is more than just commander of Eshe's provincial forces ... Speak cautiously with him as well ...* She nodded to acknowledge his call. She would make her own judgment about the defender, however.

They climbed a long stone staircase, its steps turned gray-green by moss and weather. Far below, toward the sea cliffs, lay a cemetery with many, many markers. Too many. Rün-Taran always seemed so remote from Kin-Deren and her home province's constant battles with the Ken'nar. All those markers, each one a Fal'kin's life given in service to the continent. Rün-Taran had sacrificed too many of its sons and daughters as well.

"The cliffs do not leave us much land in which to lay our dead to rest," Syne Develan said. "We Rün-Tarani place them in vaults above ground. The Ken'nar, however, have made that less of an issue these last summers. They no longer even leave us amulets to honor, let alone bodies."

If Kinderra could ever have peace, how could such crimes as these from the Ken'nar be forgiven? Two Rivers Ford. Tarq. Hadn't she done far worse?

When they entered the learning hall, the sunlight seemed to go no farther than the windows cut into the thick, black basalt walls. She followed the men down several dim hallways until they, at last, entered a large room. Near the hearth rested a bed draped with a coverlet. Two chairs were placed on either side. A small fire burned in the hearth despite the balmy air wafting through an open window.

Mirana paused when the coverlet moved. What she had thought was a blanket was the prime herself.

Eshe Pashcot appeared to have aged even more, if that were possible, since Mirana had last seen the seer prime two Quorumtides ago. The seer was not merely old, she was ancient. Long, unruly hair, white as sea foam, framed her face. Skin creased over her face like worn sail canvas. Her two milky eyes navigated in Tetric's direction but did not quite find him; the seer prime was blind.

The small, tight knot of her mouth expanded into a warm smile with Mirana's approach. "*Kin ísi Oëa*, Daughter of Pinal. Welcome," she said, her voice creaking like Bartus's ship. She held out her hands in greeting.

Mirana returned a smile and hurried over to the prime's side. "*E Oë*. I missed you last Quorumtide, Prime Eshe." She knelt at the bedside and held the woman's hands in hers. They were still strong despite the elder's age. "I'm certain *Brepaithe* Toban would have liked to have seen you one last time. He went to the Aspects Above in Twelfthmonth."

"*Ai*. I sense so many shadows on your heart, *biraena*. His passing is but one of the darkest. These old bones, however, have only one journey left in them. Perhaps your *brepaithe* and I will share stories again soon, hmm?" Eshe nodded in the Trine's direction. "Tetric."

He bowed deeply. "My prime."

"Come. Sit. Both of you." She gestured to the chairs. "Syne, you may leave us."

The defender second hesitated. "I await your call should you require me." He bowed then left. The man gave the unmistakable impression that he was as much Eshe's bodyguard as he was her Prime's Second. Perhaps that was what Tetric meant earlier.

As Mirana took one of the chairs, the old seer woman patted her hand. "I am glad you came, child. We have much to discuss."

"*Ai*, we do." The Trine remained standing. "There was a battle at Two Rivers Ford. The bridges have been destroyed and many on both sides were killed. The il'Kin are no more. The north lies unprotected. I am afraid the Aspects Above have left me the only one path for peace, but I will need your help in the Quorum of Light to accomplish it."

Mirana blinked, shocked by his directness. Then again, the prime was perhaps the most powerful seer in Kinderra, so why try to hide anything? She was done with lying.

The old woman smiled. "Would not the Seeing Aspect have allowed me to envision events of this magnitude?" She laughed, a phlegmy cackle without humor. "My Binthe lives, as does Morgan Jord. And Kaarl Pinal. The il'Kin may have faded but not completely. Would that not be more of the truth?"

The tension between the seer prime and the Trine took on weight, smothering all three of them.

Tetric sighed, acquiescing. "Pinal no longer commands the il'Kin. I assumed that with only two still living, the guard would not rise again."

"If Kaarl Pinal no longer commands the il'Kin, it could only be because he is dead." The old woman turned in Mirana's direction. "Is that true?"

She regarded the prime's hand in hers, unable to meet her unseeing eyes that still saw so much. "He is now Steward of the Quorum of Light."

"Steward he may be, but that means little to his command." The old seer nodded and pursed her lips. "Your purpose is revealed a bit more to me." She shifted her hazy gaze to the tall Trine. "As is yours, Tetric, *Ëi biraen.*" Again, she turned her head in Mirana's direction. "*U'leten Oeä u'ama o Oeä ama u'vide Oë te vertas. Placre comprende Ëa.*"

Mirana nodded. "*Ai*, Prime Eshe. I do believe you. I have learned that lesson well."

"Child, child," Eshe shook her head slowly, "so few summers you have seen to be carrying the burdens you now bear. Your parents love you more than life itself. They only sought to protect you from the Dark One, risking their own lives to do so."

"I know." She called to her Defending Aspect to shield her emotions. "Did you know I was a Trine, too?"

Tetric glared at Mirana with caution.

"Not entirely." The prime smiled, creating a new net of lines on her wizened face. "You just let me know yourself." Mirana sat back. She now understood Tetric's warning.

"No. I think that was more my parents' doing." She smiled. "You knew they were protecting me. You don't commit capital crimes without a good reason. I think you knew all along. I just confirmed your suspicion."

"Aha! Clever girl," the prime cackled. "That is a lesson no one can teach you but yourself."

The old woman shifted to face the Trine. "Hmm. The visions grow clearer. The conflict grows like storm clouds on the horizon. You need my support in Quorum for this 'one path to peace' you've mentioned. Would that be support against Kaarl Pinal, *Ëi biraen*?"

Tetric finally took a seat. "Your words hold sway in the Quorum, Eshe. *Ai*, the conflict grows, and only by uniting together as one can we stop it."

The old woman made a small gasp and tensed her bony shoulders. "By the Light! I have been such a fool, such a hopeful, hopeless fool. Oh, Tetric, Tetric. You were always brilliant, *Ëi biraen*. I never understood just how much."

He leaned forward. "Eshe—"

"Primus Magne. You seek to become Primus Magne." The seer laughed again. "Why do you need the words of an old foolish woman when you hold the steward's daughter hostage?"

"Hostage?" Mirana glanced between Tetric and Eshe. Why did people insist on speaking about her as if she were not in the room? "I am no hostage."

"I am protecting the girl," he seethed. "There are many who try to kill her."

"Not unless the Dark Trine ordered it so." The seer then turned her opaque eyes back toward Mirana. "What are you doing with him, child?"

From the corner of her eye, she saw Tetric's hands tighten on the arms of the chair, his knuckles turning white. "I...needed him."

Eshe sank back against the pillows, the sallow skin of her brows pulling together in confusion. "And now?"

Mirana shifted her gaze to her own hands. Scars still lined her palms. "He has taught me so much, but...relationships...change over time, don't they?"

Tetric leaned closer to Eshe. "There was no Trine to train me. No one who understood the burden of bearing all three Aspects. That should make sense to you of all people."

"Old wounds still bleed in us both," Eshe replied, clipping each word.

He shook his head, his eyes cast downward. "Can't we leave those wounds in the past? I have."

The old seer stabbed a gnarled finger at him. "No, you have not. Far from it." She shifted her sightless face to Mirana. "Has he not told you to be wary of me? Pulled you further from your own better judgment?"

Ai. He had. But she allowed herself to be pulled. She would never let him—let anyone!—be her conscience again. Her decisions would be her own, right and wrong, and she would accept the consequences.

"Do you need to see the mark I still bear, Eshe?" The Trine pulled his shirt away from his left clavicle to reveal a long scar.

The lines in the old seer's face smoothed into a far more menacing expression. "I cannot. I cannot see anything ever again."

Mirana tensed. If the old woman had been a defender, she would have expected fire from her amulet. She needed to find the province's clue to Jasal's Keep and leave before the Trine and the seer prime could come to blows.

"Tetric, we've been away from Deren for months and we still have sevendays of journeying ahead of us. We no longer have time for guessing games. We need Prime Eshe's help. Not in Quorum, but now."

… *What are you doing?* … he called, forcing his mind into hers.

She refused to be a thief any longer. "Prime Eshe, I seek an artifact of my ancestor Jasal Pinal. Writing from his Codex. It is important to Kinderra. And to me."

… *Mirana!* … He crossed over to her and gripped her shoulder, painfully digging his fingers in the hollow above her collarbone. The full weight of his presence pressed down on her. … *What have you done, you little fool?* …

The blind woman's opaque gaze bored into her. "I know of no such artifact within the learning hall. You seek far more than Jasal Pinal's relic, however. You have questions in your heart you dare not dwell upon. I once held those same questions. I now have answers, but they've come to me too late. There is still time for you. Do not make the same mistakes I have, Mirana."

"What are you getting at, woman?" Tetric's voice turned to steel.

Eshe curled her small, bony hands into fists, the blue lines of veins rising against the thin, sallow skin. "I now know your journey as well, my son." … *But I would have her as my master, not my servant* …

Mirana pulled herself from the Trine's grip. "I am your servant. I am a Trine, the servant of everyone in Kinderra. It has taken me too many summers to understand that." She reached for the old woman's hand again. "I have no more time to lose. We have to find Jasal Pinal's journal excerpt, my prime."

"Mirana—"

She ignored him. "I would like to search your hall."

Tetric dragged her to her feet. "I have spoken my piece, my prime. I hope you change your mind. For Kinderra's sake. And yours."

Eshe touched the amulet at her chest, pale and blue like her unseeing eyes. "Has he not already showed you how to use a power that is not your own? I see it has already left its mark upon your heart. You will never heal from those wounds. They will bleed in you for the rest of your life. Daughter of Pinal, I know you would sooner die than pay allegiance to the Dark One. You will not find your way with this man. Leave him."

He shoved Mirana from him and leaned close to the seer woman. "I once called you 'mother.' The only mother I ever knew. I pleaded with both you and your husband Lindar to understand I was using the Power from Without to help Kinderra, not to hurt her. You didn't believe me. You thought I had made some adolescent mistake and didn't understand what I had gotten myself into. And Lindar? He wanted to kill me! Please don't abandon me again. I need you, Eshe. Only a Trine will be able to stop the war between the Fal'kin and the Ken'nar. I know you have seen that."

"Tetric," Mirana interjected, "let's leave Prime Eshe to rest."

The prime nodded, ignoring her. "*Ai*, but that Trine is not to be you, *Ëi biraen*."

Mirana gritted her teeth at the seer's words. If Tetric's only solution to restore peace on the continent was the Power from Without, she would have to find some way of changing his mind.

Or fight to stop him.

She shook her head, dismissing the thought. She had enough peril on her plate, she didn't need to heap on more.

The tall Trine straightened and glowered down at the old woman. "You betray me again."

"Betray you? I did everything I could to help you. I always knew you had a magnificent place in Kinderra," Eshe replied. "I didn't realize it until you came here with the girl now. Until I could see her for what she truly is—and you. What a fool I've been. I did not want to believe what that magnificent place was."

"Because of your hate," he snarled.

"No, son. Because of my love for you." The old seer shrank farther into the bed. "I blinded my own heart as surely as you did my mortal eyes."

Mirana pulled at Tetric's sleeve. "Let's just leave—*what?*" Her hand fell from his shirt.

Tetric dropped to his knees beside the prime's bed. "Eshe. Please. Don't."

"No, Tetric Garis, I will not support you. I supported you once, long ago. And you repaid me by murdering my husband."

"He *what?*" Mirana whipped her head around to stare at the Trine. "Is that true?"

Eshe reached for her hand, creating an indelible connection to her mind. … *Vide verdas e ísi ad pacem en Oëa u'ben … As Ëo ísi …*

"You dare try to take her from me?" he growled, a deep, feral tone she had not heard from him before. "I will *not* let that happen."

A flash of violent intent was all the warning Mirana had. Tetric grabbed her by the throat with one hand and gripped his fingers across the old woman's temples with the other.

Mirana gasped and clawed at the Trine's hand as he bled her powers away. "Tetric! Stop!" she choked, but he clamped his fingers around her neck like a vice.

Eshe Pashcot writhed in pain, bringing her hands up to her head.

He dragged Mirana closer. ... *Damn you, girl ... Do not fight me* ... His hematite amulet began to scintillate, a shadowed silver luster.

She cried out in pain, no longer seeing the room as the inexorable pull of the Trine's power enveloped her. ... *Tetric, stop!* ...

The shrieking notes of the old woman's torture overwhelmed her. The Healing Aspect billowed within her, focused through the Trine's amulet burning against her palm. And into Eshe's heart.

He drove her deeper into communion with the Healing Aspect, trailing the tormented music of the prime's pain. His powers surrounded hers, at once following her and pushing her.

Eshe's pale-blue topaz erupted in light. An abrupt shift in awareness assaulted Mirana. The old prime's Seeing Aspect knifed through her mind, cutting her off from the Healing Aspect.

A field. Grasses wave high above the ocean in a freshening breeze. A tall, handsome, dark-haired youth sits astride a roan stallion. His lanky body wears the blue-and-white capricorn heraldic of Rün-Taran. The small group of fighters he leads clashes with a larger unit, an older Fal'kin defender at their vanguard, swords capped to prevent serious injuries. A regal woman, a seer, observes the sparring. The youth, hardly more than a boy, neatly blocks the older man's blade with a long sword. They fight. The youth rears his horse and makes a wide, sweeping motion. The older man falls from his saddle, landing on the ground, hard. The dark-haired boy holds the tip of his blade at the defender's neck.

He laughs then sheaths the sword. He reaches down to help the man to his feet. The defender grasps the youth's hand and pulls the boy from his saddle. As he falls, the defender grabs something from his waist. The boy cries out and twists away, his face contorting in pain and rage. He grips his amulet. The defender clutches his chest. He collapses to the ground again and lays still. The dark-haired boy backs away in disbelief. Red blooms from the hollow of his left collarbone.

The seer woman screams. The air around the youth becomes alive with a hail of arrows, but the boy does not move. He ignores the feint. He turns to face the woman. This time, he releases silvery black fire from his amulet. The woman claws at her eyes, shrieking in agony. Fighters from both groups recoil from the youth. Tears make clean tracks down the boy's dirty face. He swings back up into his saddle and charges away.

"I will not let you take her from me!" Tetric cried. His powers exploded through Mirana, tearing her Aspects from her. Her knees buckled. She fell, screaming in agony.

Eshe gave a long wail of torment, then lay still. Her life's music ceased. A deafening, sickening silence now pervaded the Aspects.

The prime's chambers snapped back before Mirana's mortal eyes. Her body shook as she gasped for breath. She stared at Tetric in horror. "What in the name of the Aspects did you do?"

He knelt and pulled her to him, embracing her fiercely. "She tried to kill you. I will never let anyone take you from me." He sat back and held her face in his hands. "You are my Trine. My child. Given to me from the Aspects Above. A father will do anything to protect his child. Anything."

She pushed him away. "Y-You killed her. You used me. Used my Healing Aspect. To kill her."

The door to the seer prime's chamber flew open and banged against the wall.

"Eshe!" Syne Develan dashed into the room.

The old defender released fiery orange flame from his amulet so close to them, Mirana felt its heat. Amulet fire slammed into the wall behind them as Tetric whirled them both out of the way.

... Run, Mirana ... Find the keep writing ... I'll draw them off ... the Trine called.

Tetric Garis had used her as a Ken'nar weapon to kill. Her Aspects had been ripped from her to feed his ruthless fury. He'd killed Eshe Pashcot. With her. Through her.

"Go!" He drew his blade. "I will find you. Go."

Syne rushed him with a drawn sword, but the Trine was quicker. In one smooth movement, he surged to his feet and blocked the old man's blade with his long sword. "Your life is forfeit, Defender." He grabbed the defender's amulet.

"No!" Mirana rammed her shoulder into Tetric's side. As the three fell, a jet of orange light enveloped the old defender. A citrine amulet lay in a pile of smoldering ash on the slate tiles.

She trembled with horror and rage and crushing disbelief. Tetric Garis had just murdered Syne Devlan with the defender's own amulet. "What have you—?"

"*Biraena*, my child, please." His desperation flooded her mind. "She would have taken you from me. They both would have. I had to. To save your life. To save Kinderra. You must understand."

Alarmed voices from the hall's Fal'kin resounded through the corridors, their calls reverberating in her mind.

Tetric jumped to his feet, long sword in hand, and motioned her quickly to the door. "I will hold them off and cover our escape. I will find you. Go!"

It was lies. All of it.

She would find Run-Taran's verse to Jasal's keep treatise—if only to make sure her mentor did not.

Mirana turned and ran as the stifling, silent cry of death echoed within her Aspects.

CHAPTER 28

"Ah, Beloved. My beloved's call is like the beckoning of the spring breeze, beseeching me to idle awhile longer. Such is the daughter of Tash-Hamar to me. Ëi ama."

—The Codex of Jasal the Great

Mirana wrapped herself tightly with the reflections of U'Nehíl as she ran through the Rün-Taran learning hall. She could not think, she could not breathe. Tetric Garis had killed Eshe Pashcot. Tetric Garis had killed Syne Develan. With the Power from Without. With the Healing Aspect. Hers.

She tore down a hallway, threw a door open with the Aspects, and dashed outside. She ducked behind a thick stone pillar as several defenders rushed by. She closed her eyes and rested her forehead against the cool stone.

She had to find the keep stanza given to Rün-Taran before Tetric did. If it fell into his hands, no one in Kinderra would be safe. She could not think about that now. She forced her mind away from what she had just witnessed, from the truth spreading like a disease within her.

Where could the writings possibly be? She bit her lip and looked around quickly. This part of the hall appeared deserted. It wouldn't be for long as word of Eshe's and Syne's murders spread.

The Rün-Tarani surged up the road on warhorses, heading north. Tetric had said he would lead them away from the hall to give her time to find the next clue.

He'd used her. Like a Ken'nar.

Mirana shook the thought away again. "Focus! Think!" The eastern sky was pale and featureless with a veil of lingering, thin clouds. A slash of blue on the horizon, the hope of breaking weather, melted with the sea. The sun cast a strange, flat light around her. It reminded her uncomfortably of Prime Eshe's eyes.

No. Later.

Running around the learning hall blindly would not help. She took a breath and forced herself to calm down. "Think."

Studying the histories in the Book of Kinderra had been one of her favorite subjects as a *scholaira*. Who would have thought her lessons would have such dire purposes? A small footnote buried in the tome mentioned Jasal Pinal's wife Antiri had traveled east from Kin-Deren after his death. The seer would have had little choice but to leave the province with their infant son, hiding Jasal's heir from the Ken'nar swearing vengeance for the death of Ilrik the Black and the growing hatred of the Fal'kin. Rün-Taran had long been a staunch ally of

Kin-Deren, and its prime in that day had been a close friend of Jasal's.

Mirana frowned. That was all well and good. She already knew there was a verse here, somewhere. If Rün-Taran was the only province that would accept Antiri, maybe she had died here. The cemetery? If Antiri was here, the verse would be with her.

She sped down a staircase of broken stones that led to the burial grounds. The wrought iron gate at the cemetery's entrance creaked as she opened it. The stairs had been carved into the side of the cliff face and reminded her painfully of Deven's Stair in the dreaded Vale i'Dúadar.

She paused and hissed. "Gate."

She turned and, with a raised hand, wrapped the iron portal with an intent of movement and closed it. She gritted her teeth at the metal's groaning and continued down.

The stairs leveled off onto a small plateau crowded with grave markers, crypts, statues, and mausoleums. Several caves yawned deep into the cliff holding other dead. High above her, more shouts rang out. She had to hide before she was seen.

In the center of the burial ground stood a large, ornately carved marble mausoleum. Bas-reliefs of rampant leopards flanked the door. Leopards? Leopards. Mirana smiled. Tash-Hamar.

She hurried to the crypt. And groaned. A chain locked the heavy iron door. She bit her lip. Would the delicate mica sheets of Teague's pendant be strong enough to hold her Aspects? The shouting above grew closer. They would have to be.

She slipped the pendant over her head and called to her Defending Aspect. She sent a thin finger of amulet fire at the links, holding back the power that wanted to rush from her. A sharp pain stabbed through her chest as thin lines began to transect the mica. She clenched her jaw. The pendant had to hold a moment longer. Tiny cracks in the mica grew, and with them, her pain. The gate chain turned red. It would have to be enough. The delicate, imperfectly perfect pendant could not hold her Aspects, forcing her to stop. She breathed hard from pain and exertion, and shoved her shoulder against the iron door. The chain broke free. She slid inside and brought the chains in with her so they would not be noticed, hissing as the hot metal burned her fingers. Unless, of course, the Rün-Tarani noticed the chains were missing altogether.

Voices and footsteps neared. She pulled the door closed behind her and guarded herself under U'Nehíl. Presences grew close. Footsteps paused. She dare not even breathe as she mimicked the life forces around her to camouflage her presence. Voices shouted again but farther away now.

Her shoulders fell as she exhaled in relief. The mausoleum stank of decay and death, as if the very air itself was a corpse. Maybe it was too soon to feel relieved.

"I don't like this," she whispered, tensing again. Why was she whispering? Anybody here was dead. Hopefully.

The tomb was much larger than it appeared from the cemetery. It glowed with a strange, blue-green light from some unseen source. The light cast eerie shadows on the walls, magnifying in dark contrast the angles of the vaults in the ceiling. Rats scurried, fleeing from her. Spiders crept higher into their webs, crawling away from her intrusion.

"Oh, I really don't like this." There was more to fear in this place than rats and spiders. It was not a living presence she felt, but a definite sense of unhappiness maybe? No, it was more than that. Much more. The sense of the place resounded with profound, all-encompassing sorrow. It carried a weight all its own.

A staircase led down to a dais. In the center of the tomb lay a sarcophagus. Carved into the lid was the relief of a beautiful woman in repose. Antiri. It had to be.

Mirana hesitated before climbing down the stairs. It probably wasn't the wise move to go charging in and set off some protection. Her shoulder blades twitched at the memory of the swords guarding Defender Prime Fasen Aldi's mosaic.

A glint emerged from the strange ambient light. She descended the steps, searching each one for a sudden and painful reason why she wouldn't make it to the next stair. When she reached the tomb, she paused again. No imminent danger called beyond the overwhelming sadness around her. She peered closer at some glyphs etched into the tomb's marble.

"*'Hac pone Antiri il'Amil, ama i'Jasal il'Pinal, nomé Ain Magne.'* Here lies Antiri Amil, beloved of Jasal Pinal, called the Great One."

She inhaled sharply. The dates of reckoning. Antiri had not even seen forty summers when she died. Now she knew why there was such sorrow in this place. Antiri Amil Pinal had died too young, of a broken heart. But was it for the love of Jasal? Or his shattering betrayal?

"You risked your life for your son and to ensure that Jasal's Keep would remain safe until its secrets could be known again to save Kinderra." ... *I swear to you, Antiri, I will not let Jasal's Keep fall to the Dark Trine ... I swear it with my life ...*

She read the epithet again. Beloved of Jasal Pinal. If Jasal had become a power-hungry tyrant, consumed and corrupted by the Power from Without, would Antiri, or whoever carved the inscription, referred to her as such? This place of utter desolation gave her more hope than she had felt since Tetric saved her life in the library—

No. Later. Kinderra depended on her.

Antiri's likeness was exquisite. Mirana's ancestress was apparently a breathtakingly beautiful woman. The sculpture was extraordinarily detailed, including the relief of an amulet, each link in the chain individually carved. The carving sparkled.

She scowled. The stone depicting the amulet's crystal was discolored, as if it were not made of the same material. "Antiri, forgive me." She scrambled on top of the sarcophagus.

The ocean air must have found its way into the tomb and corroded the marble. One small area had flaked clean. It winked as she picked at the crust with a fingernail. A crystal. It was the source of the light in the tomb. She gasped. It was Antiri's amulet. Not just a carving. Her real amulet.

Mirana took out her belt knife and pried the amulet loose, reverently lifting it from the sculpture. She scraped at the crystal, peeling off the remaining flakes of plaster.

"Why would they have covered it? To hide it from grave robbers?" Like her. She swallowed.

A noise rumbled throughout the mausoleum, stone grating on stone. "That can't be good." She remained perfectly still.

A deep vibration rattled up from the tomb's base. The crypt and the dais on which it sat began to sink deeper into the earth. She crouched down, unsure of whether she should jump off or follow the sarcophagus down. Maybe the keep stanza was buried?

She swallowed back her fear and held on to the sarcophagus as it descended. When it came to rest at the bottom of a deep shaft, she peered into the gloom. She saw nothing in the darkness, but she sensed the area had widened considerably. The grave opening yawned some twenty feet above her. It would be a difficult jump, regardless of her Aspects.

The sound of grinding stone broke the stillness. A slab rolled over the opening and sealed it off.

"No!"

There might be no way to get back out. Dread rammed its way into her brain. "Think, think, think."

Whoever built all of this must have had a way back out. Unless they did not leave.

Mirana peered farther into the blackness. "Where am I?"

She had made enough noise for anything down in the cavern to know where she was. She still breathed and all her limbs remained attached, so maybe she was alone. She stood motionless and reached out with ordinary senses and Aspects alike. She detected no other living thing. Was that a good sign or a bad one?

She smelled moisture and listened. Water lapped, like that of a pond or lake, not dripped as she expected in a cave.

Antiri's amulet, its facets twinkling, brought her attention back to the gemstone. Its shape was odd, a bit jagged on one side, not a neat oval like most amulet crystals currently worn.

She sucked in her breath again as blue-green light from Antiri's aquamarine gem erupted at her touch. A sensation, cool and soothing, wrapped around her, calling to her Aspects. Her powers surged. The amulet invited her to dwell within it as her Aspects bade the crystal to abide with her. Mirana pulled back her hand, hesitating. The last time she'd touched an amulet, an innocent man had died. No, Tarq hadn't died from Tetric's amulet, not truly—he'd died from her choice to use the Power from Without.

"Never again."

She slipped Antiri's amulet over her head and cupped it in her hands. When she called to her Defending Aspect, a beam of bright light shot out from the gem's deep blue-green depths and washed over the surface of a large subterranean lake. The light beam continued under the water's surface like the tail of a shooting star.

In the eerie aquamarine light, she could see twigs littered the cavern floor. Driftwood? No, they were white.

"Oh, Light Above."

They were bones.

Skeletons lay near the water's edge, their legs missing.

She cast out her senses, but again, detected nothing. She walked to the water's edge and grimaced at the cold water when she waded in farther. Nothing bit her in two. So far, so good. The light beam blazing from the crystal at her chest continued to a point below the water's surface.

"Aspects Above, protect me." She took a deep breath and plunged into the lake.

She swam down and followed the blue-green light, ignoring the tantalizing ruins of submerged graves and artifacts.

When she reached the bottom of the lake, she floated in front of the crumbling wall of an ancient edifice. Molded into the stone were bronze reliefs of capricorns, fish, and other sea creatures. A mosaic of a man dressed in white stood four times her height. She swam back a bit to see it all. The man battled a dark-armored warrior. Behind them, a tower blazed with snake-like tendrils arching from its pinnacle to strike the chests of other black-garbed fighters. The eyes of the man in white were inlaid with silver. Jasal Pinal.

Mirana swam back up to the surface, inhaled a lungful of air, then dove back down to the mosaic. Jasal's clue had to be here somewhere. But where?

The beam illuminated an area on Jasal Pinal's tiled chest. Another blue-green gem. That wasn't right. If the artisans knew Jasal's eyes were silver, they certainly knew his amulet was a diamond, not an aquamarine.

A presence brushed her mind. Fortunately, it wasn't Tetric. Unfortunately, it wasn't human. She whirled around, treading water, and waited for the bubbles to dissolve. Nothing moved in the aquatic ruins.

Mirana swam closer to the tiled picture. As she did so, both the gem in her amulet and the gem in the mosaic grew brighter. The crystal embedded in the wall. Could it be a shard of Antiri's amulet? It must be; that's why the amulet Mirana wore now was smaller than was typical of such gems. She touched the crystal. She felt the presence again, stronger this time. It was close. She smiled and covered the crystal in the mosaic with her palm. It was Jasal.

As within his Codex, she sensed a shadow of her ancestor's doubt. Here, he was fearful, angry, yet determined. Another portion of the keep treatise must be hidden behind the gem. She took out her belt knife and drew its tip around the edge of the embedded crystal. As if drawn to its mate about her neck, the aquamarine shard came loose to reveal an opening the width of her arm. She placed the gem fragment inside her shirt.

The Defending Aspect whispered a warning to her. Out of the corner of her eye, she caught a shimmer in the watery gloom, but when she turned, she saw nothing other than capricorn statues and eroding walls. She scowled. Jasal's writings did not hold his living presence, just a reflection of his emotions. What she felt was alive.

A little school of fish darted past her face. She batted at them in annoyance. Living presence. Obviously. Sea creatures surrounded her.

Mirana turned back to the opening in the mosaic wall. There was something very wrong about sticking her hand into a crevice protected by the Aspects that had lain underwater undisturbed for centuries, but she was running out of air and did not want to leave the spot.

Again, she glimpsed a whirl of coppery-green in the shadows of the submerged ruins. The Defending Aspect now called openly to her. She caught a flash of the scaled tail of some fish. Some enormous fish. She had seen enough.

No, she had not.

In a whirl of bronzed green and foam, a creature rammed her in the ribs, forcing the air out of her lungs. Her terrified face stared back at her, reflected in the slit-pupil eyes of a massive sea monster.

Mirana screamed out the rest of her air.

This was no mythical sea creature guarding Jasal's clue. This was a living nightmare. Suddenly, the spring-loaded sword protection from Tash-Hamar seemed tame by comparison. The lethal, curved horns on either side of its head, each as thick as her body, were the only feature that could have been misconstrued as belonging to the fabled sea-ram capricorn. Its long, sinuous body coiled like a serpent's, ending in powerful fins. Its forelegs curled into claws, each capable of ripping her open. Its demonic yellow eyes furrowed at her in hatred. Pointed teeth filled the creature's mouth. And it showed every one of them to her.

Just beyond the guardian, the crevice with the watchtower clue beckoned. But how to get past the beast and retrieve it? Maybe if she swam away slowly, it would leave her alone. She could hide, making the creature believe she had left, and grab whatever was in the opening. Which, hopefully, was not another finned and fanged friend. With small backstrokes, she moved farther from the sea serpent. It gave off an unearthly cry and whipped its enormous tail around. It struck her full on her side again and slammed her into the mosaic wall. A crack throbbed and burned through her side.

The guardian came at her again, ready to crush her with its great horned head. She twisted and swam away, pushing away the pain of her broken ribs, as it hit the wall with a thundering boom. Chunks of stone bricks fell from the ruin. Dazed, it hesitated.

She darted back to the fissure in the wall. Screwing up her face in an anticipatory wince, she reached in and touched what felt like a cylinder. She pulled it out of the crevice and kicked hard for the surface.

Her head broke the water, and she gulped a breath. Her inhale turned into a scream of pain when the creature's jaws clamped vice-like on her ankle and dragged her below the water.

The capricorn pulled Mirana back down to the ruins, swimming with powerful lashes of its tail. It shook her by the ankle, a horned, serpentine cat toying with a mouse. Agony spread up her leg. She drew a long knife and sunk it deep into the creature's snout. It let go with an inhuman cry and pawed at its face.

Excruciating pain flared in her ankle and a deep burning radiated in her side. Her lungs were starved for breath. She reached deeper for the Healing Aspect. The sea monster swam much too fast to outrace it to the surface. She swam behind a pillar, searching for another way out or at least a pocket of air.

Debris stirred up from her fight with the sea serpent flowed past her. The current tugged at her hair. The sea. Water from in the cavern must be flowing out the sea. Which meant the current led out into open water.

She swam with the current, each stroke bringing fresh torture. The capricorn glared at her with maddened, venomous fury. With a sweep of its tail, it took off after her.

Mirana followed the current flow of water into a channel. Her Defending Aspect screamed out a warning. The guardian swam a heartbeat behind her. The pain in her ankle and her side seeped through her body. The noise of their wrongness sounded through her mind, her Healing Aspect.

The channel led upward. She prayed it led to the water's surface and not some lair with the rest of the sea monster's family. The foam from the capricorn's breath broke around her legs. She would not make it unless she acted. Tetric had said her Light from Within alone would never be strong enough to save lives.

He was wrong.

She flipped around and reached deep within herself. Blue-green fire shot from Antiri's amulet to strike the capricorn's horned head. It gave an earsplitting roar and flailed in pain. Black ichor smoked the water. She wrapped the Defending Aspect around her and dug through the water with powerful strokes.

Her body burned from swimming without air, her limbs becoming too heavy to move. The shrieking discord from her wounds tried to drown out even her Defending Aspect. She was failing. Tetric was right.

No. She would make herself strong enough.

At last, she broke through to the surface inside another cave and gasped for air. The cavern lay at sea level, its wide mouth opening to the ocean. Pain raked through her starved lungs. The agony from her wounds would slow her escape. No. Pain was just a warning. Once felt, it was to be ignored.

Another alarm from the Defending Aspect shot through her. She kicked hard with her uninjured foot, her boot striking the capricorn's head. She pushed against the beast's horns to launch herself farther away.

Rejuvenated by the air, she shunted away her pain and made for the cave's mouth and safety. The capricorn once again clamped its razor fangs on her already wounded ankle, the scent of blood in the water fueling its bloodlust.

Mirana screamed, her voice ringing in the cave. She twisted over and kicking at the beast with her other boot. She unleashed blazing blue-green light from the amulet, pouring her Aspects through the crystal. Amulet fire hammered into the capricorn. The sea serpent let go of her with a howl of pain and terror. It shook off the blow and started towards her again.

She dove back under the surface and swam for the cave entrance. The guardian outpaced her, despite its injuries, to block the opening of the cavern. It lunged at her. She whirled away from its bite, its fangs missing her by a finger's breadth, but its teeth clamped on the amulet's chain. It crushed the links as easily as it would have crushed her bones. It tore the amulet from her neck, and the crystal sank into the depths.

The horror stared at her, eye to eye. Just because an opponent did not hold a weapon did not mean he was unarmed. Especially one who was Aspected. She stroked up to the surface and thrust out a hand. The creature flew back into the cave with a thrust from her Defending Aspect. Just like throwing a wine cup. A huge, angry, fanged wine cup.

Mirana sensed the sea monster marshaling its strength to lunge at her again. She bit back the pain of the salty water stinging like acid on her ruined ankle. The skin on her chest now burned. Had the thing poisoned her? Another tug at her Aspects.

The aquamarine shard from the mosaic.

She dug into her shirt and gripped the gem fragment from Antiri's amulet in her fist. She swam for the cave opening, ignoring the muscles pulling at her broken ribs.

Mirana screamed in pain as her vision tunneled to red. She drew on the Healing Aspect, reviving herself. The beast raced behind her, gaining. This time, she was ready. She pushed away her pain again and let the Defending Aspect swell within her.

Once she was clear of the cave, she backstroked and lifted the crystal shard above the water. She opened herself to the fragment of Antiri's amulet, exhilaration and connectedness again giving her the strength to fight. Blue-green lightning exploded as she willed her Defending Aspect out through the gem to pound at the mouth of the cave. Boulders fell away from the rock walls and crashed into the sea below. She poured still more of herself into her Aspects. She cried out in triumph and pain, the crystal burning into her palm. The capricorn bellowed in primal rage as the cave collapsed.

Waves from the crumbling rock washed over her and dragged her under, knocking the gem shard from her grip. It sank away. She tried to call it back to her grasp, but the agonized music of her wounds stormed through her, stealing her hold on the Aspects. The screeching disharmony of her injuries enveloped her. She screamed, inhaling water.

No. She would not give in to the pain. She would not give in to death. She had to swim to shore. She must. She must survive to unlock the secrets to Jasal's Keep. She could trust no one else now but herself.

Mirana forced her body to swim upward and gasped as her head broke the surface. The shore was only a few hundred yards away. It might as well have been a thousand miles. If she died, the secrets of the keep would die with her. No one would ever know the truth about Jasal's Keep. No one would know the truth about Tetric Garis.

She set her jaw and plied the waves as best she could, kicking with only one leg. The muscles in her side pulled brutally at her fractured ribs. Her limbs grew cold and heavy. She pulled deeper within herself, straining for the Defending Aspect. Her body refused its touch. She reached for her Healing Aspect. It, too, slipped from her grasp. The sound of the ocean's swells grew muffled as she slipped below its surface.

Mirana screamed in pain and determination, and poured all three of her Aspects out through Teague's frail pendant, still draped over her neck. She dug through the water with powerful strokes and swam for the shore.

Her knee scraped rough sand. A wave nudged her onto the thin, rocky beach at the foot of cliffs. Her savaged ankle made her whole leg pound in agony with each heartbeat. She bled from the wound, badly, a leaving sensation. Every breath made her side burn with a knifing pain. Her vision tunneled again, turning from red to black.

Darkness overcame her.

CHAPTER 29

"I am not a brave man, Beloved. If I die at the hands of the Ken'nar, it is not for honor nor ideals nor province. I die for thee."

—The Codex of Jasal the Great

The midnight constellations winked overhead when Teague returned to the learning hall in Edara from scouring the surrounding plateaus for medicinal herbs and other materials that would aid in healing or feed those that would remain at the hall when the Ken'nar attack came. Seventhmonth had arrived, and with it, the scorching heat of full summer, making foraging hard and finding supplies even harder.

A few months ago, he wanted nothing more than to leave behind the Fal'kin and the Unaspected of Varn-Erdal to begin his quest of vengeance on the Dark Trine. That was before he had known how much the Varn-Erdalans had suffered from Ken'nar attacks. The herbsfolk's apothecary barely had enough supplies to tend to a paper cut.

Illenne had asked him to find gallas leaves to sustain milk production in newly foaled mares. It would be a long time after they evacuated the city before the horses returned to their home pastures and longer still before the grass became rich again. When had it rained last? He didn't have the heart to tell her that the heat had all but withered the gallas leaves to dust. He had searched anyway. And her smile made the request difficult to refuse.

No, he would bide his time in dealing with the Ken'nar warlord until the Varn-Erdalans had a fully stocked apothecary and Ille had what she needed for her horses. And then—he twisted his mouth into a snarling smile.

He spied Morgan in the courtyard. Perfect timing.

Morgan sat on one of the wood benches under the covered portico, his back against the wall. The defender looked like he had fallen asleep sitting up. A bow and a quiver of arrows lay on the ground next to his scabbard.

A bow? Teague sank next to him on the bench. Weren't he and Liaonne teaching the seers how to use long knives?

"We are," the defender commander replied, his eyes remaining closed. "Some are finding the knives difficult."

"Bows aren't much easier."

"No, but they can fight from a distance with them."

Teague nodded. Bow and arrow? Would they suit his purpose better than a sword? He frowned. Too easy to deflect.

But more to the problem at hand, if they didn't have at least some seers who could fight, it wouldn't matter if they could call the battle or not. They wouldn't be around long enough to do so. That brought another question to his mind. He didn't want to know the answer, but morbid curiosity compelled him to ask.

"Why haven't the Ken'nar attacked already? It's been months since the battle at Two Rivers Ford. The cleaved defenders have ridden patrol every day since we arrived, but they have seen no trace of them."

"I don't know, but I, for one, am immensely grateful they have not." The defender inhaled deeply and stretched.

"They took more than a few losses, too, though."

"*Ai.*" The Fal'kin rubbed his eyes.

Teague scratched the stubble on his chin. Well, *a stubble* on his chin. "Maybe more than we thought."

"Perhaps."

He frowned at the defender's comment. It wasn't very reassuring. Maybe Morgan was just plain tired.

By the light of a dozen torches, Liaonne continued to train several seers in the courtyard. She took a glancing blow on the back of her hand and Teague winced in consolation. Her sparring partner, a youth barely out of boyhood, burst into tears at the accident. She sent him to rest.

Teague glanced at his own hand. He probably would have made the same mistake. Which reminded him.

"Um, Morgan? Listen, since so many will be leaving Edara, there won't be a lot of folks here to defend it. I wonder if we could discuss again—"

"No."

"You don't even know what I was going to—" He sighed. The Fal'kin obviously *did* know what he was going to ask. He'd let it go for now.

Teague slid off the bench to sit on the ground, relinquishing his seat to the young prime. She dropped onto the empty space and squeezed his shoulder in thanks.

"That must have hurt," Morgan said.

She sucked at the cut a moment. "It was my fault. I wasn't expecting such a good thrust. Her voice was husky with fatigue. "It's the best he's done so far. I'm hoping he'll be at least as good as his mother. How is your group doing?"

"About as well as yours."

Illenne entered the courtyard carrying a large jug of water. Teague smiled at her in greeting. Her hips swung as she walked, compensating for the weight of the heavy pitcher.

"Teague, I know you were hoping to locate more bloodsbane up to the north. Did you find any?" Liaonne asked.

Ille didn't wear skirts like so many of the girls in Deren did. The buckskin of her leggings fit her as closely as the deer the material came from. Her linen shirt hung loosely around her torso, though, only hinting at what was underneath. Leggings looked better on girls than skirts. Definitely.

Morgan reached behind the defender woman to tap him on the shoulder. "The prime asked you a question."

He shook himself. "*Ai*, of course. Uh. What?"

She frowned. "Bloodsbane. Did you find any?"

"No, but I will keep looking." He jumped to his feet and took the jug from Illenne as the washwoman followed with a platter of food. He had learned her name was Marienne. He had apologized to her for his rude behavior in the armory, but his insides squirmed every time he saw her. "I thought you left today with your father?" he asked Illenne.

"There was still so much to do." She took earthenware cups from Marienne's tray and handed them to the Fal'kin.

He poured water from the pitcher. "You can't stay."

"I have lived without a mother for a long time. I do not need one now."

"These people are starving, Illenne. Help me serve them," Marienne said as she set the tray on the bench between the defenders. "You have forgotten to eat again, haven't you, my prime? And you've been on your feet all day, Defender Commander Jord. I also know you keep watch all night. Even a Fal'kin needs to rest. Here, eat, both of you." She handed them some bread and cheese, and sliced small portions of dried beef while Illenne took the jug back from Teague and poured water into the cups.

"You should not still be here, either, Marienne," Liaonne said. "Eran will be leaving with the last of the horses soon."

The washwoman paused in dishing out the food. "I wish you would let me stay. You will need help."

The prime smiled. "*Ai*, I will, but you have done enough. You bore us six Fal'kin who all gave their lives so that the rest of us could still be here to defend Varn-Erdal now. Few Unaspected in Kinderra have sacrificed as much. You must leave tomorrow with the others."

Marienne nodded once. "*Ai*, of course, my lady."

"And I expect you back as soon as this conflict is over," the prime added. "I will most certainly need your help then." The washwoman smiled and bowed, and returned to the kitchens.

Teague watched the woman leave, her stride confident. Grief no longer held her, or at least she was good at hiding it.

"Marienne was Trein Carada's woman," Liaonne replied. "She and Trein had six children, defenders all. Trein never joined in union with her because he also had three children with Grenne Fadern, my seer second." She jutted her chin toward the courtyard, indicating the boy who had sparred with her. He watched the young seer enter the hall. Come to think of it, the boy did look like Grenne. "He did that out of respect to Grenne, but everyone knew Marienne was his woman." Her expression grew somber. "Grenne's eldest son also died at the hands of the Ken'nar. Her other two are young. The boy is fourteen, her daughter is just four summers. Grenne is no stranger to sacrifice, either."

That certainly explained the dour seer woman's bitterness. Was anyone's family whole? She still had two children, though. Marienne had buried all six of hers. He gritted his teeth, not wanting to imagine the magnitude of that kind of grief. He had enough of his own.

He took a piece of dried beef and tore a thin strip from the slice. He tugged so hard for a morsel from the jerky, his hand hit his face with the recoil. He glanced around quickly, and thankfully his dining companions were otherwise occupied. Illenne, however, made a noise sounding for all the world like a stifled laugh. She caught his gaze. Her face remained serious, although laughter danced in her soft, brown eyes.

Drei Carada, the young defender Illenne had promised herself to, must have been a relation to Trein Carada.

Teague's father had all but forbade him to see Mirana. Well, his parents were gone and so was Mirana. Wishing, hell, *praying* for things that could never be only made those things more painful to dwell upon.

He shoved another bite of beef into his mouth and put all his concentration into chewing. The soles of his boots were probably more tender than the jerked meat. They probably tasted better, too.

Liaonne sliced off a sliver of cheese from the wedge. "Drei was Trein's and Marienne's son. Their youngest. That is a loss that still hurts us. As much as losing his father." She leaned back against the wall. "As much as losing them all." She studied the cheese for a moment before putting it in her mouth.

Illenne toyed with a piece of bread but did not eat nor sit. Ille.

Teague rubbed his face. By the Light, why couldn't he hide his damn thoughts? Why couldn't he just hide, period? Why did the prime choose *that* thought to answer? If he had just kept his mouth shut, he could have avoided bringing up the whole conversation altogether.

"Illenne, why don't you sit?" he offered. "I'm beat. I'm sure you are, too." She nodded absently but remained standing. He set his food down, rose to his feet, and stepped closer to her. "I'm sorry."

She furrowed her brow. "For what?"

"For bringing up Drei."

"He was a Fal'kin. We always knew he could be killed. I accepted that." She sighed. It sounded more like determination than grief. "But thank you for your apology anyway."

Now, she smiled. And that made him smile.

"C'mon. Sit down." He ushered her to a place on the ground next to him.

Across the courtyard, Marienne lingered in the entrance to the kitchen, talking with someone. She pointed to Teague and the others. Her voice carried across the courtyard. "You need to rest. I'll bring you a tray."

Binthe stepped around the washwoman and dragged her feet as she approached them. The seer stared straight ahead, unblinking. Dark circles hung under her eyes.

Morgan and Teague rushed over and guided her to the bench. The defender crouched down in front of her. "What is it?"

She did not answer but moved a hand in front of her as if waving away an object that came too close. She gasped and covered her face.

"Binthe, what is it?" Morgan asked again and lowered her hands. "Binthe? *Dici a Ëa.*"

"I have spent too much time in communion with the Seeing Aspect. It speaks to me even when I—" She flinched.

Teague swallowed. He had seen Mirana go through the same thing. More than once. He would put her hand over his heart, forcing her Healing Aspect to take the focus away from her Seeing Aspect to sense his heartbeat. Binthe, however, was not a healer. Maybe there was another way to break her Aspect's hold? Amulets were what concentrated and focused a Fal'kin's Aspects. Maybe—

He grasped the chain of her amulet and began to lift it over her head.

Morgan grabbed his arm. "What are you doing?"

"Just give it a moment."

The seer gave a small cry as the amulet left her. She blinked and took a deep breath, looking at the group as if seeing them for the first time.

He handed the amulet back to her. "Better now?" She nodded. Illenne handed her a cup of water and she gulped it down.

"*Gratas*," Binthe said. The horse mistress filled the cup again, and the seer took another drink. "I am sorry. I have better control than this."

"You do. It's just sometimes it seems like the Aspects have even more control," Teague said. She smiled at him. As did Illenne. The courtyard suddenly felt much warmer.

Liaonne watched the seer, concerned. "Will you be all right?"

She nodded again. "*Ai.*"

"You shouldn't be the only one seeing. How are you coming with the seers?" Morgan asked.

She ran a finger around the edge of her emerald crystal. "They are strongly gifted with their Aspect."

The prime frowned. "But?"

She gave Liaonne a nervous smile. "But they are finding coordinating their efforts in the way we need to during a fight a challenge."

The defender woman kicked at a stone on the ground. "Meaning we still have no cohesive battle seer's group." Binthe took a bite of bread and did not reply.

Teague suspected half the difficulties the seer encountered had more to do with their mistrust of this young woman from the other side of Kinderra than their abilities. Centuries ago, the provinces barely spoke to each other, let alone fought together. Hypocrisy was a strange disease indeed.

Liaonne leaned forward and trailed a boot heel, making random patterns in the dirt. "Can we do this?"

Morgan slowly stood and grimaced as he stretched. "There is still time." His hand lingered on Binthe's shoulder. She covered it with her own.

"That's not what I asked."

He hesitated before answering. "There is always hope."

"Hope will not defeat the Ken'nar. Binthe, do you have any idea when the Ken'nar will come?"

"Liaonne," Teague said, "it might be too soon for her to—"

"I need an answer," she snapped. She sounded more desperate than angry.

The seer woman held the amulet a moment longer before slipping it over her head and closing her eyes. Almost immediately, her breathing quickened. She clenched her hands but said nothing. She then groaned and slid off the bench.

"Binthe." Teague rushed over.

Morgan caught her before she could fall. This time, he took off the amulet. She lay in his arms, catching her breath. She touched his cheek as he helped her to sit.

Their conversation in the hills. It was so obvious now why she had been crying then. Binthe didn't just care for Morgan as Teague had originally thought, she loved him, deeply. She feared for his life. And Morgan loved her, too. He loved her so much it terrified him into keeping his feelings for her hidden. Knowing he'd lost a wife and a son, Teague couldn't blame him.

"The Aspects Above did not show me this before." Her voice dropped to a whisper, her focus on some distant point beyond the courtyard. "Black-armored warriors stretch across the horizon. Everywhere. Yet they do not come."

Liaonne grabbed her amulet and closed her eyes briefly. Was she calling the hall's seers? "Why do the Ken'nar not come?"

"They wait. Death surrounds."

The young prime continued to hold her amulet. "What else?"

The seer scowled as if she did not understand herself what she saw. "Heat."

Illenne exhaled, sounding frustrated. "There is little open water on the high plains. Perhaps some of us should remain, my prime, so there will be more for the evacuees."

Several seers hurried over to the group, interrupting Liaonne's response. "What is it, my prime?" asked the woman Teague remembered as the Seer Grenne. A thin, red line traced across her collarbone to disappear under her shirt. One of the other seers sheathed a long knife. Grenne must have been the unlucky recipient of the tip of that long knife.

"Seer Lima has seen the battle. The Ken'nar will advance on Edara, then hold their position."

Grenne scowled, shaking her head. "We have seen nothing of this. The Ken'nar horde still masses somewhere on the outskirts of the forest."

The defender prime brought her fist down on the bench, causing him to jump. "The future, damn you. What does the future say?"

The tall seer woman straightened her shoulders. "My prime, we have been searching as many future skeins as we can. You know the Seeing Aspect only gives to us what it deems necessary."

She surged to her feet. "Then how come your Aspect has deemed it necessary to give this vision to Binthe and not to you?"

"Liaonne," Morgan cautioned.

She threw him an acid look and composed herself. "Have the scouts confirm the location in the forest you see. Binthe must see a timeframe after that."

"*Ai*, Prime Edaran." The senior seer woman started to leave then paused. She walked back to the young prime and stood close. "Liaonne, we are all working as hard as we can. We owe it to your mother. And to you." She placed her hand on the prime's arm.

"No, you owe it to Varn-Erdal." Liaonne sighed and softened her expression. "*Per Gratas Oë.*"

"You know you have my support. You always have." Grenne cupped Liaonne's cheek and kissed her tenderly. On the mouth.

The tasteless bit of meat Teague had been chewing on fell out of his mouth onto his lap. His eyebrows lifted—

A hand smacked him in the back of the head. Morgan gave him a disapproving look. The seer parted from the prime and inclined her head in a bow. She turned and left with the others.

He rubbed the sore spot on his skull and quickly averted his eyes. He concentrated on finding another mouthful of dried beef before those thoughts could be picked up by the Fal'kin, too.

"They mean to blockade us." Liaonne gripped the hilt of her sword.

"*Ai.*" Binthe nodded. Her eyes were on her amulet as she held it, not the young prime.

The gristle in Teague's stomach sat like lead. They had prepared for a sudden, violent attack. Instead, the Ken'nar planned on waiting them out. That was why they had not attacked yet. The dark warriors would surround them, and let thirst and starvation do the work for them.

He crouched down and scribbled in the dirt with a finger, making a calculation. "We've laid in supplies for three sevendays, maybe a month if we strictly ration." The drought. He sucked in his breath. All the food in Kinderra would not matter if the wells ran dry. "With the lack of rain, the wells are low."

The prime caught his gaze and for the briefest of moments, he thought he saw fear in her sienna eyes—and that frightened him. Liaonne Edaran was, by far, the fiercest defender he'd ever met.

"When do you expect them to come?" she asked Binthe.

"Soon. I'm sorry. I know you want a more specific answer. The vision I saw occurred during the day, in the afternoon maybe. I have no stars or other signs to triangulate a time reference. Let me try again."

"No. For now, that is enough. Rest. I need you whole." She folded her arms, walked away from the group a few paces, and stared out across the courtyard. "The Ken'nar surrounding us will not be within bow range, will they?"

"No, not in my vision," the seer replied, "but the skeins of time are still loose."

"We are not even fifty. How will we—?" The young defender prime cursed through her teeth.

"We have two choices now," Morgan said. "Either increase our stores tenfold and try to outlast them until Kin-Deren comes. Or we all leave with the Unaspected while we can."

The lead that had been in Teague's belly now turned to ice and quickly melted into a nauseating emptiness. "If we could have collected more food, we would have. The drought has parched everything. I haven't even seen a rabbit or a prairie grouse in days."

Binthe rose. "Liaonne, we need to give Desde more time."

She whirled to face them. "More time for what? More time for us to starve and die of thirst?"

"She will come."

"Desde has no more forces than we do."

"You're wrong. She has far more Unaspected than we do."

For the second time in as many moments, fear chilled Teague to the core. The Unaspected could not fight. Not in a war. Fending off a Ken'nar raid from one's farm was one thing. In an all-out battle, however? It went against everything Kinderra stood for. Fal'kin fought, commonfolk fed. That simple tenet was the bedrock on which society had been built. Anything else was beyond heresy, it went against the laws of nature. Then again, didn't he want to fight and kill the Dark Trine for what he'd done to his parents? For putting Illenne in harm's way?

For tearing Mirana from him.

He took a breath to clear his head. "If Prime Kellis Pinal's Unaspected are willing to fight, so am I."

Illenne smiled and took his hand. "So are we."

Morgan gave him a hard look. "Teague, enough of this foolishness. Liaonne needs you to help the herbsfolk and Illenne must ride out with her father to protect the horse herds." The defender turned toward the prime. "Perhaps we should consider leaving with them. Your horses must be protected at all costs. Sacrificing ourselves needlessly will protect nothing."

The horse mistress took a step toward the defender. "And give the Ken'nar yet another learning hall to sit in? I have heard what the other defenders said about Kana-Akün. If I am the only one to fight them, then so be it, but I will not let them take Edara, too."

"Illenne il'Talz, *obsca*." Liaonne held up her hand, silencing the girl. "Even if Desde has committed such a sacrilege, there is not enough time. With the ford destroyed, she would have to be on the march already. She will have to cross the Garnath River and the plains with an army. That would take sevendays. The Ken'nar will come before she would get even halfway. They might even see her and engage her on the open prairies. Time is against us."

Teague looked up at the sky. Stars shimmered in the cloudless heat. Illenne was right. The horses wouldn't be the only ones to suffer from the lack of water. He smiled.

"If time and this heat are against us, they're against the Ken'nar, too." The Fal'kin gave him questioning looks. "*Ai*, the Ken'nar may come ahead of the Kin-Deren forces, but that is precisely what we want them to do. After a few days of sitting out in the sun, exchanging some harmless arrow fire with us, they will grow complacent. Plus, there's nothing for them to eat or drink either."

Binthe nodded. "He is right. They will not expect a rearguard action from Kin-Deren. With Desde's troops, the Ken'nar will be the ones surrounded, not us."

Liaonne folded her arms again. This time, however, he saw a change in her eyes. It wasn't hope, but at least it was no longer fear. "You are forgetting one important thing, both of you. Desde may not be able to raise an army, regardless of what she promised. She may not come. But the Ken'nar surely will."

Illenne exhaled in disgust and picked up the food tray. She started to walk away when she stopped, turned, and slammed it back down on the bench. "May I see your bow, Defender Commander?"

Morgan made no move. "Why?"

"And two arrows."

He started to reach for them and paused. "This is not a hunting bow. It is a Fal'kin military weap—"

She snatched his bow and one arrow. "The chip in the far post." She nocked the arrow and pulled back on the string, her arm shaking with effort. She let the arrow fly. It embedded itself in a finger's-width patch of bare wood two hundred paces away. Teague's eyes went wide.

"And the other." Silently, the defender handed her a second arrow.

Again, she pulled back on the string, groaning with the effort, and released the second arrow. It sang across the courtyard to split the shaft of its mate. She handed the bow back to the defender.

"You don't need seers, Prime Edaran, you need fighters. Do not send me away like some child or useless old woman. I am willing to fight. I want to fight. I *can* fight. I will not let the Ken'nar take anything else from me—from us."

Liaonne walked over to the girl. For a moment, Teague wasn't sure what the prime was going to do. She pulled Illenne into an embrace. "I could not ask for more than your brave heart." She then held the girl back from her to look into her face.

"That's why you will go. Your father is just one man. He cannot protect every horse, every child, every useless old woman by himself. This hall, this building, is not Varn-Erdal. The horses, you, your father, and every other man, woman, and child— Unaspected and Fal'kin—are Varn-Erdal."

Illenne stepped out of her embrace. "I will not leave."

The prime's expression of sisterly devotion evaporated like the rain on the parched earth. "*Ai.* You will. You will leave tomorrow with the last of my people and my horses. *Oë comprende?*"

The young horse mistress clenched and unclenched her fists. "*Ëo comprende, Ëi Primus.*" She turned and ran off across the courtyard.

Liaonne grabbed her amulet with both hands. The yellow topaz crackled with thin streaks of light. "I'll be damned if this hall will be turned into a tomb."

Teague hurried after Illenne.

CHAPTER 30

"Ama ten u'locaraë en u'pace. Fos ta quetís Id staíonné brea."
("Love hath no place in war. Yet that is where it is needed most.")
—Ora Fal'kinnen 12:48–49

"Illenne?"

Teague ran into the stables. Hamriah whuffled at his approach. The girl brushed her horse awkwardly with her left hand. "You have to leave. Tonight. You heard Liaonne and Binthe. You could get caught behind the blockade."

"I could be. But you will be." She continued to curry the mare.

He grabbed her hand. "You can't stay here. You have to leave."

She pulled herself free and threw down the brush. "I am not useless."

"I know that. And so does Liaonne."

"Don't you think I've encountered Ken'nar before? Don't you think I've used my bow for more than hunting prairie grouse?"

"That's exactly why she is sending you with your father. She knows you are strong. And the others as well." He held her arms. "Why do you think your father evacuated the Unaspected and horses in groups instead of all at once? So the Ken'nar would not notice. They would have most certainly seen thousands of people and horses on the march. And your older seers? Your older, *experienced* seers, a few in each group? They are there to warn you and your father if the Ken'nar approach your redoubt. Ille, don't you understand? You are Liaonne's— and Varn-Erdal's—last line of defense."

She reached for his hands. "You are Unaspected as well. We also need herbsfolk to help us while we wait."

"There will be injuries here. Serious ones. I need to stay."

"There will be no one to protect the herbsfolk who remain behind. The Fal'kin will be too focused on fighting."

More emotions than he cared to understand raced through his mind. It was much easier to change the subject.

"You hurt your shoulder with Morgan's bow, didn't you?"

Illenne laughed darkly. "That thing must have a draw weight of a hundred stone if it's an ounce."

He returned her laugh. "I doubt he only draws it with his arm." Her deep brown eyes were a liqueur that spread warmth throughout his body as he drank them in. "Maybe I can help."

Teague stepped behind her and brushed her long, honey-colored hair away from her neck. He slid her shirt down to partially reveal her right shoulder. She eased back against him and rested her shoulder blades against his chest. He gently massaged the sore muscle. Illenne hissed in pain, then relaxed under his touch.

He knew enough about a woman's body, but it all had been from the medical treatises he studied, a clinical exercise. Two summers ago, he'd discovered a book of love poems his father had once given his mother. Those poems made everything he knew about women make sense in a way it never had before. Illenne's body was both a study and a poem in perfection.

Her skin was bronzed by the sun, soft to his fingertips. He inhaled her scent, sweet, familiar, but he couldn't quite identify it. He leaned closer, breathing her in.

She turned her head and brushed her lips on his hand. Warmth radiated up his arm and down his spine to settle low in his body.

"Your shoulder. It's not—" he swallowed "—it's not dislocated."

Slowly, she faced him, her lips close to his. "I am so tired of being in pain. Help me. Please."

Teague pulled her even closer and covered her mouth with his as she clung to him. Her words mirrored his agony. He would never be rid of the wound in his heart. Never. He was useless to Mirana. But maybe not to Illenne.

She kissed him back hungrily as he wrapped his arms around her. He caught her bottom lip, tasting her mouth. Her lips, her mouth, weren't enough. He wanted, no, *needed* to taste more, to forget he had ever tasted another. He kissed the tender place behind her ear, the curve of her jaw, her neck.

That scent. He now knew that scent. Almonds. She tasted of almonds from the oil she must have used on her skin. Her fingers left a trail of fire burning through him as she caressed his chest. He brought up one hand to cradle the back of her head, crushing his mouth against hers, and pulled her tighter to him with the other hand fisting her blouse at the small of her back. She parted his mouth with her lips, tracing his tongue with hers. His breathing quickened as she sighed into his kiss. So much had been left unsaid between the stanzas of those love poems, so very much.

He had once hoped to hold Mirana in his arms like this, to taste her satin skin, caress her breasts. To reach ecstasy with her. But he had failed her. He was not strong enough, brave enough, *Aspected* enough for a Trine, and never would be. No matter how much he had wanted to be, no matter how hard he had tried to be.

But Ille? She was Unaspected. Like him. Hurting. Like him. Maybe he could be enough for her. And enough for himself.

Teague poured his pain into his kiss, warring against Illenne's able, desperate tongue. He rushed her back against the paddock wall. When she pressed her hips against his, a groan of such raw need escaped his throat he might have been embarrassed if not for the lightning concentrating in his loins.

The lightning deep within him grew into a searing tempest. This lighting was a fire he understood, could control, one he could feel in the marrow of his bones. This fire was no image, no uncertainty. This fire was real. Intense. Now.

He growled in furious desire, and ran a hand under her blouse, following the curves of her body.

"Drei," she breathed.

He froze, a stone fist of shock punching him in the heart. He held her back from him. "Ille?"

She gasped in horror. "I-I am so sorry."

His heart continued to hammer at his rib cage, but now in confusion and uncertainty.

"Teague?" a voice called from farther in the stables. Morgan.

Illenne cried out in panic. She pulled her blouse closed and ran from the stables.

"Ille, wait! Come—" Teague exhaled in defeat. "Back."

"I forgot to tell you. The defenders found a stand of peda blossoms—" Morgan stood still and stared at him for a moment. "I didn't...I am so, so sorry."

"Everyone's sorry." He wanted to die of embarrassment, however, that wouldn't be nearly a quick enough end.

He sank into the straw and leaned against the boards of Hamriah's paddock. He closed his eyes and tilted his head back, letting it hit the wood with a soft thud.

Morgan cleared his throat. "Um, I've found a bucket of cold water over the head helps."

He lifted his head but kept his eyes closed. "That's not where I need the cold water."

The defender walked over to the paddock. "I am truly sorry. My mind was on preparations for battle and the seers. I should have been listening before I entered."

"And just what would you have heard?"

"I would have heard enough to know not to enter. She is a beautiful girl."

"Please, stop. Just. Stop. I think it was over anyway." He finally opened his eyes. "What did you want?"

"Earlier today, the defenders on patrol found a large spread of peda blossom. Directly east from here. About four leagues." The defender tossed down a fistful of the tiny yellow flowers. "It'll be dangerous riding in that direction now, but I thought you should know. We will need the numbweed."

"*Gratas*." He couldn't be any less thankful.

The Fal'kin rubbed the back of his neck. "Teague, again, I—"

Teague's father had said his own grandfather had been quite—what was the word his father had used?—"eloquent" when it came to curses. He'd heard a few from his father, only in rare instances, but they were eloquent, too. For once, he was glad Morgan could hear his thoughts. The defender blinked and stood back. He nodded and walked away.

"Morgan?" He heard the man's boots scrape the stable floor as he stopped. "Is it possible to love two women at the same time?"

"*Ai.*" A frustrated sigh broke the nighttime stillness of the stable. "And no."

He frowned. "That's not an answer."

"I know. If I had a better one, I would give it to you. I have yet to find one myself." The defender left him in silence.

He picked up a peda blossom. Morgan was wrong. There was indeed an answer, just not one he liked. A heart could not be divided or it would stop beating.

He was still in such agony over losing Mirana, he'd thought being in Illenne's arms would take the pain away. It wouldn't. Nothing would take his pain away. Nor hers. He threw down the flower.

Eran warned him—threatened him, really—not to hurt her. She thought she was falling in love with him, but she wasn't. Not really. Now, Teague understood. She had called out Drei's name. Ille was still so in love with Drei, she had filled her empty heart with someone else. Anything to stop the pain. Teague shook his head. He couldn't let that happen. He'd have to point out to her, that her feelings for him weren't real, but simply a way to cope with her loss. To save her life, he'd have to get her to leave, and maybe break her heart to do it.

He sucked in his breath.

To save Illenne, he'd have to break her heart.

"Oh, Light Above."

Mirana knew he'd never leave her side, no matter what evil she faced. Even if she had left Two Rivers Ford with Lord Garis without telling him, he would search for her. He *had* searched for her, stopping only when he realized there was no trace of what direction she had taken.

"Mirana."

She believed some terrible cataclysm would be wrought through her hands, and if he stayed with her, he would be killed in the maelstrom. To save his life, she had to break his heart. She had never thought him beneath her. She had placed his life above her own.

Because she still loved him.

"Oh, Miri."

Teague crossed his arms on his knees and wept.

CHAPTER 31

"The Light of the Aspects molded and shaped people from the clay of the world. The Aspects Above breathed on the people and they awakened."
—The Book of Kinderra

Teague sat in the middle of a stand of peda blossoms. The sun had traveled far into its afternoon journey and made the heat a living thing, the scorching wind its breath. He had been there for hours, hoping to untangle the jumble of emotions knotting his mind as he foraged for supplies. Binthe said the Ken'nar would come at any time and from this direction. Back at the hall, so much preparation remained. He should go back, but he couldn't. Not yet.

He had searched for Illenne that morning after their ill-fated…whatever…to tell her what was in his heart. Or try to, anyway. He wasn't sure there were even words for what he felt. He learned she and the others had left before dawn. He never had a chance to say farewell.

Mirana was Aspects Above knew where. Was that chance now gone, too, to tell her that he understood what she had done and why? To explain he didn't care if he died if he could help her? To tell her once again he loved her?

Was Mirana Pinal dead?

He clenched his hands into fists, willing himself to calm down. "I was such a fool. Such a damned fool. You have to be alive, Mirana. Please."

His gray filly, Bankin, nickered, breaking him from his thoughts. Her ears shot forward as she listened.

He jumped to his feet and pulled the heavy Ken'nar broadsword from the scabbard he had tethered to the horse's side. The sound of hoofbeats approaching fast rose above the searing breeze. He scowled. Just one horse?

He shielded his eyes from the glare of the sun. A lone rider charged toward him, the horse a sleek mare with a mahogany coat and a black mane.

"What are you doing here?" he called out as the rider cantered to a halt. He threw his sword down, burying the tip in the dry earth. "I thought you rode out with your father and the others this morning?"

Illenne Talz dismounted and ran over to him, breathless. "*Ai*, I did. I had to. Then I slipped away and rode back to search for you, but you had already gone." She wrapped her arms around him. "I am so, so sorry about what happened. It was an accident. It will never happen again. I promise."

He gently pushed her back from him. "I know. Because *we* will never happen again."

She shook her head. "Please don't say that."

He took her by the hand and walked her back to Hamriah. "You need to go. Now. It's not safe."

She threw his hand away. "I will not leave you. I love you, Teague Beltran."

He smiled sadly. "No, you don't. You don't love me any more than I love you."

She scowled in confusion. "What?"

"Ille, both of our hearts are held by people who have moved beyond us. There is no cure for that kind of pain but time." He shook his head. "I don't know. Maybe not even that."

She crossed her arms to hold herself. She looked out across the plains and said nothing for a long time.

"I miss Drei so much, sometimes it hurts too much to go on without him. Sometimes, I don't even want to try anymore," she said at last.

He swallowed down his own emotions. "It's like a knife in your heart that just keeps cutting deeper and deeper with each beat. And just when you think you can't possibly bleed anymore, you find out you can."

She wiped at her tears. "I thought—I thought—Can you forgive me?"

He held her face and brushed away the last of her tears with his thumbs. "I wanted the same thing. Light Above, how I wanted it, believe me. You deserve someone who can give you all of his heart, not just the bits and pieces that are left." He lowered his hands to hold hers. He squeezed them and stepped back from her. "I need to apologize to you, too. We may have been right wanting to help each other, but it came out the wrong way." His gaze swept the endless plains. "At least you weren't a fool as well."

"What do you mean?"

"Drei died knowing you loved him with all your heart. He carries your love with him in the Aspects Above for all time." He turned his head toward the southeast, toward Deren, toward home. "Mirana may never know how much I love her, and I was too much of a damned idiot to understand why she left me."

"Mirana?" She reached up and gently guided his face back to hers. "Why didn't you tell me?"

"I thought she didn't love me anymore. Or that maybe she never had to begin with." Tears now scalded his eyes. "Now I know she was trying to save my life."

She bent down and picked a peda blossom. "Where is she now, your Mirana?"

"I don't know." He took a long, slow breath, forcing his emotions to obey. "She is a Trine. And I am not even Aspected."

"A Trine?" Illenne's eyes widened in shock. "The Prophecy. But we have Lord Garis."

"*Ai*. We have three Trines."

"*Three* Trines?" Her eyes widened with surprise. "How could that be? Such a thing has never happened before."

He shrugged hopelessly. "It's true. I've seen her use all three of her Aspects."

"Three Trines," she repeated, her voice hushed. "Maybe one is not meant to survive."

Instead of becoming angry at her comment, Teague felt something else explode within him with much more intensity. Fear.

He exhaled a laugh of hopelessness. "Or one is false." He wanted to yell, to cry, to punch something, anything but laugh. It wasn't funny. Not even gallows-humor funny. Either of these fates embodied a fear he had no adequate way to express.

He knew with every fiber of his being Mirana could not possibly perpetrate the kind of destruction she saw in her vision of Jasal's Keep. He scrubbed at his face, refusing to think further on either of their conclusions.

She placed the peda blossom she held in his palm and closed his fingers over it. "Teague, if she is a Trine, she knows what's in your heart."

"That still doesn't change the fact that she has the Aspects," he slapped the empty place at his chest where an amulet should hang, "and I do not."

"Can you honestly stand here in front of me and say these things after what you just told me about Drei?" she replied. "Whether he had the Defending Aspect, any Aspect, and I did not never came to mind in our relationship."

A strange mixture of surprise and hope and regret stirred within him. "It didn't?"

"No." Illenne shook her head. "Drei and I knew each other our whole lives, and we loved each other for at least that long. And, *ai*, he may have been able to touch the Aspects in a way I cannot, but I am also a child of the Aspects Above. The breath of their Creation caused me to be. And you as well."

The Ora Fal'kinnen. He always thought the bible a work of beautiful but unrealistic platitudes. Could there be something more to learn from its verses? Hope began to surge over his more doubtful emotions. "'The Light of the Aspects molded and shaped people from the clay of the world. The Aspects Above breathed on the people and they awakened.'"

"*Ai*, exactly." She smiled. "The Fal'kin were made from us. We are *of* the Aspects. We do not need to touch them. The Aspects are who we are."

He nodded slowly, as much from her words as from the understanding they gave him. *The Hand of the Aspects reached out to the people with fingers as of lightning. The Power of the Aspects was bestowed to those whose hearts were touched with Light.* He was an Aspect all his own, an Aspect of life.

All the times he had let his self-loathing get in the way of his love of Mirana. Teague hung his head, wrestling once more with emotions that threatened to overtake him.

She lifted his chin and smiled. "Besides, I was a better horse rider than he was."

He laughed. "You're a better rider than everyone." He gathered her into his arms and hugged her. "*Gratas Oë,* Illenne il'Talz."

"I will never forget you, Teague il'Beltran."

"I hope very much you will."

The horses nickered. A low noise rumbled over the grassland. It sounded like distant thunder, but the sky was a perfect expanse of unbroken blue. His heart constricted inside his chest, this time for a completely different reason.

"Ille. Get on your horse. Ride."

"Why?"

He pushed her to her mount. "Ride to your father and don't stop until you reach the sea."

She swung up into the saddle. "I don't understand. What are you—?" She froze in sudden comprehension. "The Ken'nar."

"They're coming. Ride." He slapped at Hamriah's flank and set the animal off at a dead run.

As Illenne raced away to the northwest, she looked back at him, then buried her head low against the horse's neck. Hamriah sped away, her gait true. Far off to the east, a cloud drifted like smoke over the earth.

Teague pulled his Ken'nar broadsword from the ground and ran to Bankin, shoving the blade into the straps where he stowed it. He vaulted into his saddle. If the Ken'nar saw him, they might not see Illenne, and follow him instead. He waited. One. Two. The cloud drifted closer, blown by the hot wind. Three.

He kicked his heels at his mount's sides. She took off like an arrow. He gripped the reins, but he still held something in his other hand. The peda blossom Illenne had given him.

He would find Mirana. He would find her and tell her he loved her. He knew she was wrong to believe in an evil destiny for herself. Something had to be missing from her keep vision and the white light she perceived. Missing, misinterpreted, or just plain mistaken. If he could begin to see something within himself other than failure, he was determined to help Mirana see the same thing within herself. He shoved the flower into his belt pouch.

"Run, Bankin!"

CHAPTER 32

*"Like the pieces arrayed on the game board, the
armies were set. But does not war make all pawns?"*
                                    —The Book of Kinderra

Teague looked over his shoulder again. The bit of diversion
he created so Illenne could escape worked all too well. The
Ken'nar gained on him.

He gave the horse her head. She shot forward faster than
he had ever seen her run. Her hooves drummed the ground in a
single beat as she raced at full stretch.

A peculiar whistle shrieked overhead, like a raven
screeching two octaves too high. Arrows hit the ground off to
his left and made soft thuds in the parched earth. He had to get
to Edara and warn Prime Edaran and the others.

"Hurry, girl!"

More arrows soared above him, peppering the ground around him. A sudden, burning pain tore through his left arm. He screamed and slipped from his saddle as Bankin pounded forward. He righted himself with his uninjured arm before he could fall and bent low over the saddle pommel to make himself less of a target.

The learning hall's outer bulwarks loomed ahead of him—and the moat. He sucked in his breath. If the drawbridge wasn't down, he would never be able to stop in time. The moat was too wide to jump. That was the point.

The sharpened wooden pikes embedded in the gulley. Point.

Bad choice of words.

"The Ken'nar are coming! The Ken'nar are coming!" Teague prayed to the Aspects Above that whoever stood sentry heard him. Maybe he should have waited to shout his alarm until after he confirmed the drawbridge remained down.

Too late. The lip of the bridge lifted slowly. Archers on the ramparts trained on him as he neared.

"Wait! Let me in!"

Bankin launched into the air and scrambled onto the drawbridge before it could be pulled too high.

He raced through the heavy wooden doors at the entrance to the learning hall, scraping them with his legs as they, too, began to close.

He yanked Bankin's reins, pulling her head around, before he could plow into a knot of defenders in the courtyard. She pawed the air as she stopped her charge.

"The Ken'nar," he gasped, trying to catch his breath, "they're here."

"Teague!" Morgan shouted from the heights of the defensive catwalk that ringed the hall.

He quickly dismounted and grabbed his sword. "Give her all the water and oats she wants," he said to a defender, handing him the reins. "She just may have bought us some time."

He ran up the stairs leading to the catwalk. Liaonne and Binthe stood next to the defender commander. Dust stirred up by thousands of hooves created a wall cloud on the eastern horizon. Memories of the massacre at Two Rivers Ford jackknifed through his mind.

Morgan rushed over to him and grabbed his arms. "You might not be able to hear our calls, son, but we certainly heard yours. *Gratas*—"

Teague dropped his sword and grabbed his arm. "Son of rackin' grynwen whore!" He pulled himself away from the defender as pain lanced through his shoulder.

The defender instantly released him, his hand covered in blood. "You're wounded."

Teague doubled over, grimacing, and held his wound. "Well, that must be why my arm hurts so much."

Binthe rushed over. "Where is the arrowhead? Is it still embedded?"

He shook his head. "I think it went right through."

Liaonne guided him down to sit on the platform. She whistled to the Fal'kin below. "Get Palen. Tell him to bring his field kit. Now."

The seer probed the injury with her fingers. "Are you sure it went through? I don't see the exit wound."

"I know you're trying, Binthe, but I'll take care of it myself. You're not hel-hel-helping. Oh, please let go!" He yanked his arm away with a cry of pain. "I'll be fine. I just need a moment."

The prime waved over an elderly herbsman. "Palen, hurry. He's taken an arrow."

"Herbsman Beltran, what did you do to yourself?" The herbsman began to examine the wound as thoroughly as Binthe but nowhere near as gently.

He clenched his teeth so hard he thought he would crack every one. "Herbsman Palen, please. I'll take care of it myself. I just need to catch my breath." He pulled his arm away again.

Old Palen sat back and raised an eyebrow. "Suture yourself? Behind your shoulder? With one hand?"

Teague frowned and released his wounded limb to the old herbsman's care.

Palen quickly cleaned and dressed the wounds. "The Aspects Above smiled on you this time, boy. It only went through a bit of skin and some flesh. Your arm muscle is fine." He started to pack the wounds with more bloodsbane and numbweed.

He shook his head and stayed the old man's hand. "That's enough. Save it. We won't be able to make more now."

The old man chuckled. "Herbsfolk make the worst patients. Just like your *paithe*."

He blinked. "You knew my father?"

"Lad, every herbsman and herbswoman in Kinderra knew your father and mother." He groaned with effort as he stood. "I'd tell you to watch yourself for infection, but you'd only tell me to piss off, too."

"My father said that to you?"

"Bah!" He waved away Teague's surprise. "He was younger than you at the time. Your *paithe* had taken a sword scrape in the chaos, however, he was more worried about little Niah. He taught me a few things. He was a bright lad. Just like you."

He smiled up at the old man. "*Gratas.*"

The herbsman jutted his chin toward the bulwarks. "I'll head over to the outer gates, Prime Edaran."

"No," she replied, shaking her head. "I don't want you herbsfolk or the seers anywhere near the outer defenses yet until we know what we're up against. Take caches of supplies and spread them throughout the city. When the gates are breached, we'll at least have something."

When the gates are breached? Fear shot through Teague like the arrow through his arm. Had Binthe seen something? Had Liaonne's Defending Aspect called to her?

"Teague, how many were there?" Morgan asked.

He slowly rose to his feet and looked to the east. "Thousands. Five maybe."

The prime nodded. "That corroborates what the seers say. I had hoped they were wrong."

He held his throbbing arm and watched the advancing army. The Dark Trine sent five thousand Ken'nar to Two Rivers Ford. Now another five thousand marched on Edara. And Light Above only knew how many had attacked Kana-Akün last winter. Certainly some of those who had come to Edara had fought in the three battles, but not all. Probably not most of them. That meant the Dark Trine's army was much larger than any on Kinderra. Much larger.

He forced down his growing sense of dread. "Has anyone ever tried to see just how many Ken'nar the Dark Trine has under his banner?"

Binthe touched her amulet. "I've tried many times, but it's always different. I may have seen one unit dozens of times or a dozen units once."

"All these different units. Have you ever added them all together? I mean, many Ken'nar died at the ford, too, and yet here they are back at us, at full strength." He gestured with his good hand to the enemy in the distance.

Prime Edaran wiped at her face and blew out a loud exhale. She squared her shoulders. "Binthe, pull the seers back to the learning hall. I want them out of range of the arrows should those bastards decide to camp close. Call to me anything you see. I want you in my mind closer than my conscience." The seer nodded and hurried down the stairs.

Once again, Teague wished he could hide his thoughts. "I am sorry, Prime Edaran. I didn't mean to upset you."

She ignored the comment. "If they do decide to blockade us, how many days will the food last?"

The last of the Unaspected had left that morning. He chewed the inside of his cheek and recalculated now that one hundred more mouths were gone. "Three sevendays, if Eran Talz didn't take too much with him."

Morgan glanced at Liaonne, his face strained. "What if we strictly ration?" she asked.

Teague didn't have the heart to tell her his estimate was already based on strict rationing of food. "Maybe four, but folks will have to go without on some days." It was a wild guess. They might even read it as an out-and-out lie.

The prime nodded. "And the water?"

"You have five wells in this city, one of them in the learning hall. From what your herbsfolk tell me, that one has its source deep underground. The others flow from sources outside Edara."

"So, we could lose four and survive on the fifth." When he did not confirm the observation immediately, she asked again, "Teague?"

He swallowed. "If the water table holds. It hasn't rained in sevendays."

She inhaled deeply and set her jaw. "It will hold."

He took his hand from the wound in his arm as the numbweed, at last, began to work its magic. "We'll start drawing water and storing it in cisterns."

"Teague Beltran, never apologize to anyone for speaking the truth. Especially me." She gave him a curt nod and descended the stairs to the courtyard. She barked a few orders before disappearing into the hall.

He stood alone with Morgan on the catwalk. The Ken'nar stopped about a quarter-mile away. Dust hung in the air, but now and then, a black shape stood out from the haze.

It would be dark in a few hours. Would they attack then? What if the blockade Binthe sensed was just a ruse? Was it even possible to flummox the Aspects that way?

"No. I don't think so," the defender commander replied. "Unless such a thing comes from the accursed mind of the Dark Trine himself."

Teague frowned. "That wasn't helpful."

He bent down and picked up his sword. If Mirana had come here with him, he could have done nothing to protect her. Or anyone else. Someday, the Dark Trine would confront her— and try to kill her.

"Teach me to fight," he said, his voice firm.

The defender sighed, frustrated. "We've been through this."

"I have to be able to fight, Morgan. You know as well as I, the Ken'nar won't be content to stand out there forever. They will come. I'd like to try and maybe live."

"Neither Binthe nor I will leave your side. You are an herbsman. Liaonne needs you as an herbsman, not as a defender."

"I *am* being an herbsman. I am helping to keep these people alive. Am I not called to cut out a cancer to save a life? The Ken'nar are that cancer—"

The other man raised both his hands, stopping his comment. "No, Teague. I will not discuss this any further."

"You always fight the Ken'nar out in the open. Have you ever fought them in close quarters? Through the streets of a city?" He pointed to the empty hall behind them. "You heard Prime Edaran. They will breach our gates. You know this."

He had an idea, one he knew would work. And it was a bad one. Especially if the il'Kin commander took it the wrong way. When the Fal'kin turned from him and began to walk away along the balustrade, he chased after him. "Herbsfolk are sometimes paired with battle seers. They know where the wounded are. What if I'm the only one Binthe has? Are you going to let her die because you think fighting is not my place?"

Morgan whirled. His eyes flashed with anger, his amethyst amulet now glowing. "How dare you?"

Teague leveled his sword at him. "I couldn't do anything to protect my mother and father. Please help me now. Teach me."

The defender took a step toward him. "Put down the sword."

Teague refused to yield. "Teach me." His arm shook with the strain of holding the heavy blade with one hand.

The Fal'kin held his ground. "Drop the sword. Now."

He made a short thrust. "Teach me!"

Faster than he thought possible for a mortal, Morgan drew his own sword and hammered it down on top of Teague's blade, ripping it from his grip. Teague staggered back, eyes wide with shock.

The defender whirled his wrist, the blade a steel-colored blur, before he gestured with its tip to Teague's feet. "If you insist on using that tree ax, you'll need to widen your stance."

CHAPTER 33

"Aspecta'e Alta anaílé ár gente e Oëme aspecé."
("The Aspects Above breathed on the people and they awakened.")
—*Creara i'Kinderra* ("The Creation of Kinderra"), Ora Fal'kinnen 1:10

Kaarl walked among the lines of erstwhile archers as they trained in the fields along the Garnath River. He had wanted to wait longer for more volunteers before they started their march to Edara, but Desde's prescience of urgency compelled them to head out.

A handful of sevendays ago, these people had used arrows to hunt rabbits, if they had ever hunted at all. Some were a little older or younger than he would have liked but most were healthy and strong.

He lifted the arm of a woman nocking a longbow a little higher. She let the arrow fly. It hit far from the center, but at least it hit the target—clumps of sod dug from the ground—this time. He nodded and moved on to the next archer.

Desde hoped that the bowmen would cut down the first wave of Ken'nar before the remainder drew closer and had to be fought hand to hand. It was a good strategy, even routine, for trained Fal'kin. For the Unaspected, though, he hoped they wouldn't break ranks and run in terror at the first sight of their black-armored enemies.

He squinted up at the blistering sun. The heat was the proverbial double-edged sword. It hadn't rained in sevendays. The Garnath River was low and much easier to cross. It would also be an easy crossing for the Ken'nar. He frowned and wiped the sweat out of his eyes. Dozens of Unaspected hit their sod targets; many more did not.

Taul Brandt had been good to his word—with no negotiating strings attached, a small miracle in itself—and mustered more than a thousand volunteers. Of course, with numbers like that, there had been no point in trying to hide the mustering militia of commonfolk any longer—another reason to begin their march sooner than later. Furthermore, Kaarl doubted the Ken'nar would change their tactics because of a few hundred fighters, regardless of their gifts or not. The enemy simply had more numbers and more experience.

A young man—a boy, really—about Mirana's age took his place at the line. A long scar on his forearm flexed as he nocked an arrow. He pulled the string taut and let it loose with the briefest of motions from his fingertips. The arrow split one left by another archer and sank itself deep in the center of the earth mound.

Kaarl smiled. "Good. Very good. Where did you learn to shoot like that?"

The youth rested the bow on its end. "We had a few sheep. Their wool made the difference when the corn and wheat failed. I stopped the grynwen and wolves from taking what we had." He looked down at his boots. "But not the Ken'nar."

"Grynwen and wolves do not wear armor. Tomorrow you will begin working with armored targets. If you can split fletching like that, you can make the gaps in the Ken'nar armor." Kaarl clapped him on the shoulder. "Get some rest."

He started to move on to the next archer when the boy hurried in front of him. "Steward, sir. I don't want to fight with a bow. I want to fight with a sword."

"Why?"

The youth gripped the bow with both fists. "The Ken'nar took everything from me. I want to see their faces when I kill them."

Oh, he knew the taste of that particular vengeance. He knew every flavor of hatred there was for the Ken'nar. "Most Ken'nar wear helmets."

The boy let the bow drop to the ground. "Then I want to hear them scream."

He frowned. "What's your name, boy?"

"Maark Bedane, sir."

"Did you get that scar on your forearm from the Ken'nar, Maark?" He indicated the old wound.

"No, sir. After the Ken'nar destroyed our farm, I had to steal my food. I got caught. The healers' son and your daughter—they saved my arm. Because of them, I still have an arm to fight."

He wanted to embrace the boy for trying valiantly to give purpose to tragedy. More than that, he was a testament to the gifts Mirana held, the ones he had tried to hide.

"Look at those targets." He pointed to the sod mounds. "How many arrows do you see that made their marks as yours did?"

The boy frowned. "Not many, sir."

It was more like none. Toban had refused to let Kaarl choose early to become a defender with a heart full of raw hatred for the Ken'nar after the death of his father. Instead, the old prime had him serve as a scout for summers before he held an amulet. He would not waste a talent like the young archer's—a *life* like his—just so the boy could channel his revenge. He wanted living soldiers, not dead murderers. "I need you as a bowman if you'll accept the position."

The youth regarded the targets a moment longer, his frown deepening.

Kaarl rested a hand on the young archer's shoulder. "I know how you feel, son, but if we don't have good archers, many more people will die. Isn't that ultimately what we're here for? To protect people?"

"*Ai*, Steward."

"*Gratas Oë*, Maark il'Bedane." The boy picked up his bow from the ground and returned to the practice line.

… *Kaarl* … *I need you* … Desde's call burst into his mind. He ran to meet her as she raced through the lines of archers.

He steadied her as they met. "What is it? Is it Mirana?"

She shook her head. "The black line of Ken'nar. It's not a siege. It's not a siege I've been seeing. It's a blockade. They've blockaded Edara.

"A blockade? Are you sure?"

His wife nodded. "The others have seen it now, too." She held her amulet. "All of our visions showed us daytime. Without the positions of the stars, we had no true sense of time. Then I thought to watch the grass in successive time skeins. It withered and died. Edara has been trapped for sevendays."

"Wait. Has been? You mean—"

"*Ai.*" She nodded. "They're already there. We're too late, *ama.*"

He turned to the targets as the thud of dozens of arrows hitting them punctuated the air.

A slow smile crept across Kaarl's face.

Desde scowled. "What?"

"The Ken'nar are counting on the Varn-Erdalans to do something rash based on desperation, driven mad by hunger and thirst. Like, say," he shrugged, "attack them head-on. In fact, I think they're so focused on Edara, their battle seers probably aren't looking anywhere else."

His wife now returned his grin. "They're not counting on *us* to do something rash. Like blockade the blockaders with a thousand Unaspected. From behind."

"Desde, *Ëi ama,*" he kissed her, "I don't think we're late. I think we're just in time."

CHAPTER 34

"Aspecta'e Alta poneó skene i'Tempre bia Ëome, Ida fhíagn bath benedicta e u'bendicta. Qua ísi filam pon bia Ëome statam?"

("The Aspects Above have laid the skeins of Time before us, its weaving both a blessing and a curse. Which is the thread that lays before us now?")

—Ora Fal'kinnen 35:3–4

Teague hit the ground hard again. "Stop it, will you, Morgan? You're supposed to be showing me how to fight with my blade, not my butt."

It had been sevendays since he asked Morgan to train him. Shouldn't this all be getting easier?

"Then move your feet." Morgan tapped his boot with his own.

They had sparred in the courtyard of the Varn-Erdal learning hall in Edara since well before dawn, taking advantage of cooler temperatures. With the sunrise, the air had grown stifling.

Teague shook the hair and sweat out of his eyes. The move made him dizzy. Today wasn't his day to eat. Yesterday was, but he hadn't let the old Herbsman Palen know that when he'd handed out the bread last night.

He might as well stay on the ground a moment longer. He'd probably only end up there again anyway. "How can I move my feet when you throw me with your Aspect every time I get close?"

The defender commander laughed without humor. "Do you think a Ken'nar will stand politely in front of you and allow you to cut off his arm? I've told you a hundred times, you will have one chance and one chance only to bring him down." He stabbed a finger at Teague's neck. "In the gap. Under the chin. That's if he's even interested in fighting you. They think little enough of Fal'kin. They think even less of Unaspected. More than likely he will flash his amulet and be done with you, probably sucking your own life from you to do so, too. If your Ken'nar is on a warhorse, he will incinerate you where you stand and not even break stride."

Teague pulled his gaze away from the other man's hard blue eyes and remained sitting where he fell. "Are Ken'nar all men?"

Morgan laughed again, more menacingly, if that was possible. "Aspects Above help you if you encounter a female. She will cut off several other things before she cuts out your heart." The defender leaned down, his face close. "And she will enjoy it."

He drew up his knees and said nothing.

The defender straightened. "Teague, without the Aspects, you have one opportunity to stop your attacker, and maybe not even that. That is why I wish you would change your mind about this." He reached down to help him up. "Take a break. We'll try again later." He sheathed his sword then stalked off into the hall.

Teague stretched and hissed at the pain from too many sore muscles. He had spent another hot, hungry, thirsty, sleepless night checking and rechecking the supplies. After practicing for hours, he was now so parched, his tongue stuck to the roof of his mouth. Like with his food rations, he'd simply have to hold out as long as he could—which wasn't much longer.

He climbed up the wooden stairs to the catwalk on the defensive ramparts. Binthe smiled as he approached her.

"He is not sparing you, I will say that," she said.

"Sometimes, I wish he would."

He moved his left shoulder gingerly to loosen the ache in his healing arm. Thankfully, the entry and exit wounds did not fester in the heat. The sutures had hurt enough. Removing them himself had hurt much more. He'd ask for help the next time.

The black line of Ken'nar warriors stretched from horizon to horizon, not half a league away. Every one of them wanted him dead. He shivered despite the heat. It had been more than a month since their enemy had set up the blockade and Defender Prime Liaonne had received no word or sign of Seer Prime Desde's troops.

He laid his forehead on his arms. "Is it wrong to wish they would hurry up and attack? This waiting is excruciating."

"That is how they want you to feel. They hope the long hours of doing nothing but pondering your own painful death will make you do something rash."

It was working. Lifting his head, he studied the battle seer. She looked terrible—well, as terrible as Binthe Lima ever could. Long hours in the sun had turned her fair skin red, but dark circles hung under her sea-green eyes and her cheeks had become drawn. Several new holes perforated the belt holding her long knives. She had, no doubt, passed her food rations to others as well. The thought of food sent his stomach growling.

The seer dug in her belt pouch and produced a square of stale tack bread. "Here."

He shook his head. "I'm not all that hungry. You take it. Prime Liaonne is relying on you to see. If you faint away, what good will that do us?"

"I can go longer without food than you can. Please, take it."

"You can go longer, but when you have to eat, you'll need it more. I remember what my parents said about what happens to Fal'kin when they start denying themselves."

"If I faint away, there are other seers to take my place." Her voice turned brittle.

"And if I faint away, there are other herbsfolk to take *my* place. Ones that actually know something," he snapped.

She shook the hardtack at him. "But they are not the healers' son."

"That doesn't mean anything. We don't need herbsfolk, we need fighters. And I can't do either one." He gave an explosive exhale and rubbed his face in frustrated exhaustion. "I'm sorry, Binthe. I'm just—I don't know."

She smiled sadly. "Frightened?"

How did she stand it? The hours spent waiting to kill or be killed? He said nothing.

She tucked the wafer back in her belt and gently brushed the hair out of his eyes. It was a gesture his mother would have done. His hair had grown, nearly touching his shoulders. His mother would have scolded him for letting it grow this long. She would always crop it short, telling him it was so she could see his handsome face. Now, he knew it was so blood or Aspects Above knew what else wouldn't get spattered in it while caring for wounded.

"We are all frightened."

He frowned. "I highly doubt that."

"Why do you think Morgan is so hard on you? He wants to make sure you learn everything you need to survive."

He picked at the dry wood of the ramparts with a fingernail, then winced as a sliver embedded itself in the quick. He sucked at the sliver. It took him three times to spit it out. He had no spit. "You don't seem scared."

"Do you have any idea what I keep seeing?" Her voice strained in a way he had never heard before. "Every future skein is more terrifying than the next. I sense so much death." She closed her eyes. When she started to shake, she tore off her amulet.

He could be such a racking idiot sometimes. "I'm sorry." Of course, Binthe was frightened. Of battle, maybe a little, but of Morgan's death, certainly. He reached for her hand. "If anybody can make it through this mess, it's Morgan."

Binthe squeezed his hand back and slipped her amulet back over her head. She retrieved the tack bread and snapped it in two. "I did not mean to imply with my offer that you were somehow less capable of enduring this blockade than I. Here. We'll share."

They ate the stale, tasteless wafer in silence. Teague hoped whatever Mirana was eating right now, it was better than this. He toyed with the last bite. He prayed she could eat at all.

Teague placed the last morsel in his belt pouch and fished out a scrap of bandage. He unfolded it to reveal a tiny peda blossom. A petal flaked into pieces. It was now so dry and delicate, he feared putting it back into the pouch would cause it to crumble away completely. Did Mirana still have the peda blossom pendant he gave her? If he outlived this nightmare, he would swear before Kinderra and Aspects Above to make her his wife.

"Do you think you'll join in union with Morgan?"

The seer watched the Ken'nar on the eastern horizon. Her expression softened, but he couldn't tell if it was in hope or sadness. "Unlike Unaspected, Fal'kin do not need unions to have their relationships and children recognized."

"I know that. But would you if he asked?"

She now looked at her unadorned left wrist. "I would do anything Morgan asked."

He smiled. "He loves you, you know."

"The past still holds his heart. I know that as well." She took a breath. "I should not be concerning myself with the past or the future. It is the present I need to see with clarity."

He'd meant to comfort her as she had comforted him. Racking idiot. "You've seen nothing about Prime Desde and her troops?"

"I have seen plenty, but of Desde, no. Much of what I've seen, though, does not make sense. I don't know if it is this 'when' or another. I have no reference to tell me. I see other things. I see heat." She pressed the heels of her hands against her eyes, then threw them back down with an exhale of frustration. "Maybe 'see' is the wrong word. I don't see heat as much as I sense it." Her shoulders tensed and she swallowed loudly.

He nodded, not understanding but feeling the need to respond somehow. For the first time he could remember, he was glad he was not a Fal'kin.

"I'm sure Prime Desde will come," he said quietly. "She gave her word. She promised. She may be riding to us now. She might be here sooner than we think." *Ai*, it was a wild guess— and Binthe probably knew that—but just saying such things gave him at least a fool's hope.

She laughed. "You are a good man, Teague."

He leaned his elbows on the rampart railing again and rested his chin against folded hands. The Garnath River probably was low, that wasn't a lie. Four of the city's wells had sources outside of Edara, but what if they weren't spring-fed? What if their sources were fed by some underground tributary of the river? If the river had dried up—

"Oh, Lights, no."

"What, Teague?"

Without water, those who remained to defend the hall would be dead within days. The Ken'nar would not have to fire a single arrow.

He left the seer's question hanging in the dusty air and flew down the rampart stairs. He tore through the streets of Edara, checking the wells. The water had been brackish yesterday but still marginally drinkable. The buckets in all four now came back empty.

He ran back to the learning hall and entered the kitchen. It was empty, the hearths bare. There were few left in the hall to feed, and even less with which to feed them.

The hall's well was one of the few stone structures he had seen in Edara. It was enormous, as wide across as a man stood.

Three of the four buckets had been removed to prevent overdrawing during the blockade. He lowered the remaining one down on its rope. The pulley wheel squealed in protest in the stillness of the empty kitchen. The bucket should have hit water by now. He lowered it further, using most of the rope. No splash, no soft resistance returned to him. He leaned over the well opening as he held the end of the rope and let the bucket down farther still.

The bucket stopped at last. "Please, please, please." He raised it, pulling it hand-over-hand as quickly as he could. It was heavy. Hope made his heart pound. As it came over the well's rim, he pulled it toward him.

The bucket was filled with sludge.

He groaned. The water they had cached in cisterns would last a day or two, but they could not ration water with the same strictness as food, especially not in this heat. He released the rope and the bucket fell, landing with a sticky slap. He sank to the floor.

Binthe ran into the kitchen. "Teague, what happened? What's wrong?"

He lifted his head, matching her concerned gaze. "The water is gone. We cannot wait any longer for Prime Desde. We have to fight. Now."

The battle for Edara would begin, not with the roar of fighters, but with the whimper of starving children.

CHAPTER 35

"Fear shall be your ally! Death shall be your friend!"
—The Book of Kinderra

Teague stood surrounded by forty-three Fal'kin within the rampart walls of Edara. A young boy next to him fidgeted with his new amulet, tugging on the chain as if the pendant were too heavy around his neck. He was just a kid, fourteen if that. He wasn't the only one so young. Or so old. They had no business fighting. Then again, he didn't either.

While Defender Prime Liaonne Edaran addressed them, he ran through his mind all his parents taught him about stabilizing wounds on the battlefield, not to mention all Morgan had taught him about swordplay. In a grim irony, the two concerns supported one another.

Prime Liaonne assigned him to remain with Binthe. A few of her herbsfolk were likewise paired with the three other battle seers, while the remaining healing staff would be stationed in triage tents some distance away north of the learning hall. The seers would spread out through the tall grass to call the attack and would presumably learn which areas would take the heaviest losses. They would direct the herbsfolk to the wounded. He grimaced. He would be on his own to take care of any casualties.

As he hitched the heavy pack of medical supplies higher on his back, his mind returned to that terrifying night at Two Rivers Ford. The night his parents were killed. Would he join them this night? With any luck, Binthe would warn him before any dark warriors could slice him in half. Even so, the Ken'nar were as drawn to battle seers as grynwen were to bleeding prey.

His hand drifted down to grip the hilt of the Ken'nar broadsword at his waist, and he smiled tightly. He might go down, but he would not go down quietly.

Binthe leaned closer so she didn't have to raise her voice. "We will be hidden halfway toward the perimeter. We should be well under arrow coverage from the hall."

He nodded and glanced up at the sky. Stars shimmered in the sultry night but no moon. Could Fal'kin archers see in the dark? He pushed the thoughts of casualties by friendly fire from his mind and tried again to concentrate on the speech.

"The grasses of Varn-Erdal have ever caressed you like a loving mother. Tonight, they will be your shield," the young prime said. "We will not rush forth like a raging storm but be silent as the dark, moving low, a deadly viper poised to strike. You are not an army but hunters, lethal, cunning, invisible, and the Ken'nar are your prey."

He could not see her face. The torches and lamps in the city had been extinguished to get the combatants' eyes used to the darkness. Only the torches on the ramparts remained lit to give the illusion of normalcy.

"The darkness will hide our backs. You will not strike the Ken'nar until you are close enough to feel the heat of their campfires," Liaonne continued. "You will not wait for a battle cry but choose your prey and take it down at will, never revealing yourself.

"Tonight, we shall deal a blow to the Dark Trine such as he has never felt. We are not merely Fal'kin. We are Varn-Erdalans, the ever-valiant. Tonight, fear shall be your ally. Tonight, death shall be your friend. The Aspects Above have called us to destroy this foe that dares step foot on our soil. Tonight, we fight for Varn-Erdal. We fight for Kinderra. Now, onward, for tonight, my brothers and sisters, we are the Aspects Above's hand of Death. *Rememore Kin e Forte!*"

No cry went up in response to the defender prime's stirring words, no hordes surged forward in bloodthirsty glee. Instead, they crept, one by one, through narrow, hastily dug tunnels that led outside the defensive wall.

He and dozens of others scrambled through the moats and carefully picked their way through the sharp rocks and pikes. He paused to look behind him. The Fal'kin remaining in the hall had already begun to fill the tunnels to prevent the Ken'nar from using them. He, Binthe, and the others were on their own.

Teague scrambled up out of the moat and through the tall grass, following the seer. The Fal'kin fanned out in an arc to encircle the sleeping Ken'nar troops. He smiled. He could not see any of his comrades. He gasped.

Including Binthe!

"Bloody hell." He gripped the hilt of the heavy Ken'nar sword and dashed forward, keeping himself as low as possible.

He hit something hard and heard the ringing scrape of a blade being drawn. A hand shot out and grabbed him by the throat.

"No, wait. It's me. Teague," he said in a harsh whisper.

Seer Grenne took a breath and released him. "Be more careful. I could have killed you." She sheathed a long knife.

He wanted to say that they were not even out from under the protection of the hall's defenses, that he could not possibly be a Ken'nar, but he wisely kept his mouth shut. He never argued with anyone holding a knife to his throat.

Binthe emerged from the grass on his left. "This way." She disappeared again, silent as a wraith.

He crawled for what felt like hours. The first arrows had not been loosed and already his back ached from the heavy pack, his legs cramped from the awkward movement. He concentrated so hard on keeping up with the seer and staying alert for any sound that might be a Ken'nar, he ran into her back when she stopped abruptly.

She steadied him. "We will hold here."

"Where are the other seers?" he asked as he unshouldered the medical supply pack.

"I and the three others are at four points around the hall. The other seers remain within the city."

"Why aren't more of them out here to help you call the battle?"

"It is safer for those who could not wield a blade well enough to protect themselves." The dark hid her expression but not the frustration in her voice.

He sat quietly for a long time, every muscle tense. The tall blades of grass rustled against one another in the sighing wind. An occasional guttural laugh from the distant enemy drifted across the plains.

"When will it start?" A moment later, a chorus of demon howls followed by a bloodcurdling scream rose in the night.

Binthe didn't answer. She didn't need to.

*   *   *

Kaarl lay on his stomach on a slight rise, his presence tightly concealed behind U'Nehíl. Desde crouched low next to him. He parted the tall grass with a hand. Thousands of Ken'nar milled about in the camp below, their movements silhouetted by flickering torches and campfires.

So far, not even the enemy's seers suspected anything was amiss. He sneered. Nor would they. They would never think to look for this foe. He peered over his shoulder. He couldn't see them in the darkness, either, but twelve hundred Unaspected waited in the grass a half-mile behind him. His wife had staged her unit farther to the northwest.

When the homesteaders and shepherds saw the masses of Deren townsfolk on the march, that the muster had been real and not some political ploy between the Fal'kin and the province's Unaspected magistrate, they'd joined the army. It was as close to a miracle as he could have hoped for. The hundreds that had joined them were but the merest fraction of the million that called Kin-Deren province home, but he was unspeakably grateful for each one.

Without Two Rivers Ford, the only route north open to the Kin-Deren army was across the Garnath River. The heat and lack of rain had dried the mighty river to a stream, barely wetting his horse's fetlocks. The grueling march had taken sevendays even though they traveled as fast as possible. It had been too fast for some; they would doubtless have more casualties when the fighting began because of it, but there was no other way.

They were still outnumbered, and badly, but he was far too experienced in the capricious justice of war to feel a victory was impossible. Stealth and surprise remained on their side for the moment.

"It is as we feared." Desde frowned. "I estimated five thousand. I had hoped I was wrong." She shook her head. "Where could the Dark Trine have gotten such numbers? Even Jad-Anüna does not have an army this large. Kin-Deren hasn't seen this many Aspected at one time since before Jasal Pinal's time."

Kaarl fingered his sword hilt. "There is more evil at work here than we understand. We've met units a thousand, even nearly two thousand, strong over recent summers but nothing like this. After Two Rivers Ford, I thought we had seen all the Dark Trine had. Once again, he is one step ahead of us."

She tightened a strap on her heavy leather pectoral armor. "We are outnumbered five to one, *Ëi ama.*"

He gave her a cold smile. "But they don't know that."

Her mouth flicked in a quick grin at his comment, but her brow remained furrowed in uneasiness. It mirrored his own. These people had not even fought in the day, let alone at night. He gripped his wife's hand. "We are doing this to keep these people free. You know that. And so do they."

She squeezed his hand back. "*Rememore Kin e Forte.*" She gave him a quick kiss, but as she started to part from him, he held the back of her head and crushed his mouth on hers. ... *Rememore Mirana, Ëoma Trinus* ... She smiled and slipped away through the tall grass.

He crouched back down the hill to his waiting horse. As he climbed into the saddle, he looked back up the rise. Desde had disappeared as if she never existed. He chuckled. His wife was still the most cunning battle seer he had ever known.

He trotted back to his Unaspected troops. "The enemy lies in their beds. Shall we wake them?" Kaarl shouted. A cry rose from his troops, echoed moments later by Desde's forces in the distance.

He drew his sword, holding it high in the air. It glinted bloodred in the glow of his garnet amulet. He brought the blade down and thrust it in the direction of their charge. Patan, his dappled horse, leaped into motion through the grass. *"Rememore Kin e Forte!"*

Like a living cloak fanning out behind him, his troops surged toward the Ken'nar blockade. The handful of Fal'kin who rode with him loosed amulet fire on anything that moved, incinerating man and beast. Tents went up in flames, spilling dark-armored warriors into the waiting bows and swords of the Unaspected.

With a flash of his amulet, Kaarl put down a Ken'nar attempting to nock an arrow. A howling noise lifted above the shouts of men and women. Grynwen. No, grynwen *and* Desde's battalion. They would rout the Ken'nar forces to farther east, away from Edara.

The Defending Aspect rose within him. Pulling deep within himself, he channeled the power through his amulet. Red lightning licked at one of the tents, and it erupted in flames. Behind him, two Fal'kin went down under a hail of arrows. He charged his horse toward the Ken'nar archers poised for another volley. Screaming in rage, he gripped his amulet and poured fire over the Ken'nar like a wave of flame.

Kaarl drove the Unaspected forces onward and scythed through the enemy phalanx. Flashes of amulet fire, both Fal'kin and Ken'nar, surrounded him.

He allowed the Defending Aspect to fill him, no longer aware of his body or the horse beneath him. He set upon his next victim so swiftly, the Ken'nar's sword never cleared its scabbard. He raced through the blockade and cut down three more dark warriors, blasting red fire from the garnet crystal at his chest.

Once, twice, arrows flew past him, fletching burning his cheek. His Aspect stopped many, dropping them as they hit an invisible wall. His amulet incinerated others and blazed over the very archers that fired at him.

A Ken'nar screamed a command as her amulet scintillated a sulfurous yellow. Three grynwen pulled their muzzles from a body and loped straight for him. She swung up onto her mount, shrieking a war cry, following the carnivorous beasts. He reached deep within himself and poured the Defending Aspect out through his amulet, killing the grynwen before they could attack him. He cried out in fury and directed the deadly vermilion light now toward the Ken'nar. She fired her amulet. Red fire met yellow flame, a stalemate in a deadly column of orange light as each amulet sought to repel the other. He pressed closer, then slashed at the Ken'nar's neck with his sword. Her cry ended in a death's choke as his red flame washed over her. Her ashes mingled with those of the grynwen. He rode on. Killing was not to be savored; surviving was.

Desde touched his mind. ... *Ken'nar lancers* ... *Thirty* ... *Headed in your direction* ... A mental picture flew up in his mind of the oncoming dark warriors. He dashed back into the tall brush.

"Archers forward!" He raced his horse behind a line of two dozen Unaspected bowmen hiding in the grass.

He could see the lancers now in his own mind's eye, the immediacy of time and situational awareness resolved by his

Defending Aspect. He raised his sword. "Aim." Taut bowstrings creaked. Wait, not just yet. He saw the arm of one older man begin to shake. "Steady." Wait. Almost. He brought his sword down. "Now!" Unaspected arrows sang in the air and through the grass and were soon followed by screams of agony.

He pulled back on Patan's reins and dropped backward a few paces as the Unaspected scrambled around him. A moment later, seven Ken'nar lancers leaped through the dry grass, running over the bodies of their fallen comrades. Three Unaspected went down, impaled to the ground, before their fellow fighters dispatched their attackers. Two more Ken'nar dropped under Kaarl's amulet.

... Did we break the lancer line or do they still hide in the grass? ... he called to Desde. She did not answer. *... Report ...* His stomach sank. *... Desde ... Did we break the lancer line?...*

... Another army advances from the southwest ... Thousands ... came her terrified message.

He sat still in his saddle. No. After everything they had gone through at the ford, everything they had risked coming here, it couldn't end like this. He pulled himself from his shock.

"Fall back!" he screamed again to the Unaspected fighters. "Fall back!"

CHAPTER 36

"The call was given. The call was answered."
—The Book of Kinderra

Teague quickly tied a bandage on the arm of a Fal'kin too young to be fighting, Binthe next to him, holding her amulet. The seer closed her eyes, her brows furrowed in concentration. Her emerald amulet glowed brilliantly. Maybe too bright. What if a Ken'nar saw them? He swallowed.

"All right." Teague nodded to his young patient. "It's not deep. You should be fine."

"*Gratas.*" The defender gripped his forearm. "*Kin ísi Oëa.*"

"*E Oë.*" The youth disappeared back into the brush. He prayed a lot more than divine Light would protect the boy.

He had treated five Fal'kin, but thankfully, the wounds had been minor. If he found someone with more serious injuries, he'd have to move him or her to the field triage tent—nearly a quarter mile from the battle lines. That was a long way to drag a dying defender. And then how would he find his way back to Binthe? He grimaced.

All around them, the screams of the Ken'nar filled the night as the arrows and swords of the hidden Fal'kin picked them off one by one. The gibbering cries of grynwen grew louder as they feasted on their former masters. His heart fluttered in morbid curiosity. To stand up would mean not only his death but the seer's as well. He forced himself to calm down and remain alert for any cries for help or some sign of approaching Ken'nar.

"Binthe," he whispered, "I need you to find me more wounded."

Sweat glistened on her face. She sat motionless and seemed completely unaware of her surroundings. He drew his Ken'nar broadsword, just in case.

"Binthe?" The long, protracted scream of a woman rose above the other sounds of death. "Binthe, I need your help." She made no sign she had heard him. He knew she was working, but he couldn't wait any longer. People needed his help, such as it was.

He laid a hand on her arm. "Bin—"

She shoved him to the ground with a blindingly fast move, drew two long knives, and held the blades at his throat like a hideous pair of shears. She rocked back on her heels and sheathed her knives. "Do not touch a seer in the midst of calling a battle."

He did not move. "I-I'll remember that." The cries around them grew louder. "I need you to find the wounded for me."

"I cannot. I see thousands of more fighters now. I need to know—" She grabbed for her amulet.

Thousands *more*? His mind lurched. More Ken'nar? How many more could there possibly be?

"I need you to tell me where the wounded are. I can't find them in this." He picked up a handful of grass. "They will die if you don't."

She shook her head. "Two of the other battle seers have died. Only Grenne and I remain. If I take my attention away from our troops, many more will—Teague! Down!"

He flattened to the ground. Seconds later he heard the strange singing of Ken'nar arrows. Two screams rose above the dry sward, one ahead of them, another surprisingly nearby. The grass crashed down behind them and he jumped, yelping in surprise. One of the former Kin-Deren Fal'kin fell to the ground, lifeless.

"Stay down," the battle seer ordered. Another volley of Ken'nar arrows screamed overhead.

He cursed in fear and anger. "They're coming closer. We've got to move."

She did not answer.

"It's not safe here." Grass near them snapped like tinder-dry twigs. "We have to move." He grabbed her arm and dragged her up.

And ran into three Ken'nar.

*   *   *

The ponderous dark line of an army stretched farther than Kaarl could see. Their amulets glowed like demon eyes.

Fear, an old foe he thought he had vanquished long ago, returned to haunt his heart. "Mirana, *Ëi biraena*, I will not leave this life until I make it safer for you."

Two riders broke away from the column and charged toward him. He gripped his sword with one hand, his amulet in the other.

... *Kaarl ... It is Sün-Kasal ...* Desde called. ... *He's brought them ... He has brought them all! ...*

She had to be wrong. Sahm Klai had refused, in no uncertain terms, to commit his Fal'kin to defend Varn-Erdal.

... *Gratas for softening up the black-armored bastards for us, Kin-Deren ...* came the big prime's call to his mind.

... *Sahm?...* He trotted his horse in the direction of the two riders. ... *Sahm Klai? ...* He dug his heels into his mount's side and broke into a gallop. "Sahm!"

Sahm Klai gripped his forearm in greeting when they met. "Where are those black-hearted sons of grynwen?"

He shook his head in disbelief. "You came. But you said—"

Seer Second Rabb Plout grinned. "When it comes to what I see, I can be very persuasive. Some call it 'frightening.'"

The burly man waved him off. "Bah! I wasn't about to let Kin-Deren's Unaspected go down in the annals of history as the saviors of Edara while Sün-Kasal stood idly by." He turned in his saddle to face Kaarl. "I don't want to be here, but I don't want the Ken'nar here even more."

Another familiar mind touched his.

... *You are late, Ëi cara ...* Morgan's mind-voice carried a note of humor.

Kaarl laughed out loud. ... *No, we are on time ... It is Sahm Klai who is late ...*

... *I don't care when you came ... Only that you did ...* Liaonne Edaran's call broke in.

Moments later, his friend and the prime stepped from the grass with fifteen hall-cleaved Fal'kin. Kaarl swung down from his saddle and embraced the defenders.

Relief quickly replaced the concern on Liaonne's face as she turned to Sahm Klai. "How many have you brought?"

"Five thousand. Every last one of my Fal'kin," the large Sün-Kasalan replied. "Command them as you will tonight, but you'll get no cleaved defenders from me, girl."

Kaarl winced at Sahm's intentional slight of Liaonne's title.

The young prime tossed her shoulders back and grinned. "If they fight as well as they are rumored to, I will need no cleaved defenders, old man."

The big defender huffed a laugh.

… *Ken'nar bowmen* … Desde called, cutting through the defenders' conversation. … *Thirty-eight* … *Awaiting you, Sün-Kasal* … *Weakness detected in southern flank* … *Concentrate advance there* …

Kaarl noticed Binthe wasn't with the Fal'kin. "Where is Binthe?"

Liaonne's smile faded immediately. "She calls the battle from east of the hall, between it and the Ken'nar camp. Only thirty Fal'kin are left, including the hall-cleaved. Many are children."

Rabb Plout tightened his grip on the hilt of a long knife. "Then we did arrive too late."

"As long as you are here, you could never have arrived too late." Kaarl sent the seer second an intent of gratitude. "We will drive the Ken'nar to you. I'm sure you will give them the welcome they deserve."

Morgan grabbed his forearm. … *Only one other battle seer remains* … *Binthe is all but unprotected* …

… *Not for long* … he returned. His friend nodded then regrouped his fighters and crept back into the grass. "Sahm, you and Rabb push from the south. Desde's contingent is driving them down from the northeast."

Liaonne nodded. "I will advance with Morgan. We will drive them straight into your amulet, Kaarl."

His Defending Aspect rose at her words. "We will be the last thing they ever see."

*   *   *

Teague shouted in surprise as the three Ken'nar rushed them. Binthe was already in motion. She launched herself at the black-armored defenders as he dove out of the way.

The warriors were a motley group. One stood tall and lanky, a scarecrow encased in metal. Another clambered, bearlike, as wide as he was tall. The third hung back. This warrior was slightly built. The Ken'nar's sinuous armor followed the curves of her body. Morgan's description of female Ken'nar flew up in his mind. Oh, how he wished he had metal armor, too. At least from the waist down.

The seer wielded her long knives with a ruthless efficiency worthy of any defender. The reach of the longer broadswords, however, made her vulnerable.

Teague screamed in fury and charged at the lanky Ken'nar. A swing at the warrior's shoulder hit plated armor, the impact jarring through his wrists. The Ken'nar staggered back, unscathed.

The battle seer advanced on the warrior instantly and plunged one of her knives between the metal of his chest plates. He dropped to the ground, unmoving. The strike left her open. The stocky Ken'nar brought his broadsword down hard on her shoulder. She screamed as she spun away from the blow.

The two remaining Ken'nar ignored Teague for the moment, focused on Binthe. Hatred flared within him. These Ken'nar killed his mother and father. The threat of Ken'nar pulled Mirana from his life. He would be damned if they would harm his friend.

White-hot rage exploded in him. With two hands, he brought his sword down on the female Ken'nar. She easily parried the blow, not with a broadsword of her own, but with a wickedly curved scimitar like the kind favored by Jad-Anünan defenders.

"You thought you could get away with murdering the healers of Kinderra, didn't you?" he seethed. "You didn't count on me." He made a sudden jab between the Ken'nar armored pectoral plates and drew blood.

"Teague, watch out for her amulet," Binthe cried. She spiraled around and planted a foot in his attacker's abdomen. She pivoted and parried a blow from the stocky Ken'nar with the V of crossed long knives.

The female warrior rolled away from the seer's kick, her momentum bringing her back up to her feet. Teague ignored the seer's words and thrust his blade. The dark warrior, maddened by pain now, blocked his strike with bone-wrenching force. The blow from the curved blade sent him reeling. The stocky Ken'nar had recovered and now swung at Teague's neck. He ducked, the breeze of the sword ruffling his hair as it passed over him. The female Ken'nar advanced and hammered down on the point of his blade, forcing it into the ground. He yanked at it, but the hilt slipped in his sweaty hands. He fell onto his back.

The Ken'nar's scimitar came at him, intending to cut him in half. He rolled to one side as the blade grazed the back of his shoulder. He screamed in pain. The dark warrior raised the curved blade for another strike. He tugged at his sword again, and this time it came loose. He rolled and guided the blade's sudden recoil toward the woman's ankle. His sword did not damage her greaves, but it did make her stumble. He flew to his feet.

Binthe thrust out a hand and sent the female Ken'nar flying. She landed hard and lay still. The thickset assailant moved in.

The seer motioned to Teague. "Get behind me." She lashed out at the stocky Ken'nar with her long knives, bloodying him as he lumbered away.

The female warrior recovered from Binthe's throw and scrambled up. She smashed the hilt of her sword toward the seer's temple. Binthe spun away before the move could knock her out cold—and into the reach of the stocky warrior.

"Look out!" Teague sprang into action and barreled into the big Ken'nar, sending them both to the ground.

The battle seer surged forward and drove a long knife up under the female warrior's helmet into her throat. The female dropped to her knees and clawed at her neck. Her helmet rolled off as she collapsed, unmoving. Binthe staggered back, eyes wide with shock and confusion. "Gannah? But how—?"

The remaining Ken'nar did not waste the seer's hesitation.

"Binthe!" With a cry of fury, Teague rushed the remaining warrior. Before he could attack their assailant, a sensation like a kick to the chest sent him to the ground. The battle around him plunged into silence. He tried to move, but his muscles no longer had strength.

The seer fought the large Ken'nar. No matter how skilled her grasp on the skeins of the future, her knives were no match for a defender's amulet and a massive broadsword.

The warrior loosed orange light and struck Binthe in her injured shoulder. She screamed and staggered back as she slashed at the attacker with a knife. The awkward move rent the Ken'nar's chain mail but left the seer unbalanced. The warrior brought his heavy sword down on her thigh. She cried out in pain as she fell.

"Leave her alone!" Teague clawed at the ground and tried to rise to his feet, to fight, to get his body to move. His vision tunneled.

The Ken'nar gave a guttural laugh and took a step toward him. His orange amulet brightened, releasing deadly flame. Binthe swept her hand, and the fallen helmet flew at the remaining attacker to strike him squarely in his helm, his amulet fire slewing harmlessly into the air. The Ken'nar shrugged off the blow and turned to face the wounded seer.

The world snapped back into focus, and vitality flowed once again through his limbs. Staggering to his knees, Teague glimpsed skin under the Ken'nar's helmet. If he didn't do something, Binthe would be killed. He grabbed his heavy broadsword from the ground and swung, swiping the blade across their attacker's throat. The Ken'nar's head flew from his shoulders as his body sank in a brawny heap.

Teague stepped back from the headless corpse.

He killed him. Dead. The Ken'nar was alive a moment ago. Now, he was dead. He killed him.

"Teague?"

Blood gushed from severed vessels to darken the trampled grass. The circle of a bisected vertebra shone starkly white in the darkness.

"Teague, *sibe*?"

He'd decapitated a man. He'd killed him. Dead.

Binthe's groan of pain broke through his shock. He rushed to her and dropped to his knees. He stifled a sharp inhale. Had she not moved when she did, she would have lost her leg. She still might. The Ken'nar's sword had cut her leg to the bone.

"Binthe," he whispered and tried to hide his look of concern. He was pretty certain he failed.

She groaned. "Teague, go. Run back to the hall. Desde has kept her promise. She has come. Sün-Kasal rides as well. I must stay and call the battle. Morgan's out there. I must give him what help I can."

"I won't leave you." He gritted his teeth as her blood flowed over his hand. What would stop the bleeding? What? The Ken'nar was dead. Dead. His mind refused to connect his thoughts. He frantically rummaged through his medical pack with his other hand. The Ken'nar's head. Gone. Feverfew? Lungwort? No, dammit. What? The Ken'nar. Bloodsbane. Was dead. No. *Ai*. Bloodsbane.

"Just hang on." He didn't think he had nearly enough of the blood-staunching herb in his pack for her wound, but he'd use it all if he had to.

She cried out in agony and seized his arm as he stuffed the gash with the leaves. "Get out of here," she panted between clenched teeth. "I must remain to call the battle." Her skin now felt cold to his fingers. If shock set in, he wasn't sure he could help her out in the open. "Heat. Coming. Com—" Her eyelids fluttered, and she fell slack in his arms.

"No, dammit. Binthe." He whipped a long length of bandage around the bleeding leg.

"You—" She moaned again and opened her sea-green eyes. "You must leave."

The clearing made by the trampled grass around them brightened. Was it dawn already? He wiped the sweat from his forehead. "You can't stay like this. You're wounded. The Ken'nar will kill you if they find you."

"They were not trying to kill me."

"They could have fooled me."

"They never used their amulets on me. I don't understand." She gasped as her amulet flared. "Coming."

"*Ai*, I know the Ken'nar are coming, but I'm trying to save your life." He unbuckled his belt and cinched it as tight as he could around her upper thigh.

The seer shook her head. "No. The heat—" She squeezed her eyes shut and grimaced. "The heat. It wasn't a drought. It's fire. The heat I've been seeing, sensing. It's a fire!"

"What?" He looked up. The black sky had taken on a ruddy glow. "Dear Aspects Above!"

The battlefield was on fire.

He quickly replaced his belt with one from a fallen Ken'nar and slipped his broadsword into the sheath. "It's pointless to stay here. Please." She nodded weakly and put her arm around his neck as he lifted her.

"Wait. Take me closer to her." She pointed her chin to the dead female Ken'nar. "It *is* her. Gannah Tesabe. She's an il'Kin defender. I fought alongside her. For four summers. She saved my life, and I, hers. She died in the grynwen ambush. In Kana-Akün, back in Fourthmonth. I saw her die with my living eyes. How was she alive? She would never join the Ken'nar. I-I don't understand."

He frowned at the dead woman. "If she was a traitor, she deserved to die."

Teague pushed aside the grass as they ran. The smoke grew thicker, stinging his eyes and choking him. A hot wind blew and fanned the flames of the tinder-dry grass, which in turn billowed more heat and wind into the air.

They reached a small clearing in the grass created by fallen Ken'nar, grynwen, and Unaspected. A circle of fire raged around the entire battlefield. Flames leaped high into the sky, rushing toward Edara. Beyond the fire seethed the embattled armies. Thousands upon thousands.

There was no escape.

CHAPTER 37

"A Oëmea cora'e touchá cin kinema damá Ken il'Aspecta'e."
("To those whose hearts were touched with lightning
were bestowed the Power of the Aspects.")
   —*Creara i'Kinderra* ("The Creation of Kinderra"),
      Ora Fal'kinnen 1:12

Kaarl rode his horse through the fray, Patan's hooves
crushing the shards of twisted metal and stirring up clouds of
ash. He urged his mount forward through the ever-tightening
noose of Fal'kin and Unaspected, the third prong in the deadly
trident of the allied armies of Kin-Deren, Varn-Erdal, and Sün-
Kasal.

A Ken'nar grabbed a fallen lance and rushed toward him,
but instead of thrusting, the dark warrior leveled the pike down
low. Patan tripped and sent Kaarl flying from the saddle.

Instantly, the Ken'nar warrior set upon him. He rolled with the fall back to his feet and blocked the furious attack.

He made a feint, but the Ken'nar did not take the bait and brought up his own blade. Kaarl moved too late to deflect the awkward thrust and took a blow to his shoulder. He spat a curse, pain now fueling his wrath. He thrust with his sword, blindingly fast. The Ken'nar he fought hooked his blade under Kaarl's and wrested it from his hands. The move was one he had used so many times himself.

Kaarl pulled a long knife from his belt and hurled it at his opponent. It sliced deep into the Ken'nar's sword arm. The dark warrior's broadsword now tumbled away as he howled in pain.

He rushed the Ken'nar, gripping his amulet. The dark warrior drew a wicked-looking stiletto with his uninjured left hand and swiped it at him. Kaarl sucked in his stomach to avoid a slash that would have gutted him.

He drew his belt knife. He thrust and feinted, testing his enemy's skill and reach. The Ken'nar must have been young, for his body seemed lanky, as if he had not quite grown into it. His reactions, however, bordered on frightening. The Ken'nar fought as a man possessed.

Kaarl reached out to the Ken'nar's mind to heighten his attacker's sense of fear and make him hesitate. That fraction of time would be all he needed to focus his amulet, but what he touched unnerved him.

The Ken'nar's mind was empty.

The warrior stood before him, driven to kill, but no hatred nor even fury dwelled in his mind. Killing was simply his reason for being.

Kaarl crushed his fear and made another feint, thrusting wide with his right hand, leaving himself open. The Ken'nar took the bait this time and stabbed at Kaarl's chest. He brought his left arm down hard on the Ken'nar's forearm and forced his assailant to drop the stiletto, then kicked the blade away. His opponent's amulet flared and searing pain tore into Kaarl's left shoulder as a tendril of deep violet flame bit into his flesh. He stumbled backward, screaming.

The Ken'nar grabbed the knife still embedded in his right arm and smashed the hilt against Kaarl's temple. He spun to the ground. When he could see again, the Ken'nar gripped his amulet and stood still. He didn't attack but called to someone, a particular presence.

Kaarl called his sword back to him and rushed the Ken'nar. The dark-armored defender caught his own blade as it sailed through the air and narrowly deflected the blow. Kaarl reached for his amulet as the warrior swung at his head. He ducked and brought his blade up against the side of the dark warrior's helmet. The Ken'nar dropped to the ground, his helmet flying away.

Kaarl gripped the garnet at his chest, ready to strike, when he froze. The Ken'nar's face. He knew this warrior. The eyes were hollow and vacant, but he had seen them before.

"Atan? Atan Robaar?" he whispered in horror.

This was one of the Fal'kin *scholaire'e* youths who had chosen an amulet early to support Kin-Deren's provincial forces in the Two Rivers Ford campaign. He had taught this boy some sword skills himself during the rare moments he was home from a tour of duty. The young defender had died at the ford. Kaarl knew he had. He'd seen the boy go down under a swarm of Ken'nar. How could this be?

The Ken'nar's lips curled into a feral smile. "You have no hope, Fal'kin. You will soon join me. Then you will know the true power of the Aspects."

"Atan, it's Kaarl Pinal. Son, do you not remember me? Your father was a good friend. I trained you myself."

"I only know the Ain Magne's will."

The dark-armored warrior's deep blue-violet amethyst flared. Kaarl called to his amulet. Scarlet fire held purple fire at bay before overwhelming it. In a pyre of flame, the Ken'nar shrieked, as victorious as it was anguished.

Kaarl held his garnet, shaken. Why? Why would the boy have joined the Ken'nar? Atan had not tried to kill him at first. Only when the youth knew he had lost did he strike to kill. What was going on here?

... *Northern and southern Ken'nar units converging ... Heading west ... Now targeting the hall ...* Desde's piercing call came to his mind. ... *Must not break our line ...*

Whatever forced young Atan Robaar to become a traitor was far more than simple avarice.

Kaarl ran to his horse and charged back to his troops.

*   *   *

The fire roared around Teague as he struggled through the burning grass, supporting Binthe under one arm. He coughed and gagged against the smoke. "We've got to find a way through," he sputtered.

She closed her eyes and her green amulet scintillated. "Bear to the—"

"Binthe?" He wiped the sweat from her face with his free hand. "Which way? *Siba?*"

"Le—" She wilted and moaned. "Left."

She was fading. "Come on."

In his haste, he stumbled over a gopher hole and fell with the seer. She screamed in pain. He righted himself and turned to her. Her wound had bled through the bandage. The fall had sheared it open further. He cursed. "You're bleeding again." He yanked his shirt over his head. When he loosened the belt from her leg, blood rushed out from the release of pressure. She moaned and her breathing became ragged. He quickly tied the shirt around the wound and cinched the belt again. He might not save her leg. He'd be damned, however, if he wouldn't save her life.

Binthe tensed and looked at something beyond him.

He grabbed the hilt of his broadsword. "What?" He whirled around.

A grynwen padded through the grass to stop three paces from them. Corded muscles pulled taut on its four-hundred-pound frame as a line of black fur rose along its back. Pupilless red eyes tracked from his face to the seer's, then to the seer's bleeding leg.

The seer sat still. "Don't. Move."

He wasn't about to. Not even to wipe the sweat pouring into his eyes.

A scarred, black nose twitched above a black muzzle, revealing far more teeth than should be natural for any beast. Its long tongue washed over the fangs as a stream of drool dripped from its maw.

The fire burned closer. He smiled. "Do something to distract it. A feint."

A moment later, a second grynwen slunk from the grass to face the other carnivore. Lights, not *another* one!

He glanced at the seer. Her eyes were closed, her amulet bright. He fought the urge to sigh in relief; it was a very good feint.

While she distracted the real grynwen, Teague slowly reached for his supply pack. The grynwen growled at its challenger. The other beast remained silent but curled its lips upward in a threat. He had maybe three heartbeats, if he was lucky, to do what was needed. He dragged the pack closer.

One. Two. Three.

He surged upward and whirled the pack into the flames behind them. The canvas immediately ignited. He spun the bag over his head several times then hurled it at the grynwen as it leaped toward Binthe. The burning satchel struck the beast full in the chest and set its fur on fire. It yowled and writhed before disappearing into the grass.

Now, he exhaled. "You scared the *excra* out of me with that ruse." Her eyes widened and his grateful smile disappeared with the change in her expression.

A column of fire raced toward them, a tornado spawned by heat, wind, and flame.

He hauled her up. "Run! Now!"

*   *   *

"Now!" Kaarl ordered.

A dozen Unaspected bowmen released their arrows at the Ken'nar lines at Kaarl's order.

The fire around him leaped high into the night sky. Sparks showered down like shooting stars and touched off flamelets that quickly matured into a towering blaze. The air smelled of the acrid smoke of burning brush as the flames crept closer to the learning hall. The Ken'nar army stood silhouetted against the brilliant fire, a macabre scene in deadly chiaroscuro.

He and Desde brought their forces together and charged behind the line of their archers. The dark-armored warriors fell back from their troops into Morgan's Fal'kin, waiting unseen in the tall, dry grass. The defenders picked them off one by one.

A call from a Ken'nar battle seer had a unit of fighters turn sharply and run northeast, away from the allied army.

"Desde, stop them!" Kaarl screamed.

She nodded and called to Rabb Plout's mind. The air became alive with hundreds of flaming arrows. Dozens of Ken'nar scrambled to get out of the way of the deadly onslaught and ran into the hidden Fal'kin.

He smiled at his wife. … *I have fallen in love with you all over again …*

Kaarl ordered his fighters forward and drove his horse unscathed through the ruse the seers created. The metallic slither of drawn swords answered him as he rode into the dark army, clearing a path for the Unaspected fighters. He pushed the Ken'nar closer to the flames they had set.

He brought his blade down hard on another sword hidden in the grass. The recoil of the blow sent jarring pain up his arm. Morgan ran forward and gripped his amulet, poised to slay the attacker.

"Hold!" a woman shouted. Liaonne emerged from the brush, covered in blood and grime.

Desde rode over to the young prime. "Liaonne, thank the Aspects you're safe."

Kaarl dismounted and gripped the prime's forearm. "I could have killed you."

One corner of her mouth curled wickedly. "Against my blade? I don't think so. Besides, you'd have to stand in line. It seems like every Ken'nar on this battlefield personally wants my head." She wiped at a nasty gash on her arm.

The Defending Aspect surged through him. "Down!" He grabbed her uninjured shoulder and pushed her.

He brought his blade down hard on a broadsword as a Ken'nar appeared from the grass behind her. The dark-armored warrior curled his hand into a fist. Before Kaarl could reach for his amulet, his legs buckled. He fell to the ground, all feeling leaving his body. Desde shouted as she and Morgan rushed toward him.

The warrior leaped upon Kaarl and pinned him to the ground. His attacker's shin greaves dug into his chest and stifled his breath. Light swirled in the Ken'nar's amulet, the softest lavender, as the warrior locked a hand over his temples. Pain such as he had never known assailed him. Kaarl screamed, arching his back in agony.

A moment later, the Ken'nar collapsed on top of him as his wife retracted the butt of a long knife from the dark warrior's head. The force of her blow sent the Ken'nar's helmet rolling away. Kaarl dragged himself from underneath the unconscious Ken'nar, kicking the man in violent disgust.

"He's mine." Liaonne snarled as her amulet crackled with unreleased fire.

"No, wait." Desde stayed her hand. "Something is not right here. He wasn't trying to kill Kaarl."

"I wouldn't call that a friendly joust," Morgan said as he helped Kaarl up from the ground.

Kaarl rubbed at the lingering ache on his forehead. "She's right. He tried to knock me out. Another one tried as well. They both could have just as easily killed me."

His wife scowled. "Other one? They wanted you alive?"

"But why?" The younger il'Kin defender eyed the fallen warrior with loathing.

The amulet the Ken'nar used seemed almost familiar. "Wait a moment." Kaarl knelt beside the stunned warrior and rolled him over onto his back.

Desde reached down to pull him away, then stepped back and gasped. "Kaarl—"

He stiffened in shock. "What evil is this?"

"Why? Why would he do this?" Morgan asked.

"Whatever is going on here, he will tell us." Liaonne hefted her sword. "I guarantee it." She whistled to two Fal'kin. "Bind him. Take his amulet from him and bring him back behind the lines. Do not let him regain consciousness until we can question him."

Kaarl's mind still reeled at the treason of young Atan Robaar, and now this? This was not a case of bolstering someone's discontent by convincing them they stood a greater chance of victory by siding with the Ken'nar. No, this was some power unleashed from the very gates of the Underworld.

"Desde, we need to finish this madness. Now." Kaarl vaulted back onto Patan and charged back into the fray.

CHAPTER 38

"Death surrounded them, an Aspect girded in black armor."
—The Book of Kinderra

"Teague, stop," Binthe cried weakly. "I can't run anymore."

Smoke stung his eyes and obscured his vision. He wiped impatiently at them with the heel of his hand. He set her down as gently as he could. Blood had soaked through the crude bandage on the seer's leg. Unless he could pull off a miracle, she would lose her leg. No, she would die.

"Leave me. Let me call this battle while I still can." She lifted her chin. "It is my right. It is my birthright."

"You can call the battle anyplace you want, just not here." He coughed again at the smoke. "The fire is getting closer. We have to keep moving." He began to lift her again.

"No. Teague. Stop. You must go. The future skeins are clouded, but Mirana will need you. Go."

"She doesn't need me. She is a Trine. Right now, it's you that needs me. I'll not leave you to sacrifice yourself for me."

"It is my right to sacrifice myself. I am a Fal'kin. This is why I was born." She raised a hand to his cheek. "*Ëi sibe íuven.* I am not frightened."

He took her hand in his own. "Good. Because you're just going to have to live a little while longer. You can't die. You'll take Morgan's heart with you."

He had to stop Binthe's bleeding. But how? He didn't have any more bloodsbane. The bandage, even using his belt as a tourniquet, did not work.

"Morgan." She breathed the defender's name and squeezed her eyes shut.

"Your call won't do any good. He'll never find us in this."

He clawed his fingers through his hair. Sending an image of their location to the defender's mind wouldn't help, either. Everything was in flames. Morgan would have no way to tell their location from any other.

Binthe clenched her teeth and held back a cry of pain, her amulet glowing with the effort.

Her amulet! "Binthe, your amulet. Use your amulet to send up a flare."

"I can't. You know that. Only—" She coughed and gagged against the smoke. "Only defenders can bring fire from their amulets."

He shook his head and smiled. "I didn't say it had to be real. Create another seer's ruse. A fire cyclone. Send an image of the largest tower of amulet fire you can possibly imagine."

She nodded. "I'll try." She cradled her amulet in both hands and furrowed her brows in concentration. The image of a thin jet of green flame rose from the emerald gemstone. It soared into the air, only to flicker and disappear a moment later. "I can't," she panted. Her hand dropped to the ground and she fell limp in his arms.

"Binthe. Don't you dare leave me. *Ëi siba?* Binthe!" He placed her hands over the amulet and held them with his own. "Morgan needs you. If you die, you'll break his heart. That's worse than death itself. I know you love him and he loves you. Don't break his heart. Please, you've got to try again."

"Morgan." She grimaced in pain and effort.

A tower of verdant flame erupted into the sky. He turned from it and lidded his eyes from its brilliance as his hands remained locked over hers. "It's working. It's working. Keep it up."

The emerald column illusion pierced the smoke-filled night sky, brighter than the true flames it dwarfed.

She groaned again. The enormous pillar of fire sputtered once more and dissipated.

"Binthe?" He shook her. She did not move this time. "Oh, Binthe."

*   *   *

Kaarl fought close to the growing wall of fire and drained his amulet into the Ken'nar. The Kin-Deren Unaspected had converged with Sahm Klai's Fal'kin contingent, while Morgan's and Liaonne's Fal'kin fighters continued to push the Ken'nar toward them through the grass.

He raced his mount farther down the line. Thousands of Fal'kin and Unaspected fought as one, overwhelming the Ken'nar in an all-consuming tidal wave of swords, bows, and amulet fire.

... *The Ken'nar are in retreat!* ... came Desde's wide call to all Fal'kin who could hear. ... *They retreat!* ...

Like the receding tide of the ocean, the Ken'nar turned and fell back. They charged to the northeast, racing off the battlefield.

Sahm Klai clapped Rabb Plout on the back. "We've routed the black bastards!"

Kaarl gripped his saddle's pommel before he could fall from his horse. Retreat. He had never heard a more beautiful word in his life. The battle had left him far too exhausted and still too consumed in the grip of the Defending Aspect to think of a coherent prayer, but he hoped the Aspects Above could sense the overwhelming gratitude he held in his heart.

His wife ran to him and reached up to hold his arm. For a moment, he could not even find the strength to return her embrace.

Liaonne reached over to grip Sahm's forearm. "You saved the day, and a province, *Ëi cara.*"

The big prime smiled. "Just showing you how it's done, girl." The Varn-Erdalan woman crossed her arms and lifted her chin. The Sün-Kasalan smiled more broadly. "Forgive me. I'm just showing you how it's done, *my prime.*"

Kaarl dismounted, stumbling as his boots touched the parched earth. Morgan steadied him and gave him the biggest smile he could ever remember on his friend's face. "Once again, *Ëi sibe,* we remain standing. The Aspects Above really don't want us, do they?"

"I still do," Liaonne said. "I want to make sure won't circle back. I will bring in my—" She turned to the west. "No." She drew her sword, ran a few paces, and stopped. "No. Aspects Above. No."

Kaarl turned in the direction the young prime faced. For the second time in as many moments, his breath caught in his chest. Gale-force winds created by the heat of the fire billowed across the fields. The spectral outlines of an enormous wooden structure flickered within an unbroken wall of hellfire.

The young defender prime screamed in rage and brought her sword down on a corpse of a Ken'nar. She hacked at the body until it became an unrecognizable heap of flesh and torn metal armor.

"Liaonne. *Ëi siba.* Stop, Liaonne. You must stop. Liaonne!" Desde dragged her away from the dead Ken'nar.

The sword fell from Liaonne's hands as she sank to her knees, wracked by anguished sobbing.

Flames completely engulfed the learning hall of Edara.

CHAPTER 39

"Ama ísi forte i'tuda clae'e."
("Love is the mightiest of all weapons.")
—Ora Fal'kinnen 268:8

Liaonne Edaran paced like a caged animal. The flames of the learning hall of Edara illuminated her savage grimace. "They will pay for this."

Kaarl hung his head and held his amulet. He owed his life and the lives of so many others to this bit of gold and garnet, this mysterious, miraculous creation that allowed his Defending Aspect outside of himself. This time, it had failed him—and a province—entirely.

In the distance, a wall of fire consumed the once-proud ramparts and stockades of the learning hall. Flames leaped from rooftop to rooftop and devoured every structure like a ravenous grynwen.

"I don't care if the Ken'nar are in retreat. I will slaughter them as they run," the young prime spat. "Morgan, where is Binthe? I need her knives."

The il'Kin defender commander scowled. "Has she not called to you?" He looked from Liaonne to Desde. "Either of you?" The shock of realization written on the women's faces answered his question.

The young prime turned once more to face the conflagration. "She was the only experienced battle seer I had left. She took the eastern point, where the attack was most likely to begin. Teague was with her."

Kaarl's head snapped back around to the east. The fields spread before Edara had turned to an ocean of fire. "They would have been in the direct path of the Ken'nar."

"Why didn't you tell me you hadn't heard from her? I must find her. Binthe!" Morgan ran closer to the wall of fire.

Kaarl pulled his friend back from the flames. "What are you doing, man? You will be burned alive."

"Stand aside. I have to find Binthe," the defender snarled.

Sahm Klai held Morgan's arm with a massive hand. "You cannot find her if you are dead."

"Get out of my way." Morgan wrestled his arm away. "I've got to find her."

The Varn-Erdalan prime rushed in front of him and blocked his path. "You blindly search for her in there and you'll burn to death. That will save no one."

"I will not let her die. I will not let that happen again."

Kaarl shook his head. "You cannot save Binthe this way. We need to know where she is first."

The il'Kin defender flicked his wrist and held a belt knife. "Get out of my way."

Kaarl held up his hands. "Morgan, this will not bring Clarienne or Pieter back, nor will it save Binthe. Let it go."

"I was too far away. Again! I'm always too far away. I tried. I watched over my bloody sheep instead of my wife and son," he said, his voice taut with emotion he fought to contain. "And now Binthe. Out there." His hand clenched and relaxed in repetition around his belt knife. "The Ken'nar came, but Clarienne was Unaspected. She couldn't call me. I was too far to save them. I should never have left them. I was too far. I swore I'd never let that happen again. I should never have left Binthe alone in this. I must save her."

"We will, but we have to find her first," Desde said. "Please, *Ëi sibe*."

The younger man's shoulders fell in defeat. "How? She does not answer my calls. I can't lose her. I cannot."

Kaarl reached out again to hold the defender's arms. The man's mortal torment filled his own mind. "She is strong. We will find her."

"Look." Rabb Plout pointed to the middle of the conflagration.

An enormous jet of green flame rose above the orange fire into the night sky.

"Binthe." Morgan spoke her name like a prayer. "It's her. I know it is."

Kaarl scowled in awed confusion. "It can't be. Binthe is a seer. How is such a thing possible?"

A joyous smile lit his wife's face. "It is her." She laughed in astonishment. "She's created a seer's ruse."

Morgan snapped his head around toward the fire. "Binthe!" The emerald column of light held a few moments longer, then disappeared.

The young commander turned back to face Desde. "I need your horse." He cut a section of his uniform with his belt knife. He tied the cloth around his nose and mouth.

Desde held the reins, preventing him from climbing into the saddle. "Only if you promise me you'll both come back."

He nodded and took the horse's reins. He swung up into the saddle and charged toward the writhing wall of fire.

Kaarl watched him ride off. "Liaonne said Teague was with her. Morgan will need help." He grabbed a fallen Kin-Deren standard and slashed off a piece of cloth with his sword.

His wife gripped his arm. "I forbid you to make me a widow. Not after Two Rivers Ford and all of this, too."

He kissed her deeply, then tied the cloth over his face, and followed Morgan into the flames.

*   *   *

A tongue of fire licked Teague's shoulder as the breath of the searing wind blew the flames higher into the sky. He hissed and dragged Binthe farther away from the wall of fire. Her face appeared deathly pale in the firelight. She no longer responded to his voice but lay inert in his arms. He was losing her.

Deren's townsfolk had once brought a meat butcher to his parents in the healing hostel. The man's cleaver had slipped from his grasp and had taken off his hand. His parents had to staunch the bleeding before they could even begin to heal the traumatic wound with their Healing Aspect. They cauterized it—with a knife held in the fire.

"Binthe, hold on." He gently laid her down on the ground and drew his broadsword. He brought an arm in front of his face against the searing heat and held the blade in the fire. The stains of the Ken'nar's blood on the metal boiled and blackened until the ash, too, was consumed. When he could no longer stand the heat, he pulled the blade out. It glowed red.

He knelt back down, careful not to touch the sword to anything. "This is going to hurt. A lot. But I don't know what else to do to save your life."

With his free hand, he unbuckled the belt from her leg and removed the blood-soaked bandages and the bloodsbane. He carefully wedged the belt between her teeth. "I'll be quick."

He swallowed against the gorge rising in his throat. He steadied her leg, took a breath, and placed the flat of the heated sword against the laceration on Binthe's thigh. Her eyes flew open, and she gave a piercing cry. Mercifully, unconsciousness took her moments later, and she lay still once more. Where there had been a gaping wound on her thigh, now angry, burnt flesh closed the gash.

He let the broadsword fall and drew the seer back into his arms. With trembling fingers, he removed the belt from her mouth and felt her neck for a pulse. He couldn't find a heartbeat.

"No." He moved his fingers slightly and waited. "No, no, no. Binthe, please don't do this."

Had the shock killed her? Had he killed her from the pain alone? He had killed. The Ken'nar. Dead.

A weak throb finally beat against his fingertips.

He laughed, or maybe he cried, or maybe both. He no longer cared, and he let the tears come. He brushed Binthe's auburn hair back from her pale, sweaty face.

"Don't leave, *Ëi siba*. Please don't break Morgan's heart."

CHAPTER 40

"When I descended into the madness of war, you showed me the way back. Ah, Beloved! The Dove of Tash-Hamar!"

—The Codex of Jasal the Great

Teague curled his body around Binthe's unconscious form, trying to protect her from the worst of the heat, as the cage of flame slowly contracted.

Thirst and sweat had long since abandoned him and left exhaustion behind. He wanted nothing more than to sink into the thickness growing in mind and limbs. His chest rose and fell in some semblance of breathing, but he was no longer certain there was any air left to breathe. Every inhale, every exhale felt like an amulet igniting his lungs.

A shape emerged from the fire in the distance. A rider on a horse. After everything he had done to save Binthe, he would not let a Ken'nar take her now. Teague reached for the heavy broadsword, his arm shaking with the effort to lift it. He forced himself to his knees, using the sword as leverage. The rider charged closer. Teague pulled in a great gulp of searing air. The pain in his lungs revived him. With a cry of exertion, he staggered to his feet and held the Ken'nar broadsword in front of him, guarding Binthe.

The rider looked just like Morgan Jord. Teague blinked the soot out of his heat-dried eyes. Maybe that last toxic inhale had done him in, and he was already dead.

"Binthe?" the rider shouted over the roaring fire.

The seer stirred next to him. "Morgan."

"Morgan?" Teague rasped as he fought for air. He shook his head, trying to clear it.

"Binthe?" Morgan yelled. "Teague!"

It *was* Morgan.

The defender leaped off his horse. He lowered the cloth from his face and embraced him. "Thank the Aspects Above I found you." He knelt next to Binthe. "Is she—?"

"She's alive, but not for long if you don't hurry. She's gravely wounded. Her leg," Teague replied. "She lost a lot of blood. I've cauterized it. I don't know if it was enough."

The seer's eyes fluttered open. "Morgan?"

The defender cradled her in his arms. "Binthe."

She reached up to touch his cheek. "I knew you'd come. I saw it."

He brushed back the hair from her face. "I would never leave you, Binthe of the Sea." He drew her to him and kissed her deeply. "I'm getting you out of here." He lifted her onto his horse and swung into the saddle behind the seer. He placed the cloth over her mouth and reached down. "Come. We must hurry."

Teague glanced at the flames. The horse would have been hard-pressed to bring Morgan to them. With two riders, it would be all but impossible to ride back out. With three?

"Get her to safety."

"Teague."

"I've done all I can for her. If you don't leave now, you'll never make it."

The defender reached down and gripped his forearm. "I will return."

His friend certainly wanted to come back for him. There simply was little chance, however, for the man to do so. So, he just nodded.

Morgan stabbed his heels into his horse's flanks and raced away.

Teague jogged for a while, following the il'Kin, but soon the heat and smoke overcame him. He sank to his hands and knees, choking and gasping for air. Just hours ago—had it only been hours?—he'd wondered if he would see his mother and father before the battle for Varn-Erdal was over. He had expected death from a Ken'nar's blade, not fire.

He pushed himself up again and staggered forward a few more steps. The fire approached nearer and stole the air as it fed off the grass. A howling wind from the firestorm buffeted him. The ground rushed up at him.

The end must be near now because Morgan's horse paused and split into two. One horse disappeared while another galloped toward him. Maybe it was a Ken'nar after all. He had never been so glad to see one in his life. He'd rather take a blade than burn to death.

Morgan had said Teague's parents had consecrated him to save lives, an oath no less than that of the Fal'kin's own. Teague had killed. It was a Ken'nar, and he did so to save Binthe's life, but he had taken a life. Maybe the debt would now be repaid.

The rider raced toward him, his mount, a white and brown dappled horse, hardly larger than a pony. It certainly didn't look like a warhorse. It didn't matter. He didn't matter. All that mattered was Mirana. Maybe by saving Binthe, Morgan would have the courage to go on. Maybe he had saved Mirana by saving both of his dear friends.

He no longer felt the heat. He no longer felt much of anything. He closed his eyes and, at last, gave in to the suffocation blanketing his mind.

"Teague?" Someone called his name, dragging him back to consciousness. "Teague! Wake up, son!"

Strong hands jostled him. He opened his eyes as slits. The Ken'nar looked like Mirana's father, Kaarl. He wanted to tell her father how much she meant to him, and he had been too much a fool to understand she had been trying to save his life.

"I'll get you out of here. Hang on, *biraen*."

The man with silver eyes—they were just like Mirana's eyes—put him on the dappled horse. He tied something over Teague's nose and mouth. Teague couldn't breathe as it was. He fought weakly as the world plunged into darkness.

"We're almost there, Teague. Stay with me."

The pounding hooves of the steed jarred him awake once more. He had to speak to her father before he faded for good.

"I loved Mirana. Tell her I loved her, and I wanted to make her my wife. My wife. For forever."

"You'll have to tell her that yourself." The man's voice sounded, well, sounded *happy*. Strong arms tensed about him.

"Hold your breath and shut your eyes. Do not open them, do not breathe, until I tell you."

The air around him became living heat. He fought a scream of pain and terror. His lungs ached. His skin burned. He could not hold back any longer. He screamed when the icy wall of cold air hit him.

"Teague, it's all right. You're safe now, lad."

His eyes would not open now. Maybe they had been seared shut. They felt that way. Each knifing breath stabbed through his lungs. Other arms now carried him, other voices shouted. He wanted to cry out again. His skin hurt; their touch was so painful. It hurt to breathe. Everything hurt. Why wouldn't they leave him alone so he could sleep? Were his mother and father still in pain, wherever they were? *Paithe. Maithe.*

When he was a part of the Aspects, when Mirana touched them, she would know how much he loved her. When he was with the Aspects, he would be with her forever.

Mirana.

CHAPTER 41

"Comé ísi Verdas?"
("What is Truth?")
—Ora Fal'kinnen 300:1

Teague lies on the stone, life bleeding from him. She calls his name. He does not answer. The Dark Trine's sword comes at her. It tears through her abdomen. She sinks to her knees. Blood flows hot over her hand. The Ken'nar overlord crosses behind her, brushing her hair back from her neck to clasp the chain of an amulet. His touch is gentle, his fingers like ice. Betrayal overwhelms her more than any mortal blow.

Mirana awoke with a start and clutched at her chest.

"Mirana?" Tetric Garis held her, calming her thrashing. "You had the vision again, didn't you?"

She pushed herself out of his arms and did not reply. Too many words needed to be said, and each one more painful than the next.

"You saw more this time." His words were a statement, not a question.

She placed a hand on her stomach. The gaping wound she expected to find was not there. Her neck was free of the heavy burden of an amulet. Everything was as it should be. Except that it was not. It would never be again.

The Trine reached for her again. "Mirana?"

She grabbed his wrist and stopped him from touching her.

Small trees dotted the landscape around them and waved in the wind under the bright midday sun. Birds sang to each other in the branches. Far off to the east, the Dar-Jad Al Mountains rose a misty purple from the green line of the distant jungle. A salty tang hung in the humid breeze.

The horses still had their saddles on. How long had she been unconscious? How long had he lied to Kinderra? To her? "How did you find me?"

The kind, concerned smile he offered crushed her more than the flat, cold expression of murderous vengeance. "I hold your Aspects closer than my own."

"Ashtar." Mirana rose to her feet on legs that had yet to find their full strength and stumbled over to her horse, when she stopped abruptly. Her ankle. It was whole.

"What did they send after you?" he asked. "I nearly had to take your right foot from you. You must eat. Healing takes much more from the patient than it does the healer."

She ignored him and wrapped her arms around the warhorse's massive chestnut neck, inhaling his musky, sweet-hay scent.

Tetric rummaged through his stallion's saddlebag and held out some dried fruit, but she refused to take it, tightening her embrace on the warhorse. The Trine set his mouth in that now-familiar hard line and put the fruit back in the saddlebag. He withdrew the alabaster cylinder. "Here. You apparently fought quite hard for it, you should be the one to open it."

She eyed him for a moment before taking the container. Shades of several emotions seeped from his mind as she touched his hand. Anticipation, certainly, but something deeper. Worry. No, not worry. A sort of sadness, a muted dread. About her. He knew her feelings of betrayal and so much more threatened to pull them apart.

He gestured to the cylinder. "Well?"

Her own emotions defied simple labels. Doubt—or, more truthfully, denial—was left behind with the dead bodies of Seer Prime Eshe Pashcot and Defender Second Syne Devlan.

"How can you just stand there and act as though nothing has happened?"

He looked out over the grass and pulled his head to one side, stretching his neck muscles. "So, her poison has already taken effect?"

"Her vision of you attacking that man was the final piece, not the first. Tetric, you killed her. And you used me to do it. You took my Healing Aspect with your Power from Without and used it to kill Eshe Pashcot."

He whirled on her. "She was trying to separate us, destroy our bond. Mirana, we must. Remain. Together. Or Kinderra will fall. I did what I had to, to save your life."

She stepped closer, meeting his challenge. "It wasn't only her vision separating us. It's you. And-And all the *evil* you hold as good."

"Evil?" His black gaze bore down on her for a moment longer before he finally released his anger in a soul-weary sigh. "I would have never believed *Matura* Eshe would have done this to me. She only let you see what she wanted you to see."

"I saw you kill that man. I saw you blind her. You killed him with your Healing Aspect fueled by the Power from Without. And you killed her now for showing me what you did. I once thought you gave me hope. All you've given me is lies. My parents—Oh, Light Above! I was such a fool!"

"Mirana, you are as dear to me as any child could have ever been. Why are you abandoning me like this?"

He was the one who had abandoned *her*, abandoned Kinderra, with the very lie of his existence.

When she refused to answer him, his shoulders fell. There were no thoughts of his now that she could not see, no emotions she could not feel. His grief threatened to magnify her own.

"I never knew the woman who bore me, nor the man," he said with a hushed voice. "Eshe and Lindar Pashcot brought me into their home when I had nowhere else to go. I was just a boy, not more than a summer older than you. I did not know my strength. Rumors had preceded me. Eshe is—was the wisest of all Fal'kin. Surely, if anyone could show me the path to become a Trine, what I needed to become for Kinderra's sake, she could. She said she could. She and her husband, both.

"When Lindar learned I used the fullness of the expression of the Aspects, he didn't just seek to stop me, he sought to kill me. I went to him, to talk sanity with him. He drew a sword on me and called me an abomination. I went to Eshe and begged for her help. When I told her that Lindar plotted against me, do you know what she did? Do you know how she helped me? She laughed at me, Mirana. I loved her as the only mother I had ever known. And she laughed at me. She refused to believe her husband would have done such a thing.

"Did Eshe show you any of this? Did she show you how many of her own Fal'kin's lives I saved, her own Unaspected, using my powers from Within *and* Without? Did she show you how hard I tried to convince Lindar I was not the monster he portrayed me to be? He took advantage of me. Of my trust, my love. On that practice field. Did she show you that? Did she show you the knife he tried to drive through my heart as I helped him off the ground?"

Mirana shook her head slowly. "No."

"And why do you think that was? Because she would rather have been chained to the ignorant belief that the Power from Without has no place in Kinderra. You know that's not true. You understand something that she, in all her summers, in all her immense Aspect, had refused to understand and accept. *Ai*, I killed her husband. *Ai*, I blinded her. And had I not acted when I did, I would be dead. Had they succeeded in killing me that day, what would have become of you in Deren's library?"

She curled her hands into fists and stalked close, feeling the heat of her Defending Aspect reflected in his amulet. "You would have never lived to become the Dark Trine! The prophecy would still be a half-forgotten legend. And I wouldn't have been tortured by it to the point where I tried to kill myself!"

He did not change his stance. "It is a myth, Mirana. I told you that before. A fable created by the narrow-minded and those unwilling to change their beliefs for peace. You have used the fullness of the Aspects. You know what it can do."

She laughed at the tragedy of his disbelief. "The only myth, the only fable is the one you've accepted about yourself. That the horrors you perpetrate on Kinderra and her people are somehow justified because you think they will stop the war.

How can you believe you'll be Kinderra's savior when you believe the Soul Harvest is a blessing gifted to you by the Aspects Above? When you accept the stealing of life to add strength to your power is a *good* thing!"

He lifted his head to the sky. "Mirana, I have made mistakes. Serious ones. Those feral folk we fought in the Vale i'Dúadar are some of the most heartbreaking. Beings who used to be men and women, who I thought, in my arrogance, I could turn into allies of a sort through the Soul Harvest. *Ai,* I used it before I fully understood it. Now that I do," he leaned toward her, his eyes flat and black, "I have saved *thousands* with it. Men and women who rightfully should be *dead!*"

His words chilled her. She wanted to run from him, to distance herself from his words, from her ignorance having once abdicated her conscience to him.

"You will never become the Trine Kinderra needs you to be if you do not accept all the power the Aspects Above have given us," he continued. "If you do not, the evil you see in your keep for yourself will become an indelible path, and you will be consumed by it."

She squared her shoulders. "It will become my path if I do. The Power from Without is a murderous weapon of the most insidious kind. I will not use it again, knowing what I know now. It is an abomination."

He hung his head. "If this is the truth you cling to, then there is nothing I can do to change your mind."

She kept her distance from her once-mentor. "It's not my mind that must change, Tetric. It's yours."

… I thought you understood what I was trying to do?…

"I did. Until I realized it was all an illusion wrapped in half-truths. You will not rebuild this continent through the Power from Without. You will just impose on her a new form of destruction buried under false wholeness."

He stalked closer still, towering over her. ... *You understand NOTHING! ... I have given my entire life, all that I am, to save the people on this continent ... To stop Kinderra from destroying herself ... Such is the destiny the Aspects Above have given me ... It is why I have come into this world ... I will see this through.... Any way I must ... There is no choice in this ... It is the way it must be ...*

She turned her face from him, from his imploring amulet, his imploring mind. No emotions could ever express the betrayal she felt.

"I trusted you," she whispered in tortured understanding. "I believed in you. I turned my back on my parents for you. I loved you just as much as I did my father." She clutched the alabaster cylinder and the precious writings it contained to her heart. "I will no longer choose your lies over the truth. If we are to be enemies to bring true freedom to Kinderra, so be it. *That* is the way it must be."

... *Please don't leave me, Mirana ... Please don't ... You are my child now ... You belong to me ...*

She ran to Ashtar. In a single, fluid movement, she vaulted onto his broad back and dug her heels into his sides.

... *Do not leave me ...*

She raced away from Tetric Garis as bitter acceptance, a suffocating pall, smothered the torn shreds of her heart.

CHAPTER 42

"Quistempre'e Ëomus u'vide trevia, per trevia pone et bia Ëome."
("Sometimes we cannot see the way, yet the path lies there before us.")
—Ora Fal'kinnen 198:18

A fireplace sat in Teague's lungs—with the fire still in it.

Full consciousness came at him like a battering ram bent on vengeance. He lay on his side, the position aggravating a dozen different aches. He rolled over onto his back. That hurt a lot more. He coughed. That hurt far too much to do a second time. He cried out in pain—or meant to—giving a sort of whimpering moan instead.

"He's awake. Oh, Teague. Thank the Aspects Above!"

Raising his eyelids took more effort than he expected. "Illenne?" He blinked. She appeared travel-worn but otherwise unscathed.

He lay on a straw pallet under a tent, some muslin thrown over several poles, its sides open to the air. Raindrops seeped through the cloth to patter on the ground. Other wounded, hundreds of them, convalesced around him and in dozens of other similar shelters. Scorched fields spread into the distance. Beyond the blackened stubble, a few timbers smoldered despite the rain.

Edara.

He turned his head away. It was not a dream after all.

Mirana's mother, Desde, knelt beside him. "How are you feeling?" Standing behind her was Mirana's father, along with Defender Prime Klai and Seer Second Plout.

He didn't know how to answer her. He should not be alive to breathe, let alone do anything else. "*Ëo anaíle; Ëo aspece*," he said at last.

"You are a very brave young man," Kaarl said, smiling.

"No, I'm not, sir." He coughed again and gritted his teeth. "You and Morgan are the brave ones. You rode through the fire to save us."

The steward crouched down. "Teague, Binthe told me what you did."

"I could have wounded the Ken'nar." Morgan and Binthe had been right. His parents died sacrificing themselves so that he would live on to carry on what they had taught him about saving lives. He took that sacrifice and made a mockery of it. "I could have rendered him senseless. But I didn't."

Mirana's father shook his head slowly. "No, you couldn't have. They fight with inhuman tenacity. Had you not done what you did, that Ken'nar would have killed you and Binthe both. You saved her life."

He sat up too quickly, and his head swam. "Wait. Binthe's all right?"

Kaarl nodded and pointed.

The Rün-Tarani seer stood on a hastily made crutch, her wounded leg bound in a dressing, Morgan Jord by her side. She smiled as she approached. "The herbsfolk say I should be able to outrun grynwen in a few sevendays. Thanks to you."

He worked his mouth before his brain could think of any words. "You're standing." How did she still have her leg? Cauterizing the wound might have stopped the bleeding, but the procedure could damage flesh as much as the wound itself.

Morgan knelt and gripped his forearm. "You are truly your mother and father's son. *Gratas Oë, Ëi sibe.*"

He averted the il'Kin defender's gaze and pulled at a bandage on his other forearm.

Defender Prime Liaonne Edaran entered the tent. "You are awake. That is good." She gave him a curt nod. "You have wasted enough time sleeping. I need your help with my people."

Cuts and scrapes covered the young Varn-Erdalan prime's limbs, and angry red blisters marred the skin on her forearms. He scowled. Why weren't the wounds on her left shoulder and right thigh bandaged? Knowing Liaonne, she'd probably refused. "Was anything spared?" he asked instead.

Her hollow expression gave him all the answer he needed. "We were able to free what horses were still in the stables. Your Bankin is fine."

That miserable, obstinate, wonderful, courageous nag. She was alive. He wiped at a raindrop that fell on his cheek through the tarp. "The rain must have helped." Strange, the drop felt warm.

Prime Liaonne blinked back some rain that fell on her own face. "It came too late. Nothing stands now. Edara is gone."

"*Ai*, my prime, but we still live. Your horses still live," Illenne Talz replied. "My father and the others, we did not lose a one. Horse, aged seer, or Unaspected. We live. Did you not tell me yourself that Edara, Varn-Erdal, was not a building, but us? All of us? Together?"

The defender woman swallowed and nodded. "We will rebuild. We must."

In the distance, the dilapidated remains of the learning hall appeared gray and ghostlike in the rain. "My parents once told me," Teague cleared his throat of the logjam that had lodged there, "they told me healing, the recovery, is the slowest, most painful journey there is, but also the most important." He fiddled with a thread on the linen bandage. "Even the most rewarding."

Where would they even start, though? If Kana-Akün was under Ken'nar control, how would Varn-Erdal get the timber it needed to rebuild? Or any other province, for that matter? The Reckoning would turn before wood from Jad-Anüna would reach Varn-Erdal.

Prime Liaonne nodded. "You are correct, Teague."

He frowned. "You heard that?"

"We all did." Prime Desde smiled. "It is another facet of your bravery. You tend to think what we are all too afraid to say aloud." Then her expression hardened. "It is as the Ken'nar said. The Dark Trine is waiting on our doorstep."

Teague scowled in confusion. "Ken'nar? You captured a Ken'nar? How? Don't they usually light themselves up like a Quorumtide bonfire if they're ever captured?" The Fal'kin must have taken his amulet before the warrior could fire it. Unless the Ken'nar wasn't a defender.

"We captured a Ken'nar," Sahm Klai answered and exchanged a furtive glance with the other Fal'kin. "He tried to attack Steward Pinal as the battle wound down. Prime Kellis Pinal rendered him unconscious, and we had him brought back behind the lines to interrogate him."

Teague rubbed at his burned chest and quickly wished he hadn't. They said the Ken'nar told them the Dark Trine was waiting on their doorstep—present tense. He was poised to strike? Now? "Have you asked him about the size of the Dark Trine's army?"

Rabb Plout shifted nervously. "We cannot get close enough to question him."

He didn't have to be able to read their thoughts to understand they weren't telling him everything. "When he was unconscious, didn't you take his amulet?"

Steward Kaarl glanced at Prime Desde, maybe even calling something. "We did, but he is still very dangerous."

He coughed and grimaced with a laugh. "Other than toss you on your butt," he smirked at Morgan, "a defender can't really do anything to you without his amulet. A seer can barely do that much."

"He's neither a defender nor a seer," Illenne said.

"*Obsca, biraena*!" Prime Liaonne hissed.

The horse mistress threaded her arm through his and held him protectively. "He deserves to know."

His mind lurched. "The Ken'nar is a healer?" He struggled to get his feet under him. "I want to see this man."

Morgan steadied him back down on the pallet. "No, Teague. It's much too dangerous. He has injured anyone who has come close."

"Let me go. I want to see him—"

Kaarl held up his hand, stopping the comment. "Teague, no."

With Illenne's help, he clambered up. "I am Unaspected. He may not perceive me as a threat."

"Teague," Desde said, tears embedded in her voice, "the healer we've taken. He may be…that is, he appears to be…your father."

His mind halted, hard. He heard her words, but they wouldn't connect into meaning.

Kaarl squeezed his wife's hand. "Son, it looks like him, but the Ken'nar have done something to him. That-That creature is no longer your father. Give us some time. Maybe we can—"

Hope burned like an amulet in his heart. "Where is he?" he demanded.

Illenne nodded toward another tent, some distance from the makeshift village.

He ignored the Fal'kin and walked toward the tent. Cautiously, he pushed back the flap and held his arms out at his sides as he entered.

No. It couldn't be. It could not be. It just looked like him, that's all. Just like they said. The same hair, the same face, the same eyes. The dark warrior stirred. Teague stopped, just outside of the tent.

The man stared right at him, expressionless, no joy at seeing him, no recognition. No love.

Aspects Above, no.

He took a step closer. The man made a low snarling noise.

Teague's heart drummed in his chest. "Let me see his amulet."

The steward shook his head. "Son, he isn't—"

"Now."

Kaarl hesitated then reached into the folds of his torn and stained uniform. He pulled out a pale purple sapphire, the color of spring lilacs, centered in a gold amulet.

Teague had seen this amulet every day of his life. He turned to the Ken'nar.

"Father?"

"Come closer, boy." The man's voice oozed between his ears, at once soothing and edged with ice, something familiar yet not.

He could not feel himself breathe nor the ground beneath his feet. All he knew was his father was alive. "Father, it's me. It's your son, Teague." The Ken'nar healer remained silent.

Teague rushed over to the man who had been Tennen Beltran and wrapped his arms around him, tears streaming down his face. "Father! You're alive! You're alive!"

"Teague! Don't!" Someone shouted behind him to warn him.

"I thought you were dead. What are you doing dressed as a Ken'nar?" When the warrior did not answer, he asked again, "Father?" He lifted his head from the man's shoulder. "It's me. Teague. Don't you recognize me? What has happened to you? Have the Ken'nar poisoned you? Where is Mother?"

Morgan and Kaarl rushed into the tent, Prime Desde and Binthe just behind them. "Stay back," Binthe cried, "or he'll kill him."

His father was alive! No matter what the Ken'nar had done to him, his father was alive and Teague would find a way to heal him. Teague loosened one of the chains binding the Ken'nar. "I can help you, Father. I know I can."

"No! Don't!" It sounded like Prime Desde's voice, but he ignored it.

"Bring your friends closer," the Ken'nar whispered. "The Kana-Akün has yielded a rich harvest indeed. I would add these to the Ain Magne's bounty."

He backed away from the Ken'nar as horror crept through him. His father no longer recognized him. Or cared. "It's me! Father! What have they done to you?"

"Call your Fal'kin friends. I will ease their pain."

"Father. No." Teague sat rooted to the spot, allowing the tears to blind him from what he no longer wanted to see. "Come back. Please." It was a stupid thing to say, pitiful, desperate words uttered because he had no other way of making sense of the shell left behind from the Ken'nar's evil. His father was gone. Nothing remained that could return.

Somehow, the Ken'nar had subverted, perverted the man who was once his father, and had turned him into a mindless minion. They had turned his father's blessed gift of Healing, the rarest and most precious Aspect of all, into a tool for his own ends.

No, not they. He. Only the Dark Trine, the thrice-cursed had the power to do something so hideous.

The Ken'nar leaned close, and his arm brushed the amulet Teague still held in his hand. "The Ain Magne has use for them. But not you." The pale lavender sapphire burned against Teague's palm.

Someone gasped. "Teague! Get back! Now!"

The chains wrenched free behind the post and fell away. With lightning-fast reflexes, the Ken'nar healer grabbed the back of Teague's neck. He struggled in the man's grip, the warrior's fingers like a vice. The Ken'nar's thumb dug into his windpipe as the amulet brightened in Teague's hand. He tried to release the crystal, to throw it away, but he was no longer in control of his own body.

He opened his mouth to scream but heard nothing. His existence turned into one of blinding agony. A sword of fire lanced through his brain. His body curled into itself as every muscle contracted at once. He writhed against the Ken'nar grip.

Kaarl barreled a shoulder into him, knocking him away, and leveled his own amulet at the Ken'nar.

Teague pushed himself up on his forearms. "No! Please! Don't!"

The red amulet fire slammed into the dark-armored healer. The Ken'nar turned into a column of flame and shrieked in pain and rapturous release.

Teague rushed over to the incandescent pyre. The steward grappled with him and held him back.

Kaarl dragged him over to Morgan. "Get him out of here."

"Let me go." Teague wrenched himself free and staggered to the pile of ash that had been Tennen Beltran. A breeze stirred the embers only to have the rainwater wet the ash into dark gray silt. He sank to his knees. With trembling fingers, he touched the ashes.

Illenne knelt beside him in silence.

"Teague, *biraen*, he tried to kill you," Mirana's father said. "That creature was not your father."

The ashes were still warm. *Paithe.* He dug his father's amulet out from the soot. The soft purple sapphire glinted in the dull daylight. "But he was. Once."

Teague lurched to his feet and stumbled out from under the tent, his legs like two columns of lead. Far to the east, past the tinder grasslands of Varn-Erdal, rose the green forests of Kana-Akün.

"It is just like Atan Robaar," Kaarl murmured.

"He fell at the ford." Desde sounded like she was unsure of her own words.

The steward shook his head slowly. "No. He was alive. Here. He tried to capture me."

"That's impossible," Morgan said. "We saw him go down at the ford."

Binthe brought her hand to her mouth then curled it into a fist. "Gannah Tesabe. She attacked us in the fire fields. She would have killed me if it hadn't been for Teague distracting her. The Dark Trine must have captured her after the grynwen ambush outside of Falantir and healed her. He turned her into another one of those monsters. Somehow."

"But Gannah was already dead when we were forced to leave." Kaarl's voice had grown soft with disbelief. "Tetric Garis tried to heal her. She died in his arms. You saw it. We were all there."

Teague turned to face the empty, scorched binding post. "He used the Soul Harvest. Everyone thinks it's just a story, a myth. But it's not. I heard my parents talking about it one night when they thought I was asleep. They were talking about a time they as children learned their Healing Aspect in Kana-Akün from Prime Belessa Tir. Lord Garis had been studying Healing there, too, only a few summers older than they. They found him reading an old scroll. He picked it up and left before my mother could read it all, but she saw enough. The Soul Harvest is a technique only Aspected healers can perform. They said—"

Healers or Trines. A conclusion pushed at his mind, and he shoved it away with as much insistence.

He wiped at his face and at the memory of his parents' conversation. "That's how the Dark Trine has been building his army. He's been using healers to destroy the minds of the Fal'kin he's captured from the battlefield through the Soul Harvest. He's been using my—" He swayed on his feet. When Illenne rushed to help him, he held out his hand, stopping her, and steadied himself.

Binthe held her amulet. "Maybe Gannah wasn't truly dead but unconscious. *Ai*, Lord Garis healed her wounds—we all saw that—but maybe the Dark Trine found her after we left and revived her somehow." She took a deep breath. The pang of terrified comprehension flashed in her sea-green eyes. "The Dark Trine has been doing this for a long, long time." She turned her head to the southeast.

Teague watched her for a moment. Was she thinking of Deren or someplace farther? Rün-Taran, her home, lay in that direction, too.

"How could Lord Garis *not* know if Gannah was alive or not?" Morgan demanded. "He's a bloody Trine, for Aspects' sake!"

"Maybe—" Kaarl swallowed. "Maybe he realized she was too far gone and there was nothing more he could do for her." He glanced at his wife. "*Ai*. He put her in some sort of stasis to make her passing easier. The Dark Trine found her before she could succumb."

"Which begs another question," Morgan said. "If Garis's second, Rendel, and the rest of the Trine's troops are in Kana-Akün, how did that mean little bastard of a seer not detect five thousand Ken'nar leaving for Edara? Why didn't the Dar-Azûlans come?"

No one answered. A tightness built within Teague's chest, having nothing to do with his burnt lungs. Mirana's father had just lied to her mother. The dread in the man's eyes told Teague he had made the same chilling conclusions and tried to push them away for the same reasons.

"We're certain the Ken'nar bastard sits in Falantir, so he could have captured your defender and taken Prime Tir to use her to enslave Fal'kin." Rabb Plout made no effort to disguise the disgust in his voice. "But how could the Dark Trine have harvested Tennen Beltran if he was in Kana-Akün?"

The Dark Trine wasn't in Kana-Akün. Again, Teague's mind fought against the conclusion.

"He was at the ford," Prime Liaonne spat. "That massacre was unlike any bloodshed I've ever seen."

He wholeheartedly agreed with the defender woman. However, the Dark Trine had been preoccupied with more than calling troop movements. "A unit of Ken'nar drove straight for us as my parents and I and the other herbsfolk waited in the Dar-Anar foothills outside of the ford. The warriors hadn't found us by accident. They knew exactly where we were."

During his parents' hushed midnight conversation all those summers ago, they had said Healer Prime Belessa Tir had a treatise on the Soul Harvest. They had seen it once when they were at Falantir as young *scholaire'e* and had snuck into the prime's office. The room hadn't been empty like they had expected. They had found Lord Tetric Garis, a youth himself at the time, studying with the healer prime, in Belessa's office. Reading the forbidden treatise.

No.

"The only reason why my parents had been in the foothills in the first place was that Tetric Garis ordered them there."

Kaarl gently laid a hand on Teague's shoulder. "Lad, I know you have been through much, too much, really, but I know Tetric Garis. I have fought alongside him. It cannot be."

Prime Desde began to shake. "She's with him, Kaarl."

The steward drew closer to his wife and held her arms. "We know nothing. Let's not draw conclusions based on fear. You know all too well not every image that comes to a Fal'kin's mind is sent from the Seeing Aspect. You, Rabb, Binthe, even Mirana never saw anything about a harvested army."

"We have bigger problems than sullying Tetric Garis's character," Sahm Klai said. "The Dark Trine is encamped in Falantir, not two hundred leagues from here. Why wait for him to move south and lay waste to the rest of us? Attack him at his garrison in Kana-Akün." He pointed to the northeast.

The steward shook his head. "We'd have to know what we'd be fighting first. If we fought five thousand at the ford and another five thousand here, Aspects Above only know how many fighters he truly has."

Teague dragged his fingers through his hair. Tetric Garis had ordered his parents to a location precisely where the Ken'nar knew to look. Gannah, the il'Kin defender woman, supposedly died in the man's arms in the Kana-Akün forest, but he and Binthe had been attacked by her here at Edara. Trine Garis even warned of the attack on Two Rivers Ford but never made any mention of prescience about an attack on Falantir. Mirana had been given to the Trine as his *scholaira*.

Mirana was with Tetric Garis.

Teague had heard enough. He clutched his father's amulet and walked away from the group.

"Where are you going?" Morgan asked.

"We have to find out what the Dark Trine has in Falantir," he replied, his back turned to them.

The il'Kin defender stepped in front of him. "You cannot do this."

"I am tired of everyone telling me what I cannot do. I am going to do what I will. I am going to see what the Dark Trine is hiding in Falantir. We don't know how long he's been enslaving Fal'kin to fight for him. Look what he did to my father. The Dark Trine might still have my mother."

"Teague, your mother may be—" Prime Desde began.

He pivoted to face the group. "My mother may be what? Say it. Dead?" He shook his head quickly. "The Dark Trine wouldn't kill her. In fact, he'd make damn sure she'd live. She's too important to his plans. Especially now." He held up his father's amulet. "She's alive."

"Teague, please." Desde crossed over to him. "There is no guarantee that your mother is in Falantir. The steward is right. We need to think about this and make a sane plan, and not rush off like misfired amulets."

Teague pointed to the northeast and Falantir. "What if my parents weren't the only ones captured at Two Rivers Ford? He could have harvested—" His arm fell to his side.

Mirana's vision.

Was this what she saw? Herself turned into a mindless drone, a living amulet controlled by the Dark Trine's will? Bile burned his throat. He clenched his jaw so hard the pain stabbed up his temple.

Whether her father heard his thoughts again or came to the conclusion on his own, they shared the same expression. The steward set his face like flint but sheer terror shot behind his silver eyes.

He pinned Kaarl with his glare. "I am going to Falantir."

Kaarl stood over him. "No. You will not. It's far too dangerous. I will go."

"With all due respect, sir, the Ken'nar know you," Teague replied. "Whether by your face, your voice, or your presence from within the Aspects, you'll be found out and killed." He brought a hand to his empty chest. "I am Unaspected. The Ken'nar have never touched my mind. Nor would they even have cause to do so. I mean nothing to them. They won't even bother with me."

Prime Liaonne gave a displeased sigh and frowned. "He has a point."

"The boy will not go alone." Morgan tightened his sword belt. "I will go."

Binthe cleared her throat. "Let me understand this," she said, her green eyes twinkling with humor. "An herbsman and a defender are going to crawl past Aspects know how many Ken'nar, infiltrate their ranks, learn of the Dark Trine's battle plans, rescue a healer, *and* still find a way back out? Alive?"

Morgan pursed his lips. "Perhaps I should take along a second knife."

She grinned. "*Ai.* And you need to take along someone who can actually see what you're getting yourselves into."

Ai! Wait. No. Teague frowned. Binthe and Morgan were dear to him. He didn't want them to come. There was no one else in Kinderra, however, he'd rather have by his side. "What about your leg?"

The seer woman let the crutch fall and balanced adroitly on one leg. "Unless I am mistaken, a horse is ridden from the seated position."

"Binthe, *siba.*" He walked over to her and held her arms. "You lost a lot of blood. You're too weak. There's no cure for that but time."

She smiled. "My horse will be the one running, not I."

He handed the crutch back to her and embraced her. "I cannot thank you enough."

"Liaonne, do you have any detailed maps of Falantir?" Morgan asked.

"I did," she replied. "I'm not sure what has survived the fire."

The defender nodded. "I will help you look."

Binthe smiled. "*We* will help you look."

As the Fal'kin left, Teague studied his father's amulet in his hands. Raindrops beaded on its facets, creating miniature reflections of the crystal. He rubbed at some dirt caked on the gold setting. It would not come off. He looked closer. It was blood.

Teague gripped the pale amethyst amulet tightly. He had planned on infiltrating the Ken'nar ranks and taking down the Dark Trine with his sword. That was ludicrous—he would die before he could even think of drawing his blade, and he knew it. His father, however, once said knowledge cured more patients than herbs or even the Healing Aspect. There might be another way to take down the Ken'nar tyrant—with knowledge. And maybe, just maybe, Mirana would then be safe.

"You were right, Father."

"I have no right to ask it of you, but I must. What if Drei was not killed?"

He turned. "Ille—"

"I know, but what if he's still alive? What if he's been—" She scowled. "What if he's been *hurt* like your father? Or what if they have not yet erased his mind? They could be waiting to see if they need him. If he's alive and whole, I know he's been trying to escape all this time."

He reached for her hands. "If I find Drei, I will bring him back to you. I swear it."

She nodded and swallowed back her tears. "You must come back, too. If you do not, your peda blossom will never bloom again. You wouldn't do that to her, would you?"

If he had to search the entirety of Kinderra or storm the gates of the Underworld to find Mirana, he would stand by her side and brave the white light from her Jasal's Keep vision to save her from the Dark Trine.

"No, Ille," Teague said. "I will never leave Mirana again."

CHAPTER 43

*"Now, I fear they wish me to take up another Burden.
I do not want it. Yet there is no one else. Thou Aspects
Above! Why dost Thou torment me?"*
—The Codex of Jasal the Great

Trine Tetric Garis stood on the windswept coastal grasslands of Rün-Taran. Like the once-mighty bridges of Two Rivers Ford, he collapsed into the abyss of his despair.

Mirana Pinal was gone.

He had remained at their camp for days. When she didn't return immediately, he waited days longer still. The Rün-Tarani drew closer, vengeance over the deaths of Seer Prime Eshe Pashcot and Defender Second Syne Develan roiling off their minds to pollute the Aspects. He could wait no longer. He must leave.

If the girl would not come back to him, he would find her and bring her back to his side. Kinderra depended on her. *He* depended on her. She would give him Jasal's Keep. With the keep in his possession and Mirana as his heir, this senseless war would be over, at last. This senseless, contemptible, damnable war would be over.

Only if she returned to him.

He could no longer deny it. Mirana Pinal was the daughter of his heart, of his Aspects, bequeathed to him by a trinity-deity to which he swore supreme allegiance. He loved Mirana, by the Aspects how he loved her!

Tetric buried his face in his hands.

No one understood the blessing and the burden of carrying all three Aspects. The horror of a prescient vision where hundreds, even thousands, were to die and little could prevent it. Of killing without hesitation in the furious embrace of the Defending Aspect only to be consumed by the crushing emptiness of death meted out by one's own hand sensed within the Healing Aspect. No one knew the agonizing guilt of being lauded as a hero one day only to have those same adorers slaughtered the next. No one knew the rapturous glory of the three gifts uniting as one within the communion of a flawless gemstone at one's chest.

No one knew these things, except for Mirana Pinal.

He had once desired a child, an heir to whom he could pass on his beliefs and ideals. His paternal love. That dream belonged to another man, to a woman, dearly cherished and now long dead. By some miracle known only to the Aspects Above themselves, they saw fit to give him that child. Mirana had brought joy back to his heart when he thought such a thing was impossible. He now had a caring, a *need* even, to make a future beyond himself. For her.

Mirana had hidden her presence from him because she was terrified, not of him, but of her own power. What other reason could there be? She couldn't possibly hate him enough to shut her mind from him permanently, to leave him forever. Surely, she would come back to him once she had a chance to digest the revelations of the recent days. All she needed was time. And him.

She now knew the glorious strength of the Power from Without. She now understood its limitless potential. No mortal frailties bound its capacity like the Light from Within. *Ai*, the Power from Without had to be released as soon as it was brought within, but that was its purpose—to be taken then given back to the world from whence it came, a cycle repeated until the threat to life no longer existed. How was that abhorrent? How was that a sin?

No one had shown him how to understand this, let alone wield his Trine gifts together through the Power from Without. He had yet to see eleven summers when he first tasted it, fifteen summers when he no longer feared but embraced its promise, seventeen when he exploited its magnificence—with disastrous results. He paid for his ignorance with a price that would haunt him for the rest of his days. Instead of running in fear from the Power from Without, however, he learned to grasp it with both hands.

He would ensure Mirana never made the same mistakes, faced the same agonizing failures, he had. He would show her how such power was not to be feared but to be controlled. He would make certain she never feared the power—or herself—again.

Only if she returned to him.

... *Answer me, my second* ... Tetric called, pouring his will into his mind's voice. He waited long moments in silence. The bitter taste of dread pooled in the back of his throat, a flavor he thought now foreign to him. Had the boy been killed at Edara?

... *Ëo hac* ... his second returned at last.

Relief washed away the concern. ... *Why did you not answer me immediately?* ...

Again, there was a pause in his second's call. ... *Edara was not as successful as you saw it might be* ...

... *That is immaterial now* ... *Mirana Pinal has left me* ... *She rides north* ... *You must stop her* ...

... *Do you not even care what happened at Edara?* ... Anger tinged with pain, physical and otherwise, colored his second's mind words. ... *We lost thousands* ... *Thousands!* ... *Against my judgment, the judgment you instilled in me, I followed your plan, not mine, and waited* ... *I could not wait any longer* ... *But it was already too late* ... *We lost before we fired the first amulet* ... *Sün-Kasal came with five thousand Fal'kin* ... *And Kin-Deren?* ... *Desde Pinal arrived with a thousand Unaspected* ... *A thousand Unaspected, Ain Magne!* ...

Trepidation filled Tetric and added its heaviness to his grief. It blotted out his fury at his second's disobedience. ... *Did you find horses?* ...

... *There were no horses* ... his servant returned, his mind's voice thick with accusation. ... *We were only able to harvest a handful of Fal'kin before one of the healers was captured* ... *I believe he is dead now* ... *He returns no calls, I sense no presence* ... *Do you not understand?* ... *We were the ones who were massacred* ... *Us!* ... *Your Ken'nar!* ... *We lost because you were not here to lead us!* ... *You no longer listen to reason* ... *Nor to me* ...

He would suffer his lieutenant's impudence no longer. He forced his presence further into his servant's mind. ... *You blame this failure on me?* ... *I put you at the head of my armies, an honor no other has held* ... *Ai, I failed* ... *I believed in you, that you could accomplish what needed to be done—* ...

... I AM NOT YOU! ...

Tetric winced, as much in discomfort from the force of the call as in surprise that his seer could leverage such strength from such a distance. *... No, you are not me ... And never will be ...*

His second was now silent for long moments.

... I have given you everything ... I am the only one who dares to tell you the truth ... Even when you do not wish to hear it ... the seer returned at last. A sense of sorrow colored his mind-words. *... I warned you your plan to blockade Edara would not be successful ... You nearly killed me for it ... Have I not done all you have ever asked of me? ... Did you even bother to see if I lived or died after Edara? ... And now you tell me you don't believe in me? ... Why, Tetric? ... Why? ...*

His servant worshipped him. He knew this and had cultivated it. He had shown more of his true self to his seer second than any other save Mirana.

... Sido, Sido ... You cannot fault yourself for just holding the Seeing Aspect ... Nonetheless, the fact remains you are not a Trine ... And Mirana Pinal is ... he called. *... You are asking something of me I cannot give you ... Ai, you have had your uses, and I shall always be grateful to you for them ... But she will ensure Kinderra remains under my guidance ... She will be my legacy ...*

Once more, long moments passed before his second's mind reached out to him again. *... Mirana Pinal will only give you a legacy if she is at my side ... I have seen this ... I have told you about this ... Again, you wanted to kill me because of this truth ... Only together can Mirana and I give you the legacy you have always wanted ... If you continue to press her, she will be your death ... If she is with me, I can save you both ... And Kinderra ... I have seen it ...*

Anger flared within him, his hematite amulet like a firebrand against his chest. *... You will not touch her, Sido ...*

... I am the only true disciple you have ...

... You want her only to feed your appetites ...

... I am trying to save your life! ... Do you not understand that? ... Tetric, please ... You have been more of a father to me than the man who gave me life ... Do you not love me as a son?...

Tetric grew silent. He owed Sido Rendel a truthful answer for all his summers of service, but such an answer might open a chasm between them that would never close. To lose Sido and Mirana was unthinkable. Unthinkable.

... I do need you, Ëi Seconde ... I require you so I can rebuild Kinderra ... But you are no child to me ... Be content with how much I do rely on you ... Find Mirana Pinal ... Bring her back to me ... I will accept no failure from you in this ... Ëo comprende? ...

He let his communion with his seer second fade without waiting for his returned reply.

If Mirana did not return to him, if he could not find her before she found the last stanza to Jasal's Keep, if she did not choose the Power from Without, she would become his enemy.

Dread seeped through him like blood leaking from a mortal wound. He had made his second show his fealty with dire, brutal actions when the seer had passed but fifteen summers. Surely the Aspects Above were not asking brutal actions from himself?

Mirana had told him a swordsman would vanquish her at the keep.

He was that swordsman.

He covered his eyes with his hand and squeezed them shut. For the first time in his life, he did not want to see any more.

Tetric raised his fists in the air in defiance. "Never once have I turned back from what you demanded of me! No matter the cost! Or the pain! Have I not given you enough? I beg of thee! Do not ask this of me! Not this!"

... Come back to me... he called again. *... Please, Mirana, Ëi biraena ...* No answer returned.

The Ain Magne hung his head. The Aspects Above demanded his own show of fealty, but in the end, there was no choice. He would do whatever was necessary to stop the war from destroying Kinderra. If Mirana Pinal did not return to him, he would not allow her to threaten the land.

He would have no choice but to kill her.

CHAPTER 44

"End and beginning in One, in Both."
—The Trine Prophecy,
The Book of Kinderra

Heat. Heat. Heat.

Swords clash against a backdrop of flames. Arrows and grynwen sing in the night. Hazy multitudes fight against black-armored warriors. Unaspected! Unaspected have taken up arms! Fal'kin, Ken'nar, Unaspected, the music of their lives stills. An inferno reaches into the night sky.

Heat. Heat. Heat.

Jasal's Keep juts into the night sky.

… Do you not understand you have the power to end this war? … The Dark Trine's mind-voice resounds in her head. It blots out the clamor of the battle seething far below the watchtower.

... The deaths of your friends, of innocent Unaspected children, will rest on your head, not mine! ... Who will be called the 'Dark Trine' then? ...

"Mirana! Don't give it to him!" Teague cries. He collapses to the pavers. Bleeding, bleeding, away, away. Teague. Her. A body lies next to the young herbsman, a man's, the face, the presence blurred in a time yet to be. Friend or foe? The music of his life is nearly gone.

A flash of pure white light, like the inside of a lightning bolt, blinds her.

Heat. Heat. Heat.

"No!" She snapped open her eyes and brought Ashtar's pounding gallop to a halt.

Wind scuttled clouds across the sky and tugged at the tangles in her hair. The grasses of Rün-Taran's northern coastal prairie whispered and rustled in the breeze. The scent of rain—and something else—wafted through the air. She sniffed again, and this time, drew on the Aspects to heighten her senses. Smoke.

Fire.

A conflagration burned somewhere. The wildfire, though, was more than a collision of nature and man.

No dream had awakened her. The Seeing Aspect brought to her a battle amid flames, with thousands fighting, Unaspected among the combatants. The sense of the vision, its panicked immediacy—the vision was a skein of the present.

The rain she smelled now would come too late, too far from the battlefield to save its parched earth.

"Another province is in ruins, Ashtar."

Like her own heart. An inferno of desolation and rage swelled in her, driven by the cyclone of her guilt.

She had given Tetric Garis her trust, her love, everything she had. She placed him before her father and mother. She turned away from her most deeply held belief and accepted his tenet that the Power from Without would be the saving grace that she had sought for so long. Now, a demon in hero's armor continued to roam Kinderra, a monster she should have slain to save her beloved homeland but had been too blind to see the lamb was a serpent.

Light shall be dark; Dark shall be light. In one. In both.

Yet, did he not save her life, as she did his? Did he not want to unlock the secrets of Jasal's Keep, as she did? Did he not want to stop the unending summers of violence and death as much as she did?

She turned in the saddle. He was out there, somewhere, searching for her.

Did he not want peace as desperately as she did?

Mirana slipped from Ashtar's back and buried her face against the warhorse's neck.

She was nothing more than a muddled mixture of noble passions and honorable purpose woven together with bitter sins and failed intentions. How was she better than Tetric?

Ashtar whuffled and butted her shoulder with a velvet nose. She lifted her head and stroked the white stripe on the horse's broad face.

"The more I tried to run from becoming the Dark Trine, the closer I came to emulating him."

He'd tried to turn her into another Dark Trine, an acolyte who would carry on his ideals of perverted justice.

Light shall be dark; Dark shall be light. In one. In both.

Again, rage at his betrayal burned within her.

The misty mountains of Jad-Anüna soared above the verdant valley far to the north, their heads lost in clouds painted purple and gray by the setting sun. A thousand leagues farther still rose the granite shoulders of the Trak-Calan Mountains and the quest's conclusion for Jasal Pinal's writings and identity.

"We have to find the last of Jasal's hidden writings before Tetric does. If that watchtower is a weapon or a beacon, he'll call his Ken'nar to Deren and there will never be true peace."

Her shoulders fell, the enormity of the quest lying before her overwhelming her anger, the weight of her arms exaggerating the ache in her weary back.

She held onto a saddlebag for support and felt a rounded object within.

The alabaster cylinder. In her flight, she had completely forgotten about it.

She removed it from the satchel. Twice as long as her hand, the receptacle had no glyphs or markings that indicated what it contained. Wax sealed its lid.

She drew her belt knife and picked off the seal. Her heart drummed against her ribs as she worked loose the tight-fitting lid. She paused before lifting the cover. What if there were some sort of protection on the cylinder itself?

"Think, Mirana. If you fought off a sea monster and an army of crazed marauders, you can fight off whatever the cylinder could release." She hoped.

She held the container out from her. Closing one eye, she braced herself and loosened the lid. It came off in her hand without incident. She exhaled. Small victories were still victories.

A piece of parchment lay curled inside the cylinder. It was in far better condition than she would have expected after having lain at the bottom of the ocean for more than a thousand summers. She unfolded the page and read the ancient words:

Only in Their unmatched Wisdom could such a design be conceived. We are to be stripped of Their greatest treasure and give back that which was given unto us as a testament to the Light. With these, I will build our tower, our Protection. I claim it not as mine, for it is of the Aspects Above, but only claim the responsibility for the accomplishing of it. I am but Their humble carpenter; They are the Architect. Their mighty Tower will stand at the very heart of Deren. A pillar unto the heavens!'

She thinned her lips in frustration. The journal entry was as cryptic as the others. She read it again, trying to understand Jasal Pinal's state of mind when he wrote the words. His emotions rang of desperation perhaps? Determination? *Ai*, but something more than that. Hope. Jasal was desperate, desperate that what he was doing would work, but hope filled his heart. He was out of options, and he believed this keep tower was the only choice open to him. It had to work. It simply had to.

"Work? But work how?"

She dug in the saddlebag to retrieve the other pieces of parchment and flopped down on the ground, laying them out before her.

She studied the Kin-Deren verse. … *Help me, Jasal … I need to understand* … Under her fingertips, a reflected sense brushed her mind, an echo of Jasal's thoughts and emotions. "'This is a time of great peril. My visions have disheartened me once again. The Walls and the Gates in which I had placed all my hope are doomed to fail.'"

It was self-explanatory. Jasal believed the design of the keep was divinely inspired, but he felt thoroughly overwhelmed by the task. Despite that, determination to see Deren safe compelled him to continue.

She tapped her finger on the loose leaf of parchment from Tash-Hamar. It spoke of the keep's construction, so perhaps it was next in the sequence.

"'With a great price do we labor on the tower.'" She bit her lip again. No, he was considering the design first. Maybe the one from Rün-Taran might come second. "'Only in Their unmatched Wisdom could such a design be conceived.'"

She groaned in frustration. "Think." *Ai*, Jasal believed the Aspects Above gave him the idea for the tower's construction. He said so again in the Rün-Taran verse, *They are the Architect*. The Rün-Taran verse told her nothing.

No. Not quite. The ingeniousness of the design left Jasal awestruck but overwhelmed, too. More than overwhelmed. The directive terrified him to his core.

What was so ingenious about a tower? *Ai*, the keep was tall, but it was made of stone. She gritted her teeth. What was she missing?

She read again one of the Rün-Tarani stanzas. "'With these, I will build our tower.' What are 'these'?"

Mirana traced her finger on the verse before it and recited, "'We are to be stripped of Their greatest treasure and give back that which was given unto us as a testament to the Light.' Hmm. The Light?"

The *Exultante* from the Ora Fal'kinnen, recited every Choosing Ceremony as the newly ordained Fal'kin chose their amulets, spoke of the Light. "I exult in the glory of Thy Light! The Light to See, the Light to Defend, the Light to Heal. Thy crystal resteth like a star against my breast. Thy servant is glorified in the name of the holy Aspects! Is that what you mean, Jasal?"

She pursed her lips. "'With these, I will build our tower, our Protection.'"

Protection. Testament. Treasure. Light.

Her breath caught in her throat. Jasal's verse from Rün-Taran. *Testament to the Light. We are to be stripped of our greatest treasure*. Treasure. Jewels. Crystals. *Given to us as a testament to the Light*. Testament. *With these, I will build our tower, our Protection*.

Tash-Hamar. *We lay aught else we have to give.* Kin-Deren. Commitment to protect. Protect.

"Dear Aspects Above!"

Jasal's Keep was made of amulets.

Mirana sat, stunned. Jasal had asked the Fal'kin to sacrifice their amulets to build the keep.

One massive, ultimate protection.

And if Tetric managed to take control of the keep before she did—

"I will not let you gain control of the keep. I will not!"

If she could not find the fourth and last piece to the puzzle of the keep, if she could not decipher the secrets of its power and use it to save Kinderra, the Power from Without and the Soul Harvest would reign. Her homeland would die, heartbeat by heartbeat, under a gilded fallacy of oppressive peace and false enlightenment at the hands of a benevolent tyrant.

One will come forth, thrice-cursed, to destroy. One will come forth, thrice-blessed, to rebuild.

"While I still have breath in my body, I will destroy the war that has ravaged us for three thousand summers and rebuild Kinderra."

Tetric Garis was the Dark Trine.

And if she could not alter her destructive fate to become the Light Trine, even hope would not remain.

THE SAGA CONTINUES...

Trine Revelation
The Kinderra Saga: Book 3

TRINE FALLACY
The Kinderra Saga: Book 2

Dramatis Personae

Kin-Deren—1ˢᵗ Hall. Standard: gold field with red eagle

ANTIRI il'Amil Pinal (2094–2127): Seer. Joined in union
with Jasal Pinal. Son, Jasan (b. 2122). Born to Tash-Hamar
province. Amulet: blue-green aquamarine.

ATAN Robaar (3350–): Fal'kin *scholaire* Defender. Chooses
early to support the Battle of Two Rivers Ford. Amulet: red
ruby.

DAV Koehl (3319–): Defender. Defender Commander of
Kin-Deren provincial Fal'kin forces. Amulet: blue sapphire.

DESDE il'Kellis Pinal (3319–): Seer. Prime of Kin-Deren.
Served as il'Kin battle seer before elevation as Prime's
Second. Joined in union with Kaarl Pinal. Mother of Mirana
Pinal. Amulet: yellow topaz.

GANNAH Tesabe (3345–3367): Defender. Member of the
il'Kin. Born to Jad-Anüna Province. Killed in a grynwen
ambush in Kana-Akün forest in 3367. Amulet: yellow
sapphire.

GEMMA il'Lakumbe Piaar (3318–): Unaspected. Senior
herbswoman at the Healing Hostel of Kin-Deren. Born to
Jad-Anüna province. Husband Baden Piaar (deceased).
Mother to five children (three sons, two daughters) killed in
a Ken'nar raid in 3350.

HAARLEN Lasen (3312–): Unaspected. Quartermaster of the Learning Hall of Kin-Deren province.

ILRIK Maldaar (2089–2122): Defender. Ken Defender of the Dark Triumvirate. Also known as "Ilrik the Black." Amulet: deep red-purple garnet.

ISEL, Wend (3317–): Defender. Horsemaster of Kin-Deren province. Oversees the stables in Deren and the province's warhorse herd. Amulet: yellow zircon.

JASAL Pinal (2092–2122): Trine. Primus Magne and Prime of Kin-Deren. Amulet: diamond.

KAARL Pinal (3314–): Defender. Defender Commander of the il'Kin. Named Steward of the Quorum of Light after the death of Toban Kellis. Joined in union with Desde il'Kellis Pinal. Father of Mirana Pinal. Amulet: red garnet.

MAARK Bedane (3352–): Unaspected. Orphaned when his parents were killed in a Ken'nar raid of their homestead and farm in 3365.

MIRANA Pinal (3351–): Fal'kin *scholaira*, training as a seer. Daughter of Kaarl and Desde Pinal.

MORGAN Jord (3334–): Defender. Commander's Second of the il'Kin. Amulet: purple amethyst.

NIAH il'Sahli Beltran (3325–): Healer. *Priora* of Healing Hostel of Kin-Deren. Born to Tash-Hamar province. Joined in union with Tennen Beltran. Mother of Teague Beltran. Amulet: rose quartz.

NIALL Corran (3318–): Defender. Commander's Second of the Kin-Deren provincial Fal'kin forces. Amulet: red beryl.

TADDIE (Taddeus) Egen (3362–): Fal'kin *scholaire* Seer. Apprenticed under Defender Wend Isel as a stable hand.

TARN Salka (3315–3365): Defender. Member of the il'Kin. Killed in a Ken'nar skirmish near Thyre's Crossing in the Trak-Calan highlands in 3365. Amulet: blue zircon.

TAUL Brandt (3320–): Unaspected. Magistrate of Deren.

TEAGUE Beltran (3351–): Unaspected. Son of Healers Tennen and Niah Beltran. Apprenticed as an herbsman in the Healing Hostel.

TENNEN Beltran (3322–): Healer. *Priore* of Healing Hostel of Kin-Deren. Joined in union with Niah il'Sahli Beltran. Father of Teague Beltran. Amulet: light-purple sapphire.

TOBAN Kellis (3272–3367): Seer. Former Prime of Kin-Deren, Steward of the Quorum of Light. Father of Desde il'Kellis Pinal. Amulet: light-yellow beryl.

YENIRA Irasda (3349–): Fal'kin *scholaira* Seer. Chooses early to support the Battle of Two Rivers Ford. Amulet: blue topaz.

Trak-Calan—2nd Hall. Standard: gold field with green tiger

HINSAH Parn (3348–): Defender. Commander's Second of Trak-Calan provincial Fal'kin forces. Amulet: medium-green peridot.

KOBEN Ryotan (3314–): Seer. Prime of Trak-Calan. Raised as a foster brother to Tetric Garis. Amulet: dark-orange garnet.

SHALAS Yutan (3245–3330): Seer. Prime of Trak-Calan. Foster father and *patrua* mentor of Tetric Garis. Amulet: golden topaz.

Rün-Taran—3rd Hall. Standard: white field with blue capricorn

BINTHE Lima (3343–): Seer. Battle seer of the il'Kin. Granddaughter of Eshe and Lindar Pashcot. Amulet: green emerald.

ESHE il'Bahane Pashcot (3270–): Seer. Prime of, Rün-Taran. Joined in union with Lindar Pashcot (deceased). Grandmother to Binthe Lima. Amulet: pale-blue zircon.

LINDAR Pashcot (3268–3330): Defender. Defender Commander of Rün-Taran provincial Fal'kin forces and Prime's Second. Joined in union with Eshe il'Bahane Pashcot. Grandfather to Binthe Lima. Amulet: red-orange carnelian.

SYNE Develan (3289–): Defender. Prime's Second and Defender Commander of Rün-Taran provincial Fal'kin forces. Amulet: orange citrine.

Tash-Hamar—4th Hall. Standard: purple field with red leopard

FALANNAH il'Aldi Sadhi (3308–3350): Seer. Served as a battle seer in the Tash-Hamari provincial Fal'kin forces. Mother of Timir Sadhi. Sister of Fasen Aldi. Amulet: pink morganite.

FASEN Aldi (3303–): Defender. Prime of Tash-Hamar. Uncle of Timir Sadhi. Brother to Falannah il'Aldi Sadhi. Amulet: blue sapphire.

TIMIR Sadhi (3333–): Defender. Prime's Second and Defender Commander of Tash-Hamari Fal'kin provincial forces. Nephew of Fasen Aldi. Amulet: deep-orange citrine.

Kana-Akün—5th Hall. Standard: green field with gold hart

BELESSA il'Isofar Tir (3279–3367): Healer. Prime of Kana-Akün. Presumed killed in the Battle of Falantir, winter 3367. Amulet: green tourmaline.

THIEER Pannen (3321–3367): Seer. Prime's Second and Seer Commander of Kana-Akün provincial Fal'kin forces. Presumed killed in the Battle of Falantir, winter 3367. Amulet: yellow apatite.

Varn-Erdal—6th Hall. Standard: white field with red horse

CLARIENNE il'Hadten Jord (3336–3359): Unaspected. Shepherd and homesteader. Wife of Morgan Jord. Died with infant son, Pieter, in a Ken'nar raid in the Varn-Erdal plains in 3359.

DREI Carada (3348–3365): Defender. Son of Trein Carada and Marienne Tans. Attacked by Ken'nar, winter 3365, presumed dead. Amulet: deep-magenta rhodolite.

ERAN Talz (3315–): Unaspected. Horsemaster of Varn-Erdal province. Oversees the stables in Edara and the province's warhorse herd.

GRENNE Fadern (3325–): Seer. Elevated to Prime's Second of Varn-Erdal before the Battle of Edara. Two sons (deceased), one daughter (deceased) by Trein Carada. Previously coupled with Trein Carada until his death. Coupled with Liaonne Edaran. Amulet: deep-pink tourmaline.

ILLENNE Talz (3349–): Unaspected. Horse herd mistress and archer. Daughter of Eran Talz.

LIAONNE Edaran (3342–): Defender. Prime of Varn-Erdal, elevated after the Battle of Two Rivers Ford. Daughter of Vallia Edaran. Amulet: yellow topaz.

MARIENNE Tans (3318–): Unaspected. Learning hall attendant and laundress. Mother of Drei Carada. Coupled with Trein Carada until his death. Bore five other children (three sons, two daughters), all defenders, deceased.

NATHEN Keldir (3298–): Defender. Senior defender on Prime's Council. Father of Liaonne Edaran. Amulet: amber citrine.

PALEN Clar (3298–): Unaspected. Senior learning hall herbsman.

PIETER Jord (3358–3359, d. 6 months): Unaspected. Son of Morgan and Clarienne Jord. Died in a Ken'nar raid in the Varn-Erdal plains.

PIOL Lidan (3295–): Defender. Senior defender on Prime's Council. Amulet: green chrysoberyl.

TREIN Carada (3317–3365): Defender. Attacked by Ken'nar, winter 3365, presumed dead. Amulet: blue apatite.

WESAL Pettan (3293–): Defender. Senior defender on Prime's Council. Amulet: dark-pink zircon.

VALLIA Edaran (3317–3368): Defender. Prime of Varn-Erdal. Perished in an ambush during the Battle of Two Rivers Ford. Amulet: red ruby.

Jad-Anüna—7th Hall. Standard: blue field with gold lion

ABER Hebari (3328–): Defender. Prime's Second and Defender Commander of Jad-Anünan Fal'kin provincial forces. Amulet: green spinel.

NAMBRE Dinir (3302–): Defender. Prime of Jad-Anüna. Amulet: red-brown andalusite.

TILENATETE Nasta (2835–2867): Trine. Prime of Jad-Anüna. Elevated to Primus Magne during the Red Plague of 2864–2866. Killed by Ken'nar when she tried to offer aid during the pandemic. Amulet: pale-green chrysoberyl.

Sün-Kasal—8th Hall. Standard: red field with white bull

BYSTRA il'Tari Klai (3312–3350): Defender. Joined in union with Sahm Klai. Two sons (deceased), one daughter (deceased). Amulet: blue-gray cordierite.

RABB Plout (3328–): Seer. Prime's Second and Seer Commander of Sün-Kasal provincial Fal'kin forces, serves as battle seer. Amulet: red-brown topaz.

SAHM Klai (3308–): Defender. Prime of Sün-Kasal. Joined in union with Bystra il'Tari Klai (deceased). Two sons (deceased), one daughter (deceased) with Bystra il'Tari. Amulet: smoky-brown quartz.

Dar-Azûl—9th Hall. Standard: black field with argent silver griffin

SIDO Rendel (3345–): Seer. Prime's Second and Seer Commander of Dar-Azûlan Fal'kin provincial forces, serves as battle seer. Born to Kana-Akün province. Amulet: light-green peridot.

STAINE, Kev (3325–): Defender. Amulet: medium-blue kyanite.

TETRIC Garis (3313–): Trine. Prime of Dar-Azûl. Amulet: hematite.

TRINE FALLACY
The Kinderra Saga: Book 2

Glossary of Terms and Words

-á .... past perfect tense; joined to word it modifies. Example: had created = creará.

a .... to

a nehíl .... (you are) welcome; literally "a nothing;" not to confused with a greeting "Ben ve" as in "good coming."

accepte, acceptem .... accept, acceptance

ad .... at

adam, adamé, adamá .... forget, forgot, forgotten

agen .... again

ai .... yes

ain .... one, whole, complete, only

aire .... air

alainne .... beautiful

alta .... above, high

ama .... love

amausar .... steward, stewardship, manage; literally "loving use" amula .... amulet; Amulets allow an Aspected to further focus and use their innate Aspects, especially outside of themselves. An Aspected's life force harmonics will resonate with one specific crystal, except in the case of a Trine. Because they possess all three Aspects, Trines have the innate ability to modulate their life harmonics to adapt to any amulet.

amulets .... The sacred tool and relic containing a gemstone used by the Aspected to manifest their powers outside of themselves. While all Aspected have certain abilities without an amulet (e.g. telekinesis, telepathy), to produce major actions with their Aspects requires the use of an amulet. Typically, when they've reached 18 summers old, Aspected choose a single amulet for life through a mystical union of life harmonics matching the natural harmonics within the gemstone's crystal structure. The connection is unique and indelible. The loss or destruction of an amulet causes untold anguish on the Aspected individual, most committing suicide. Only Trines, those with all three Aspects, can choose more than one amulet. (see Aspects, Aspected, Choosing Ceremony, Trine)

an ....an

anaíl, anaíle ....breath, breathe

anelies..another

animale...animal

Anqa Lingua.......................................literally "old tongue"; the ancient language of Kinderra

aonta...union

aquete, aqueté ....water, watered

aquila ....eagle

ár...on, upon

as...as

aspeca...life

aspecaem...soul, spirit

aspece, aspecae ....live, alive

Aspecta('e)...Aspect(s)

Aspecta'e Alta .... Aspects Above; This is the trinity-like deity that Kinderrans believe created the universe and all living things. They are the source of life and the powers of the Aspects.

Aspected... Generic term for one who possesses the powers of the Aspects. In the culture and beliefs of Kinderra, the Unaspected were the first peoples created by the Aspects Above. Some of these were chosen by the Aspects Above and touched with fingers of lightning, bestowing upon them the powers of the Aspects to become the Aspected, stewards and protectors of all of Kinderra. The expression of Aspect powers occurs in about one of every 1,000 births.

Aspects, Powers of the .... The powers of the Aspects occur in three types: Defending, conferring extraordinary reflexes, speed, strength, and situational awareness, as well as the ability to manifest amulet fire from one's amulet; Seeing, conferring the ability to see into the past, present, and future; and Healing, conferring the ability to stimulate the healing of injury and illness thousands of times faster than normal. Major expressions of the Aspects require the focus of an amulet. For example, while it is possible for a healer without an amulet to suppress pain in another to a degree, to set a broken bone would require an amulet to focus the Healing Aspect. All Aspected have certain innate abilities that do not require an amulet, including telekinesis, telepathy, and some ability to shunt away pain and enhance endurance.

aste..star

atuda...together

aud, audé...hear, heard

avera...long for, want

ban..white bath .... both

bé .... by

ben .... good, kind

Ben dië .... good morning, good day

Ben iré .... farewell, goodbye; literally "good leaving"

Ben kin; B'kin .... hello, hi (informal); literally "good light"

Ben nöc .... good night

benedicta, benedictaé,
benedictan .... bless, blessed, blessing

besa .... kiss

bhéth; bhéth en aonta .... join; join in union (marry)

bia .... before

bir .... bring

biraen, biraena, biraen'e .... child/son, daughter, children; often used as a term of endearment

biran .... birth; literally "bring forth"

Book of Kinderra, The .... Historical reference of Kinderra written before the Sundering by Aspected and Unaspected scholars. Considered one of the two revered books of the Fal'kin

along with the Ora
Fal'kinnen.

braith, braith ár................................depend/rely, depend/rely on

brea...great, most (quantity); (see
also magne)

bremaithe..grandmother; also term of
respect for female elders

brepaithe...grandfather; also term of
respect for male elder

buai...win

caela...sky

call..telepathic communication
("He called a warning to her
mind."); also the act of
telekinesis ("He called a cup
into his waiting hand.")

calora, calorae ....warm, warming

cara, caran; Ëi cara('e).....................friend, friendship; my
friend(s)

cëos; cëosan......................................choose; chosen

cerebus..brain, mind

Choosing Ceremony.......................The sacrament where
Aspected *scholaire'e* choose
their gemstone amulets
through the mystical union of
their life harmonics with the

harmonics of a gemstone's crystal. The ceremony is held annually for those who have reached 18 summers old.

chosant .... protect

cin .... with

cinen .... within

cinstandan .... withstand

clae .... sword, weapon

Codex of Jasal the Great, The ...... The journal of Jasal Pinal. Written between 2117–2132. There have been several attempts throughout history to destroy the work, but none have succeeded.

com .... like (similar to)

comé .... what

compre .... know

comprende, comprendea .... understand, understanding

confian .... trust

consente .... agree; Example: I agree, okay = Ëo consente

corem .... face

covrir (v.) .... cover

crear, crearé, creará ....create(s), make; created, had created

il'Crearae (The Creation)................The creation psalm from the Ora Fal'kinnen. Also; also creation or a euphemism for Kinderra or the universe

culpa; Ëo ad culpa............................fault; "I'm sorry" (literally, "I am at fault")

cunaré (slang) ....derogatory term for female genitalia

daingaen...stable, solid

dam...give

dar...mountain

defecta, defectim ....fail, failure

defende, defendeä, defendeo.........defend, fight, protect; defender; defense, protection

defender...An Aspected individual who possesses the Defending Aspect

Defender Commander ....Highest-ranking officer in a Fal'kin provincial army; (see Second)

Defender's Second..........................Second-in-command of a Fal'kin provincial army; (see Second)

derra ....earth, land, world derranen .... foundation; based on the root word for "land"

dhái .... past

dici.. speak, say

dië... dawn, day, morning

digita .... finger

diu .... long (length)

doma.. home, house

dúa... between

-'e.. plural suffix (pronounced 'eh'); joined to word it modifies. Example: friend/friends = cara/cara'e.

-é... past tense suffix; joined to the word it modifies. Example: created = crearé.

e .... and (pronounced 'ee')

Ëa .... me

Ëam.. mine

Ëi .... my

elies .... other

ëllenas .... fill(s)

empe, a'empe.................................... begin, had begun emplecti ....embrace, hug

en ....in

engre (n.), engren (v.) ....anger

enigma...puzzle, riddle

Ëo ....I, I am

Ëo anaíle; Ëo aspece........................"I breathe; I live." A
defender's adage.

Ëome...us

Ëomus...we, we are

et ....there

eta(n) ....there was/were

etim...still

etís...there is/are

expel ....Punishment for a capital
crime among the Fal'kin
where the condemned is
forced to leave Fal'kin
society and his/her province.
In the most extreme
circumstances, a Fal'kin's
amulet is taken. Most Fal'kin
would prefer death than
being kept from their calling
to the Aspects, their amulets,
and their province.

il'Exultantae
(The Rejoice) .... A psalm of praise from the
Ora Fal'kinnen

exulte .... exult, exalt, praise

fal... follow

Fal'kin; Fal'kinnen .... "They who follow the
Light;" the whole body of
the Fal'kin. These Aspected
people believe in the
philosophy of the Light from
Within. They use their innate
powers of the Aspects within
themselves as their sole
source of power. To draw in
life forces to augment one's
power is considered the most
extreme crime one could
commit. Fal'kin caught using
the Power from Without are
relieved of their amulets and
expelled from the province.

fár.. for

fárdam, fárdamen;
Ëo fárdam Oë .... forgive, forgiven; "I forgive
you"

fhí, fhíagn, a fhí.............................. weave, weaving, to weave

filam... thread

fin... at last, end, finished fissura ....crack, fissure, split

forma ....form

forte ....fort, keep (building), strong

fos ....yet

fuádain ....fleeting

gainem ....sand (n.)

gemma ....crystal, jewel

gente, -n, -na ....people, man, woman

gháinn, gháinn'e ....grain, grains

gloria, gloriae, gloriaé ....glory, glorify, glorified

Gratas, Gratas Oë ....thanks; thank you

grynwen ....Massive, wolflike carnivores
known for their pupilless red
eyes and their viciousness. It
is believed they use some
type of primitive Aspect-like
senses to hunt.

gryphus ....griffin

hac ....here

hale ....holy

har ....hill

healer ....An Aspected individual who
possesses the Healing Aspect

i'.. of; joined to word it modifies

-í.. future tense suffix, joined to
word it modifies; Example:
will create = crearí.

id (m.), ida (f.)................................ it(s)

Iëa, Iëam Iëas .... she, her, hers

Ië, Iëm, Iës.................................... he, him, his

il'- .... of the; joined to word it
modifies. Often used as a
prefix in formal surnames,
especially matrilineal names.

il'Kin .... The Fal'kin strike force
comprised of defenders and
battle seers from all nine
provinces. The il'Kin is a
special operations unit
serving all of Kinderra and
augments provincial forces in
times of need. It is under the
direction of the Steward of
the Quorum of Light and led
by a defender commander.
Historically, the il'Kin has
served Kinderra in the
absence of a Trine's
provincial forces. Only the
most highly accomplished
Fal'kin are invited to join its
ranks.

imbecilae, -t.....................................ignorance, stupidity;
                                               ignorant, stupid

impatientia......................................impatience

inaspeca (n.) ....free will, will

incendio ....burn

infera ....below, under

inimica...enemy

íre..go, leave, journey

ísi(é) ....are, be, is; was (preposition);
                                               (see pronouns)

íuven; íuven sibe/siba....................young; younger ("little")
                                               brother/sister

ken ....power

Ken'nar; Ken'narren......................."They who use the Power;"
                                               The whole body of the
                                               Ken'nar. Ken'nar believe in
                                               the philosophy of the Power
                                               from Without. They use their
                                               innate Aspects and their
                                               amulets only to pull in the
                                               life forces around them and
                                               pour out that power back
                                               through their amulets,
                                               providing a seemingly
                                               limitless supply of power.
                                               They believe the use of the
                                               Aspects should not be

limited by one's innate powers.

kin .... light

Kin ísi Oëa .... Light be yours; a formal greeting. The reply is "E Oë" (And you).

kinema .... lightning

len .... gentle, soft

leten .... allow, let

locarae .... location, place

luve .... rain

luveclae .... storm, tempest; literally "rain sword"

ma, maís .... may, may be, maybe

maent .... meant

magistrate .... the highest-ranking government official of a province's Unaspected, akin to a Fal'kin prime

magne .... great (honorable); (see also brea)

maithe .... mother; has the connotation of "mommy"

manë .... hand

marca ....brand

matrua ....aunt; also can mean
                                                              "godmother," "teacher," or
                                                              "mentor"

mer..sea, ocean

mercare, mercaré ....buy, bought

minia..little, small, tiny

mista ....mist

morte, mortea,
mortean, mortes ....dead, death, die

mor...more

nome ....name, call; also a telepathic
                                                              call of communication

necesit ....must

nefas, nefas'e....................................sin, sins

nehíl...nothing

nöc...night

nubla..cloud

numbers, 1-10
(cardinal, quantity) ....primus, seconda, trina,
                                                              quatra, quinta, sexta, septa,
                                                              octa, nonta, decema (see also
                                                              "ain")

nun...nor

nunqa .... never

-ó .... present perfect tense; joined
to the word it modifies.
Example: have created =
crearó

o .... or

obsca; Obsca Oëa osa .... close, shut; "Close your
mouth" ("shut up")

Oë .... you

Oëa .... your, yours

Oëma .... who, whom

Oëme .... they

Oëmea .... those

Oëmus .... them, their

onoír .... honor

Ora Fal'kinnen .... Literally "Prayer of the
Fal'kin." The major religious
work of the Fal'kin, detailing
their relationship with the
Aspects Above, the powers
of the Aspects, and Kinderra.
Considered one of the great
books of the Fal'kin along
with The Book of Kinderra.

osa .... mouth oscuil, oscuil'e ....eye, eyes

pace...peace

palibre ....word

passenae (n.), passen (v.) ....passage, hallway (n.); pass (v.)

paithe...father; has the connotation
of "daddy"

patientia ....patience

patrua ....uncle; also "godfather,"
"teacher" or "mentor"

pecta ....breast, chest

penilaré (slang)...................................derogatory term for male
genitalia

per...but

periclaem ....fear

pericul, periculus ....danger, dangerous

pián..pain, suffering

placre..please (v.)

potest..possible

pon, pone ....lay/lay down, lies/rests

potem...after

Prime..The Aspected leader of a
province's Fal'kin

Prime's Second...............................The Aspected next in line for primeship (see Second)

Primus ....Anqa Linqua for "prime;" used as a formal reference

Primus Magne ....A dictator-like role elevated from among the Aspected to lead the entire continent's Fal'kin. This role is enacted during times of extreme duress in Kinderra, such as a pandemic or other widespread calamity.

priore (m.), priora (f.),
priore'e (pl.) ....The head of a healing hostel or infirmary, something akin to the chief of staff

pronouns...are capitalized; Ëo (I), Oë (you), Ëomus (we), etc.; state of being implied. Example: I am here = Ëo hac.

proxi...against, close, near

qua..which

quen ....when

quet, quetís......................................where, where is

quis...some

quistempre('e).................................sometime(s)

quod ....because

Quorum of Light............................The council comprised of all
the primes and seconds from
the nine provinces of
Kinderra. The Quorum
discusses the state of affairs
in Kinderra, and sets policy
and laws affecting the Fal'kin
of every province.

Quorumtide.....................................The major holiday time in
Kinderra, marked by feasting
and celebration, and often
fewer military actions due to
impending winter weather. It
coincides with the Quorum
meeting, which occurs in
Deren for one sevenday each
Reckoning in Fifthmonth.

reace ....reach

Reckoning..The literal number of the
year. Example: Mirana Pinal
was born in the Reckoning
of 3352.

rememore ....remember

Rememore Kin en Forte................Remember the Light in the
Keep

Rememore Kin e Forte ....Remember the Light and the
Keep

responara... answer

requa .... require

revelar... reveal

risa... rise

rith... run

robare.. steal

runh... secret, hide

sana .... health

Sana e Kin a Oë............................... Health and Light to You; a
                                                        formal greeting

sanare, sanarente, sanareä.............. heal, healing, healer

sculpte.. sculpt, shape

scinane, scinané, scinaneá.............. shine, shined, shone

scholaire (m.), scholaira (f.),
scholaire'e (pl.) .... Aspected students learning
                                                        how to use their powers.

Second... The second-in-command of
                                                        a province's Fal'kin (Prime's
                                                        Second) or Fal'kin army
                                                        (Commander's Second). This
                                                        is an extremely influential
                                                        and pivotal role, requiring
                                                        much vetting and
                                                        interviewing, and provides an
                                                        immediate and seamless

transition of power upon a prime's or defender commander's death or incapacitation. Final approval for either role rests with a province's prime, although in the case of a Commander's Second, the Defender Commander's choice strongly influences the decision.

Seconde...See Second

seer...An Aspected individual who possesses the Seeing Aspect

seer's ruse ....A seer technique for projecting visions through an amulet to be viewed by others. (see also Visi Externa)

servad..servant

settan...set

siba, Ëi siba ....sister, my sister

sibe, Ëi sibe ....brother, my brother

siber (n.), sibere (v.) ....sieve (n.), sift (v.)

siniúint ....destiny

skene...skein

solis .... alone, apart, separate

staíonnae, staíonne .... need (n.), need (v.)

statam .... now

standan .... stand

Steward of the
Quorum of Light .... The influential facilitator of
the Quorum of Light is
elected by the primes and
seconds of the Quorum. The
steward has no vote for
his/her province but can cast
a single vote by proxy for
another province unable to
attend Quorum meetings as
well as cast a tie-breaking
vote in the rare instance
when it occurs.

straitéis.. strategy, plan

summer.. Euphemism for a calendar
year, especially in reference
to age (I am sixteen summers
old; the man has seen thirty
summers); also the literal
summer season. (see also
Reckoning)

ta... to

talus('e) .... claw(s), talon(s)

te ....from

tempre..time

ten...has, have

testus; Ëo testus................................swear (an oath); I swear

tha..than

the..then

thet...that

toucha ....touch

todhái ....future

traiseh...treasure

tré...through

treor..command, guide

trevia...direction, way; (see also íre, passenae)

Trine...One who possesses all three powers of the Aspects (i.e. Defending, Seeing, and Healing). These individuals are exceedingly rare, perhaps one born only once every several hundred summers. In Kinderran culture, it is believed the Aspects Above create a Trine to save

Kinderra from some great
impending calamity.

tuda .... all

tudempre .... always, eternal, forever;
literally "all time"

tudsa .... also

tuil, tuilé .... earn, earned

u'- .... not, un-; joined to word it
modifies. Example: u'kin
meaning dark or "not light."

u'ai .... no

u'ben .... evil; literally "not good"

u'bendicta .... curse; literally "un-blessing"

u'cin .... without

u'gen, u'gente .... none, no one

u'kin .... dark; literally "not light"

u'len .... hard

U'Nehíl .... Literally "false nothing." The
practice of masking one's
presence from within the
Aspects by manipulating
one's Aspects to mimic or
reflect the "life force" noise
in the general vicinity.

u'pace ....battle, war; literally "not
                                           peace"

u'verdas...falsehood, lie

u'vide...blind, sightless, often
                                           derogatory; "u'vide vermihn"
                                           meaning "sightless maggot"
                                           as someone without the
                                           Aspects.

u'vide excra (slang)..........................Unaspected; literally
                                           "sightless shit"

Unaspected.......................................those without the Aspects

upacaem...destruction; based on the
                                           root word for "war"

usar ....use

ve ....come(s)

verda, verdas ....true, truth

vermihn...maggot, worm, or any
                                           vermin or disgusting
                                           creature; often used as an
                                           insult

vide, vidé, Videä, Vidë...................look/see, looked/saw, Seer,
                                           Sight

virtú ....bravery, courage

visi..vision

Visi Externa......................................A seer technique for projecting visions through an amulet to be viewed by others; also known as a seer's ruse

voide...void

year..see Reckoning; see summer

ABOUT THE AUTHOR

While other kids read comic books under the covers with a flashlight at bedtime, **C.K. DONNELLY** wrote fan fiction and fantasy stories.

She used her love of writing to pursue a career in journalism and was honored with several press awards for business and economic reporting. She has also held careers in healthcare, and currently runs a freelance writing and marketing support firm.

She resides in Arizona with her oh-so-patient husband and her little black dog (who is equally patient). She no longer writes under the covers by flashlight. Usually.

Printed in the USA
CPSIA information can be obtained
at www.ICGtesting.com
LVHW092109190824
788668LV00004B/448